COLD ALLIES - ~~the~~ prestigious *Locus* magazine readers' poll for best first novel of the year.

'The best first novel of 1993 . . . The perspectives keep switching like turns of a kaleidoscope . . . vivid prose, masterful plot handling, and an overall humane intelligence. Read it!'

Locus

'Gripping and realistic . . . an assured, imaginative, and distinctive debut'

Kirkus Reviews

'An enormously capable first novel . . . so fluidly readable that I went through the whole thing in one sitting. It should herald the beginning of a major career'

Darrell Schweitzer, *Aboriginal Science Fiction*

'Stirring . . . an original blend of political intrigue and unique speculations on alien first contact'

Booklist

About the author

Patricia Anthony's short stories have appeared in major science fiction magazines and anthologies. *Cold Allies* was her first novel and she has published two others so far, *Brother Termite* and *Happy Policeman*. Her fourth is imminent. She lives in Dallas, Texas.

Cold Allies

Patricia Anthony

NEW ENGLISH LIBRARY
Hodder and Stoughton

Copyright © 1993 by Patricia Anthony

First published in Great Britain in 1995
by Hodder and Stoughton
A division of Hodder Headline PLC

A New English Library paperback

An episode of this book first appeared, in a different form,
in the July, 1992 issue of *Isaac Asimov's Science Fiction Magazine*,
under the title 'Blue Woofers'.

The right of Patricia Anthony to be identified as the Author of
the Work has been asserted by her in accordance with the
Copyright, Designs and Patents Act 1988.

10 9 8 7 6 5 4 3 2 1

British Library Cataloguing in Publication Data
A CIP catalogue record for this title is available from
the British Library.

ISBN 0 340 61842 6

Printed and bound in Great Britain by
Cox & Wyman Ltd, Reading, Berkshire

Hodder and Stoughton
A Division of Hodder Headline PLC
338 Euston Road
London NW1 3BH

To Charlie Ryan, editor of *Aboriginal Science Fiction*,
who pulled me from the slush pile and gave me his kind,
tireless encouragement. And to Mary Ryan and
Laurel Lucas and the rest of my extended family.

CHAPTER 1

AUTUMN, NEAR KSAVEROVKA, UKRAINE

The artillery shell passing overhead made a noise like tearing paper. It was a huge sound, the noise God might have made rending the sky in two.

"Major Shcheribitsky!" Lt. General Baranyk shouted, emerging from his BRDM scout just as the dun grass before him blossomed into fire. A heartbeat later, tardy as thunder to remote lightning, came the dull boom-booms of the strikes.

"Major Shcheribitsky! What is our position?"

But the major was already out of his tank, shouting into his radio phone.

The spread of Ukrainian vehicles, fragile dots on the ocean of grass, was caught in a tempest of red and black, a sudden fall hailstorm of flame and deep-throated sound.

No. This can't be, Baranyk thought. Everything was out of position. The Arab National Army should be east of him someplace, sandwiched between his own regiment and General Ilschenko's. Baranyk should be flanking the enemy, not riding directly into their line of fire.

Baranyk's BTR-80 personnel carriers were still loaded, the majority of the infantry providing convenient cannon fodder. The armored BMPs traveling with them had loosed their Sagger missiles. White trails scratched the sky.

Above his head another errant enemy shell went over with a loud shurring sound, the tissue-paper noise of his battle plans ripping apart.

"Shcheribitsky!" Baranyk called, bringing his field glasses to his eyes.

Apocalypse rode the meadow. Most of his tanks had stopped to adjust their positions so they were face-front to the town on the horizon. Some were moving blind, crashing into each other in confusion, their commanders either under cover or dead. The personnel carriers and BMPs were lurching forward, angling in front of the two tank battalions and driving right into the defended opponent.

"Order the infantry to withdraw!" Baranyk lowered the glasses in time to see the stricken look on the major's pitted face.

"I can't get through to them, general," he replied. "They have driven too far ahead and the Arabs are jamming."

Too far ahead, Baranyk's mind echoed numbly. Yes, too far ahead. His infantry had somehow got in front of his tanks. If they kept going as they were, they would not need to fear the enemy. Ukrainian shells would kill them.

Baranyk crawled up the deck of Shcheribitsky's T-80 to the angular turret.

The wiry little major followed, snatching at him. "Get down, sir. They will have our range."

Frantic, Baranyk twisted out of Shcheribitsky's grip. He reached the closed hatch and stood, lifting the glasses to his eyes.

The Arabs had found the first tank battalion bunched, and now its funeral pyres littered the field. Like startled rabbits, the second battalion had frozen in place. They were at last firing back, and had loosed smoke from their baffles; but a whimsical wind whipped the smoke to and fro, obscuring the vision of the commanders behind as much as confusing the enemy.

If his tanks were blind, his infantry was deaf. Never hearing the order to retreat, the BMPs and personnel carriers rushed toward the enemy artillery.

Oh, Baranyk's mind voiced in an eerie, graveyard hush. *So sad*. The only order his regiment had heard was that morning's Order of the Day: they were to attack that afternoon. In the midst of fire, they could not, would not, be flexible. Good Ukrainian soldiers, good mothers' sons, they did what they were told.

Major Shcheribitsky climbed up next to him. "Sir? What are the orders?" he asked.

For once Baranyk had no answer. Carried on the fretful wind was the sour smell of autumn and the prickly scent of cordite. Through the glasses the general watched as his tanks stalled and his infantry hurried to oblivion.

There in the southern town of Grebonki the ANA lay hidden: Iranians, Iraqis, along with more familiar killers— Uzbeks, Azerbaijanis, and Muslim Cossacks. Those wayward children of the Red Army, his former comrades, were going to murder them all.

"Sir! Sir!" a corporal on the ground was shouting. Baranyk took his eyes from his glasses and glanced down. "Corporal Zgursky from Reconnaissance," the man announced. "I was trying to tell my captain, but he wouldn't listen, sir!"

"Not now!" Baranyk snapped. Zgursky blanched, and suddenly Baranyk forgot his rage. He noticed how young the corporal was, how smooth-cheeked and fresh-faced and innocent. *What a good soldier Zgursky must be*, Baranyk thought. So polite he was, a proud mother's son. "Go ahead," the general said, tempering his voice. "If it's important, tell me."

The corporal shifted his weight, uneasy under the combined gazes of Baranyk and the major. "Grebonki, sir. I'm from Grebonki. And I was trying to tell my captain the town to our south is Ksaverovka. We are seven kilometers from what the captain thought was our position."

Baranyk whipped his head toward the battle. Even without the glasses he could tell it was a rout. Through his chest, through the soles of his feet, he could feel the hollow bass thuds of the shells. Smoke curled toward the cloudless bowl of blue sky: gray smoke from the tank baffles, black smoke from the burning T-80s.

"I can deploy the artillery," Major Shcheribitsky said, his tone disheartened and unsure.

"No use," Baranyk whispered, his words carried away by the ripping sound of a shell.

"What, sir?" the major asked, cupping a hand to his ear.

"No use!" Baranyk shouted, finding his voice. "They are still on their tractors, and it will take over thirty damned minutes to get them deployed! Move those tanks forward! Tell them to attack!"

Seven kilometers out of position, his infantry bare and unprotected as a baby's ass. Seven kilometers and the maps were all wrong.

"Sir!" the major screamed over the noise. A shell hit uncomfortably near, making Shcheribitsky flinch. "Sir! Did you say attack?"

Baranyk turned so fast that the small major stumbled back, nearly losing his footing. "Yes! Attack!" Seeing the major's incredulous expression, he screamed, "Don't blame me! Blame the Russians! We plead for help and what do they give us? Outdated, erroneous Soviet maps!"

The major's thin mouth tightened. A moment later he called down to the communications officer.

The general brought the glasses to his eyes again. What he saw in the binoculars confused him. At first he thought the ground itself must be moving. The brown earth, like a turgid sea, crested and rolled. When he realized what he was witness to, all hope left, even the thready hope of stalemate.

"Retreat!" Baranyk ordered, climbing off the tank.

Shcheribitsky followed him. "Sir. Only the tanks can hear us. The others—"

Baranyk whirled. "It is a human wave! Retreat!"

The major's tone was soft, doubtful. "But our infantry," he said.

"I know."

There was nothing Baranyk could do, nothing of use Shcheribitsky could tell him. Baranyk knew it all. He knew that his infantry was dead, that the battle was lost, that

Pogrebnyak's and Ilschenko's divisions could not hold. The Arabs would roll into Kiev, all for a seven-kilometer mistake, all because a captain would not listen to a corporal.

"I order you to call a retreat," Baranyk said. The tranquil aftermath of defeat surprised him. He should be sorrowful, he thought. There should be self-recriminations. Instead he felt peace descend, the peculiar serenity of despair. "Do it now, major, and do it fast."

The major snapped his fingers, and a sergeant ran up with the radio. "Where do we retreat to, sir?"

"West," Baranyk replied, not considering any particular location. There were no places to hide; only places they could run. After a pause he climbed onto the back deck of his BRDM and stepped through the cupola.

Standing on his seat, Baranyk watched what was left of his tanks begin to roll out of the fog a scant five kilometers ahead of the deadly human sea.

"Shcheribitsky?" Baranyk called just before he fled the battle.

The major glanced up from his field telephone. "Sir?"

"Tell them not to stop and pick up the wounded."

As Baranyk watched, he saw Shcheribitsky's gaze grow hollow, as though the little major were staring through the vacuous eyes of the dead. "But they take no prisoners, sir."

"I know that," Baranyk replied.

It was forty-five minutes later, well out of sight and sound of conflict, that Baranyk discovered how fleeting, how fragile defeat's peace could be. Three mechanized rifle battalions, he thought. One tank battalion. Of the 2,250 men he'd taken into battle, at least 1,500 were gone.

His composure burst. From simple exhaustion, he didn't try to suppress his tears. Out of respect for the dead, he refused to cover his face.

CHAPTER 2

SPRING, CRAV COMMAND, TRÁS-OS-MONTES, PORTUGAL

Even though he had overslept that morning and had to be dressed in two minutes flat, Sergeant Gordon Means stopped dead on the porch of his barracks. Cocking his head, he listened to the low, angry rumbling from the south. He stood, his non-reg Nikes unlaced, his fatigue shirt tucked messily into his unbelted battle dress trousers, wondering if the base was under attack and whether he should go get his M-16 or hide under his cot.

Across the mist-shrouded, pine-scented yard ambled two Brit officers, one still chewing on a piece of toast. Gordon watched them pass.

Yoo-hoo, guys. We're under fire, he wanted to call. Christ. Hadn't they heard it?

" . . . ball went right between the goalie's feet," the Brit captain said to the major, sounding as though he were not in a war at all but auditioning for the BBC.

The low thuds came again. Gordon fought the urge to dive for cover. *Oh,* he thought, recognizing the sound for what it was and feeling more than slightly stupid.

Thunder. Just thunder. The ratcheting of his heart began to slow.

When he felt steady enough to walk, he left the porch and trotted to the bunker. On its pad an Apache helicopter dripped condensation down its sleek, greenish hide. The sun, just under the eastern horizon, was backwashing the overcast sky with gray light. To the west, feather boas of fog caressed the shoulders of the mountains.

Glancing at his watch, he noticed it was past 0700. He was late for duty again.

Hurrying, he took the four flights of cement steps a pair at a time until he was deep in the fluorescent-lit guts of the bunker. He rushed down the olive-painted hall, past the other blast doors, and paused before the third from the end on the right. Performing his morning ritual, he took a skip-step, brought his right leg out hard, and kicked the ill-hung and often recalcitrant door under the knob. It popped open, colliding with a bang against the block wall.

Gordon landed in the entrance, crouched in his killer-karate posture, and froze. Someone was sitting in his room. And not just any someone. Between Gordon's upraised hands was framed the solemn, unsmiling figure of Colonel Pelham.

"As you were," the colonel said.

Gordon automatically straightened. As he did, his pants slid to his bony hips. He caught them before they fell any farther.

"They killed another satellite," the colonel told him.

Gordon glanced up from buckling his web belt. Pelham's round face was the exact color of semisweet chocolate; at his temples was a dusting of sugar-white. Had his expression been kinder, he might have resembled a Hershey elf.

"We've tracked the laser pulse to the Pyrenees again," Pelham went on. "You didn't get all the cannon."

"Oops. Sorry about that, sir. But begging the colonel's pardon, if I had some backup, maybe the lasers would be easier to get."

"Convince the French, sergeant," Pelham said dryly. "You just go convince the French the Arabs are up there. They keep telling Centcom-West that the Arabs are firing from the Spanish side, not theirs."

For a moment there was quiet. Gordon could hear the faint clack-clack of Stendhal's unit from the other room.

He wondered where Stendhal's CRAV was headed and if it would survive.

"Close the door," Pelham said.

Gordon eased the door to and gave it a shove, jamming it more or less closed. When he turned, the colonel was eyeing him. Gordon wished he could hide his Nikes, wished he had made it to work a few minutes earlier, wished he hadn't come Kung-Fuing it through that door.

"Sit down," the colonel ordered.

The only other place in the room to sit was at the controls of his CRAV. Gordon perched uneasily on the padded seat, his eyes darting away from the wire-basket gloves and the black plastic goggles.

Gordon hated people watching him work with the robot, even though, with the goggles on, he could see nothing but what the CRAV unit saw, could hear nothing but what its microphones picked up. Still, he figured, it was like sex: he could get deaf-and-blind involved in that, too, but wouldn't want anyone making notes on his performance.

"Mitsubishi's here. Their munitions product manager will be monitoring you."

Gordon snapped his head toward the colonel.

Pelham must have caught the panic in his expression, Gordon thought, because the colonel smiled. It wasn't much of a smile, but, then, the war was going so poorly that that was all Pelham could probably manage.

"Don't sweat it," the colonel told him. The man had a voice that mimicked the semisweet chocolate of his face: it was thick and dark and smooth. "Just the usual contractor curiosity. He wants to monitor all the operators. I told him, as far as performance was concerned, you were probably the best."

Pelham, perhaps wisely, let the compliment lie. He sat, his hands clasped over his taut, camouflage-covered belly, and stared. He watched Gordon the way a psychiatrist watches a new patient.

When the silence between them grew uncomfortable, Gordon finally asked, "When's he going to be monitoring, sir?"

"Beginning today. Answer any questions he asks. Treat him with the proper courtesy." The colonel stood up, all lean six feet four of him. He was, as usual, ramrod straight, his bowed head the only concession to the low-ceilinged room. "I've downloaded the targeting to your computer. Lunch, of course, will be brought in. This is a Till-Kill mission." Suddenly his face softened. "You're late again. Get any breakfast?"

"Yes, sir. Sorry, sir. I didn't feel like breakfast," Gordon lied, not wanting to admit he hadn't awakened in time to drop by the mess hall.

"Take out that laser, sergeant," Pelham said, his gaze heavy with allotted responsibility, settled on Gordon. "And do it fast. If they shoot down our last Super Keyhole and discover you're still alive and kicking, they may put two and two together. They'll fire on the civilian AT&T satellite, and you won't have an operational CRAV anymore."

On his way out, Pelham patted Gordon's shoulder absently and fought with the door until it opened. When he was gone Gordon slipped his hands into the gloves of his Computerized Robotic Assault Vehicle and set the opaque goggles over his face. To boost his morale, he started to hum the CRAV corps song.

THE PYRENEES

It was like waking up for the second time that morning, or like God creating the world: first there was darkness; then Gordon jerked his head twice to the right, activating the unit.

He was deep in the forest. Somewhere to his right a lark trilled in the fog. He slipped his feet into the control shoes, finding them blind, and pressed down on the accelerator. The CRAV came to life, the hum of its nuclear motor so quiet that the bird never stopped singing.

Tipping his head left, Gordon brought the Global Positioning System on line. The military satellite's lime-green map superimposed itself over the mist-bound forest. To the lower left of his vision field his own software noted that all weapons systems were functional.

So. Here he was. Yes, sir. Right in the mountains just below the town of Bagnères-de-Luchon. Like a caution light, a yellow dot blinked at the head of the valley. That's where the pulse laser was presumed to be, along with a company of pissed-off Arabs.

Shuffling his feet, Gordon brought the piano-sized robot up out of the trench he'd dug for it the night before. The engine's mosquito hum rose to a faint squeal. The bird stopped its singing mid-verse.

According to the engineers, CRAVs conveyed no sense of touch, but all the operators felt things anyway. They talked about it sometimes, but only among themselves. At that moment Gordon could feel the knobbed backbone of the mountain under the treads of the robot, could feel the belly-soft, pine-needled loess in between. He'd felt the artillery shell that killed his first CRAV. Sometimes it seemed to him he'd died right along with it.

Hey, hey, Ma, he'd written to his mother, who was living in a refugee camp somewhere in Arkansas. *I died today.*

Died not as he had thought he might two years ago, of hunger and thirst in the Nebraska desert the Greenhouse Effect had wrought. No. He'd died quick and hard, in a hot-air burst of shrapnel in the rain-soaked Pyrenees.

It had been weeks before he talked about the loss of the unit. After that, he joked about the experience with the other CRAV freaks, but only a little. Almost a year later, it still bothered him. The diamond vapor-plated CRAV was a heroic extension of his scrawny body, a Superman Doppelgänger of titanium and steel. It was, in a way, his better half.

Carefully, cautiously, he made his way down the mountain until he was in sight of the road. There he stopped, engine idling. Pressed into the narrow asphalt trail were the serrated prints of tanks.

He strained to listen, but there wasn't much to hear: no growl of diesel engines, no voices. In the still air, the fog lay thick across an enamel-green pasture.

"Da-a-angerous, deadly," he breathed. The wraparound goggles shut off all sounds from the command room, even his own. He sang on in silence. "A missile clutched between our che-e-e-ks."

There should be some noise, he thought. The village wasn't that far, just a mile to the west. He should be hearing the lowing of cattle, the tinkle of goat bells.

"Ro-o-bot geeks."

He pressed his foot gently, dubiously, to the accelerator. A half-mile up the road he found a body.

An old peasant woman. Black shawl. Gray hair beginning to revolt from the tyranny of its pins. She was lying on the other side of the road, head resting on her arm, body curled as though in sleep. Blinking once hard, he activated his telescopic vision. There were goddamned flies crawling on her face.

He blinked again quickly, more a reaction of surprise than a command. His vision returned to normal, and suddenly she was just an old lady who had decided to plunk down where she was and catch a few Zs.

There was no blood on her. No wounds. Her eyes were open, her lips fish-mouthed. Her face a dusty blue.

"Scene One, Act One of *Night of the Living Dead*." Gordon whispered, even though he couldn't hear himself talk, even though he knew he was four hundred and fifty miles away.

He trundled on nervously, knowing where there was one gas victim, there were bound to be more. At the next turn of the road he found them, sprawled over a yellow and white buttercup-massed pasture. All of Bagnères-de-Luchon was there. The Arab National Army had obviously marched them into the flower-bedecked meadow. And the people had stood and waited, wondering what would come next.

Death had. Only a few, it seemed, had figured out the mystery early and tried to flee the helicopter's spray. They lay on the road, they hung over fences, they sprawled loose-limbed in the sweet grass of the roadside ditch. A yellow hound was feeding on a body.

"Whoa. Stephen King does France," Gordon whispered.

Abruptly the dog yelped and bolted, glancing to the field in alarm.

His heart doing a triple-step, Gordon turned to see what had scared the dog. At first he thought it was his imagination, the morning was so misty, the thing moving in the pasture so subtle. A cold thing, neon blue.

He blinked. The pasture clicked into close focus. The blue light was real. Not much brighter than the fog, it flitted from corpse to corpse, like a butterfly among flowers.

The light halted. Gordon had the eerie sensation it was regarding him. A sort of wintry lassitude weighed him down, the same placid comfort that proceeds a death by freezing. His eyes started to close. Faintly, in the back of his mind, he could hear the monotonous tap-tap-tap of sleet striking a window.

He shook himself out of the half-sleep, and his eyes popped open to darkness. He'd inadvertently shut down the CRAV.

He gasped. Violently he jerked his head twice to the right. The vision field came back. The blue light was closer, right at the fence; and he could sense, as he could feel his robot arms and treads, the light's intense curiosity.

"Arm missiles!" he screamed.

The head-up display sprang into life. The blue light was square in the center of the kill box.

The words MISSILES ARMED, MISSILES ARMED marched in red across his vision.

He touched the stud in the little finger of his left glove and tried to bring it into contact with his thumb. His hands were shaking like a drunk with the d.t.'s. Jesus God. He didn't have the strength to push his fingers together hard enough to fire.

The thing was closer now, moving through the log fence like a ghost. The sound in his mind grew louder, the tap-tap-tap more authoritative now, hail more than sleet. Gordon was afraid that he would freeze where he sat and that the duty officer would find him at lunchtime, arms and legs encased in ice, mouth open like the gassed dead in a last, airless shriek.

A few clustered anemones bowed their heavy heads at the light's passing. It eased over the body of a teenaged girl, ruffling her hair, her clothes.

Gordon's thumb finally found the bulge at his little finger, finally steadied a bit. He backed up a few feet to move the light into the kill box. Out of the corner of his vision he could see the robot fingers mimic his hand's firing position. The steel hand, too, was trembling.

An explosion of light and sound. In the chaos something scraped his cheeks, nicked the bridge of his nose.

"Don't fire!" Colonel Pelham was shouting. "For God's sake, don't fire!"

Gordon struggled out of his command chair, but a female MP caught him in a bear hug. In front of his startled, disbelieving eyes was the boxy computer unit of the CRAV, the blank olive wall. They'd pulled off the goggles too fast; he felt dislocated from his body. He arched his back, and his forehead collided with the MP's cheek.

"Settle down," the MP growled.

The control room was crowded with people, and Colonel Pelham was taking Gordon's gloves off so quickly that the leads scraped his skin.

"Print that!" someone snapped.

Still dazed, Gordon turned to the voice. A stocky Oriental man with a black-and-yellow Mitsubishi windbreaker was staring at him.

"Help that soldier," the man said when he caught Gordon's glance. "You took him out of CRAV reality too abruptly."

Gordon's ear stung from the goggles. Warm blood trickled down his neck.

The man from Mitsubishi popped the floppy disk out of its drive and handed it to the colonel.

"Get my unit," Gordon said, but no one was listening to him. No wonder. His tongue and mouth were thick, his words mushy.

"My unit." They'd left his CRAV out in the field, out in the goddamned road. Left it vulnerable to the attack of that cold, blue light.

Pelham pocketed the disk and looked at Gordon curiously. They were all staring at him now, the contractor representative, the colonel, the MP.

"You let that thing get my robot," Gordon said and, to his shame, started to cry.

IN THE LIGHT

Lieutenant Justin Searles snapped awake to find himself in a high-backed seat, a blanket rumpled around him. Except for the faint growl of the engine, the bus's interior was burdened with silence, the sort of sticky, late-night silence in which nothing moves.

Beyond the night in the window, a bloated moon coated the desert with fish-belly light. He stared out, wondering where he was. An old, established desert. Arizona. Maybe New Mexico. The rocking motion of the bus and the musty smell of long-enclosed places lulled him to sleep again.

He shut his eyes and dreamed of the persistent tap-tap of cold fingernails against his bedroom window, a sound like the dead wanting in.

Jackknifing forward, he jerked himself out of his doze. It seemed to him that he had had this dream before; and it seemed that he had never quite awakened from it. His heart was doing a heavy-metal rock number in his chest, and his breath came hard and fast and painful. Panicky, he blinked into the potato-chip bag- and magazine-littered darkness.

On an aisle seat near the door an elderly man was snoring softly, mouth ajar, hand around a bent-spined paperback. Reading lights haloed the heads of the sleeping passengers, as though the small group were dozing away the miracle of Pentecost.

Justin's heart started to slow. The ache in his chest subsided. Peering over his shoulder, he noticed someone else awake. The girl had brown hair and huge brown bon-bon eyes.

An American girl, he thought. As his mind formed the words, he could see her smile flicker and die.

Somewhere pellets of ice rattled against rocky ground, the sound of their impact so loud that he wanted to cover his ears. Instead, he yanked the blanket to his neck and looked out the window in time to see a shooting star flash orange across the desert sky.

"Hello. My name is—" a voice said.

He turned. The girl was sitting next to him, but he couldn't, for the life of him, remember moving over for her. *I must have, right?* he asked himself. *I just moved over and forgot about it, that's all.*

Her brows furrowed in thought and then cleared. "Ann," she said after a moment, as though she had just then decided on the name and thought her decision charming. "My name's Ann. Where are you headed?"

"I—" He couldn't remember. He couldn't remember where he was going. "I think there's something wrong," he hissed.

The clatter of frozen rain was so intrusive, the noise made him forget what else he was going to say. It was so loud he began to wonder if in the morning he would find the inside of his skull coated with ice.

Swiveling, he stared out the window and saw the orange smudge against the sky again.

No. That burning thing wasn't a falling star. Oh, God. It was an F-14 crashing.

"Read me your book," Ann said.

Her voice startled him. He looked down at his hands and saw he was holding a Navy manual with the words TOP SECRET emblazoned in white across the dark-blue cover.

"Read it to me aloud," she told him, leaning toward him intimately.

He opened to the first page.

CHAPTER ONE, it said in large, sans-serif type.

And under that was printed:

MAYDAY

MAYDAY

MAYDAY

With a spasm of fear he slammed the book shut. At his shoulder the girl was staring at him.

"What's the matter?" she asked. Suddenly her face began to sag, the features drooping, as though its underlying structure was as boneless as a snail.

He tried his best to get out of his seat, but the blanket held him down. "Jesus God! I'm not on a bus. Where am I?"

She put her hand on his arm. There was a mushy, arctic feel to her flesh. "In a moment. I want you to read me the book now."

He moaned and twisted. The book dropped from his lap.

"Don't be afraid," she told him. "We won't hurt you."

The bus was rolling side-to-side like a ship on a slow sea. Down the aisle came the bus driver, steadying himself by the tops of the seats.

"What's the matter, boy?" he asked angrily. The bus driver's face was jowly and the armature of his skull nearly buried in fat. And Justin knew, he knew for sure, that if he dared touch the man's cheek, his hand would sink into that gummy flesh.

"Don't you want to fuck her?" the driver asked.

The fat driver, the boneless girl, had him trapped against the window. He turned to look out, to see if there was some escape.

The F-14 was going down in a blaze of glory, twin dandelion fluffs of parachutes behind it.

"Take her to the back," the bus driver said. "There are empty seats in the back and no one's looking. You can fuck her all you want. You can fuck her brains out."

With a moan, Justin tore his gaze from the window and looked at the girl. His gaze flash-froze there. Behind her blank eyes he could sense the strange, chill weatherhead of her thoughts.

CRAV COMMAND, TRÁS-OS-MONTES, PORTUGAL

Sometimes it seemed the lesson the Army most wanted to teach Gordon was how to wait. After being dragged from his command chair, he'd been taken to a small, windowless room, where he sat for an hour. He had the time to contemplate his situation (screwed) and his bladder (full).

Someone in the next room was making coffee, and soon the smell began to remind him that he'd missed breakfast.

An MP finally came for him, the same MP he'd bumped faces with. She didn't smile. Gordon didn't either. With some chagrin he noticed her cheek was turning purple.

When he asked, she took him down the hall and let him use the bathroom. She didn't offer him a cup of coffee and she didn't mention lunch. When he came out of the john, she marched him straight into Colonel Pelham's empty office and left him there.

Gordon was fucked. He'd been about to shoot a missile off into—what? An optical illusion? They'd get him on a mental for sure.

Morose, Gordon sat and studied the room. Behind the colonel's high-backed chair were taped maps of the war. The red arrows of the ANA's movements were, in essence, a march from famine, an exodus from the greenhouse heat. Gordon's eyes followed the Arabs' desperate journey north through Spain, through Almería, Valencia, Barcelona. A smaller red arrow spiked up from the Black Sea to Bucharest, where the Syrians had stalled. From the east came the largest and most ominous of the red arrows, sweeping north across the Carpathians, losing part of its width in the tragic struggle through Ukraine and then spilling toward Poland. No, the war wasn't going well, and even if Gordon hadn't been able to read defeat in the maps, he could smell it in the stale air of Colonel Pelham's office.

The sound of the door opening behind him brought Gordon up and out of his chair. He dug his right toe in the linoleum and pivoted into a crisp, military salute, a real poker-up-the-butt salute. Only two things were wrong with it: the squeak his Nikes made during the pivot, and the fact that Pelham was nowhere around. Right hand to his eyebrow, Gordon stood staring at the man from Mitsubishi.

Quickly he lowered his arm. For a moment the two men studied each other. When the moment approached the point of awkwardness, Gordon bowed. He dipped his head the exact instant the Oriental stuck out his hand. He nearly got an eyeful of thumb.

"I am Toshio Ishimoto," the Japanese said in a clipped, Morse-code grunt.

Gordon straightened quickly enough to see Ishimoto jerk his hand back and give him a small, answering bow.

The rep had a low-center-of-gravity build, the kind of body that looked impossible to tip over. "I look forward to working with you, sergeant."

Before Gordon could respond, Pelham entered. Gordon hastily saluted again.

"At ease," Pelham said, shutting the door carefully behind him. "And sit down."

Gordon perched on the edge of his hard-backed, hard-seated Army-issue chair. Pelham dropped into his seat with a weary sigh. Ishimoto remained standing, hands clasped behind his back, looking more Army than Gordon could ever hope to look.

Pelham opened a drawer, pulled out a small tape recorder, and set it on the desk.

"Tell us everything," Pelham said.

"Yes, sir," Gordon replied. "What does the colonel want to know?"

"Your impressions," Ishimoto explained.

"From the moment you saw the blue light."

Gordon sat straighter. The blue light. So it hadn't been a figment of his imagination after all. "Scared, sir."

"Why?" Pelham asked.

"Why, sir?" Surprised by the question, Gordon glanced from Ishimoto to the colonel. Neither was giving clues. "Well, it was weird, sir."

"Weird?" Pelham asked.

"Yes, sir. And there were all those bodies. I mean, for a minute there I thought I had clicked into a Channel 27 rerun of some old John Carpenter film."

Pelham sighed, shook his head, and said to the manufacturer's rep, "Sergeant Means here is our resident comics and science fiction expert."

"How appropriate." The flicker of a grin lightened the Samurai scowl. "Did you feel the light acted intelligently?" Ishimoto asked suddenly in his machine-gun grunt.

The question made Gordon's jaw drop.

"Did you get that feeling, sergeant?" Pelham insisted. "This is subjective, here. We have the visuals. Now we want to know how you felt."

"Well, yes, sir. I mean, I never stopped to consider it. I just—"

"You just what, sergeant?" Pelham leaned forward.

"I felt it was curious about me."

Ishimoto and Pelham exchanged looks.

After a while, Gordon asked, "Sir?"

"Yes?" Pelham answered.

"What about my CRAV unit, sir?"

"Safe. Mr. Ishimoto sent it into cover."

Gordon shot a hard look at the manufacturer's rep. Having someone else use your unit was a little like having someone else use your girlfriend. "Thanks," Gordon muttered.

"My pleasure," Ishimoto said.

"Anything else you can tell us, sergeant?"

Gordon forgot protocol utterly. He simply shook his head.

"Well. You will never discuss this meeting or what you saw today. You will not mention it to the other operators, you understand?"

Gordon stared into Pelham's brown eyes. "Yes, sir."

"And if you encounter this object again, you are to treat it as a friendly."

"Okay," Gordon said. "So it's an object, okay, sir? That's cool. And I'll consider it a friendly. If it wants to come up and mate with my CRAV, I'll lift my tail for it, begging the colonel's pardon. But, goddamn, I mean if I'm not supposed to talk about it, can't I even know what it was?"

The other men exchanged glances again and then both stared at Gordon.

Ishimoto was the one who answered. "We don't know what it was."

Very quietly, very slowly, Pelham reached out and turned off the recorder. "Dismissed, sergeant," he said.

Gordon was so glad to leave the room that he realized only later that he still had his stripes and that he must not have fucked up too badly. And it was only after lunch, much too late to go back and bother the colonel, that he remembered the odd sound the blue light had made in his mind, that clattering sound of sleet.

CENTRAL ARMY HOSPITAL, BADAJOZ, SPAIN

Be a pediatrician, her mother had told her. *Go into obstetrics. That's the field for a woman.* Even now, Rita Beaudreaux thought, she could be back in the States running a general practice, wiping children's snotty noses and lancing boils on working-class butts. The National Guard captain considered her mother's advice as she pulled the overhead microphone closer and tapped the foot pedal to turn on the recorder.

"Body that of a well-nourished male between the ages of nineteen and twenty-five."

Scalpel in hand, she stared at the mutilated white boy and wondered what advice his mother had given him.

Be careful was the most likely, but this boy's job had compelled him to disobey.

"Severe blast trauma to the face has sheared away the mandibular structure," she said into the mike. "A few centimeters above the geniohyoid, the tongue is gone. Right orbit empty, the ethmoid sinus exposed."

She paused before going on. "No blood present in the wound."

No blood. She wondered if the mike had picked up the tremolo in her voice. The single intact eye of the boy on the table riveted her for a moment.

When wounded, he might have wanted to scream, but could not have managed more than a gurgle. A hiss. The palate, all its teeth intact, made a pale gothic arch over the ruins of the missing jaw, a grotesque half-cathedral. She lowered her gaze to his chest.

"Through the center of the sternum, a hole seven millimeters in diameter. The edges of the hole are clean and well defined."

As if made with a cookie cutter, she thought.

Clearing her throat, she added, "With no evidence of bruising."

Too neat for a bullet hole. She'd seen enough of those during her six years as a forensic pathologist at Bellevue. No, firearm trauma made a mess of the muscles, it liquefied fat.

Her scalpel cut through the corpse. The flesh made a peculiar sound, like tearing silk. "Fascia layer shows evidence of desiccation."

The corpse's underlying muscles were marbled, the color of port cheese. She followed the neat, perfectly circular hole down through the brittle balsa-wood sternum until she came to the empty pericardium. The hole that had caused the boy's death was small; but through it something or someone had neatly cut the aortic arch and lifted out the fist-sized heart.

There was no smell. There had been no predation. Of course not. All the fluids, all the red corpuscles were gone.

Disease? she wondered for the third time. But no disease she knew of could deliver this sort of full-body punch. The Army must not have thought so either, because they hadn't bothered to give her a clean room and her own sterile air supply. Still, the worry persisted somewhere in the dim med-school part of her mind. When studying oncology, she had imagined lumps in her breasts; and cardiology had made her await fearfully the occasional flutter of her heart. Now, looking at the corpse's flesh, she felt her skin begin to dry and tighten.

Chemical agent? Perhaps even now it was active. Perhaps it could penetrate her gloves. Her fingers began to itch.

Impossible. No disease, no chemical could drill through muscle and bone to suck up a living heart.

She was struck again by the horror on the young boy's face. Could her own face wear that horror? And under her coffee-and-milk skin would be parched coffee-and-milk flesh.

"Well?"

The voice came from behind her. She nearly dropped her scalpel. Whirling, she came face-to-face with "Loon" Lauterbach. The Saceur, NATO's Supreme Allied Commander in Europe, looked nattier in his camouflage BDUs than most men did in full dress.

"Damn it!" she snapped. "Don't sneak up on me like that!"

Lauterbach blinked in surprise, then laughed. "At ease," he said.

"Crap," she said under her breath and turned back to the corpse. She heard Lauterbach's approaching footsteps. He stood beside her, looking down. Most people, even Army people, wouldn't have had the guts for that.

"I thought you were in Portugal," she said.

"Flew in this afternoon." The small, balding four-star general did not lift his eyes from the corpse. "What killed him?"

"I don't know."

"Is it possible the shrapnel injury did?"

She began the caudal incision, making the tail of the autopsy Y a few inches higher than normal. Even the intestines, she noticed, were dehydrated. A little dust drifted up in the glare of the light. Cellular dust, creamy pale. She stepped back reflexively. Lauterbach didn't.

"Well?"

"I don't know," she told him.

"This soldier was alive yesterday. What could have done this to him?"

"Nothing could have," she answered.

"Well, something did."

"True desiccation reduces mass, and there is no sign of that here. Look at him. Just look at him, general," she ordered. "He's still a pudgy-cheeked boy. If he were mummified, those cheeks would be sunken and drawn."

At the last word, Lauterbach glanced up at her sharply. His yellowish hazel eyes were dispassionate, the eyes of a puma, a wolf. "You're not getting enough sleep."

"Neither are you," she shot back.

His expression wavered, his gaze became furtive. "I'm flying to Poland tonight. It's important for me to know. Did the shrapnel kill him?"

She looked at the wound. In one lightning-from-God instant, the kid had lost half his face. "Given medical attention soon enough, he would have lived."

The corners of Lauterbach's mouth dipped in revulsion. She could almost read his thoughts: *For what?* "Do you suppose he wanted to die?" he asked quietly.

Rita glanced at the general curiously. His face was so weary that he seemed close to illness. War was a lamprey, a sucker of life. It found its victims in battle where death came easy, and even in bunkers where it did not.

Lauterbach was a hands-on commander, flitting from one front to the next, exhorting his tired army. Maybe his dearest wish was that his plane would go down. The young white boy on the stainless steel table must have ached for a desperate peace like that.

"Yes. I'm sure he did," she told him.

The general nodded. "Then it was as though he were killed by friendly fire."

"Friendly?"

"Loving fire." His voice was so soft, it could barely be heard above the sound of the circulated air from the ducts.

ARLINGTON, VIRGINIA

Linda Parisi trudged home from the city bus stop, suitcase in hand. The gig in Boston had been a killer: too little money, too many strange people. They'd come up to her after the lecture, their eyes wide with hope and desperate invention, to tell her how they, too, had talked to the Eridanians, and how the Eridanians had turned their lives around, blah, blah, blah.

She limped up the concrete steps of the red-brick apartment house, staggering under the weight of her battered Samsonite.

Maybe, she thought, some chivalrous or impressionable soul would hear her and come out to help. As loud and slow as she made her progress, however—banging her suitcase pointedly against the walls as she passed—no one hurried to the rescue.

The hall of the apartment house was dim and littered. At her chipped steel door she fought the usual battle with her keys: two for the twin deadbolts, one for the regular lock.

Inside she found that her poodle had thrown up on the carpet in revenge for her trip. Farther in, she discovered the full extent of the obtuse dog's retaliation. Lacy had spilled his water and carpeted the kitchen with soaked and crumbling Kibbles and Bits.

The light on the answering machine was blinking. On her way to the cramped closet for the broom, Mrs. Parisi hit the MESSAGE pad on the phone.

"Call me," said the machine.

She found the broom and dustpan and was toting them to the kitchen by the time the beep sounded and the next message came on.

"I'm not kidding." The same voice. "Call me."

"Oh, ca-ca," she replied, unleashing the irritation she'd kept in check the entire weekend. "Oh, ca-ca on you. I hope you find yourself chin-deep in the smelly."

Mrs. Parisi knew the voice, of course. Feet aching, she halted in the door of the kitchen and surveyed the chaos. Next to her sat Lacy, tail a-wag, obviously delighted with his handiwork.

Beep. "Call me at home, call me at work. Just call me. Our lives are in danger."

Sighing, Mrs. Parisi swept the dog food into a pile and used the dustpan to dump it back into Lacy's bowl. "Din-din," she said with a venomous smile.

Before she called her editor/publisher, Mrs. Parisi took off her sensible pumps. When she was comfortably settled on the sofa, she lifted the receiver, hit the 1 button, and listened to the rapid, tuneless tones as the phone automatically dialed.

"Tau Ceti Publications," the receptionist chirped. The girl sounded very dim and very young.

"Is Tad Ellis there?"

"He's on another line," the girl said. "May I take a message?"

"This is Linda Parisi—"

"Oh!" The girl was so startled that the perkiness left her voice. She sounded older, and even intelligent. "I know he wants to talk with you, Mrs. Parisi. Please hold."

Mrs. Parisi was treated to Muzak: the Valium String Quartet's rendition of *Evergreen*. Then the tenor voice of Tad Ellis came on. "The pogrom's started," he said.

Mrs. Parisi didn't respond. She sat contemplating the ache in her elbow and pondering the indigestible Kibble that Ellis had just fed her.

"You there?" Ellis asked at last.

"Of course."

The IRS? Parisi wondered. *The Justice Department?* Just who did silly Ellis think was after them this time?

"Two guys in dark suits came by," Ellis went on. "They asked about you. They asked about your *books*."

Mrs. Parisi's eyes fled to the shelves where *Meeting the Eridanians*, *The Eridani Way*, and *In the Bright Eridanian Light* were displayed.

"It's started, Linda," Ellis said in a breathy, conspiracy-theory voice. "They asked for your address and phone number. I gave them your old one, but they're bound to catch up with you sooner or later. They're *very* interested in what we know about UFOs. They've picked up Gene. They got to Sally."

"Well, bless their hearts."

"Are you listening to me?"

"Yes, dear. I am."

"Get out of town," Ellis said in a firm voice and hung up, leaving Mrs. Parisi listening to the hum of the empty line. She put down the receiver and stared at the watching dog.

"Sillies, Lacy," she told him with a sigh. "This business is simply packed full of sillies."

CENTCOM-EAST, WARSAW, POLAND

Lt. General Valentin Baranyk looked up from his doodling and caught the eye of the German commander, Kurt Weiderhausen. The German was young, probably no more than forty-five or -six, so there was no way for him to remember the Great Patriotic War. Still, Germans were sensitive about the subject. The smooth-faced German looked uncomfortable, and Baranyk wondered if that was because of the progress of the eastern campaign, or the fact that the American was late, or simply because he found himself at the head of another invasion of Poland, however friendly.

Andrzej Czajowski, on the other hand, seemed placid. The Saceur-East was smiling as he toyed with his coffee cup, smiling as though remembering some childhood song. It was easier, Baranyk knew, to find a pleasant spot in your memories and tuck your mind away there. He himself had made reliving childhood a habit. To keep from remembering Kiev.

That was where it had all got away from him, everything: his peace of mind, his good name, his army. The battle out of control, the troops spilling through his incapable fingers like water. At night, when Baranyk closed his eyes, he could hear the squeak of the tanks, the thuds of the artillery. And could see, painted on the smoke-dark southern sky, the glow of Kiev in flames.

Baranyk was startled from his reverie when an aide announced the American. Dourly he watched the German and the Pole look up. They stared at the door as though God and His archangels were about to make an entrance. *Stupid,* Baranyk thought. No one, not even the Americans, could save them.

"Gentlemen," the entering American said with a nod. Lauterbach was an intelligent-looking, small, spare man, too small, Baranyk thought, to be a warrior. He fought small and smart, too, like a trapdoor spider, popping out of his hole at the oddest times. The Arabs fretted and plucked at him without effect, as though he had somehow got into their clothes.

Before the American even sat down, he began a rapid-fire monologue as though he realized, even better than the men in the room, that time was running out.

"Two days ago, we lost a pilot," the American general said. "A Lieutenant j.g. Justin Searles. He was flying an old Super Tom. It was hit by flak and went down. He and his radio intercept officer bailed out at the same time. The RIO made it to the ground. Searles did not. If we are to believe the RIO, the Woofers captured him."

Baranyk shifted his gaze to the other commanders at the table. The German looked worried, but that was his usual expression. The Pole seemed stunned.

"Then they are not simply observing," Czajowski said.

"No." The American linked his hands on the table, ignored the coffee the aide poured for him. "We must consider them a player. But that does not necessarily mean they are an enemy."

"The mutilations?" Weiderhausen asked. "You are having them, too?"

Lauterbach nodded.

"If they are killing our soldiers . . ."

"We're not sure of that," the American said quickly. "The mutilations might be a form of mercy killing. They take only the severely wounded. Besides, as many Arabs have been found mutilated. We must not forget that we are dealing with an alien mentality—"

"You assume aliens," Baranyk blurted. "*You* assume, general. Perhaps the rest of us believe something else."

Lauterbach gave him a level, appraising look. "The lights are extraterrestrial ships. And the beings who control them are centuries ahead of us in technology. If you fire on them, you may find it the worst command decision you've ever made."

"Kiev was my worst command decision. The rest, as you Americans say, is uphill from there." Baranyk glanced up from his own entwined hands in time to catch the pity in the German's face.

Baranyk tore his gaze away from Weiderhausen's pale blue eyes and back to the emotionless hazel eyes of the American. "These Woofers have nothing to do with the war. They are irritants only. Where are our supplies? You cannot fly planes on piss."

"Nobody has fuel," the American told him quietly. "And the Gibraltar Dam keeps our tankers out of the Mediterranean. If you want oil, why don't you go to your old comrades in Russia? Siberia's oil-rich."

Baranyk snorted and shook his head. "The Russians bartered my Ukraine for their own safety. They wouldn't give me adequate maps; why should they give me oil? In the meantime we are losing a war."

"I still say our best chance is to get the Woofers to join the fight with us," Lauterbach told him.

"If you insist they are alien," the Ukrainian replied, "then how can we communicate? We fail to understand the Arabs. How do we understand little blue lights?"

"Oh, Valentin," the American sighed. "I think I understand the Arabs. They're just hungry."

Baranyk dismissed the Greenhouse Effect with a wave of his hand. "Let them eat dirt."

The American's lips tightened. "I thought that's what we were trying to do."

A short, introverted silence in the room. The Pole took another sip of coffee. The German stared off into middle distance. Lauterbach regarded the table.

"I have feelings for the victims of famine," Baranyk said when the silence grew unbearable. "The Chinese have suffered, for example, but they do not start wars."

"No, they die very quietly, the Chinese," Czajowski murmured.

From the end of the table, Lauterbach spoke, his voice barely above a tired whisper. "One thousand Americans die of starvation every day."

Baranyk caught the wince in the German's face, in the Pole's. The Americans had their famine, but Europe had its war. To Baranyk, one debt canceled another. The Americans had no heart for battle, even though they had sent their best commanders, their soldiers, their magical weapons. It was not America that was being invaded. And if worse came to worst, they could pull out and go home.

"God. Don't you see how sad it is?" the American asked, spreading his arms. "These aliens have traveled across space to find us starving, to find us killing each other. Yes, there are mutilations. I don't deny that. Perhaps they lack a concept of death. Or perhaps they have a higher notion of it." His weary eyes settled on each of the men at the table. "Sometimes I wonder if they might be appalled that we hold life so cheap."

CHAPTER 3

NEAR CALHAN, COLORADO

They'd started from Texas, were turned back at Missouri, and need had driven them west. Just past Topeka, his Pa died, and he buried him on the side of the highway, scooping up the hard earth with a crowbar, burning his hands on the sun-scorched rocks.

Only when the state troopers stopped him outside Colorado Springs did Jerry realize he'd run out of traveling room.

To Jerry's right was a makeshift refugee camp, a hardscrabble nightmare of a place, all tin and canvas and plywood. It squatted on the beige desert floor, nearly all a color with the sand and stinking of heat and shit and death. Behind the Colorado State policeman with the bermuda shorts and the mirror sunglasses stretched a broad expanse of desert. In the bright distance blue-purple clouds were sitting on the ground.

"It gonna rain?" he asked the trooper with awe.

The man stopped reading aloud from Colorado Injunction 236 to look back over his shoulder. "Huh?"

"Rain. See them clouds?"

"Shit. Those aren't clouds," the trooper laughed. "Those are mountains."

Jerry didn't hear the rest of what the trooper was reading.

He was busy looking at the mountains. It was like looking into the face of God.

"Hey! Hey!" the trooper finally said, waving a hand in Jerry's face. "You with me here, or what?"

"Yes, sir." It was hot, just as hot as it had been in Texas, a long way to drive, Jerry thought, not to escape the heat. He kept trying not to stare at the mountains or stare at the cop's bare legs, either. He'd never seen a trooper in shorts before.

"This truck outfitted for propane?"

Jerry stared into the trooper's face, trying to read the expression behind the mirror sunglasses. "Yes, sir."

"How the hell old are you, anyway?"

"Eighteen," Jerry replied quickly, upping his age by three years.

"You got a license?"

"Huh?"

"A license to drive this thing. Are you paying attention, son?"

"Wasn't no place to get one in Texas," Jerry replied, this time truthfully. He looked out over the desert again to the blue mountains. They were cool and pretty and distant, like the faces of women in magazines. "Cain't I get through?" he asked all of a sudden, which brought a cautious frown to the trooper's face. "I drove a long ways."

The trooper finished writing the ticket and stuffed it into Jerry's sweaty hand. "We don't have any facilities for you here. Go on home."

"Cain't do that," Jerry said firmly.

"You'll die here, son."

"I'll die the fuck back in Texas, too," Jerry said.

At Jerry's tone, the trooper looked up. "All right. Then put your goddamned iron-heap truck in the camp and set your tent along with the rest of the Texas trash. See if I give a shit." With that he walked off to his solar-powered van. Jerry watched him go, wondering if there was air-conditioning inside. Probably. The trooper's shirt hadn't stuck to his skin the way Jerry's sweated tee shirt did.

Licking his lips, Jerry walked back to his truck and, after

a few tries, started the engine. He found a spot about fifty yards from the other refugees and struck camp alone.

Funny how lonely he felt, his old man dead and buried in a shallow grave four hundred miles back. Jerry's Pa hadn't been much of a man; hadn't even been much company; but his absence felt strange, like the emptiness left in the jaw from a rotted-out tooth.

As the sun sank below the western mountains, Jerry started a dinner of beans and jerky. Above his head the bowl of sky darkened to a fragile violet. By the time the stars were out, a girl wandered over from her tent and sat down.

She was his age, Jerry guessed, or a little older, and she sat with her legs spraddled. He kept trying to look away, but the sight of her bare legs drew him as the mountains had. A night wind picked up, carrying from the camp faint tatters of voices and the dense, earthy smell of sewage.

"Where you from?" she asked after a while.

"Texas."

"Huh," she huffed. "Sure wasn't smart of you to come here. Bury people every day here."

Jerry's hand froze on the spoon. "They die?" he asked.

"Course they die. Otherwise you wouldn't bury 'em, stupid."

"Oh." Her tongue was so sharp, he was afraid to ask what they died of.

The girl was watching him. Her legs were skinny and her eyes too big, like the eyes of an owl or some other night predator. "I'll do you for a plate of beans," she told him.

The wind lashed the flames this way and that, sending firefly sparks into the dark.

"I'll do you good."

She pulled her skirt up to her hips, and between those skinny legs were shadows secret as evening. He looked away quickly, down into the snapping fire.

Jerry dreamed of women, of course, but he dreamed of eyes as blue as lakes, hair dark as rain, skin cool and water-smooth. This girl looked like something the desert had coughed up. She frightened him a little.

"I like to do it," she said.

In the fire, black embers crawled with red. The smoke smelled clean and pungent, as if it had come from an evergreen. "I'll give you some beans, anyways."

"I really like to," she whispered.

When the beans were done, Jerry fed the girl just to send her away, then lay for a while alone under the dusty tarp.

The camp was quiet, all the cook fires out, when Jerry got up from his blanket. Shivering a little in the desert cold, he walked out into the sand and stared west.

I could walk there, he thought. Maybe be in the mountains by morning. There would be pine trees and the clear streams he had seen in magazine ads.

If he went to a place where it rained, Jerry figured, he could live off the land easy. You could see the fish in those rivers, he knew, down in the transparent water, like under plate glass. Moss would grow there, and ferns fine as a lady's hand.

To the south, a single thunderhead sailed its bulk over the desert, yellow lightning warring in its belly. He'd watched schooner-shaped clouds move across the Llano the same way, bearing their load of moisture to other, greener places. As Jerry stood staring at the thunderhead, he thought he saw a flash of cold, neon-blue. Deep in his mind he heard the nearly forgotten tap-tap of chill rain falling.

Memories of coolness and moisture drew him. He took a few dreamy steps south and the tap-tap-tapping hushed.

He stopped and the magic vanished. *Rain*, he thought. *Somewhere it's raining*.

Maybe tomorrow or the next day, he thought, he'd walk to Colorado Springs.

ARLINGTON, VIRGINIA

An official knock at the front door jolted Linda Parisi awake. In the darkness she felt Lacy flinch and jump from the warm spot he had made for himself on the covers. By the time the second determined rap came, the dog was fully awake and barking.

With a groan, Linda pulled her stiff body out of bed and

shuffled to the door, turning on the living-room light as she went. Through the fisheye lens of the peephole she saw two men in dark suits waiting in the hall.

"Mrs. Parisi?" one of them shouted.

"Silly, stupid ass me," she whispered to the yapping poodle. The men had probably seen her light come on.

Could Tad be right for once? Was a man who saw spies under the bed capable of seeing more than his own imagination?

"Mrs. Parisi? We know you're in there."

The man's voice sounded reasonable, even friendly. Scooping up Lacy with her good arm, she fumbled with the keys and opened the door as far as the chain would permit.

"It's very late," she pointed out, keeping her voice pleasant but chiding, the same tone she used on the IRS.

All she could see of the first man was a brown eye and part of a dark suit. "We're from Army Intelligence," he said quietly, pressing his ID to the gap in the door. "We'd like to talk to you. May we come in?"

"Perhaps if you had called first—"

"Talk to us now or talk to us later, ma'am," said the other man. "We'll stand out here all night if we have to."

"All right," she told them. "Hold your itty horses. Just let me get decent."

She padded into her bedroom, retrieved her old terry-cloth robe from the still-unpacked suitcase, and on the way out shut the door firmly in Lacy's face.

When she undid the chain, one of the men said, "Sorry about the time." They were both tall, young, and conspicuously well-groomed, just the sort of spook clones Tad Ellis might have dreamed up.

They didn't wait to be invited in. One man walked over to her bookshelves and began rudely scanning the titles. The other went to her coffee table, opened a briefcase, and sat, without permission, on her floral-print sofa.

"We want to know about these," the man with the briefcase said as he spread photographs across the glass top.

Mrs. Parisi pulled her bathrobe tighter. She knew those

photos better than she remembered the face of her long-dead husband. They were the photos she had taken of the Eridani ships.

"Dear me," she said, making her tone puzzled, less like the UFO researcher they had come to see and more like the old widow she resembled. Helplessness, she had learned early in life, could be used to devastating advantage. "I don't suppose you've read my books?"

"We've studied them at length," the man at the bookshelves said. "What we want to know is if you can talk to these aliens."

"Well," she said and paused, her mind working furiously. She bent to study the photos. "If I could, what would you like me to say?"

The man on the couch gathered the pictures and put them back in his briefcase. "The Supreme Allied Commander of Western Europe will tell you that when you get to Spain."

Mrs. Parisi blinked. She looked at the man on the couch. "Spain?"

"Please get dressed. Pack your things. Don't worry, the Army will see to the upkeep of your apartment."

He stood, snapping the briefcase closed. *Don't worry*, had the ridiculous man said? But they were fighting a war in Spain.

In the bedroom, Lacy's barking was hysterical and shrill. Lacy was an excitable animal, and Mrs. Parisi knew that if she walked into the room at that moment, she'd find her pet yapping in aimless, frenzied circles, circles that mimicked the frantic whirling of her thoughts.

"Oh, I don't know if I can," she demurred.

Just as the men from Army Intelligence wore the same type of suit, they shared the same type of eyes. Hard, level eyes. "Pursuant to the Martial Law Act, I am placing you under detainment," the man by the bookshelves said. "Please pack your things now. If we have to do it for you, I'm sure we'll miss something you'd want."

Giving up the battle with a sigh, she nodded and walked to the bedroom, careful not to let Lacy escape. Well. Imagine that. Her fame had spread far and wide, so far that the

Supreme Allied Commander of Western Europe wanted to talk to her. She wondered what he would say when he found out the photos were a hoax.

CENTRAL ANA COMMAND, BARCELONA, SPAIN

Colonel Qasim Abdel Wasef, nicknamed by his troops al Saiqah, was feeling decidedly unThunderboltish. Wearily, he drove his Fiat through the cobblestone streets, preferring to retain command of his own life, his own auto, than put them in the hands of some illiterate Algerian driver.

Despite his exhaustion, despite the grimness of the war, Wasef found himself smiling. On the Spanish side of the Pyrenees the sunlight had the familiar diamantine quality of Alexandria. Edges were sharper than on the rainy French slopes; and the warm breeze reminded him of home.

The road was crowded with new troops, men fresh off the battlefield and famished. He passed a vegetable market already stripped of its produce. On a street corner stood two Libyan noncoms, cutting into a melon with their bayonets. The thin flesh parted and juice poured out, staining the sidewalk like pale blood.

Wasef looked hurriedly away. There had been too many corpses lately. The French had stopped him at Gerona, exacting ten thousand casualties. And the American general, Lauterbach, nibbled at the heels of his infantry battalion.

Wasef made a right at the bombed ruins of the Museu Marítim and drove past the green swatch of grass at the Moll de Bosch. The flowers, he noticed with dismay, had been trampled. Tank tracks scored the lawn. In his rearview mirror he caught sight of the shattered spires of the cross-harbor cable car.

Too bad, he thought wryly. The Gibraltar Dam had not only contained the rising Mediterranean; it had also kept the Allied navies out. Nothing had protected Southern Europe from the Arab advance. Nothing. And now war, not the ocean, had made its high-tide line in Barcelona, coming in on rolling breakers of metal.

He parked his car on the Passiq de Colom and walked

into the Western Command Center through a press of loud, ill-dressed soldiers awaiting orders.

On his way up to General Rashid Aziz Sabry's office, he shared an elevator with a young private with Moroccan insignia on his shoulders. The boy was eating a jar of Apricot Facial Scrub with crackers, probably thinking it was some sort of gourmet Western dip. Wasef considered enlightening him, but was stopped by the happy look on the boy's face.

The colonel got off on the fifth floor. In the anteroom, an Algerian lieutenant was berating a Libyan sergeant at the top of his lungs. From what Wasef could glean from the tirade, the NCO had started a fire in his room, thinking to cook a piece of meat.

Neither looked up as Wasef made his way around them. The lieutenant was too furious, the sergeant too abashed.

Wasef knocked at the commander's door and waited for an answer. When none came, he entered anyway, and surprised his fellow Egyptian in the middle of reading field reports. The corpulent, bearded general, seeing his colonel, rose. Sabry gestured at the closed door and the noisy harangue beyond.

"You see we are a rabble," the general said with a pained, lopsided grin.

Wasef saluted, but Sabry waved the salute away.

"They steal things out of stores," Sabry went on. "They murder shopkeepers. It is a terrible war when we shoot merchants."

"Hang them," Wasef suggested, taking a seat.

Sabry sighed. "Hang them for stupidity, and we would have to hang them all. They are young boys mostly, our soldiers. Sheepherders and mechanics."

"Not enough mechanics," Wasef said. "Not nearly enough for our tanks." He glanced out the window and caught an unexpected, heart-stopping sight of the Mediterranean.

Sabry had apparently followed his gaze. "It reminds me of Alexandria, doesn't it you?" he asked. "Alexandria before Egypt died and the Nile became a trickle."

"They should have shared," Wasef said bitterly. He turned

and saw the general regarding him, bemused.

"The Nile?" Sabry asked.

"The food."

The shouts from the anteroom stopped. Either the lieutenant had finished dressing down the sergeant, Wasef thought, or he had strangled him.

In the silence, Wasef could hear the general's soft sigh. Food was an old argument, a moot argument now. Still, Wasef persisted. "The Greenhouse heat was a genocidal plot of the industrialized countries. They hoped we would be as the Chinese and not fight back."

"You don't mean that," the general said gently. "Surely you have not caught the paranoia of the masses, colonel. No one wanted the new deserts."

"No," Wasef replied, refusing to be chided. "The sin of the Westerners was simply that they did not care."

Sabry gave a dismissive wave, indicating that he wished to change the subject. He asked, "And as to the roadway across the mountains?"

"Secure," Wasef said. He pushed aside a memory of corpses lying in a buttercupped meadow like children napping on a bedspread. "When we disable the last military satellite, we can begin troop movements. Yours is a brilliant plan. The French are complacent. They will never expect a flank attack."

"Good, good," the general said with a vague nod, ignoring Wasef's praise. "Better to get our inevitable victory over with quickly than to obtain it by attrition. Better for both sides."

"The Americans have a new weapon," the colonel told him.

Sabry grimaced, as though Wasef had committed a dreadful faux pas.

"A surveillance weapon, I believe," the colonel went on. "So far, it has not fired on us."

Sabry drew his hands down his swarthy cheeks. "We know of the small remote vehicle," he said. "You surely don't mean that."

"No, sir. A pilotless airborne."

The general hefted his bulk from the chair, walked to the window, and looked out to sea. A white pigeon flew up from the street, flashing across the teal sky like a scrap of errant paper.

"A blue light," Wasef added, speaking to the old man's back.

Sabry muttered something into the open window, but the freshening wind blew the words away. Wasef lifted his head and drank in the breeze, as though his lungs were thirsty as the Nile Valley.

"What, sir?" Wasef asked.

The general turned to eye him. In Sabry's round, bearded face Wasef read a weary lack of surprise. Whatever the blue light was, the general had already heard of it.

"Have you fired on the light?" Sabry asked.

"Yes, sir."

Sabry closed his eyes a moment, then opened them. They were sad. "Have you hit it?"

"Not yet, sir."

"Don't fire on it again, colonel," he said. "It is my belief that the blue light is not American. In fact, I think the blue light belongs to no one we know."

DULLES AIRPORT, VIRGINIA

Whoosh, they'd taken her from her apartment. Whoosh, they'd driven her to the airport. At Dulles, Mrs. Parisi tried to engage the agents in conversation, but the pair didn't seem interested.

"I had a young boy looking after my dog," she told the green-eyed agent. "I told him I'd be back Sunday. Lord only knows what Lacy will do for food."

The man cast a mildly sympathetic look in her direction. The agent with the green eyes was the nicer one, she decided. The easier to work on.

"Don't worry, ma'am. We know about the dog. We've made arrangements," he told her.

"He needs to go out, too. Oh, my. He can make such a mess."

The man gave her an impartial smile and turned away, attention and charity depleted.

Doodles, she thought in irritation. Mrs. Parisi was a master manipulator, had earned her stripes in cuteness as a child and junior officer rank by her sex appeal as a teenager. Now that she was getting on in years, fragility had given her a stunning new weapon. It frustrated her when foiled.

Her gaze was drawn to the window and the planes queued up in the darkness. She couldn't con these men, and in twenty-three minutes—whoosh—she'd be swept off to Spain. Asleep in her apartment one minute, on her way to Europe the next. It took one's breath away.

One's breath.

A sly grin tugged at the corners of her mouth. The two agents were seated tensely, surveying the airport as though they thought the ANA or the Eridanians might be sneaking up on them.

With a subtle gasp—it was important that the scene not be overplayed—Mrs. Parisi put her hand to her chest.

The nicer agent looked at her, and his expression changed from blankness to alarm. "Are you all right?" he asked.

"Oh, I'm fine," she told him in a squeezed voice. And began gulping air.

The agent motioned to the second man. "Kevin," he said.

Through shuttered eyes, Mrs. Parisi saw the other man leap to his feet. Around the terminal, waiting passengers were starting to look her way.

She had to fight down a victorious smirk when the green-eyed agent turned to his partner and in a satisfyingly frantic voice snapped, "Call an ambulance."

THE PYRENEES

Gordon didn't find the laser. What he found was a T-72 tank on the side of the road, its engine cover up and no soldiers around.

Through the screen of trees he caught a flash of blue.

The blue light had been there when he came on line, and it had stayed with the CRAV since, following it like a shy stray dog.

Ignoring the light, Gordon pushed through the undergrowth that paralleled the road. At the crest of a hill near a burned-out farmhouse, the trail forked, one gravel-and-mud path leading west, another, even more rugged, leading east. He drove the CRAV forward and studied the ground.

No more treads to follow. But tire tracks. Big ones. The mark of the Brazilian-made Laser Deployment Vehicle. The tire tracks went east, straight up the mountain.

Gordon jerked his head left to bring up the display. The road to Spanish Vielia was a mile or so ahead. A good road, he saw, a decent French highway. The LDV wasn't going up that. Oh no. It had to go the hard way around, up through the goat trail to the Pico de Forcanada.

What the hell? Are they lost? Gordon wondered.

He looked up at the exposed grassy slope. What the LDV had climbed was a muddy pasture, complete with cow patties the shape of cinnamon rolls.

No telling what was on the other side of that hill. It might be a long haul, and his stomach and bladder were telling him it was break time. He eased the CRAV to the back of a destroyed barn and buried it in a manure pile while two rubbernecking Guernseys and blue Rover looked on.

CRAV COMMAND, TRÁS-OS-MONTES, PORTUGAL

Gordon closed his eyes and felt the odd sensory jump as the CRAV powered down. Taking off the gloves and goggles, he stood, stretched. It was past break time, apparently. His dinner lay, gelatinous and cold, on the side table.

Jerking open the warped door, he walked to the end of the corridor, to the restroom. After a pit stop, he paused at the refrigerator to grab a can of Coke. In the freezer, stacked next to the icemaker, he discovered a cache of Snickers.

Chewing on the ice-hard chocolate, he ambled back toward his room, halting dead at the open doorway of Stendhal's cramped command center.

She was obviously in the midst of a difficult move. Her head was thrown back, her face streaming sweat. Her gloved hands plucked the air.

Not all the operators minded being observed. Stendhal, Gordon figured, relished it. Her camouflage blouse, as usual, was open all the way down, exposing her Army-issue undershirt. Sweat had darkened the olive cloth between her small breasts, and her nipples were at erect attention.

It was only because she couldn't see him that Gordon dared look at all. Stendhal wanted the other guys' eyes on her, he knew, not his shy, cowlike regard.

He was so engrossed in Stendhal that he didn't notice the man from Mitsubishi approach until the rep was right beside him. Gordon jerked his gaze away from Stendhal's nipples and nearly choked on a piece of Snickers.

Ishimoto, following the line of Gordon's leer, raised an eyebrow.

"She is good," the Japanese said.

"Huh?"

"A good operator. I monitor her as well."

Gordon pressed his lips together and fought not to let his gaze slide back to Stendhal.

"You put your unit into a dung heap," Ishimoto said.

"Yeah."

Ishimoto's impassive expression broke, his lips cracking upward into a smile. "A very clever maneuver. So. After you eat, you will follow them up the hill?"

"Yeah," Gordon replied, then remembered his Army manners and amended it to "Yes, sir. Of course I'll use the hill as a defilade, but, hell, the Arabs could be just on the other side. And I'd sure like to know where those helicopters went."

"Ah," Ishimoto nodded. "The helicopters with the nerve gas."

"Yes, sir."

For a moment they stood there, staring at each other.

Black lashes made an awning over the most expressionless eyes Gordon had ever seen. Looking at Ishimoto, in some ways, was like looking into the face of his own CRAV.

Just inside the door Stendhal was grunting and huffing her way to some sort of CRAV-maneuver climax. Then suddenly she smiled, sighed in exhaustion. Her arms dropped.

"The blue light," Ishimoto said.

Gordon whipped his head away from the slumped, happy girl. "Sir?"

"It follows you. Why?"

"I don't know, sir."

"When *I* operate the CRAV the—what we call a Woofer goes away. When you operate the CRAV, it comes back." There was an emotion now on the Japanese's face, but Gordon wasn't sure whether it was suspicion or envy.

"It just took a shine to me, I guess, sir."

Ishimoto nodded and walked away, to the monitoring room, taking one final look at the breasts. After a moment of thought Gordon, too, went back to work.

THE PYRENEES

Manure fell off the turret like wet brown snow. In the muddy yard, Gordon swiveled his head. The Guernseys had gone off to seek other entertainment, but Rover was there, hovering a foot or so above the sodden grass.

As he watched the light, Gordon felt the tap-tap-tapping begin, a sound like someone knocking at the base of his brain.

"Stop that," he said.

The rain sound quieted to a cold, pouty hiss.

Pressing the accelerator gently, Gordon rolled up the long, open incline. Near the top he paused to raise his missile tubes. As the opposite slope came into view, he noticed the pasture was empty. The heavy tire treads of the LDV disappeared in a curve to the right.

Gordon swiveled his head. Rover was hovering a few yards away. "Where'd they go, Boo-Boo?" he asked.

The only answer he got was that eerie whisper of falling sleet.

IN THE LIGHT

Ann and Justin were in the very back of the bus, on the long bench seat. He was using his blanket as a pillow, and Ann was on top of him, riding him to climax. He was coming, the bucking of his hips frenzied. He grabbed her at the bunched skirt and squeezed tight, feeling the cold sponginess of her waist underneath.

The next instant there was a throb, a spurt of release. He'd come, but there was no real pleasure in it. Ann crawled off him and lowered her skirt. "Will you read me your book?" she asked politely.

Dazed, he sat up and noticed his zipper was open. He should have been wearing his speed jeans and helmet, but they had disappeared somehow. He zipped up his flight suit while outside the window an F-14 crashed in the desert and two chutes came down over the twisted skeletons of burned Arab tanks.

"I crashed," he whispered to her.

"What?"

"I remember now. I crashed."

"Read me your book," she said.

"My name is Justin Searles. Lieutenant j.g. Justin Searles. And I crashed my F-14."

"Read me your book now, Justin."

He shoved at her. "Jesus God! You captured me."

The Arab National Army must have captured him, must have started feeding him drugs. Justin pounded on the window, trying to get out, and the bus driver was back, wanting to know what was happening.

"Come on, boy," the bus driver said.

Outside the window the desert flashed by. A burning oil field blossomed on the horizon like a night flower.

"Come on, boy. Don't you want to fuck her again?"

Ann leaned over and grabbed at his groin. Justin elbowed her hard in the chest. His arm plunged into her, went right through her pink sweater, right through chilled blood and putty-soft bone until it hit the bus seat.

He screamed.

"Now you've gone and done it," the bus driver was saying.

He'd gone and done it. God. He'd gone and done it. There was something he should remember, he knew, but the terrible din of sleet battered all thought out of his brain.

"What do you want?" Ann asked. "What will make you happy?"

He grabbed the nubby material of the seat in front of him and held on for dear life. "Please let me go home," he said.

THE PYRENEES

Below Gordon's leafy hiding place, the huge pulse-laser tractor was mired in the mud. A platoon, thank God not a company, just a platoon, were standing around the vehicle scratching their asses and apparently wondering how to get out of this mess.

Nearby a Palestinian NCO was giving hell to a Libyan corporal. The corporal, Gordon saw with his telescopic vision, was staring down in confusion at a map.

"Arm missiles," Gordon whispered. At his voice command the screen flickered to life. He touched his thumb to his middle finger and the words MISSILE 1 LOCKED lit up in red.

The instant before Gordon could press his fingers together, something blue flitted through his sights.

"Jesus, abort! Abort!" Gordon shouted as the Arab platoon leaped to its collective feet.

Arabs were running everywhere, grabbing their AK-47s, grabbing their mortars. The NCO stopped screaming at the corporal and started screaming at his men. One soldier was firing into the blue light so fast, he overheated his rifle and jammed it. The driver of the LDV flung himself into the seat and started the engine. The huge maw of the laser swung blindly in Gordon's direction.

"Oh, shit! Bring in the stuntman!" Gordon cried. Rover

was skimming back and forth across the ground, still drawing small-arms fire, still blocking Gordon's aim.

And then the corporal pointed. He pointed right up the slope to the CRAV.

Ping-ping. Rounds bounced off Gordon's diamond-hard hide. Bullets tore through the branches, causing a green rain of debris.

"Lower missiles!" Gordon ordered, hoping he could save his fragile tubes.

Below, the sergeant had more or less got his men into order. They had dropped belly-down into the mud and were firing up the hill, alternately loosing rounds into Rover, into Gordon.

Gordon pushed his feet into the controls and tore backward, slamming the rear of the CRAV into a sapling. The tree fell on the turret, leaves dangling over his sights like a lady's Easter veil.

In the muddy pasture, the corporal with the mortar was calmly finding Gordon's range. Trailing branches, Gordon floored the accelerator. But just as he was up and over the lip of the small ridge, his visuals exploded into red fire and brown dirt.

"Jesus fucking Christ! They killed me again!" he shouted. But a heartbeat later, seeing rocks and trees flash by, he realized the CRAV was still functional. It had simply lost its footing and was tumbling into a ravine.

He hit the center of the shallow stream with a bruising thud and a loud splash, coming to rest right side up. Panicked, he goosed the accelerator. The CRAV lurched over the rocky bed, a scant hundred yards ahead of the pursuing Arabs.

CHAPTER 4

CENTCOM-EAST, WARSAW, POLAND

Ever since childhood, Baranyk liked the hour just before sunset. This preference, he knew, made him an odd duck: most people preferred the garish sunlight at the middle of the day.

Subtle dusk spread over the fields like smoke. Shadows stretched lissome along the ground. At twilight in the country, the cows came clanking home. Birds flew to nest. Dusk felt as though the hectic day sat down to a good dinner and a warm fire; that it had the leisure to lean back and prop its legs on the hassock.

Lingering outside the prerevolutionary palace which housed Centcom-East, Baranyk contemplated a stand of birches and felt his heart grow still.

When the opening door behind him threw a rectangle of golden light across the yard, he turned and saw the compact form of the Saceur-West ambling toward him.

Now, Baranyk thought, the mood would be destroyed. The American would be jovial the way Americans always were. He would make a joke and laugh too loudly, and think Baranyk morose because he would not laugh with him.

That didn't happen. Lauterbach simply came up to his side and stood gazing across the meadow at the Kampineska forest beyond.

The wind flirted with them, tugging at the American's jacket, at Baranyk's battle-dress blouse. The Ukrainian thought he caught the whiff of whiskey from Lauterbach, light and sweet, like blended perfume.

"Tell me about nuclear scientists," the American said in a voice nearly as quiet as the breeze. "Which ones are missing?"

Night was deepening fast. Now, in the dying light, the American was indistinct. He might have been a familial Polish ghost haunting the darkness of the yard; or a sorrowful Ukrainian one haunting Baranyk himself.

"We don't know. When the breakup came, it was hard to keep track," he replied.

The American grunted, a neither-here neither-there sort of grunt. In the gloom Baranyk saw him lift a hand to his mouth. He heard the rattle of ice, heard him swallow. Lauterbach had brought his glass of whiskey with him.

"Word from the CIA has it that twenty top experts went east about five years before the hostilities."

Baranyk sniffed derisively, "The CIA."

"Yes, granted. Most intelligence is crap. But if it *is* true, the Arabs would have had time to build bombs and the delivery system to go with them. Then there are those seven tacticals missing from the old Red Army list. The propellant has certainly degraded, but the missiles can be refitted."

"What if—" Baranyk began and then looked away hurriedly. The question was so shameful and so terrifying, it was best, when it was asked, that one's face be hidden. "What if the war seems lost? Would you actually consider using nuclear weapons on European soil?"

Baranyk heard ice tinkle against the sides of the glass. "That's a Presidential decision," the American said.

Out of the quiet of the birches an owl hooted. *Early to be hunting*, Baranyk thought. Perhaps it was searching for a mate. The owl's song was as lonely as the whistle of a night train.

"Goddamn it," Lauterbach whispered. "Here."

Baranyk turned. There was just enough light left to see

that Lauterbach was holding something out to him. He took it. A book, he thought in surprise, running his hands over the slick cover.

"Read it," Lauterbach said. "Then think about what I said at the meeting."

The book was too large to fit in his pocket, so Baranyk clapped it to his stomach and folded his hands over it like a choirboy. "I will."

"Promise me," Lauterbach said. Then he laughed. It wasn't an American laugh at all, but a low, sad, Ukrainian one, a laugh so sad that it seemed to be a necessary part of the evening. "I know you don't believe in them, but they're out there. And they're wiser than we are. All that knowledge there for the asking. Think about the miracle."

The American left, and Baranyk was alone with the night. He watched the owl fly off, pale wings spread like a death angel.

A jeep near the road started its engine. The shielded headlight beams were twin, slitted eyes. Baranyk turned and walked back into the grand entry hall of the Command Center. He stopped and glanced down at the cover of the book. *The Eridanian Way,* by Linda Parisi, it read.

FAIRFAX HOSPITAL, FAIRFAX, VIRGINIA

Mrs. Parisi had been suitably poked and prodded. Internists and cardiologists had mumbled over her chest. They'd put her on a monitor for a while and run an EEG. Not finding anything, of course, they'd finally stuck her in a room just to keep an eye on her overnight. She'd known they would.

Just before dawn she rose and padded to the small closet. As she suspected, her clothes were gone; but her sedated roommate's were not. When Mrs. Parisi took the purple tent dress and sandals, the sleeping woman didn't miss a snore.

The dress hung on Mrs. Parisi, of course; because Mrs. Parisi, unlike her fat sow of a roommate, had been careful to keep her figure. Glancing in the dresser mirror, she saw that the grape Kool-Aid color didn't flatter her, either.

In her roommate's purse she found a driver's license made out to a Sally Glenndarning. A Discover, a Visa, and a MasterCard. And Sally had left one hundred and thirty-five dollars in her wallet, a dreadful temptation for the hospital help.

Putting Sally's thick wallet back in the purse, she slung the awful, clashing leatherette bag over her shoulder and tiptoed to the door.

Mrs. Parisi had always been a meticulous planner. She'd wanted to make her move all evening, but knew she should hold out until four.

By three in the morning the body processes started to creep. Eyelids became heavy, the heart slowed. Between three and four, most people who were going to die peacefully quit breathing. The live ones, though, were sleepy at three and comatose an hour later.

Peering out, she saw one agent asleep in his chair a few feet down the hall. The other was nowhere to be seen.

Scrunching up her feet to keep them from flopping out of the oversized sandals, Mrs. Parisi walked to the stairs. She limped down three flights and came out in the lobby. No one, not even the uniformed guard, watched her leave.

She walked three long blocks before she found a pay phone. Using Sally's AT&T card, she dialed Tad Ellis in Maryland.

"Huh? What?" Tad said sleepily, catching the phone on the third ring.

"Wake up and listen."

Mrs. Parisi heard a rustling on the other end of the line. Probably Tad's bedcovers. "Linda?" he asked in a mumble.

"Yes. Now listen carefully. I want you to go out and rent me a car. Better yet, a van."

Tad was awake enough now to cough. As with most heavy smokers, it was the thing he most wanted to do upon arising. In the middle of his hacking fit he managed to say, "But it's four o'clock in the *morning*."

"Go to National Airport. They rent cars at all hours there.

Bring money, Tad. At least a thousand. Go to as many ATMs as you have to."

"It's not the ATM," Tad said with a yawn. "It's the *card* that determines the credit limit. I could go to one ATM and get as much as I wanted."

"Oh. Is that right, dear?" she asked with counterfeit admiration for the boy's fiscal acumen. There was nothing Mrs. Parisi loathed more than being corrected; and so to teach Tad a memorable lesson in manners, she added, "Then perhaps you'd better make it two thousand. I'll take a cab to—" She thought for a moment. "The Lincoln Memorial. You meet me there."

Yes, Mrs. Parisi decided. The Lincoln Memorial. That should suit Tad's clichéd sense of adventure perfectly.

"Are you listening, Tad?"

"Jesus, Linda. Can't this wait till nine?"

"Tad," she told him somberly. "Army Intelligence is after me. They want to take me to Spain. Do you hear what I'm saying, dear? To the war front. They'll make me tell them all I know."

"Oh, my God," he breathed, and Mrs. Parisi knew that not only was Tad fully awake at last but she had hit all the right paranoia buttons. "Drugs. Torture. They'll get everything out of you."

"That's right," she agreed, feeling more than a bit foolish standing in Sally Glenndarning's absurd tent dress and grossly wide sandals. "You must help me, Tad." Then she added darkly, "Or the Eridanians won't understand."

CENTRAL ARMY HOSPITAL, BADAJOZ, SPAIN

Dr. Rita Beaudreaux lifted her head from the microscope and rubbed her blurred eyes. Beside her lay the slides from the hole in the sternum. The hole had parted the cells so neatly, they were stacked like boxes in a warehouse. Nothing—no laser, no scalpel, nothing—could have made such a neat incision.

The sound of the door opening behind her brought her head around in a snap and set her heart racing as though she was afraid she'd see something supernatural there.

It was only Lieutenant Colonel Martinez. The short, swarthy officer had his hands stuck into the pockets of his camouflage jacket, and it didn't look as though he was expecting a salute. "Hi, Rita," he said. "It's late."

She grunted in reply, her mind still on the slides.

Martinez slumped down in one of the hard-backed, vinyl-covered chairs. "You've found that the cellular structure of the hole in the chest is undamaged," he said.

She stared at the slides in idiotic disbelief. The hour was so late and she was so tired that she wondered for a moment if she had already told him. They might have had an entire conversation she'd forgotten.

"There have been other injuries like that," he explained. "We had another pathologist studying them, too."

"Other injuries?" she asked, bringing her head up so quickly that her vision swam. "What caused this?"

Martinez's Aztec features creased into an embarrassed half-smile. Hispanic, but he was at least three shades darker than she was. "Aliens," he said.

Had she not seen the seriousness in his eyes, she might have laughed.

"Look," he told her, "I know you're not much of a soldier. None of our Reserve or Guard doctors are. You people don't take orders well." He laughed.

"But aliens?" she asked, grinning. He was an affable sort, the lieutenant colonel. He'd had to adapt to a bunch of subordinates who habitually reminded him, in subtle or not-so-subtle ways, that they were not only better educated than he but better paid. There were times Rita felt sorry for him.

"Aliens. I'm sending you to Lérida to study them."

She blinked, thinking at first that she hadn't understood him or that he was talking about some other Lérida, one in Portugal or northern France. "The Lérida near the Pyrenees?"

"That's right. General Lauterbach wants a pathologist to view the bodies in situ. I've assigned you a platoon and given you a veteran lieutenant, Helen Dix. Look, Rita, I know you'll take this the right way: Don't pull rank on her. If Dix gives you a suggestion, don't stop and ask why. Don't argue with her as you do with me. There won't be time for that." His broad-cheeked face was pulled down in sympathetic lines.

"God almighty, colonel! They're shooting people out there!" Fear made her tone harsher than she'd intended, and Martinez paled. She felt an immediate regret. Throughout her life the lash of her tongue had driven away those she cared for.

"You'll be under fire at times, yes," he said, keeping his voice low and calm and soothing, the way doctors did when giving a patient bad news. "But Dix is a superb field lieutenant. Keep your head down, and she'll get you out of trouble."

Rita took a calming breath to keep from offending the likable Martinez again. But she was angry, angrier at the Army bureaucracy than she had ever been at the enemy. "Surely you have somebody in the regulars to send."

He patted the air with his hand—a suggestion, not an order—to keep her protests in check. "It wasn't my decision. It was General Lauterbach's. He likes you. He has confidence in you."

She jerked her head away and glared at the microscope. "If he likes me so much," she said, "why is he sending me out to die?"

THE PYRENEES

Gordon had driven the CRAV far. The Arab Hind searching for him was a couple of miles back. He could hear its motor noise, a distant grumble on the night wind. His rear-engine compartment blanketed by mud to escape infrared, Gordon took a short break.

He dozed with his eyes open, a trick that CRAV operators learned quickly. Close your eyes for more than thirty seconds, and the robot would shut itself off.

Gordon was in a half-sleep now. The liquid sound of the stream was lulling. His night vision had automatically cut in as the sun set, and the boulders on the other side of the stream were fuzzy greenish lumps.

A bird roused him from sleep by its sharp, startling shriek. A few minutes later, a deer came down to drink, and Gordon moved his head to watch it. After the deer left, a misty rain began to fall.

When he caught sight of the glow coming up the ravine, Gordon stiffened, believing at first that the Arab platoon had finally found him.

It was Rover.

The light floated happily toward him over the rocks like a dumb, friendly dog.

"Go away," he whispered.

Rover stopped, hovered. The sound of the helicopter changed from an indistinct growl to a quiet flutter.

"Get the fuck away!" Gordon hissed.

Reaching out, Gordon grabbed a nearby tree limb and pulled it over the front of his unit. A few yards from him Rover was bobbing up and down in place, a balloon at the end of a tether.

Whop-whop. WHOP-WHOP. The Hind was just above Gordon, coming in low over the trees. Suddenly the north side of the stream lit up in sickly shades of night-vision green.

Above Gordon's head came a sound as if something heavy and soft had fallen from a height, the noise of an ATGM leaving its tube. Instinctively, Gordon shut his eyes. A second later the missile hit with a comic book KA-BLAM that set Gordon's ears ringing. Mud and small stones pattered on the CRAV's exposed hull.

When Gordon opened his eyes, he saw that both lights were gone. The clear stream was making a waterfall into a newly dug crater.

THE LINCOLN MEMORIAL, WASHINGTON, D.C.

The rising sun turned the Reflecting Pool what Mrs. Parisi might have decided was a charming color had she not been waiting so impatiently.

It was so like Tad to be late.

The morning had turned from peach to gold by the time the publisher pulled up in an electric-powered Chevy van and stopped.

Tad was chain-smoking. His little effeminate face was pinched. "Oh my God, Linda," he blurted. "Are you all *right?*"

"Did you bring the money?" she asked.

He handed her a thick envelope. She opened it and peered inside: the tractable boy had brought all two thousand. The bills, she saw at a glance, were newish but not stridently so.

"What are you going to *do?*" Tad wailed.

Glancing up at his disheveled blond hair, she twisted her mouth in disgust. The least the man could have done was make himself presentable. She wondered if he had rented the van with his hair all stuck up like that. "Well, I'm leaving, dear."

"For *where?*"

"I think it's best you don't know. You might inadvertently tell them."

Tad's pale-blue eyes darted toward the traffic on Constitution Avenue. "Oh, God," he said under his breath. "They'll get me, too, won't they. No telling what I'll say under torture."

"That's right." She handed him the purse. "Now listen," she told him. "I want you to take this back to Fairfax Hospital and give it to a Sally Glenndarning. Tell her I am so appreciative of the loan of her dress, and that I hope she won't file charges."

Tad's blue eyes widened. For an instant he actually seemed intelligent and awake. "File charges? Oh, God. What about the van?"

"You should probably pay for it, dear. That's what the Eridanians have told me."

"Okay," he said glumly. "I rented the nicest they had. It'll be expensive," he added.

"Tad, if you'll remember, the Eridanians have no concept of money. And you mustn't complain. They can sense that, you know."

Still morose, Tad nodded.

"But, just to show I love and trust you, I'm leaving you my dog."

She jerked open the door pointedly. After some hesitation, he clambered out.

"Can you drop me off at National?" he asked so pitifully that she was almost inclined to take him. But it was best, she knew, to get on the road early, before the heavy traffic began.

Climbing into the seat, she slammed the door and looked out at him. Really, the boy needed a comb and a few hours more sleep. "Why don't you take a cab," she suggested, keying the ignition.

The van started with a soft hum. The dash readouts came on, the charge light reading FULL. She drove off, leaving Tad standing in the parking lot, staring forlornly after her.

As Mrs. Parisi sped over the Arlington Memorial Bridge, she rolled down the window to blow some of the cigarette stench out of the car.

Tad was so silly. If he had a brain in his head, which he didn't, he would know she was headed west. There was a network of fans out west. Wealthy fans. Someone would certainly be kind enough to rent her a condo. There would be plenty of spending money. And maybe, if it ever bothered to snow decently again, she could even go skiing. She'd heard there were good slopes around Colorado Springs.

NEAR CALHAN, COLORADO

Jerry Casey sorted through the blankets and clothes in the back of the pickup. When he was finished, he went through everything carefully again, a knot of horror tightening in his belly.

His food and water were gone.

It was hot, and already his mouth felt cottony. To the east the sun was peeking over the flats, making a dull, glinting mirror of the sand.

Yards away in the camp, cookfires had already started,

and the heady smell of coffee mingled with the stench of old urine and shit.

Grabbing his cup, he walked to the nearest tent. Just outside the flap, he saw, a hollow-eyed woman was sewing a child into a shroud. The body's small legs were covered, but the face was still exposed. The corpse's skin was a sickly gray, the same color as the tattered sheet she would be burying him in.

The woman glanced up. Her eyes were like glinting seepage at the bottom of a shadowy well. "Something to drink?" she said.

Her question confused him. Then he realized she saw his cup. "Yes, ma'am," he told her. "Somebody done stole my water."

Her face was all dry cliffs and arroyos, the flesh so thin he could see the bones underneath. A hard, desert floor of a face. "Got to watch what you drink around here. My kid didn't," she said furiously.

See what happens? she might have shouted at her son if he could somehow still hear her. *See what happens when you don't do what you're told?*

The dry wind teased at the sheet, flapping it back and forth over the corpse's neatly folded hands. The fluttering disturbed Jerry more than anything, because he knew the tickle of it was something only a dead person could stand. An almost overwhelming urge came over him to reach over and tuck the sheet in. "Yes, ma'am."

"Get into everything, them kids," she said, shaking her head.

"I'm sorry," he told her, but she didn't seem to be listening.

"You come a long ways?" She was staring out over the desert now, rocking a little.

"From Texas."

"We come from Oklahoma, but to them damned Colorado troopers we're all Texas trash."

Jerry wanted to get away from the woman with the skull face. He couldn't leave without saying something else, though. He didn't remember his own Ma real clear, but he remembered the manners she had taught him. The only problem was, he couldn't think of a thing to say.

"You're alone, I noticed. Young boy like you. Don't seem right."

"My Pa died back on the road."

She looked down at her son and the winding sheet with mild surprise, as though she had forgotten he was dead. "Well, you'll be wanting some water, most likely. Get you some of mine," she offered, nodding her head toward the tent. "It's boiled."

"Yes, ma'am. I sure do thank you." Jerry turned away from the boy's corpse and pulled open the tent flap. Two other children were sleeping inside. One little girl's face was bone-dry, her cheeks high-colored, as though she had a fever.

Quietly he made his way to a washpan, dipped his cup in the water and took a drink. The water tasted flat, the way all boiled water did. Without disturbing the children's sleep, he made his way outside.

The woman was still sewing.

"Thank you, ma'am," Jerry said again.

The boy's folded hands were disappearing into the sheet. Another few moments the face would be covered; and Jerry thought that when it was, it would be a good thing.

She didn't look up from her work. "You're a good boy," she said.

THE PYRENEES, ABOVE BAGNÈRES-DE-LUCHON

Colonel Wasef stared down into the stream bed at the destruction his men had wrought. The action of the water, he noticed, had already smoothed the sharp edges of the crater, so that the mistake seemed to have been made years before, and the earth had nearly forgotten.

"Qasim," his captain and childhood friend began in apology. "My brother—"

Wasef waved the apology away tiredly. "I'll assure General Sabry that there was no way for you to know. Are you sure you hit it?"

"The helicopter pilot is positive. He saw nothing get away."

Wasef looked at the small tread marks leading downstream. "Something did," he grunted.

He turned and saw Yussif pressing his lips together in chagrin. Yussif was such a pudgy-cheeked man that the gesture made him look like a scolded child. "Don't do that," Wasef told him.

The captain's expression altered to one of bewilderment, and Wasef laughingly explained, "Don't make such a face. It is like when you were in school and the teacher called on you for the lesson."

Captain Mustafa grinned. A positive sign. It was hard, Wasef knew, to keep up the men's morale. In Egypt, women and children were dying. Wasef had lost his own wife, Zahra, on the dusty march from the plagues in Sinnūris. But Yussif's family had been in Cairo, he remembered. Surely they were safe.

He thought to ask the captain about them, but didn't have the heart. *Soon*, Wasef thought, soon they would make another move into France. The Eastern army would push through Poland and then through Germany. The two fronts would meet, hammer and anvil. And, even though it was too late for him, the other men could bring their families out of that sandy hell.

"I've sent a platoon downstream," Yussif said, motioning with his hand. "The helicopter has searched, but there is so much leaf canopy, the pilot could not see anything. I ordered the T-72 to the Garonne river. The stream comes out there."

Wasef nodded. "A good plan. Very good," he said, seeing the pleasure in Yussif's face, an unimportant backdrop to the disturbing memories of Zahra.

"We will get the robot, colonel."

"Yes. Of course you will."

Before they left, Wasef glanced down at the stream bed again and suppressed a shudder. There wasn't much that Colonel Qasim Wasef feared. But this. This scared him to death.

There was the crater, tangible and real as the stones, with no signs of a kill around it. Yet something other than the robot had gone into the ravine and not come out.

Allah must be punishing them for abandoning the desert, he decided. For leaving the women, the old men, the children to their prolonged deaths. Wasef had the cold thought that perhaps General Sabry was wrong. Perhaps the blue lights were not UFOs but some sort of avenging angels.

IN THE LIGHT

A calm voice said, "Go ahead. Call your mother."

It was suddenly quiet. Lieutenant Justin Searles dropped his hand from his eyes and saw that he was standing in one of those bus rest stops. To his right was a pay phone. Before him, a long bar where silent passengers, motionless as stuffed animals, hunched over their coffee. The place smelled of onions and grease.

"Call your mother," Ann said.

Justin turned to the pay phone and realized there was a quarter between his forefinger and thumb. He put the coin in the slot and dialed the old number.

"Hello, Justin," a voice in the receiver said.

The voice was female; it wasn't his mother's.

"Mom," he said anyway. He wasn't feeling much like a fighter jock anymore. He was so scared that his voice cracked like a little kid's. "Mom. Where am I?"

"You're close. Just picture home in your mind. Picture it very, very hard."

He thought of Florida, the squat, blocky pink house, the mango tree in the front yard, the lemon tree in the back. The thick, sweet, green grass and the gray thunderheads in the humid sky.

But Florida wasn't like that anymore, was it?

"They'll let you come home," his mother said kindly, "if you'll read them your book."

He slammed the receiver on the hook and stared in horror at the phone.

Oh, sweet Jesus. The ANA had him and he would never go home. The Arabs had him by the short hairs and all he was allowed to tell them was his name, rank, and serial number, and he could remember only two thirds of that.

He glanced out the plate glass window of the diner. In the dark sky an F-14 was going down in flames, the blue lights of Woofers around it.

"Good thinking," a familiar voice said.

He whirled. Lieutenant Commander Harding was standing there.

"Name, rank, and serial number." The XO nodded. He was dressed in his whites, and there were huge rings of sweat under his arms. It was always hard to stay cool in the desert. "Tell you what, lieutenant," he said. "You've come through this test admirably. Let's go have a cup of coffee."

Harding put his huge hand out. Justin took it. The man's palm was firm and dry. Light winked on the XO's balding dome and the embossed anchors of his brass buttons.

"A test, sir?" Justin asked, afraid not to believe it.

The XO clapped him on the back. "Sure, kid." His voice was so gentle that it made Justin want to cry. "Don't you remember the test? Well, I guess the drugs are still working on you. Let's have that cup of coffee and wipe the cobwebs out."

There weren't any cobwebs in Justin's mind. There was only scattershot ice so slick that his thoughts kept sliding.

Justin sat down on a stool next to a glass container of donuts. The waitress pushed a white cup and saucer in front of him.

Saucers. He stared at the dish. Something nibbled and fretted at the edges of his memory.

"You run into many Woofers, son?" the lieutenant commander asked, taking a cautious sip from his steaming cup.

"Always run into Woofers lately," Justin answered, pulling his gaze away from the saucer. The waitress was staring at him. Something in her cold eyes, her pulpy face, reminded him of Ann.

The XO said, "Tell me your story. Everybody's got a Woofer story, don't they?"

The XO's spoon made a musical, frosty sound against the thick sides of the cup.

"The first time my radio intercept officer saw one in his screen, it scared the shit out of him." Justin laughed into the sudden, vacuous silence. "Then he got where he could identify their fuzzy return and they didn't worry him anymore. I've seen 'em fly off my wingtip and follow me like a dog, like they were curious or something."

"Oh?" the exec asked with a strange, flaccid smile. "Do you think they're curious?"

"I guess so, sir. They're like big, friendly dogs." Justin's coffee was strong and hot. The sip he took burned the roof of his mouth. "When we get down, my wingman makes a joke of it. Hey, Justin, he'll say. You had a blue Woofer sniffing up your tail, a Woofer with a twenty-foot hard-on."

Abruptly he had the jarring thought that his wingman was downed over ten minutes ago. Behind him in the pit, Tyler was screaming, "Approaching Woofers!," but Justin, who was preoccupied by the AAA they'd taken in the port engine a while back, was fighting the stiffness of the stick and the crazed bumpy-road feel of the plane.

MAYDAY

MAYDAY

MAYDAY

"Eject," Justin said as he turned, expecting to see his RIO. Lieutenant Commander Harding was there instead.

"Eject?" the exec asked pleasantly, lifting one eyebrow.

"I had to punch out. We were losing hydraulics," Justin said. Or were they? Or was the AAA part of the test, too? He whirled around on the stool to stare out the plate glass window. Over the desert mountains streaked the red dot-dash-dot of tracers. Chaff sparkled in the dark. From a desperate, evading plane hot pink flares fell like garish beads from a broken necklace.

"Look into your coffee," the exec said.

Justin looked. The inside of the cup was a green radar

scope and at twelve o'clock was a tight pattern of white blips. Fuzzy bogeys.

Woofers.

"What do you think they are?" the XO asked.

Justin started to sweat. In the back of his nostrils was the ghost of a stench, the smell of burning insulation. "I don't know, sir."

"Look it up in your dictionary."

Justin had a book in his hands. WEBSTER'S COLLEGIATE DICTIONARY, the cover read. Below that was printed TOP SECRET.

It wasn't the words that made him remember. It was something else. Maybe the frigid blue of the executive officer's gaze, maybe the wintry chatter in his mind.

He remembered the numbers in his Head-Up display counting down to minimum controllable airspeed; the way the nose of the plane began to dip.

Oh, he remembered.

He remembered Tyler's screams of "What, Searles? Are you crazy?" and reaching, reaching to pull the face protector down, setting in motion the automatic ejection sequence. With a burst of fire the canopy blew, carried away on the hurricane wind. Tyler was rocketed out first. A second later, Justin, too, was blasted upward, his speed jeans inflating as he pulled breathtaking Gs.

He remembered hearing the lacy flutter of the deployed parachute above; he remembered seeing the F-14 plummet to the dark earth below. And, almost peripherally, he noticed that some sort of light was painting him blue. His parachute harness was blue. His palms were blue. And there was something cold at his shoulder.

Something inquisitive.

"Oh, Jesus God!" Justin screamed. He lurched up from his seat at the counter and ran to the window where an F-14 was going down in flames and a Woofer was snaring its slow-falling prey.

He launched his body through the window, shattering the paper-thin glass. On the other side of the broken window, the air didn't have that scorched-metal smell of the desert or the humid, sweatsock smell of the land near the Gulf. Instead, the atmosphere was blue and moist and January cool and suddenly Justin realized beyond a reasonable doubt, beyond the blind high confidence of a fighter jock, that there were some things he was better off not knowing.

THE PYRENEES, BELOW BAGNÈRES-DE-LUCHON

Gordon had pulled his CRAV into some brush, caught an hour's nap, some chow, and bathroom time. Now he was up again and running, running as fast as he could.

The helicopter was still after him. He would hear it close in every once in a while. When it passed overhead, he'd dig his way into the debris at the side of the stream and hide as best he could.

Earlier that morning he'd tried dragging brush to obliterate his tread marks; but the scoring in the mud looked suspicious. He'd given up hiding and had fled, knowing that, with the helicopter after him, the laser deployment platoon wouldn't be far behind.

Gordon was breaking no land-speed records. The stream bed got rockier, and the fastest he could go was a daredevil ten miles an hour.

The sides of the gully were so steep now that he could barely see above them. God only knew what was up there. A road, maybe. With trucks. A BTR-80 full of soldiers.

He'd miscalculated the whole thing. The banks to either side were pure, sheer shale. If he tried to climb them he'd tip over, and Gordon didn't want to spend time on his back.

Not now, when he was being hunted.

The stream bed widened. At a bend, dead branches and trash were piled from earlier flooding. He rolled on a bit and stopped in alarm.

He'd come out at the fucking Garonne river.

Goddamn it, he thought, staring in dismay at the boiling rapids and realizing he would have to double back and fight it out with the LDV platoon.

Swiveling, his treads clacking against the stones, he looked up at the opposite bank and froze.

A T-72 was trundling down the slope. The scene, as in a good movie, was all eerily clear: the camouflage paint on the tank's armor; the gaping black hole of the 125mm muzzle. The grass. Gordon could see every damned blade of grass, every fucking green leaf and pine needle. He could see the dark eyes of the tank commander standing in the cupola rim, and God, Gordon could hear things, too—Dolby Sound distinct. The muted squeal as the turret turned, finding its bearing. A bird singing somewhere in the brush.

"Arm missiles!" Gordon screamed, shaking himself out of his trance. His display sprang into life, along with the words: SYSTEM MALFUNCTION.

"What the hell's the matter with you?" he shouted; but the software was already working on the problem. The kill box blinked out. A schematic came on.

TUBE COVERS STUCK, the display said after a second's pause.

Oh, Christ. It was the mud. When he'd dug himself into the stream bank, he'd accidentally jammed shut his tube guards.

Slamming the CRAV around, Gordon splashed downstream, heedless of the rocks. Behind he heard the squeal of the cannon as it tracked him.

No time to run. No time to think. Those shells were goddamned sabots, armor-piercing. At this distance, the depleted uranium boot would squash him, diamond plating and all, like a bug. He backed up fast, clanging hard against an outcropping, and stared at his readout, hoping he'd dislodged the clay. No such luck.

And then he wondered why the tank hadn't fired; if maybe it had come down with constipation of the automatic loader.

Gordon looked. The tank commander's helmet was off, and his head was lowered to his outspread arm. The cannon was aimed at a spot Gordon had been a moment ago.

Gordon splashed through the shallow water to the left.

The cannon did not follow. On the hill the tank stood quietly, its gun aimed at the ravine as though it were a statue of a man pointing.

Look, the tank might have been saying. *Look*.

Jerking the CRAV into reverse, Gordon bounced off the shale bank like a pinball.

MISSILES 4–8 AVAILABLE, the readout said.

Trundling right, he got as close to the bend in the stream as he could to get a better view of the opposite bank.

The tank commander's face was turned slightly, his chin resting on the metal deck. His dark eyes were open and his skin was the almond color of the Hotpoint refrigerator in the bunker. There was a neat, perfectly circular, absolutely bloodless hole in his forehead.

From the graveyard hush that had fallen, Gordon figured the gunner and the driver were dead as well.

He stood befuddled, his CRAV patiently waiting for a kill order that was unnecessary now. He stared until his eyes teared from fatigue, until a flash of blue at the edge of his screen caught his attention.

Rover was back. The blue light hovered near the lifeless tank, happy as a dog that has just brought in the morning paper.

IN THE LIGHT

"Read me the book," Harding said.

Justin Searles looked down in his lap and gently stroked the XO's balding head, leaving imprints of his fingers in the skull. Clack-clack. Clack-clack. The interior of the bus was dim, and the sound the carriage made against the steel rails was soothing.

Smiling, Justin turned the first page.

"Chapter One," he read. "Procedures on Encountering UFOs."

The words were meaningless. Justin saw them and mouthed them. The book seemed to please Harding, though. The XO settled down and sighed with satisfaction.

On the seats around them sat the bus driver and the

waitress and Ann, their eyes huge and dark with wonder, as though Justin was telling them the most fascinating story.

Justin read.

His mind was an albatross running over the snow, taking to the air on its wide clumsy wings. The wind caught him and boosted him into the glowering clouds, where there were no missiles, no hot flak.

He looked up from his book to smile into the freezing rain of their gazes.

CHAPTER 5

CRAV COMMAND, TRÁS-OS-MONTES, PORTUGAL

Someone squeezed Gordon's upper arm. Obeying the command, he closed his eyes. When the CRAV had powered down, he pried the glasses off and saw Pelham standing over him, Ishimoto behind. The two were breathing hard, as if they had run all the way from the monitoring room.

"Out of the chair," Pelham said.

"But, sir—" His CRAV was sitting somewhere out there, only half its missiles working, the Garonne in front of it, the LDV platoon behind. And Pelham was asking him to *leave the chair?*

He began to protest, but Pelham had his stern colonel face on, a scowl that erased all resemblance to a friendly Hershey elf.

"You're not security-cleared for this, sergeant. Out. Consider yourself dismissed."

Military training took over, like the thoughtlessness of instinct. Gordon freed his hands from the controls and leaped off the seat. Quickly Ishimoto sat down and began putting on the gloves.

"Sir—" Gordon said.

Pelham rounded on him. "Get out," he said in a cold, hard voice. "That is an order."

Gordon flinched away. He wrestled the door open, and turned back once, in time to see the Mitsubishi rep putting on the glasses.

He trudged up the three flights of stairs. In the middle of the fog-bound yard he felt the impact of what had just happened. He stopped dead, a silent wail of loss in his brain.

"Hi," a female voice said.

Gordon whirled to see Stendhal next to him.

"Listen. Pelham's been on my ass," she was saying. Her BDU blouse was open, the light wind whipping at it so Gordon was getting a now-you-see-it now-you-don't peek at her nipples.

"You know the CRAV better than anybody, and I thought, well, if you're not busy or anything, maybe you could give me some pointers."

Gordon wasn't listening. He was feeling his outrage grow from a small, toothless thing into something huge and fanged and clawed.

Ishimoto had never taken a CRAV into battle. He didn't know tactics, and would be unprepared for the little eccentricities of the unit. Each robot had its own particular feel. Gordon's CRAV was skittish, needed a light touch on the accelerator; firm, slow pressure on the brake.

Stendhal was looking at him funny, and Gordon knew he should say something. But all that wanted to come from his mouth was a shriek.

"You okay?" Stendhal asked.

"Yeah. Sure."

Gordon had always been the odd one out, the loner, the guy the jocks beat up in middle school. When he was a kid, Nintendo had allowed him to pretend he was strong, courageous, deadly; then the CRAV came along and made that dream come true.

"I hate to bother you, but is now a good time?" Stendhal was saying, "Or after dinner? Maybe we could even go to the mess hall together or something. I really need some help."

Gordon turned and, leaving Stendhal open-mouthed behind him, ran back down the steps to the third level of the bunker.

The monitoring room was empty, he saw as he halted in the doorway in surprise.

"Colonel?" he called, walking inside.

Five screens peered down from their brackets on the ceiling. Only two were on. In the first, someone was thrashing through brush by a mountain road. The other screen was showing a closeup of a shale bank and a robot hand clutching a thick tree root. The picture shook, and droplets of water were beaded on the camera lens.

Gordon felt a splintered-ice shiver of alarm. The second screen was the visuals from his CRAV. Ishimoto was going to try to swim the Garonne river.

Is he fucking crazy? Gordon wondered, his panic blossoming into hysteria.

"Colonel Pelham!" Gordon shouted, pivoting to the open doorway. Then he caught sight of something that brought him up short: to better analyze Rover, an ambient temperature gauge and an electromagnetic counter had been plugged into his CRAV's monitor.

He looked at the screen again and saw that Ishimoto had brought up the CRAV's diagnostics. ALL MISSILE TUBE COVERS CLEAR, they read.

Then the CRAV was moving, hand over hand, grasping for purchase. The shaking of the screen lessened, and suddenly the CRAV was free of the riverbank. It dropped to level ground and bounced on its stiff McPhearson struts, its camera pointed directly down the ravine.

"Whoa, mother," Gordon said under his breath, admiring the Mitsubishi rep's skill in spite of himself. Jesus. Talk about iron balls. Ishimoto had dipped the missile tubes in the river to wash the mud out.

Fascinated now, Gordon watched the CRAV trundle its way up the stream bed, missiles armed and ready. Ishimoto the Fearless was setting out to destroy the LDV platoon.

The trees and rocks blinked out so quickly that Gordon reflexively took a step back, bumping into a rollered chair.

The CRT monitor was blue. Bright, neon blue.

The screen was shaking now, as though Ishimoto had once more plunged the CRAV into the rapids of the Garonne. Gordon glanced down and saw the numbers on the digital of the thermometer dropping: 53, 37, 16. The needle on the electromagnetic gauge leaped into the red.

"Colonel Pelham!" Gordon screamed, running from the room. In the hall he was stopped by the thought that there was only one place the colonel could be; that there was only one kind of emergency that could have taken him from the action. Gordon raced down the hall to the men's bathroom.

He threw the bathroom door open so fast, it banged against the wall with the noise of a howitzer.

No one was standing at the urinals. But two feet showed under the door of one of the stalls. A pair of camouflage pants sagged around the silent ankles.

"Colonel Pelham?" he called.

There was a long moment before a reply came, as though the owner of the feet was hoping that Gordon would go away. "Yes?" the colonel finally asked.

"Sir? I was just in the monitoring room. The Woofer's attacking Ishimoto."

From behind the stall door came the frantic sound of paper flapping. A *People* magazine dropped to the tile.

"I'll be right there!" Pelham called in a high, tight voice.

Gordon stepped into the hall. A moment later Pelham wrenched open the door and hurried out, his face grim and urgent.

"Where is he?" the colonel barked. "Is he all right?"

"I don't know, sir," Gordon admitted, running to keep up.

At Gordon's door Pelham stopped, put his shoulder to the green-painted metal, and shoved. The door popped open, and Gordon peered around Pelham.

Ishimoto's back was arched, his body convulsive-rigid. Pushing the colonel aside, Gordon stumbled into the room and grasped Ishimoto's upper arm. The man was trembling so violently that the metal leads of the gloves mimicked the noise of chattering teeth.

"Power down!" Gordon shouted even though he realized Ishimoto couldn't hear him. "Power it down!"

But the Japanese paid no attention to the bruising clutch of Gordon's fingers.

Pelham took a breath. "We'd better get him out."

Gordon tore the goggles from the rep's face and then jerked him out of the seat. Ishimoto landed with a thump on the floor.

"Sorry, sir," Gordon said to the astonished Pelham as he climbed into the chair and slipped on the gloves. "But I'm getting my CRAV out of this shit."

THE PYRENEES

The moment Gordon had the goggles on, he could feel the bone-numbing cold, could hear the thunderous clatter of sleet in the back of his brain.

"Back off!" he shouted at Rover.

Suddenly there were trees again, the calm stream trickling over the rocks. A few yards away Rover skipped through the air, and the din in Gordon's mind became a chill hiss.

"You'll burn out my controls with that electromagnetic crap, you asshole!"

Raising his arm, Gordon checked the fine three-fingered claws of his unit. The metal was coated with a thin film of frost just now burning off in the sun.

"Now stay behind me," Gordon said, swinging his arm a couple of times to show Rover the way. After a few moments of either confusion or petulance, the blue light floated to Gordon's rear and stayed.

Gordon moved out through the shallow water of the stream, and Rover kept his distance, bobbing along behind the CRAV. It was later—much too late to do anything about it—that Gordon realized the chance he had missed. Stendhal had talked to him. And he'd been so rude, she would probably never speak to him again.

IN THE LIGHT

Justin woke up to see Harding and the bus driver staring at him. "That was an interesting book," the driver said. "Thank you for reading it to us." His eyes were dark, luminous holes in his spongy face.

Harding sat down so close to Justin's thigh that Justin could feel the chill of his body. "Tell us about war, now," he suggested.

Outside the window the night was flashing by. The F-14 was gone, left miles behind. Justin pulled the blanket around himself. "It's cold in here," he said to no one in particular.

"Would you rather tell Ann about the war?" Harding asked.

The sound of sleet was softer now, a comforting hiss, like the song of tires on a wet road. "No," Justin said.

"We can call her, if you'd like," the bus driver told him.

Deep in his blanket, Justin shivered. He felt as though his bones had turned to ice and nothing, nowhere, could warm them. "She bothers me," he said.

"I'm sorry." The meager light winked on Harding's bald head and the brass buttons. "We thought she would make you calm."

"She just bothers me," he told them.

Harding reached out and put a nerveless hand on Justin's arm. "Then we'll tell her to stay away. Would you like to drive the bus?"

"Would you like that?" the driver asked, leaning forward intently.

"Yes," Justin said. "Oh, yes. I'd like that a lot."

He was in the high metal-and-vinyl seat, the starry highway spread out before his windshield. Harding and the driver were beside him, grinning.

"Go ahead," the driver said encouragingly. "Go ahead, son, and take her up."

Justin pushed the gear shift forward slowly, feeling the rumble of the engines through his legs, his spine. The bus

shot down the spangled road. When he thought he had
gained enough speed, he pulled the steering wheel toward
his belly. The bus soared up into the night.

"Do you like it?" Harding asked.

Justin was smiling so broadly, he couldn't answer.
Euphoria caught the words in his throat, as though he'd
glutted himself on joy. Ahead of him the stars merged,
clustering in the center of the windshield. An instant later
they turned a frail, lovely shade of blue.

"Where would you like to go?" Harding asked.

Feeling the speed of the bus like a glad ache in his
chest, Justin considered the blue-shifted stars. "Florida,"
he told him.

"Then fly there. Go ahead and fly there. And when you
reach Florida, will you tell us about war?"

"If I can reach Florida," he whispered, "I will tell you
everything I know."

CENTCOM AIRFIELD, BADAJOZ, SPAIN

The M-16 propped awkwardly between her legs, Rita
Beaudreaux stared at the boxes of supplies around her and
listened to the sound of the Sikorsky powering up.

"Dear God," she whispered. Her voice was covered by
the angry whine of the rotors, and that was fine with Rita;
she didn't want the pilot to overhear. Rita's mother, when
she was alive, had grumbled that she'd never taught her
girl anything; but she had bequeathed two unforgettable
childhood lessons. One, iron with the weave of the fabric;
two, always pray aloud.

"If you get me out of this weirdness, God," Rita promised
quietly, "I'll start going back to church. Really. I mean it.
Amen."

God wouldn't have much time, it was all happening so
quickly. Another moment or so, she'd be airborne, and
a couple of hours after that she'd be hiking through the
minefields near Lérida. Her fingers toyed with the fat metal
attachment on the bottom of her M-16's muzzle. A grenade
launcher. Some idiot had given her a grenade launcher. And

not bothered to ask if she'd like a user's manual.

The scream of the rotors overhead lowered to an idling whine.

"Rita?"

General Lauterbach clambered into the passenger compartment.

"You okay?" the general asked.

Rita crossed her fingers and waited for miracles.

After a cursory glance around, Lauterbach took a seat atop a box labeled MRE—HAMBURGER PIZZA. He took off his helmet and put it in his lap.

"Glad I could catch you before you left," he said.

Before you left. Rita felt her religious faith sink back into agnosticism.

Lauterbach leaned across and peered closely at her rifle. "I see someone gave you a grenade launcher," he chuckled.

"Yeah. Like I was a real soldier or something," she said dryly.

His smile died. "Something's come up. Something important." His yellowish hazel eyes were calm, the gaze of a lion aloofly considering a gazelle. "I need to know if there's any way to duplicate those alien mutilations."

"No," she said. "I already told you, nothing I know could do that."

Lauterbach nodded. "I see. Your orders have changed."

Rita caught her breath.

"I'm going to try a little psychological warfare on our Arab friends. If you come across mutilations, I want you to leave the Arabs in place. The mutilated Americans who can pass for Arabs are to be stripped and their uniforms replaced with BDUs you get from dead, nonmutilated Arabs. You understand?"

Rita ran her hand through her short, curly hair. She was sweating, she noticed. Sweating like a pig. "No, general, I don't."

"The mutilations are rare: about one percent of the dead. You and the platoon can handle that. The Arabs don't wear dog tags, so the ruse should work. When you strip the Americans, remember to take off socks, underwear, everything. I doubt the Arab doctors will look close enough to notice differences in dental work. At least that's what I hope."

"You're telling me to desecrate corpses?" Rita snapped. "What kind of order is that?"

"Not desecrate—" he began.

She didn't let him finish. "What about those American boys' parents? Their wives? Lord, general, has the Greenhouse Effect changed us that much?"

Lauterbach was staring at her, his mouth open. Finally he managed to say, soothingly, "I didn't mean to upset you."

"You didn't upset me," she said. "You offended me."

He reached out, put his hand, wiry and warm, on hers. "We're losing this war," he said. "Our weapon stockpiles are low. We can't make armaments, we can't fight a war without fuel. Rita, for God's sake." His voice was so low and intense, she had no choice but to listen. She would have heard that voice even if miles away. It was a voice to make Allied soldiers weep from Lisbon to Warsaw.

"If we don't get help," he told her, "our surrender is inevitable."

He pulled away first. His fingers trailed over hers. She wondered if the gesture was accidental or affectionate.

"You know what they call me?" he asked with a sad, lopsided smile. "Loon. They call me Loon. You know why?"

Guardedly she shook her head.

"Everyone thinks I'm crazy. Good. Let the Arabs think that." There was a manic glint in Lauterbach's yellow eyes, a hard, topaz sparkle that scared her. "No one believes me, Rita, but there are aliens out there. God's given us a wild card. God's given us a miracle. And I have it in my hand."

The rotors idled quietly. Outside in the overcast day a Humvee sped across the tarmac, its engine growling. One soldier called to another, laughter in his voice. The breeze from the open door smelled sweet, but it didn't lighten the atmosphere in the helicopter. Rita could feel the weight of the air on her shoulders. It was thick and soupy, like the false environment in an aquarium.

"I want more than life itself to talk to those aliens." In his voice was a startling tremolo of desire. "But if I could communicate with the lights," he said, "it's possible they wouldn't help. They might not understand armed conflict."

Then the general gave her an unexpected, disarming smile, and to her profound astonishment, he winked. "But maybe we can trick the Arabs into thinking the lights have joined us. No harm in that, is there?"

THE PYRENEES BELOW BAGNÈRES-DE-LUCHON

Someone had painted a crude symbol on the T-72, Colonel Wasef noticed. A sign to ward off demons.

The tank commander must have been nearly out of the hatch when the blow fell, or else the impact of it threw him partially out. He lay half over the deck, his eyes wide with surprise. The bloodless hole in his head went straight through to the other side. An impossible wound, bordering on the ridiculous, a wound that might be made in a cartoon character.

Hearing footsteps approach, Wasef started. It was only Captain Mustafa. Quickly Wasef smoothed the fright from his features, but knew that Yussif had seen.

The captain's face was so taut, Wasef knew that his friend, too, was having trouble keeping the fear in check.

"The engine has not been shut off," Wasef said.

"No, sir."

The two stood for a moment listening to the agitated grumble of the diesel engine. The T-72 needed a tune-up, Wasef thought, and from the wreath of smoke around the rear of the vehicle, smoke that stank of carbon and unburnt fuel, he decided it could probably do with a ring job, too. All the vehicles were old: the planes, the trucks, everything. Only spit and baling wire held the Arab army together.

"Someone should turn off the engine," Wasef told the captain. Yussif paled, the blood draining from his face so much, his skin mimicked the pallor of the corpse.

Mustafa wasn't merely frightened; he was paralyzed.

"I'll do it," Wasef said quickly, and wished he had not volunteered.

Skirting the driver's entrance, he climbed up the deck and peered around the dead TC into the hatch. On the floor of the tank lay the gunner. He was an odd, yellowish color, the shade of spoiled goat cheese.

Sometimes Allah was unexpectedly kind. The T-72 gave a last chugging twitch and fell silent. It had run out of gas. Relieved, Wasef clambered down to the grass.

"Could the blue light be American?" the captain asked.

"I don't think so," Wasef told him. "If they had such a weapon, we would now all be the color of cheese and have holes through our bodies."

Yussif leaned over to whisper into Wasef's ear. "Yes. If one possesses such a weapon, one uses it to destroy armies, not a single tank."

Wasef gave a nervous nod.

"Yet it trails the American robot," Yussif went on, pointing down into the ravine. "See the marks of the treads?"

Yes, Wasef thought. The blue light was not American, but it had some special relationship with the Allies, a relationship Wasef was not canny enough to understand. He stared at the tread marks in frustrated dismay.

"The robot has gone back up the ravine," Yussif said. "The platoon will kill it."

And then what? Wasef wondered. He had the impulse to tell the captain to pull his platoon out and send them back to base.

"The men are frightened," Yussif admitted. "They are illiterate, mostly, and superstitious. Once they believe the Americans are protected by djinn, they will not fight."

"Superstitious, yes," Wasef said absently. His own master's degree in electrical engineering was no insulator against such unfounded and primitive fear. Before the killing heat came to Egypt, he had imagined himself one link in a long proud line from the builders of Giza, a line superior to the filthy Algerians, more intelligent than the backward, sheepherding Libyans. Now he wasn't so sure. They, at least, knew the methods of dealing with the supernatural.

He glanced over at the squad who were standing near a tree, as far from the tank as they could get without being reprimanded. No one was sitting down; no one was squatting. They fingered their weapons and looked nervously around the glade.

Wasef cleared his throat.

"What, brother?" Yussif asked, leaning forward to catch any word of wisdom, any hint of direction. Loyal Yussif, Wasef thought fondly, would jump off a cliff if he were asked. But, like the rest of the army, he needed to be shown the path up the mountain.

Wasef gave the captain a level, encouraging look. "Tell the men these deaths are proof that we do battle with the forces of darkness. Tell them that, as Allah is good, justice will prevail."

Yussif smiled as though he had been granted a generous and unforeseen absolution. "Yes, Qasim. As Allah is my witness, we shall prevail."

IN THE LIGHT

He drove the bus through the sharp edge of night into day. Below, in fierce, bright light, Florida stretched, its white sand a chalk line between the cobalt blue of the sea and the enameled green of the land. Justin saw home, and his hands clenched on the wheel so hard, they trembled.

On a small side street of a quiet subdivision in Boca Raton, Justin brought the bus down and parked before a pink cinderblock house.

"Don't you want to go in?" the exec asked.

Justin stared out the bus window. The house was just as he'd remembered: the mango tree, thick-trunked and wide-leaved, dominating the front yard; the bed of jasmine and bird-of-paradise blooming just beyond. An ocean of emerald grass lapped at the pavement.

"You've come all this way," the bus driver said. "Don't you want to see your mother?"

The bus doors opened, and Justin stepped out. Above his head, he noticed, the palms made a clattering sound in the breeze. He bent to pick up a fallen coconut and held it to his chest, running his hands along its smooth, green surface.

Florida smelled the same: lush and moist and verdant, as though the air itself were about to bloom. Above the roofs of the houses, toward the sea, blue-gray clouds massed, the sight of them at once languid and anticipatory.

"Do you like it?" the exec asked. "Is it what you were looking for?"

Without answering, Justin skirted the house and headed for the backyard. There was the screened porch he remembered; here the budding lemon tree. And there stood his mother, hanging laundry on the line.

"Mom," he said.

She turned and gave him a smile. The features didn't stay put long enough for recognition. Her nose grew short, and then long. Her mouth rearranged itself several times indecisively. Her hair went chameleon-like from brown to salt-and-pepper to white.

"I see you've brought friends," she said. Her voice was undecided, too, changing from alto to soprano and back again. The timbre of it was all wrong. "Let's go in and have some milk and cake."

He trailed after her, a chick inescapably captured in the gravity of a mother hen. The screen door, which always needed oiling, squeaked just as he remembered. The kitchen was the same, too: all sunshine yellow and white.

"I've missed you," Justin said as he took a seat at the kitchen table. To his left sat the bus driver, chair faced the wrong way, arms resting on the metal bar of the back. To Justin's right Harding sat, fingers laced on the Formica.

There was the sugar bowl he remembered from childhood, the ceramic one with the flowers on the side. The coconut in his lap, Justin watched his mother take down four plates and carry them to the table.

"Do you hear it?" he asked his mother.

She glanced up at him curiously, her eyes shifting from blue to hazel to black. "What?"

"That sound of the palm trees tapping. Do you hear it?"

"It's just the wind," his mother told him.

"Yes," he said. "Just the wind."

She poured milk in four glasses and set the chocolate cake on the table.

"Justin was just going to tell us about war," Harding told Justin's mother.

"Were you, dear?" his mother said.

The palm trees in the front yard rattled like icy castanets. Justin looked up into his mother's face and saw that her eyes had changed to green.

"How *is* war?" she asked.

They were all staring at him now, the bus driver and Harding and his mother. The clatter of the palm trees was so huge a sound, he could scarcely think.

"I'm scared all the time," he whispered.

The air in the kitchen was cool and thick. "Tell me," his mother said.

He remembered planes erupting into fire, coming down over the desert in graceful orange arcs, like falling stars he might have once wished on. The worst, he remembered, were night landings, the carrier below in the darkness, a lit postage stamp in the immensity of the sea. The carrier was such a tiny thing, he was constantly amazed to find it. Sometimes, when the seas were high, he pictured the hook not catching and his plane tumbling and crashing on the deck.

Wrapping his body around the solidity of the coconut, he said, "I wish I could go home."

He flinched when he felt Harding's mushy hand touch him. "You *are* home," the exec said.

But Justin had remembered the thing he most wanted to forget: Boca Raton as it truly was. At high tide, he knew, fish swam in empty houses, crabs scuttled through backyards, and walls and fences stood like reefs against the pummeling of the long breakers.

"I wish I could go home," he whispered, and neither Harding's touch nor the cool sound of his mother's voice was any comfort.

IN THE PYRENEES BELOW BAGNÈRES-DE-LUCHON

Pelham hadn't ordered him out of the chair, so Gordon went on, making slow and cautious time up the ravine, Rover bobbing behind his unit, keeping out of sight.

Gordon's tubes were erect, his missiles armed. He drove with his thumb on the firing stud.

Lucky, that, he thought, when he rounded a bend in the stream and found an Arab detachment waiting.

There was the guy with the mortar calmly settling the CRAV in his sights; there were the rest, not thirty yards away, hidden in the boulders as best they were able. And here was Gordon, tubes upraised, ready for the showdown.

It was Dodge City all over again.

Before Gordon had a chance to react, a few AK rounds pinged off his hide. Surprise brought his thumb down on the stud.

Missile One launched with an ear-splitting hiss, rocking the CRAV on its springs. The blast of the propellant blinded Gordon; an instant later he was deafened by the missile's explosion. Even before the CRAV was fully steadied, even before he could see where he was going, he spun right, hoping to avoid the returning fire.

There wasn't any. Looking down into the clear stream, he saw the water was threaded with syrupy crimson. Funny how blood mixed with water, he thought. Funny how beautiful it was. It made delicate, curlicue feathers, deft as a painter's strokes.

When the smoke cleared, he saw the small Rattlesnake missile had hit the rocks to the rear of the squad. The burst of shrapnel and stone had been intensified by the contained space. Men and pieces of men were tangled like flood debris.

The knot of shredded corpses stirred. Slowly, gradually, a man crawled out from under, dragging pink streamers of his own intestines. Rover drifted past Gordon and settled, gentle as milkweed fluff, on the soldier. When the blue light lifted a moment later, the man was no longer moving.

"Get back here!" Gordon shouted, embarrassed and sickened at the same time, as though he had caught his dog worrying a neighbor's pet rabbit.

Rover floated toward Gordon and stopped a few feet away. In the back of his mind Gordon could hear a chill, questioning rattle.

"You don't do things like that, damn it!" he shouted. "Shit, that's . . . Jesus, that's . . ."

The dead soldier was a funny almond color now, and there was an expression of stunned relief on his face.

CHAPTER 6

NEAR LÉRIDA, SPAIN

Rita clambered out of the Sikorsky and trudged cumbersomely across the tarmac. The duffel bag was weighing her down, and somehow the M-16 and she kept colliding butts.

Beyond a Chinook, an absurdly petite soldier stood near a machine-gun-mounted Humvee. Helen Dix, Rita decided; and she found herself wondering if the lieutenant had a problem finding size-three BDUs.

"Capt'n Beaudreaux?" the lieutenant asked as Rita got within earshot.

It was a moment before Rita remembered to return the junior officer's salute.

"I'm Lieutenant Dix. Glad to have you aboard," the woman said in a Georgia-cracker drawl.

Rita's heart sank. Lauterbach was a man of contradictions. A man who had the sense to put her in a woman's platoon and the stupidity to forget that the officer was a redneck.

"Thanks, lieutenant. I appreciate that," she replied, steeling herself for some good old-fashioned prejudice. "I'll try and stay out of your way."

Although dainty, Dix had wiry forearms that would have looked more natural on a boy. Her denim blue eyes had that long-distance stare common to front-line soldiers.

Dix blinked at Rita. Her gaze seemed to narrow its focus. "Where you all from?" she asked.

"Louisiana originally—"

Suddenly Dix smiled. "Lordy, Lordy," she said. "A Southerner. Thank God. Come on, capt'n. We got us some driving to do."

Surprised by the genuine welcome in the lieutenant's voice, Rita climbed into the Humvee. Dix had gone shopping for her platoon, she saw. The passenger floorboard and the backseat were filled with string bags of fruit.

"That there's Specialist Jimmy Hoover," Dix said, gesturing with her head in the direction of the machine gun. The young, angular Hoover was sitting with the gun between his legs.

Dix keyed the ignition, gunned the engine, and peeled rubber on her way out of the base.

"You all take your stop-up pills, ma'am?" Dix asked, taking her eyes off the road.

Rita kept hers straight ahead, figuring that at the speed they were going someone in the Humvee should be watching. "Please don't call me ma'am," she said in a strained voice. They took a corner too fast, the fenders brushing a yucca and a close-packed fence of blooming cactus.

"Begging the capt'n's pardon, but what do you want me to call you?"

"Call me Rita. Just Rita." They were zipping down a straightaway now. A white goat barely escaped being a road kill.

"Well, Rita. You take your stop-up pills, or what? I mean, if it ain't the worst thing that can happen getting your period in the field, it comes close."

"No, I haven't taken . . . I mean, nobody gave me . . ."

"Shit. Ain't men all alike?" Dix asked rhetorically, reaching into her BDU blouse and bringing out a plastic bottle. "They just plain overlook the essentials. My old boyfriend? He used to climb my ass about spending too much money on Tampax, like crotch wicks were jewelry or something. Here. You just take one of these, sugar. There's a canteen down there on the floorboard someplace."

Rita took the pill bottle. She was prying the canteen loose from a bag of yellow Spanish cherries when the Humvee slowed.

Startled, Rita lifted her head. Dix was driving grim-faced now, careful not to hit the refugees massed on the side of the road.

There were hundreds of them. Perhaps thousands. Old men with canes. Begrimed children holding tight to their mothers' hands. They were walking west, all with the same blankness in their faces, all wearing the same shroud of dust. A line of migrating ghosts. The mass of people moved with the communal, dull purpose of herded cattle.

Rita stared hard at a man in a three-piece suit, a basket of clothes in his arms. Had he not looked so exhausted, so desperate, she might have thought he was on his way to the laundry after a long day at work. When the Humvee passed, his eyes tracked it, hot and urgent.

"Where do they come from?" Rita asked. There were so many, it seemed all Spain was emptying.

"Little towns around here. Hey," the lieutenant said in a bright voice. "I hear you know General Lauterbach. He as much of a hard-ass as everybody says?"

Hard-ass? Rita wondered. Funny. She had never thought of the general that way. "Not that I've noticed," Rita said.

"Huh. Maybe he's just nicer to you than he is to his staff."

"I've been told I have the general's every confidence, whatever that means," Rita said distantly, wondering when the march of homeless Spaniards would end.

"No, honey," Dix laughed. "I hear he *likes* you. That he's what the girls at Robert E. Lee High used to call 'namored on you and all."

As she swallowed the Mens-Ex and clamped the top back on the canteen, Rita's mind returned to the helicopter, to the touch of Lauterbach's hand on hers. "I doubt that."

"Well, I got it straight from Major Tubbs who got the word from Lt. Colonel Martin who heard it right from the great man himself, that we were to treat you like Steuben crystal. Ain't that just the most romantic thing you ever heard? Steuben crystal. And here I was expecting you to be some Junior Leaguer, not some tough broad with a grenade launcher on her weapon."

Rita frowned. "I'm simply important to the general as a researcher. That's all that means."

Taking her eyes from the road, the lieutenant gave Rita a sly look. "Ain't what Lt. Colonel Martin says. Fact is, Lt. Colonel Martin understood that General Lauterbach had a particular interest in you and that your safety and well-being was paramount to the general. Paramount, he says, like if anything happened to you, the army would chew ass past my tailbone. Sugar, that may not be love, but that's heavy like."

Rita remembered the first time she met the general. She'd been in an aircraft hangar sorting out the bones of five men who had burned to death in an APC. Two of the bodies were drawn up in the typical burn victim's pugilist stance. The other three were in charred-bone pieces.

She remembered she had spread out the dental charts and medical records and had just identified one body by an old spiral fracture of the tibia when someone walked into the hangar.

Hearing footsteps, she had looked up but saw nothing important about the visitor in the shadows. She returned to her task.

"You're taking a long time with this," the man said. "Why don't you just approximate the way most of the other doctors do?"

She spun around. "You'll get your IDs when I say you get your IDs. Families will be burying these bodies and they won't want to cry over some stranger."

He took a step forward into the floodlights and she saw two things at once: the disarming smile on his face and the four stars on his collar. "What's your name, captain?" the general asked pleasantly.

"Doctor," she shot back. "Doctor Beaudreaux."

The smile faltered. "Well. Carry on," he said with a vague nod. Then he left the room.

It was only afterward that she realized she hadn't saluted

and that he hadn't chastised her for that.

It's obvious he loves me for my tact, Rita thought. *Or my nappy hair. Or my training-bra-sized breasts.*

On the way to the staging area, Rita told Lieutenant Dix of the new orders and tried to picture herself in bed with the general: him on top; her on top. None of the positions seemed to work. And ringed around the bed, the displaced civilians of Spain were looking on with their huge, empty eyes.

CRAV COMMAND, TRÁS-OS-MONTES, PORTUGAL

Even after the CRAV was safe abed, Gordon sat in the black silence of the goggles, letting his nerves settle like fizz off a Coke. When he felt his legs and arms were steady, he pried off the headgear.

Ishimoto was sitting next to him.

They looked at each other. In the close quarters of the command center their knees were almost touching. Someone had installed a secondary screen on the table near the CRAV computer.

Ishimoto sat unmoving, even his breathing kept to a minimum. As spare and abstract as a haiku.

"It bothers you," he finally said.

Gordon didn't need an explanation. "Yeah," he agreed. "It bothers me." They'd snuck into his room, rearranged his furniture, and then sat there and watched him work. He hadn't known a thing.

"We leave impressions on all we touch," the rep said. "I have used all five CRAVs in this place. The mark you leave on your unit is strong. That is why I think the Woofer follows you. It senses you in it. It senses your equanimity."

Ishimoto sat back, as though to allow Gordon to digest what he had said.

Equanimity? Gordon thought. *What the hell does equanimity mean?*

"What?" he asked.

"Detachment. Tranquillity," was the reply. "One must detach oneself from the world in order to be at peace with it. You have this quality, but it is an indifference I do not understand. I follow the Eightfold Path because it has been taught to me. You follow it unknowing. It is possible that you may be a true master."

Gordon scratched his cheek. "Huh?"

"I am Zen Buddhist," the rep replied, his voice and his face passive. Jesus. And Ishimoto thought Gordon was tranquil. If the Japanese had been any more tranquil, he would have been asleep.

"No kidding?" said Gordon, intrigued. "And I could be a Zen master?"

Ishimoto's lips split into a broad smile. "No kidding."

Gordon sat back in the command chair and grinned at the boxy computer.

The Japanese stood. "You will be hungry."

In the empty cave of Gordon's belly an appetite awakened, a bear rousing from hibernation. "Right. Let's go to the mess hall or something. You eaten?"

Ishimoto shook his head. "I have waited for you."

As they left the room, Gordon glanced at Ishimoto again. "Hey. Are you all right now?"

Ishimoto raised a placid eyebrow.

"I mean, after what happened between you and the Woofer. You okay?"

It was as though a wall had come down between them, a soft wall, but it was there nevertheless.

"Yes," he said simply.

Gordon hesitated before asking the next question. "How did it feel? What did you see?"

Ishimoto took a long, deep breath. His onyx eyes settled on Gordon. "I saw a great emptiness," he said.

NEAR CALHAN, COLORADO

That morning the supply truck had traveled the twenty miles from Calhan out to the camp, bringing just enough food to make people hungrier. The cops had strutted around, as if the delivery was the next best trick to the loaves and fishes.

There had been a lot of cops with semiautomatic rifles, and when two men fought over a packet, the cops pulled them out to the road and shot them down in front of God and everybody, just like that.

Nobody said a word.

Jerry had seen people die before. Hell, his own Pa had sat in the truck dead an hour before Jerry finally figured out he wasn't mad or just not in a talkative mood. But the way Jerry had been raised, it was right that there should be a respectful silence when someone passed on. Jerry had always believed death made people thoughty, like they were considering their own road to glory and worrying about sin.

One man just stood there, as though he thought the cops were kidding. The other one fell to his knees and started crawling—Jesus, crawling—toward them. Jerry would never forget the expressionless look on the cop's face, and the way the top of the man's head disappeared in blood and brain, like a watermelon hit with a hammer.

And he'd never forget the way the people had just stood around, looked at the bodies and then walked off, eating and passing the time of day.

Things weren't right in the camp. It was a place where people weren't people anymore.

As dark fell, he counted his supplies again. It didn't take him long. Six crackers in a neat little package, and a carton of water the size of the servings of milk he used to get in school.

When it was full night, he set out into the desert, keeping his pace slow, his eyes on the Rockies. After a few minutes he came to a dry creek bed. As soon as he was over the lip of the ravine, a light hit him in the face. Blinded, squinting, he froze.

"Look what we have here," a man said.

Another man: "More Texas trash."

Blinking in the glare, he watched two state troopers get out of their jeep and walk toward him.

"What do you think you're doing?" the first cop asked.

The second didn't wait for an answer. "Sneaking west. Hey! Don't you know by now that Colorado doesn't want you?"

Jerry bolted, but the cops were faster. A hand grabbed a fistful of his hair. The pain brought him to his knees.

"Hey, boy." Laughter behind him. "You know what we do to assholes who try to sneak west?"

A boot hit Jerry's thigh, toppling him the rest of the way to the dirt. Another kick in the small of his back. He sucked up powdery dust.

"Texas trash," a cop giggled, a startlingly feminine sound, something that could have come from a teenage girl. Had the cops been drinking? When men were drunk, they pushed too hard, they hit too hard. Jerry knew what whiskey blows felt like.

Something touched him between the shoulder blades. A *zzzzt* knifed through him, front to back. It felt as though the hand of God had reached out and tried to jerk his soul from his body.

"Do it again," one of the cops said.

Jerry tried to squirm away, but the muscles in his chest and arms were twitching. His lungs quivered. His breaths came in gulps, so that his screams emerged as slapstick ah-ahs.

"What are you saying, boy?" a voice asked. "Are you back-sassing us? Len, I think he's back-sassing us. I think he's resisting arrest."

A touch, and another jolt snapped his head back, compressed the air in his lungs.

A cop laughed.

The touch of the stun gun clipped the end of Jerry's cry. His knees shot up to his stomach. His arms, out of control, flailed in the sand. The violence of his convulsion sent him tumbling into the ravine.

His face smacked rocks as he rolled. When he hit bottom, a gravel slide came with him, pattering on his eyes, his open mouth.

Lying there, helpless, he saw the beam of a flashlight

play around the ravine. It came to rest on his face. A soft chuckle drifted down with the light. Then the beam clicked off, and Jerry was alone in the dark.

When he heard the clatter, he tried to get up and failed. But the clatter, he realized, wasn't stone against stone. It was cooler and smoother than that.

The ravine was awash in blue. The knife-edged creases of the arroyo were blue. The rocks were blue. In his mind he heard the soothing tap of rain.

He closed his eyes and listened. Autumn rain, like the showers that used to drum on the corrugated roof of their shed. It was a silver sound, and secretive, like minnows flashing underwater. On his cheeks, on his eyelids, on the exposed skin of his arms he could feel a chill prickle of mist, a touch light as imagination.

When he finally dared open his eyes, he saw that the entire world was blue, horizon to horizon, and the air smelled of rainy October, a scent of promises.

He opened his mouth and drank life in, filling his lungs with it. He drank the blue even as the light was going away.

Jerry lay under the stars, and the mist slowly evaporated into the desert air. After a long while he got up. Afraid to attempt the mountains, he limped, strangely satisfied, back to camp.

NEAR TOPEKA, KANSAS

Mrs. Parisi first noticed the change in Kansas City. She'd visited the place as a child and had thought then that it was a presentable enough town, if somewhat provincial. Now all sorts of undesirables huddled around the Kansas City stores.

And the lawns. For heaven's goodness sakes. The lawns were all brown.

Of course she'd heard about the Greenhouse Effect, and that was all well and good; but one had to have a sense of pride. Perhaps if the citizens of Kansas City had taken care of their lawns, none of this Greenhouse thing would have happened.

The highway from Kansas City to Topeka was a mess, with cars every which way and people wandering around with knapsacks. Some even had the poor taste to bring their children with them. When she passed the children, Mrs. Parisi waved, but they never seemed to want to wave back.

She refused to let her optimism be hampered. "Ca-ca on you!" she shouted merrily as she passed. The windows on the van were rolled up, keeping in both the air-conditioning and her words. She waved. "Ca-ca, you little worthless runts."

On the highway out of Topeka a roadblock was set up. For some odd reason there were a great many people wanting to get in. She was one of only two cars wanting to leave.

"West?" the highway patrolman at the roadblock asked in surprise. To either side of the highway, Mrs. Parisi noticed, careless farmers had let their fields go untended.

"Yes, dear. West. Out to Colorado Springs."

"Ma'am? Are you absolutely sure you want to do that?"

The policeman was nice enough, but his solicitousness was beginning to wear. "Of course I am certain. I'm a writer, you know."

Mrs. Parisi used her credentials as a writer both often and well; but the trooper didn't seem impressed. He wandered to the back of the van and opened the rear door. Turning around in her seat to peer at him testily, she noticed that he was studying her supplies.

"Colorado Springs," he said, his voice echoing in the steel confines of the van.

"Yes. Would you care to arrest me for that?"

The trooper shot her a look. "Stupidity is no misdemeanor, ma'am," he replied, slamming the door so hard, she jumped.

She drove past the long line of filthy people waiting to get into Topeka. They stared at her with hollow eyes. And even though she waved at them, waved until her arm was sore, no one as much as lifted a hand to cheer her on her way.

NEAR LUBLIN, POLAND

Michów, Baranyk's new center of operations, consisted of a handful of houses lined up along an asphalt road. There were no chickens pecking in yards, no women walking their way to market. Although there were soldiers there, plenty of soldiers, Michów had a sad, abandoned look.

Baranyk, who lost his driver two weeks before and still hadn't the heart to replace him, drove the borrowed American Humvee to the end of the pockmarked road. At the church a group of Germans and four new tanks were waiting. He got out and returned the German captain's salute.

"It is, ah, pleasant to see you again, general," the German said in halting Polish.

Baranyk nodded vaguely in Reiter's direction, his eyes on the Mercedes tanks. They were short, he saw with surprise. Tough-looking. Fast-looking.

Captain Georg Reiter must have noticed the direction of Baranyk's gaze. When the general turned, he saw the German was gloating. "*Ausgezeichnet, ja?*"

"Pretty," Baranyk said indifferently and was pleased to see the German's smile fade. The captain seemed to be trying to decide whether the indifference was insulting or had merely sprung from Baranyk's own incomplete grasp of Polish.

Reiter's mouth moved indecisively before he spoke, as though he were searching for vocabulary, syntax. "It is good . . . a good weapon," he finally blurted. "It will serve you."

"The better to die for you and your soft-bellied country," Baranyk muttered in Ukrainian. His eyes lifted to the group of Germans, and he saw Zgursky standing among them. The young, peach-faced sergeant had slapped his hand over his mouth to suppress a laugh.

With a conspiratorial wink to Zgursky, Baranyk turned

back to the German captain. "So," he said. "We will try them out."

"Yes. *Gut*," Reiter agreed. "We have four Ukrainian teams. I will be, uh, glad for you to see how they—perform."

"No," Baranyk said. "You and two of your men. Myself and the sergeant there." With his head he indicated the startled Zgursky. "And one other Ukrainian. We will take two tanks out. You have promised me the tanks are easy to manage. If my men are to fight in them, I wish to know their simplicity firsthand."

Reiter seemed to be struggling for translation. Finally his face uncreased. "You are joking," he said with a smile.

"I am quite serious. Call your men."

Dispiritedly, Reiter turned and motioned two Germans out: a stocky, pink-faced lieutenant and a dark-headed noncom.

Baranyk laughed and called out to Zgursky. "Come, sergeant," he said in boisterous Ukrainian. "Come show me I was right to give you your stripes. I have always wanted to be chauffeured in a Mercedes."

Zgursky shuffled forward like a shy crab.

"Call the lieutenant with the German father," Baranyk said softly. "Maybe he can translate for us. What's his name? Goose?"

"Gutzman. Pavel Gutzman, sir," Zgursky said.

"Gutzman!" Baranyk called with a rumbling laugh. "Step forward and enter destiny!"

A tall, blond-haired man in Ukrainian uniform threaded his way through the knot of Germans.

"Yes, sir?" Gutzman asked, drawing himself up into a snappy salute.

"At ease," Baranyk told him with a jovial smile. "And come tell me all about this miracle of a tank."

The two told him. They told him at length. As they got into their lecture, they seemed to forget the differences of rank. Their voices grew more assured. Their eyes were bright with pleasure, the eyes of children with new toys.

"It goes fast. Very fast, sir," Zgursky was saying.

Gutzman blurted, "And the nuclear motor is very quiet. There is some material they use which mutes the sprockets."

The two were grinning at Baranyk, eager, effervescent grins.

"A miracle," Baranyk said, smiling back.

"Yes, sir. A miracle," Gutzman laughed.

Baranyk climbed onto the deck of the German miracle and stepped through the hatch—not onto the utilitarian seat he had been expecting but a padded captain's chair. The inside of the tank was spacious. No colliding noses and butts, as sometimes happened in the T-80s. The driver's cubbyhole was fully open to the gunnery compartment.

There were buttons and dials and gauges everywhere. Digital read-outs, computer screens.

Zgursky pointed to one of the computers. "A small on-board radar."

Gutzman explained brightly, "So the tanks will not run into each other."

"As the 1st Armored did at Kiev," Baranyk said.

The comment threw a pall over the pair's enthusiasm. Zgursky met Gutzman's eye, then looked quickly away.

"Yes, sir," Gutzman whispered. "The radar will prevent some of what happened at Kiev."

Zgursky bent over the computer and brought up two helmets. He handed one to Baranyk. The sergeant was grinning again. "Put it on, sir. You will be our weapons officer for the run."

Goggles were built into the helmet, Baranyk noticed, and a thick cable ran from it into the wall of the tank. He slipped the helmet on and opened his eyes to blackness. Zgursky fiddled with something, and suddenly the world came to life.

It was as though he were sticking his head out the turret. There was Michów: the short stretch of paved road and the church. Disoriented, he flung out his arm and bumped into a chair.

A hand grabbed him. "Sit down, sir," Zgursky said. "The

first view through the goggles is unsettling."

Baranyk knew where he was: he was in the tank. Yet he was out in the open, too. His mind told him he should be feeling the breeze on his face, should be smelling the heady scent of spring grass. Yet his nostrils brought in only the smell of rubber and new plastics.

Someone gently guided him to his seat. He groped for the armrest.

"A network of fiber optics, sir," Gutzman was explaining. "It produces a sort of holographic image in the brain, much like the eyes themselves."

Across the way Baranyk could see the Germans crawling into their own tank, Reiter looking disgruntled. He watched a sparrow flutter across the sky and land on the church roof.

"Ready?" Reiter said quietly into the left ear of Baranyk's receiver.

"Ready," Zgursky countered in Baranyk's right. "We will take lead position."

Gutzman told him, "We will be moving now, General Baranyk. The sensation will be strange. If it bothers you too much, take off the helmet."

Zgursky forgot enough about rank to add a small anecdote: "The lieutenant threw up the first time the tank moved, and the Germans got very angry."

The sergeant laughed; Gutzman didn't. "Eight degrees at ten kilometers per hour," he said.

In Baranyk's left ear, Reiter repeated in his crude Polish, "Eight degrees at ten."

There was no rumble of diesels, no whine of turbines. The tank simply moved. Baranyk could feel the tickle in the soles of his feet as it crept from the side of the road into a meadow. At the edge of his peripheral vision a flock of birds leaped skyward. He turned to watch their flight, heard the slight rumble as the turret turned with him.

A miracle. The tank was a miracle.

"Increase speed to twenty," Zgursky said.

The tinny voice of Reiter replied, "Twenty, *ja*."

They passed through an open gate, and Baranyk swiveled

his head to see that the second tank was following.

"Will you fire on us, Hammer One?" Reiter laughed. "Or do you sightsee?"

Quickly Baranyk moved his head back, the turret turning with him.

"Hammer One?" the German called. "We will be—" Reiter let off a string of German, apparently searching for vocabulary from someone else in the tank. "*Ja, ja*. We will be entering a plain ahead. Would it be good to show the general our speed?"

After a pause Zgursky replied, "Increase to fifty."

"You are not courageous, sergeant?" Reiter challenged.

"Seventy-five," Zgursky muttered.

Baranyk gasped as the tank shot forward. He put his hands out, hit something. Red lines sprang up in his vision.

"*Achtung, achtung*," a woman's calm recorded voice was saying into his left ear.

"General!" Gutzman's tone was tense.

The woman was saying something else, but it was in German and Baranyk couldn't understand. He felt the lieutenant fumbling at him. A hand clutched his.

"Here," Gutzman said. "Here is the stick. No, no, sir. Not that thin one. That is the remote-control machine gun. This thick one here to your right."

Baranyk gripped it. Short. A knob on top and a rounded stud.

The rocking of the tank sent Gutzman's shoulder into his. "You have activated the fire controls. Here. Here is the lever to shut them off."

The lever was a ribbed thing on the side of the stick. Baranyk depressed it, and the red lights went away. The jostling at Baranyk's shoulder ceased: Gutzman had evidently decided that the general was not about to destroy the tank and felt safe enough to return to his own post.

The Hammer zipped over a tree-shaded bridge at a speed that took Baranyk's breath away. He should be feeling the wind in his hair; but there was nothing but dizzying exhilaration.

Out of the corner of his eye he saw the other tank draw

abreast. They were running over the soft loam of a field now, and he could see the treads of the second Hammer kicking up mud.

"A race, Sergeant Zgursky?" Reiter asked, his voice clear and diamond-sharp in Baranyk's ear.

"A race, then," Zgursky agreed.

Baranyk would have thought the tanks could not go any faster. He was wrong. The force of the acceleration pushed him back into soft upholstery. They lunged across the field, clattered over an asphalt road, and into the flower-dotted meadow beyond.

Ahead of them birds burst from a tree and flew, a shower of black sparks. "Beautiful," he said in awe.

"What, sir?" Gutzman asked.

"It is so beautiful."

Turret-to-turret they flashed past a burned-out farmhouse, past an intact but crumbling barn. Then a small town, the houses beaded up along the dirt road as if they had condensed there. Lubertnów. How had they got there so quickly? Baranyk wondered if Reiter realized how far they had come or if he was simply caught up in the excitement of the demonstration.

"Angle left," Zgursky said, obeying his own command and skirting the southernmost building.

Baranyk glanced around. Reiter had turned right.

"Left! Left!" Zgursky snapped.

"*Ja*," came the abashed voice in Baranyk's ear. Reiter had obviously mistranslated. By the time they passed the last house, the Ukrainian tank was well in the lead.

"Shit!" he heard Zgursky shout.

In the field beyond Lubertnów squatted a hornet-shaped Hind, its rotors motionless and sagging. The helicopter crew nearby leaped up from their lunch, panic in their eyes.

Baranyk's own eyes widened. The approach of the tanks must have been so quiet that the Arabs had failed to hear. He watched as the men sprinted for their chopper.

God. Where were the controls again? He thrust his hand forward and found the stick.

"Fire!" Zgursky was screaming. "Fire, sir! Sight in the

kill box and depress the stud!"

Now was no time for instructions, Baranyk thought. The pilot was wrenching open the chopper door. The general fumbled at the lever. Red lines sprang up before his eyes.

"*Achtung*," the woman's pleasant voice warned him. "*Achtung*."

At the corner of his vision he saw the German's tank move forward, the cannon coming to bear. An instant later, before Baranyk could find his own firing stud, the second tank's muzzle belched flame. The shell whizzed past him and hit the helicopter broadside.

There were two quick explosions, one after the other. Pieces of the Hind spouted upward to rain down like black hail.

"*Achtung*," the woman said.

What did she want this time?

Der something *ist ge-*something. From Baranyk's one year of German language in school, a class he had failed, it sounded as if she was telling him that the hat was on the roof.

"Vehicles ten degrees," Gutzman said, his voice tight with fear.

Baranyk turned his head. Holy Father. There were four Arab AFVs rolling out of the cover of some birches. The first let loose a round from its 73mm gun. The shell hit a few meters away, kicking up clods of thick dirt.

"*Achtung*," the woman was calmly saying.

Baranyk wished she would shut up. His hand was sweating, his fingers sliding nervously around the stick. The display was confusing. Did he have the AFV centered or not?

Still unsure, he pressed the firing stud. The Hammer's engines might have been quiet, but its self-loading cannon was not. The boom of the 120mm gun made Baranyk's ears ring. A quick jolt passed through the tank. Reflexively he closed his eyes. When he opened them again, he saw he had annihilated an outhouse.

The German tank advanced and fired. An AFV received

a round that went straight through it, right side to left. The vehicle shuddered and burst into flame.

To his right, Baranyk saw a white plume from one of the AFVs and knew what it meant. A Sagger missile was headed straight at them. With the unrestricted view, he felt that he was standing alone and helpless in the field, his pants around his ankles, watching Death ride up.

"Brace for impact!" he screamed.

The explosion rang the tank like a gong. The Hammer rocked back on its treads and then steadied.

"Radar out!" Gutzman was shouting. "Hydraulic controls normal! Reactor normal!"

Baranyk opened his eyes in astonishment. He hadn't realized he'd shut them. What he saw nearly made him close his eyes again. An AFV was a mere twenty meters away. He aimed his head at it, put the dot of the kill box right on the cupola, and depressed the stud. The Hammer recoiled as the shell left the muzzle. The AFV was suddenly wrapped in orange flame.

"Hit the smoke! Hit the fucking smoke!" Zgursky wailed.

Baranyk wondered frantically if he had the smoke controls and, if he did, where the hell they were.

"*Vorsicht pass auf*, Hammer One!" Reiter barked.

"*Ja, ja, gewiss*, Hammer Two," Gutzman replied, then added dryly in Ukrainian, "Christ, what a time to tell us to be careful."

Careful? But we're on fire! Baranyk thought in alarm, then realized that the white smoke had come from the Hammer's own grenades.

The Mercedes tanks drove faster, saw better, and produced more smoke than any tank he'd ever seen. They were in a fog now, Zgursky rumbling through the grass slowly, as though feeling his way.

To Baranyk's right the mist flashed red. The ground shuddered as a shell hit home.

Reiter or the AFV? Baranyk wondered. Then Reiter's voice in his ear solved the mystery. "*Du musst heraus*, Hammer One! *Raus!*"

There was a heavy metal clunk. The tank quivered.

"Did we hit something?" Baranyk cried. "I can't see a thing!"

"Just me," Gutzman said, embarrassed. "I was trying to fix the radar, and I deployed the mine sweep."

"*Raus* where?" Zgursky wanted to know. "Where is the AFV and where is Hammer Two?"

Gutzman's reply was testy. "How should I know? The radar is out."

The radar was out, and they were inching through the mist like a ship lost in a fog with icebergs.

"Advise, please, Hammer Two," Gutzman said quietly. "Which way do we turn?"

"LEFT!" Reiter screamed, his voice losing the last shreds of its composure. "Turn left immediately!"

The tank slewed left. Zgursky punched up the power.

"*NEIN!*" Reiter let loose a flood of German that ended with, "*RIGHT! I MEAN RIGHT!*"

Something loomed in the fog. Big and green and metallic. The Hammer slammed into the armored backside of the last AFV. The collision threw Baranyk out of his seat.

Zgursky backed away, and Baranyk could see the damage they had done to the AFV. The mine sweep had gutted its engine. A small electrical fire had started. The Arab soldiers were hurriedly dismounting from the vehicle and running across the field to the birches.

"Now we leave," Reiter said wearily, finding his misplaced Polish.

"Understood," Gutzman said. "Leaving the field."

They returned to Michów. Gutzman was fretting about the damage sustained by the Sagger hit, although Reiter's tank drew alongside and said the damage was minimal.

The tank didn't seem to mind. It rolled happily across the moist meadow as if no battle, no Sagger strike, had ever occurred.

Watching the fields whisk by, Baranyk found himself smiling.

"What is it, sir?" Gutzman asked, seeing the general's expression.

With two tanks there had been four AFV kills. *And* a helicopter. He mustn't forget the helicopter. "I am thinking how nice it is," Baranyk said wistfully, "to be on the winning side for a change."

CHAPTER 7

IN THE LIGHT

Helping his mother take the clothes from the line, Justin buried his face in a towel and breathed the flowery smell of fabric softener.

What was it he was supposed to tell her? he wondered.

Oh, yes. He remembered now.

His mother was opposite him, her right hand on the corner of a sheet, her left plucking at a wooden clothespin.

"I fly an old plane," he said.

"And where do you fly?" she asked, her voice sliding the scale from soprano to pulsating alto.

"From the carrier in the Gulf to the oil fields." He gazed up at the heavens to see an eagle skimming the clouds. "What used to be Saudi Arabia, Iran, and Kuwait. I fly reconnaissance, mostly. Sometimes I fly CAP for the bombers. The bombs go off like fireworks. The wells burn like orange stars. In a lot of ways it's pretty."

"Is it?" she asked, her voice sinking to a man's bass. He was afraid to look at her, afraid to see what might be happening to his mother.

Keeping his eyes on the circling eagle, he said, "This scares me."

"War?" she asked in a voice like an oboe.

"Yes. No. This. This scares me, too." He reached out

and grabbed the towel, pressed it tightly to his cheek.

And now he was seated across from his mother at the kitchen table, Harding and the bus driver bracketing him. The towel was gone.

"I'm scared every time I go up," Justin admitted, with a sidelong glance at the Lt. Commander.

Harding was smiling. But his lips, like worn rubber bands, had trouble holding their shape.

"I'm scared over the target when the bomber goes in for its run. I'm scared of the AAA, and I'm scared of landing. God. Landing on that carrier in the dark."

"Tell me," his mother said.

"I didn't use to be scared," Justin whispered.

The three were sitting as still as rag dolls. "I don't know what happened to me. Sometimes I think—I think—I'm expendable, just a lieutenant j.g. They give me shit with wings to fly. I'll never come back. That's what'll happen. I'll go down like Peterson and Cucullo and the others. And then it's over, and landing, somehow, is worse. Landing is the worst thing of all."

He looked at his folded hands and wondered if the eagle was in the sky outside, and, if it was, what it was hunting.

"If you're afraid, why do you do it?" his mother asked, taking a bite of cake. The hand clutching the fork was wrong, as if it contained one too many fingers.

The palms were tapping at the window. Justin turned and saw that the trees had moved closer. They were crowding the hibiscus outside.

"If you're afraid, why do you do it?" his mother asked again, her voice now a foghorn moan.

His own voice rose giddily high. "I don't want to. I *have* to."

"Why do you have to?"

His mother's interrogation reminded him of Pastor Gilbreath's questions when Justin had thought to join the ministry. Back then, the pastor's inquiries were as sharp as the arrows that pierced St. Sebastian. His mother's questions clattered against his bones.

"The Arabs attacked us, didn't they? They attacked us."

"Why did they attack you?"

He threw his head back. The ceiling rose to blue, cloudless infinity. "Damn it! Because they were hungry!"

His mother and the bus driver and Harding were staring at him, their loose faces puddled in confusion.

"If they were hungry," his mother said, taking a sip from her glass of milk, "why didn't you feed them?"

Justin pushed himself away from the table and stood, his chair toppling. He fled to the living room and halted, breathing hard. There was the floral sofa he remembered. There was the table made from a cross section of oak. Atop the TV sat the model he'd made in middle school: the gray plastic model of the Nimitz.

He walked over and picked it up. The hull was slick and smooth; the square elevators delineated. The deck was no larger than his two hands. The planes were tiny as midges.

Putting the model down, he walked outside. In the front yard the mango tree was heavy with orange fruit, and the postman was making his way up the walk.

"If they were hungry," the postman asked, "why didn't you feed them?"

Lightheaded, Justin swayed on his feet. The front yard was filled with a pattering-rain sound. The air was cool and dry.

"Here," the postman said, handing him a letter.

When the postman walked away, Justin tore the blank envelope open.

>FROM: Pastor Gilbreath
>TO: Justin Searles
>MEMO: Why didn't you feed my sheep?

Justin balled the letter furiously in his hands.

It *was* raining. Warm drops slid down his cheeks. His legs gave way, and he sat hard on the grass. A few minutes later, Harding came out and sat beside him.

"There isn't any God," Justin told him. Then he whispered, "There wasn't any food."

He looked into Harding's eyes. They were dark bubbles

now, swelling from forehead to chin.

Justin swiped angrily at his cheeks. He wouldn't cry. The grief was over, years ago buried, and he'd cried enough then. It was raining, that was all. He could hear the tap-tap-tap on the pavement, the clink of the drops on the palms.

"My own mother died of hunger," Justin told him, but when he looked up, Harding was gone.

NEAR LÉRIDA

Rita opened her eyes to find she was squeezed into a dark, grave-shaped place that smelled of earth. She sat up. In the rectangular slit above her head an eerie dawn was breaking.

The side of the pit was an acidic, artificial pink. Close by, someone was whispering, the voice airy.

I'm in a foxhole, she thought. *That's right. I'm sleeping in a foxhole.*

She got to her feet and peered over the lip of the trench. Pink stars were drifting, ghostly and serene, across the night sky.

"Get down, captain!" a man's voice hissed.

The stars painted the valley Day-Glo bright. Through the orderly rows of trees to Rita's left something huge stalked the inky shadows.

A tug at the back of her pants. "Get your head down, sugar," Dix whispered.

Rita looked into the pit and saw the bulge of Dix's helmet, a quarter-moon in the slanted light.

Like an itchy, vague prescience of danger, the bomber came. It tickled the pit of Rita's stomach; it tingled down the back of her neck. With a turbined howl, the plane burst into being. The orchard bloomed yellow, and kept blooming, a showy, apocalyptic spring.

Dix grabbed her waist and pulled her down.

"Sssh," she whispered.

The light at the mouth of the trench turned throbbing orange. The hurricane roar of burning trees made a tempest of the night. Something massive barked. The earth quailed, shaking dust into Rita's face.

Gasping, she clawed her way out of Dix's arms and lurched to her feet. Scrambling up the lip of the trench, she tore her fingernails to the bloody, stinging quick. Someone grabbed her belt.

Caught in a battle of dragons, the ground quaked. A monster peered over the rim of the western knoll and belched blue-and-yellow flame.

The flares drifted off, dying pink suns on the wind. All except for one, the monsters retreated. The last turned and came through the burning trees toward them.

"Down!" Dix hissed.

Rita couldn't tear her eyes away. It was closer, moving fast. Coming straight for them, a huge creature of basso profundo rumbles and absurd tenor squeaks.

Dix tackled her. They toppled onto someone else.

The noise was deafening. Rita wondered what would happen when the tank fell into the hole. She imagined her skin giving way like the tender flesh of a strawberry; imagined the crack her bones would make as they splintered. She reached out and clutched Dix, burrowing her helmeted head into the lieutenant's chest. On her back she could feel the dull knife-points of blunt fingernails.

Rita smelled sweat, tasted the salt bite of her own tears. Who was shaking so hard? Oh, Christ. Which one of them was sobbing?

Grinding, pounding clamor. Rita raised her head and saw something immense blot out the sky. Suddenly Dix squirmed on top of her, between her and the oncoming treads.

Whump. The soil above compacted under terrible weight. Rocks clattered down the sides of the trench, pinged against helmets and clutched weapons.

Deep in Dix's tiny body Rita could feel the tick-tick-tick of a frightened heart, swift as the pulse of a bird.

The tank's engines screamed, the treads clawed dirt. Suddenly the air in the trench was filled with dust and diesel exhaust. In the slit above shone quiet stars, a waning orange light. The rumble moved away, was smothered by distance.

A man laughed. "You all right, lieutenant? Captain?"

Dix climbed off Rita. "Go on back, Garza," she said, her voice calm. "Go on back and get some sleep."

"You see what that tank did, ma'am? Goddamn. It rolled right over our foxhole."

"Go on back to your sleeping bag," she told him. "Go on, now. You hear what I said?"

"Yes, ma'am," he whispered, and crawled away.

Down the hill the burning trees crackled soft and low. Rita's teeth were chattering. Shivers worked their way from her chest down into her stomach, her legs.

"First time's the worst," Dix told Rita. "First time's the hard one. But you got to suck it up, girl, all right? You're a captain, all right? You may be National Guard, and you may be just a doctor and all, but you can't fall apart on me, okay?"

After a hesitation Dix picked up her handset. "Forward OPs? You okay?" Dix whispered. "Hoover?" she prompted.

A voice from the speaker replied, "All here, lieutenant."

"Sergeant Dunbarton? You still with us?"

The handset spat static. "Yeah, lieutenant. Ruined my sleep. How about yours?"

"Keep down and keep quiet," she replied. Putting away the handset, she turned back to Rita. "It'll be all right, sugar. It'll be all right now."

Rita didn't reply. She was too exhausted, and there was nothing really to say. Somewhere in the distance the battle continued. Artillery rumbled like remote thunder. The earth twitched in its bed.

THE PYRENEES, NEAR THE SPANISH-FRENCH BORDER

The laser tractor was tucked safely in the mountain tunnel like a spider in its hole. Wasef stared at it in amazement, his mind fuzzy from lack of sleep.

They'd actually made it. For a while, the night before, he didn't think they would.

His soldiers had slept and eaten, grumbling because Wasef had refused them cookfires. The colonel himself hadn't napped, and now he was paying the price of that poor decision. His arm muscles were jumpy, and there was an annoying tic under one eye.

Sunrise had turned the lichened rocks around him to peach. Blue shadows pooled in the crevasses. He shivered in the brittle air and walked farther out into the sunlight, hoping to find warmth. Around him peaks rose like mosques into the lavender sky.

A sound drew his attention. He looked down to see a jeep making its way up the Spanish slope.

"Captain Mustafa?" he called.

Instantly, as though the captain had congealed from the shadows, he was at the colonel's side.

"Get five men with rifles and hide them in those rocks."

Yussif glanced at the approaching jeep and nodded. Wasef drew back against the tunnel wall and watched the men scatter into position.

As the jeep neared, the colonel saw the insignia on the side and motioned for the squad to lower their weapons.

One man. A captain without a driver. The jeep rolled into the tunnel and stopped, engine idling loudly in the confines of the granite.

As Wasef made his way over, the captain killed the motor and got out. "Colonel?" he asked with a smart salute.

Wasef returned the salute and noticed that his hands were trembling, perhaps from cold, perhaps from exhaustion. Quickly he put his arm to his side.

"I hope this is no imposition," the man said. "But I have asked to be assigned to you." The captain was curly-headed and swarthy, thin as a sapling and eager-eyed. Wasef's gaze dropped to the stenciled nametag.

RASHID, it said.

He looked up and in the man's face saw a suggestion of a familiar, indolent smile. "You're General Rashid Sabry's son, Gamal," Wasef said in surprise. "You look just like him."

The young man's grin widened. "Thinner."

"Yes," Wasef laughed. "Thinner." He held out his hand in welcome.

Gamal clasped it.

"I understand you studied astrophysics at Cal Tech," Wasef said.

A flicker of emotion in Gamal's face. Wasef could feel the hand stiffen in his own. *Guilt?* he wondered. *And does he feel guilty because he lived with the enemy, or because he is now murdering friends?*

"I myself studied in the U.S. for a while," Wasef told him and instantly felt Gamal's grip relax. "It was a pleasant country once," he added softly.

Gamal's own voice was cautiously formal. "Yes, it was, colonel. A pleasant country."

Yussif wandered up, curiosity no doubt spurring him. Wasef made short shrift of the introduction and leveled a curious glance at Gamal.

"You asked to be assigned?"

"Yes," he said, remembering his mission. "You have been having a problem pinpointing the satellite. I thought I might be of help."

Wasef saw Yussif's lips tighten. The colonel knew the man was jealous of his duties. He hugged them to himself and refused to share, like a young boy with a handful of candy. Of late the captain's jealousy had gained a mean streak. Yussif was indeed failing to hit the satellite, and even Wasef's patience had become strained.

"There is no real problem," Yussif said.

"Well, of course there is," Gamal replied, either not reading or ignoring the warning in Yussif's expression. "But it's nothing to be ashamed of. It's hard to distinguish between microwave sources unless you know what you're looking for. And it's doubly hard to shoot one down."

"Would you care for some breakfast?" Wasef asked before Yussif could rebut.

"Please," Gamal said, a childish delight in his eyes. "I skipped dinner last night."

"Captain Mustafa? Will you get something for our new laser fire officer?" Wasef ignored the effect of this rebuff and blandly turned to Gamal. "Your father agreed to this?"

"Yes," Gamal said. "And he thought I might get a closeup

look at the blue lights. He said you were having some activity."

The chill on Wasef's wind-whipped cheeks moved to his chest. "Sit down," he murmured.

The boy took a seat against the granite wall of the tunnel. Wasef hunkered next to him, wishing that the boy would change the subject, wishing he had never come. Since the deaths of the tank crew, the men had begun looking over their shoulders. They'd painted warding signs on their rifles, their trucks. Even Yussif had come to believe the lights were supernatural, and Wasef himself . . .

"They are a heat sink, you see," Gamal was saying. "I have instruments in my jeep. Infrared, a gravimeter . . ."

Yussif walked up and shoved a can of sardines at Gamal.

The young man stared in surprise at the sardines before muttering a dubious "Thank you. So anyway," he said, "I was hoping to get a closer look, to determine what the blue lights are. I have some theories of my own—"

"They are the devil," Yussif snapped.

A small smile tugged at Gamal's lips, a smile not of mockery but simple disbelief. "Surely you don't—"

"They are the devil! If you had seen men killed as we have. If you had seen the blood sucked from their bodies—"

Gamal was shaking his head. "Superstition . . ."

"Islam is not superstition," Yussif said.

Gamal stopped. His face was bewildered, unsure. "I never said that."

Wasef caught Gamal's questioning glance. "Here. Let me open the can for you," the colonel said, gently taking the sardines from his hand.

"Allah has nothing to do with the blue lights, Captain Mustafa," Gamal told him, "if they are alien."

In a voice that was too loud, a voice that drew the attention of the men, Yussif exclaimed, "Allah has everything to do with everything!"

Lips pursed, Gamal sat for a moment, watching Wasef open the can. The smell of fish rose like an oily cloud in the thin air.

"What I meant was," Gamal went on quietly, "these lights

put out a radar signal and microwave noise. They are a physical presence, captain. Not ghosts."

"It is not up to us to question the nature of demons."

Wasef handed Gamal the open can. The boy looked around, as though in search of a fork. Finally he gave up, pinched a sardine out with his fingers and stuffed it into his mouth.

"You know?" he asked as he chewed. "Humans must question the nature of the universe. It was not my choice, Captain Mustafa, to think of aliens. I am a scientist above all. However, given Occam's razor—"

"You are *stupid!*" Yussif spat.

"Stop it," Wasef said, looking from one to the other. "Stop arguing like this. If you wish to debate this point, I'd suggest you not use words but tanks."

The pair were staring at him now in surprise. He got to his feet. "Famine aside, isn't Western objectivity and Eastern passion what this war is all about? Gentlemen, I will get some sleep now. Wake me at dusk. And in the meantime confine your discussions to less inflammatory topics."

Shaking his head, he walked off to his sleeping bag. Seated around the laser, his soldiers watched him. They also snuck sidelong glances at Gamal Sabry. Glances full of righteous indignation, ignorance, and fury.

NEAR LÉRIDA

"Wake up, capt'n," Dix said.

Rita opened her eyes. She was lying alone at the bottom of the foxhole. Someone had thrown a coat over her. The air was cold. The bluish light of dawn trickled into the trench.

"Get up, capt'n," Dix said, looking down. "We're moving out."

Rita sat up, her sweaty uniform sticking to her skin. She yearned for a toothbrush, Colgate, and a hot shower with lilac-scented soap. Then she caught sight of the trench. It startled her. The tank had plowed into the left side of the hole, its treads scouring a track some three feet wide and two feet deep.

"You want some breakfast?" the lieutenant asked. Below her helmet, Dix's blue eyes were as cold and tranquil as the dawn.

Rita shook her head, looked around for her own helmet.

I could just hide here till the end of the war, she thought. *That would be good.*

"You coming, ma'am?"

"Yeah," Rita sighed. "I'm coming."

Tossing her gear over the edge of the trench, Rita clambered up after it. In the orange grove, the fire had not gone out. Gray smoke drifted into the violet sky. The abandoned hut where Dix had parked the Humvees was flattened.

The patrol lounged around in the grass and rocks, just finishing a cold breakfast. Rita slipped her coat on and noticed them watching her. Their gazes were level and, in their dispassion, frightening.

"Forward OPs tell me there was a doo-wompus of a battle due south," Dix said as she ambled up, her own breakfast in hand. "ANA and the Allies done caught each other with their pants down. Left their dead on the field. We all heading up there. Might be bad," she added, her cornflower eyes settling on Rita's face.

"I'm a pathologist, Dix," Rita said. "I've seen bodies up closer and nastier than most."

Dix nodded. "Listen here, capt'n," she said quietly. "I sure do hate to say it this way, but—"

"Just say it."

Dix took a deep breath. "You all a senior officer and everything. And you been put in my care. But don't you go endangering my troops. I give everybody one free freak-out, okay? Last night was yours. With all due respect, you done shot your wad."

"I'll hold it together," Rita assured her, wondering if somewhere in those Spanish hills she'd find her missing courage.

THE PYRENEES, NEAR BAGNÈRES-DE-LUCHON

Gordon had overslept, and by the time he got the CRAV out of its hiding place, the sun was up and the birds were singing. Now it was past noon, and he still had no idea where the laser was.

The first thing he'd done that morning was find the cow pasture. He saw the marks of tank treads in the grass, and the knobbed mark of tractor tires. The Arabs had used a tank to tow the vehicle out of the mud.

Then, somewhere on the road, he lost the trail. The tank had gone back to its base, but he wasn't sure the LDV had gone with it.

Center yourself, Toshio had told him the evening before, over supper. *Center yourself, find the quiet, and knowledge will come.*

Yeah. Okay. Only nothing was springing to mind.

He turned his head and looked up the road. Where the timberline ended, rocky peaks rose, snow snuggled around their shoulders like a soft, tasseled shawl.

Suddenly he knew. The tank had gone down the mountain and the LDV had gone up. Up to try another potshot at the satellite.

The Arabs were pushing their luck, two firings in three days. The laser probably needed all sorts of maintenance. But Gordon also knew they wanted that last satellite bad.

He glanced behind him. Rover was playing over the rocks, Gordon's blue, happy albatross. As soon as he looked Rover's way, he could hear the clatter start up in his mind.

"Noisy son of a bitch," he muttered, and was jolted to feel the light touch of Toshio's hand on his arm.

Normally Gordon hated that. He hated when someone touched him while he was on-line. The sensation was eerie, disorienting, like bilocation.

But Toshio's touch seemed soothing, as if reminding him that he wasn't really in the mountains and about to get his ass kicked.

"No problem," he told Toshio, breaking another cardinal CRAV rule of solitude.

Gordon headed into the naked rocks, keeping to the side of the road. Behind him Rover appeared to be trying to stay out of sight.

A jet passed over, and Gordon dived for whatever cover he could find. It was a Mirage, either a French sortie looking for the LDV or an Arab sortie protecting their own. Hoping he hadn't been seen, he trundled out from behind a boulder and continued his trek.

The incline steepened. Hollows in the granite cupped creamy mounds of snow. The trees had given way to a few patches of juniper and alpen roses.

Gordon looked across a gorge at a gossamer waterfall. Close by, a falcon called out with its raucous, tuneless voice. He raised his head and saw it turning lazy circles in the sun.

Something in the sky glinted. An instant later he heard the air-ripping scream of an approaching plane. The Mirage dropped from the glare of the sun and headed straight toward him.

"Oh, my God!" Gordon shouted. There was no place to hide, nothing but sheer wall on one side and precipitous drop on the other. He gunned the accelerator. The CRAV shot forward.

The Mirage was so close, he could see the clear bubble of the canopy, could count the missiles on each wing. Suddenly one fell free of its mount, spraying a mist of propellant.

He ducked, a completely futile gesture. The CRAV didn't understand *duck*. It only knew *run*. It knew *hide*.

The missile hit wild, blasting a hole in the stone above Gordon's head. Debris flew. The CRAV shivered on its springs. Then the Mirage was rocketing past, up and over the mountain.

"Ha, ha, asshole! You missed me!" Gordon laughed.

Hearing a curious rumble, he looked up in time to see the granite wall above his head slough off. A heartbeat later, part of the mountain thundered down on him.

MICHÓW, POLAND

Baranyk stabbed his pointer at the map. "Here, Major Shcheribitsky. The Arabs have been here at Lubertnów, and there are reports of skirmishes at Parczew. Gaze into your crystal ball and tell me what you think they are doing."

The small major, his wedge-shaped badger's face grim, eyed the map reluctantly, as though it might bite. "They are sending scouts to our flank, general." He drew a line with his finger, arcing up over Lubertnów, Parczew, and straight to Warsaw. "When they move . . . if they move, they will go north."

The general grunted. "I want a reconnaissance flight south." He stabbed the pointer into Lipsko, leaving a dent in the paper.

"Yes, sir," Shcheribitsky said calmly, as if he planned to get to the order sometime that afternoon. "But then Landsat shows no major incursion."

"Landsat is a blind bitch. She sees only during the day, and then with not enough resolution. They could be hiding in the villages and moving only at night. Perhaps our scouts are lazy, and keep to the main roads."

Baranyk stared at the map, and suddenly the Arab plan coalesced. He saw it clearly, as though the red arrows had already been drawn and the battle commenced.

"Now, major," he snapped. "Fly the recon now!"

The major motioned an officer to his side and whispered into his ear. The man nodded and hurried out of the room.

Baranyk went on. "And let us send a tank battalion out to meet them at Parczew where you think there is a company and I think there may be much more. Include those German miracles, those new Mercedes tanks. And give me air cover. Helicopters. Those BO-105s with HOT missiles Reiter has given us."

Baranyk saw Shcheribitsky's pockmarked cheeks pale.

"What?" Baranyk asked, impatient.

"Fuel, sir," Shcheribitsky said. "The diesel has arrived for our tanks, but the jet fuel—"

"Call the Poles," the general growled.

Shcheribitsky was apologetic. "They say they have their hands full themselves, sir, with the battle at Kraków. And they have no fuel, either."

Baranyk brought his pointer down on the table so hard that it broke, a piece flying off and narrowly missing a lieutenant. "May the fuel be fucked!" The gathered officers flinched. Baranyk scarcely noticed. He was looking into the mind of the Arab commander as though the man's skull were made of glass.

"We are using alcohol for some of the flights, general," Shcheribitsky said quickly, "but the Polish alcohol is unreliable. Sometimes we find it mixed with water. We have enough fuel, perhaps, for the reconnaissance flight and two helicopters, but—"

"Listen to me!" Baranyk said, thrusting his face so close to the major's that the man stumbled back, his russet eyes wide. "I smell it. Only one time has my intuition left me, and that was at Kiev."

In the sudden silence, he gazed again at the map. "No, gentlemen," he said to his officers. "I believe the Arabs mean to surround us, and, to save ourselves, we must attack before the net is closed."

CHAPTER 8

THE PYRENEES

When Gordon had stopped screaming, he felt Toshio's hand on his arm. The Japanese wanted him out of the chair and, judging by the grip, he wanted him out quickly.

Gordon ignored the order. He was still trembling. His unit's visuals were up and running even though there was nothing to see but gray-shot black.

When the panicked snag in his breathing unkinked and the ringing in his ears subsided, he tipped his head to bring up the diagnostics.

The avalanche had disabled his missiles. Everything else looked good, though. The small reactor was intact, not bleeding radiation into the valley. The turret was probably movable, even though he couldn't, with the rock slide's weight on it, coax it to turn.

As an experiment, he eased his foot down on the accelerator. The CRAV's engines whined, but the unit stayed put.

Toshio's hand was cutting off his circulation. With a furious jerk Gordon pulled his arm away. Servomotors screamed. Rocks shifted uneasily. Gravel rattled on the CRAV's turret.

Gordon pushed again at the rock. The stones on his left gave a quarter-inch. Outside his grave he could hear a grinding noise as part of the slide gave way.

No one touched him again. Face grim, Gordon settled in the chair, licked his lips, and set about, stone by stone, to dig himself out.

MICHÓW, POLAND

In the quiet of his field office, Baranyk lifted the phone and punched the eleven-digit number, listening to the noise of the circuits clacking through. A secretary answered, the protective and suspicious kind. She immediately tried to take a message.

"Get him," Baranyk said. "Trust me. He will know who I am. Tell him Lt. General Baranyk is calling from Poland."

Baranyk consulted his watch. It was a full three minutes before Fyodorov picked up the phone.

"Valentin Sergeyevich!" the senator cried in a voice so hearty that Baranyk knew it had been rehearsed.

"Vassily Petrovich!" Baranyk replied in a tone equally lighthearted. "Did you know you can gauge the importance of a man by timing how long it takes to get him on the phone? I clocked you at three minutes. To get me would take four."

Fyodorov laughed. It wasn't the deep-bellied laugh Baranyk knew. There was a distance to it. Fyodorov must be wondering why the general had called. "How are you, my friend?" he asked. "And how go things in Poland?"

Baranyk dropped all pretense of cheer. "I call my debts," he said.

In the silence on the line Baranyk imagined he could hear the slow, heavy tread of the years rolling back. Afghanistan. Fyodorov was remembering Afghanistan.

What was Fyodorov like now? It had been ten years since they had last met, and ten years could change a man. Was he fat, his Italian suit packed tight as a sausage? Was he bald? Ah, worse yet, was he complacent?

Fyodorov laughed again, this time more circumspectly and with a sort of sadness. "I am too old to put on battle dress and take up my gun again, but, if you need me, *tovarich*," he said, using a term Baranyk knew he had not used for years, "I will come."

"I wish you to make an appointment for me with Pankov."

Silence. Baranyk could hear his question rattle against the sides of Fyodorov's mind. Now Baranyk knew the answer as to how Vassily Petrovich had changed. The man would still die for him; but he hesitated to be embarrassed because of him. Fyodorov had become a politician.

"Well," Fyodorov replied, "as you must know, he is very busy. There is unrest. Siberia has its farmers' strike, and the coal miners are out again."

Baranyk fought a surge of temper. First Russia was elder brother to his Ukraine, pushing and pulling and insisting on its own way. Then, when the Greenhouse heat had made the tundra arable, Russia began to play solitary games.

"Surely, Vassily Petrovich, you are not out of favor so soon?"

"Out of favor?" Fyodorov replied with a defensive chuckle. "With democracy there are no ins or outs to favor."

"Please," Baranyk said, using the most deadly weapon in his arsenal, the poison arrow of guilt. "Please. I beg you on our friendship."

If Fyodorov wanted him to crawl, then Baranyk would crawl. If he wanted him to cry, then Baranyk would force tears to his eyes. He would not, could not, see his army destroyed again.

"God. Do not beg," Fyodorov whispered, sounding not at all like a politician. "I will ask him."

"Send a plane for me to Warsaw. We have very little fuel."

"*Da, da.* I have my own plane now, you know. A little Cessna. Very pretty. Yellow and white. You will like it."

Baranyk pushed the matter of the plane aside. "Will he meet with me, you think?"

The senator sighed heavily. "Pankov is a whore. He will meet with anyone." Swiftly he added, "I never said that."

"Shoot you, would he?" Baranyk chuckled.

"Ah, worse than that. Pankov has been known to be petty. He would have my office redecorated as he did with Shulubin." Fyodorov was laughing happily. "I would be stepping over painters for years."

Baranyk laughed along.

Fyodorov's laughter sputtered and died. In a quiet voice, a voice much like the young, frightened soldier he'd once been, he said, "He will meet with you, Valentin Sergeyevich, but I don't know if he will give you the answer you want."

NEAR CALHAN, COLORADO

When someone crawled under the blanket with him, Jerry Casey woke up. An arm slipped around his hip and skinny fingers tugged at the waistband of his underpants.

"I'll do you for something," a voice said in his ear. "Whatcha got?"

He pulled away and sat up. The girl he'd met the first night was lying next to him. Her hair was all stuck up on her head. A smudge of dirt ran down the side of her cheek, and just under it was a single bruise like the dot of an exclamation point.

"What happened to you?" she asked him. In the shadows of the lean-to, her eyes were dark and wide.

He put a hand to his throbbing face and felt around the torn skin, the congealed blood. "Troopers caught me sneaking out west."

"Lucky you wasn't killed."

A silence fell. Jerry didn't bother to break it.

"I like to sit out and watch the buzzards go wheeling," she said wistfully, staring out of the lean-to with a faint smile. "Pretty the way they do, all big and easy, like black airplanes, you know? Then sometimes I think about what they're circling around, and it makes me kind of sick. There's lots of people who think they can make it out of here. Not a one of 'em does."

The sky outside was blue and empty. The sight of the mountains to the west set his heart to racing again.

"I seen something last night," he said softly. "I seen something pretty."

"Yeah?" She scrabbled around on the blankets, then settled down like a dog trying to make itself comfortable. "What was it?"

"I dunno."

"What'd it look like?"

"Heaven," he told her.

Desert mirages were already shimmering across the flat burial ground, and the mountains were reflected over the graves. Suddenly he knew there was no point going to Colorado Springs. No point hiking to the cool; not when the best cool of all was coming to him.

"It talked to me," he told her.

She was right at his shoulder. He could feel the heat from her body; smell the sour odor of her sweat. "Yeah? What'd it say?"

"I don't know. I couldn't understand the words."

Tonight, he decided. Tonight he'd go back and see if he could understand those clattering voices.

NEAR LÉRIDA

They'd been moving out for hours. Rita's shoulder was sore from the weight of her gear bag's strap; her feet hurt all the way to her ankles.

Before Lérida, she had thought she was in good shape. But now Lauterbach had thrown her in with a bunch of twenty-year-olds, and she was beginning to understand that aging wasn't just something that had happened to a body on a steel table. Aging, down and dirty and intimate, was happening to her.

She'd taken her coat off once the sun began climbing the sky. Now she was dusty and sweating. Her stomach reminded her that she'd missed breakfast.

She watched Dix. The diminutive lieutenant had a stride like an energetic boy.

Trudging up a hill, Rita lowered her head and studied her feet. Marvelous, she thought, how feet could move while the brain kept begging them not to.

Mesmerized by boredom, by the sameness of the gray-green grass and the stones, she bumped into Dix before realizing that the lieutenant had halted.

"We all here," Dix said laconically.

Rita stared dully down the hill. In the center of a demolished town, an M1-A1 tank and an M-113 ambulance were still burning.

There were bodies everywhere. The ones in Arab uniform had been caught on the slope. Some still lay in orderly ranks, rows and rows of them, toppled like green dominoes.

"You can see what happened," Dix said, drawing a line of imaginary fire with her finger. "Some dimwit of an Arab colonel told them to take Balàguer, and those folks kept coming and coming, just like they had sense."

There were ANA tanks there, too, the camouflage paint charred to black. An AFV squatted like a burned alphabet block some child had failed to put away.

"We're gonna find most of the Allied boys down there in the streets," Dix told her.

Balàguer bore only a passing resemblance to a village. The houses that weren't gutted had become gray, formless rubble.

Staring numbly at the destruction, Rita caught a flash of blue. When she looked, the blue disappeared behind a wall.

"What?" Dix asked.

"I think I saw something."

Instantly Dix crouched and motioned the others down. Rita fell to her knees beside her.

"Probably just the wind," Dix whispered. "Or your eyes playing tricks. Still, no point taking chances. You keep up with me."

Suddenly Dix was sprinting, still crouched, to a boulder. Rita hurried after the lieutenant at a limping trot.

When she reached the pooled shadow at the base of the rock, she turned and saw the rest of the platoon spread out, moving down the slope stealthily.

Then someone shouted, "CBUs!" and the next instant she

heard a small pop. A soldier's leg disappeared in a mist of blood.

"Shit. Goddamn," Dix was muttering under her breath. She whirled on Rita. "Get the hell out of here up that hill. Just the way you come, understand me?"

But instead of backtracking, Rita started moving across the hill. A soldier was coming from the opposite direction, a medic with a field emergency kit over her shoulder. The medic was staring intently at her feet. Rita looked down and saw a small, olive-green metal ball to the right of her boot. She froze, her pulse beating a rapid tattoo in her neck.

"Capt'n! Capt'n Beaudreaux!" Dix was shouting.

Rita took a deep breath and moved forward, reaching the screaming man a few moments after the medic did.

"Start me an IV drip, stat. Quarter grain of morphine," Rita told the medic. She looked into the soldier's terrified eyes. He was a black kid, and something about him, maybe his vulnerability, maybe the shape of his face, reminded her of her nephew, Allen.

For the first time since her arrival at Lérida, Rita felt competent. She might be rusty at surgery, but at least the tools were familiar. No damned little bomblets. No baffling grenade launchers.

Rita examined the wound. The foot was gone. Inches above the ankle, the peroneal artery was pumping bright red. Both tibia and fibula had shattered to push shaved-ice splinters of bone into the surrounding fascia.

With quick, sure motions she snapped on her gloves and tore the suture pack open.

In his drugged confusion, the boy was trying to move his leg. Rita steadied him with one hand and caught the steel tip of the needle in the tough, rubbery shaft of the peroneal artery. In five quick stitches she had it closed. Tying off quickly, she moved to the saphenous vein.

"Look!" the medic shouted. "*Madre!* What's that?"

Heart faltering, Rita looked around.

A blue globe of light was drifting lazily from the village, moving against the gentle, dry breeze. As Rita stared, her hand still raised over the boy's leg, she thought she could hear a sound coming from the light, the tap-tap-tap of sleet.

The platoon was paralyzed with fear, spellbound by wonder. The blue light moved in silence, the macabre, inexorable silence of death.

"Don't fire!" Dix suddenly screamed. "Don't fire!"

But none of the platoon had brought their weapons to bear. The light seemed too ghostly for bullets to stop it.

It was so close now, Rita could feel the cold radiating from it, could feel a slight breeze pulling at her blouse.

The medic stiffened as if poised to flee. Too late. The light was close enough for Rita to touch. Her shoulder was freezing cold, her right hand, her suturing hand, shook from the chill.

Then a thought sprang to mind, a thought so clear, so foreign, that it might have been planted there. The light was curious, she realized. It was taking in the scene, it was asking clattering questions.

"Go away," she told it firmly.

Logic said run; but fascination held her. There was something at once ghastly and serene about the light. Something seductive. That corpse she had autopsied, had the boy's single eye been wide with fear or awe?

"Go away," she said.

After a hesitant, almost winsome moment, it began to float back down the hill, light as thistledown, blue as a gas flame. Suddenly it arced up into the sky, its speed astonishing. A heartbeat later, it was lost in the turquoise Mediterranean sky.

WITH THE CRAV IN THE PYRENEES

Light, damn it. Not a lot of light, but light all the same, seeping through a hole in the jagged rocks.

Inching his arm up, Gordon pushed his hand out the hole. Rocks shifted, clicked, rolled down the mountain to his left.

When his hand was free, he groped blindly in front of him. The engineers who built the CRAV would have thought Gordon crazy, but he knew he was feeling the chill stones.

He dislodged a few at a time at first. Then, in gathering excitement, he was knocking them away, causing his own mini-avalanche.

There were only two feet now between him and freedom.

He brushed at the rocks harder. They pattered down, raising dust. He put his foot to the accelerator. The motor strained. Stones pinged against the turret.

"Go, baby. Go, baby," he urged under his breath as though rooting for a befuddled pet or unsteady toddler.

Something big dislodged and rang against his crushed missile tubes.

"Go, baby," he pleaded.

The nuclear motor rose to a high whine. The treads lifted, grinding rock.

The world crumbled. There was an ear-splitting crunch. When the dust cleared, he was looking at the road.

For a while he just sat there, his arms cramping. The light outside his rocky grave was blue and shot here and there with brass. Sunset. It was sunset. And somewhere up ahead of him the laser was preparing to fire.

Frantically he pried his right arm from the rubble. When it was loose, he battered the wall again. This time it gave. At the rear of the vehicle he heard the slide shift like a beast from sleep. The treads found purchase, and suddenly he was lurching, bouncing, over the lip of the wall.

As soon as the treads hit the asphalt, he gunned the engine. Behind him was a Judgment Day roar as the rocks tumbled the rest of the way down the mountain.

WITH THE LDV IN THE PYRENEES

Standing atop the LDV tractor, Colonel Wasef gazed at the night sky, dimly aware of Gamal mumbling beside him. The air was thin and sharp, the gathered stars strewn ice chips.

"There," Gamal said at last.

Wasef looked down. Bathed in the glow of the screen, the fire control officer was smiling. Among the cross-hatched green of the VDT lay four red dots. A fifth dot, a stuttering red shadow, was moving slowly north-to-south across the screen.

"There are the three communications satellites," Gamal said, lightly touching a forefinger to each. "This moving signal is an old Keyhole in a low polar orbit. In the center is the newer, geosynchronous KH-176."

"He is wrong," Yussif grunted. The colonel turned to stare, but it was too dark to read Yussif's expression.

"It is all out of position," Yussif went on. "The one there in the middle. That is the target."

"I am not wrong," Gamal said.

"Tell me," Wasef urged quietly. "Tell me why you think you are right."

"The azimuths. The signals. They are as distinctive as fingerprints," the boy replied. "Look," he said, pointing over Wasef's head. "There is Jupiter. There Mars. There Betelgeuse, Rigel, and the Pleiades." Gamal's tone was hushed, as though he were reciting the names of angels.

"I know the stars, the planets, the satellites," Gamal said. "I have known their names since childhood. My family had a place in the desert, and we would go there, my father and I. He gave me books and a small telescope, and I would map the heavens for him. I know what is up there," Gamal said, "because when I close my eyes, I can see the stars."

Wasef stared up into the shimmering heavens. *So far away*, he thought. The satellites were so far away, one would think they were untouchable.

"The one in the middle is the target," Yussif said sternly. "It is in the correct position."

"The Allies have moved it. Placed it in with the others," Gamal said. "They think to hide it from us."

Yussif grabbed Wasef's arm. "Don't listen to him. He is a traitor."

Wasef caught his breath. Yussif was a man-shaped spot where the viscous night had clotted.

A traitor. It was possible. How many years had Gamal

been away from his people? What loyalties had the boy forgotten?

Yussif's grip tightened. "He will fire on the wrong satellite and it will be weeks before we know."

A cold wind whipped down the mountain, tugging at Wasef's coat.

"Traitor?" the boy said in a tiny, intimidated voice. "But my father—"

"Target the satellite, Captain Rashid," Wasef ordered, his voice harsh.

Gamal turned back to the screen, tapped the data into the computer. On his arm Wasef could feel the fierce weight of Yussif's hand.

The servomotors of the laser hummed. Majestic as Allah's accusing finger, the barrel raised slowly into the night, its bulk eclipsing the stars.

"Check coolant pressure, captain," Gamal said, his voice now firm and sure.

"Check the coolant pressure, Captain Mustafa," the colonel said.

With a grunt, Yussif walked to the second VDT and sat down. "Coolant pressure optimum," he muttered.

The laser powered up. Its low throb pulsed in the pit of Wasef's stomach. The servomotors halted with a heavy clunk.

"Locked on," Gamal said.

Traitor? Wasef wondered, looking down into the green-lit boyish face. The colonel felt helpless, as though fate were rushing at him, huge and inescapable.

"Give me a pressure readout," Gamal said.

Yussif glared. "Optimum, I tell you."

"A readout, please."

"Four-oh-one," Yussif barked.

Gamal nodded, intent on his screen. The throbbing hum of the laser might have been the slow heartbeat of the mountain.

"Firing," Gamal said.

Wasef looked up in time to see an arrow of green shoot starward. The peak was bathed for a moment in emerald glow. Then darkness crashed down. The laser's hum lowered to a dull headachy beat.

Wasef heard another noise. A strange noise. A clanking. He turned. Something was rushing at them from the tunnel.

WITH THE CRAV IN THE PYRENEES

Gordon dashed from the tunnel the instant the laser went off. GPS MAPS DOWN—AT&T SEND FUNCTIONAL flashed in red across his visuals. The Arabs had hit the last Super Keyhole.

Soldiers scrambled for weapons, but the platoon didn't have a chance. Arms spread wide, Gordon hit them at his top speed of sixty-eight miles per hour.

His metal treads ground bodies. Bones popped and cracked. Someone screamed, a high-pitched sound of despair.

Gordon screamed, too, caught in a paroxysm of fury and an intoxicating adrenaline high. He slewed the CRAV around and made for the truck. Shoving his hand through the radiator, he tore off the grille. Green fluid gushed like exotic blood.

He rushed the laser and grabbed a corner of the housing, the only thing he could reach. Above him he saw three startled Arabs looking down at him: two by-God captains and a fucking colonel. In his metal hand the housing tore like paper, came loose, fell, bringing a shower of sparks and two keyboards with it.

The smaller captain ran. Gordon rounded the back of the tractor to follow. Behind him the survivors of the Arab platoon, recovering from shock, were firing their AKs.

"I'm fucking, goddamned Superman!" Gordon shouted, punching a nontactical dent in the tractor's chassis as he passed.

AK rounds chimed off his diamond-plated skin. Bullets hit the rocks, spraying dust, sparking fireflies on the steel sides of the laser tractor.

Gordon could see the shorter Arab captain frantically

trying to set up a mortar. Before the man could aim, Gordon was on him. The captain howled in agony as Gordon threw him into the night.

"I'm a goddamned assault vehicle, aren't I?" he shouted as he turned, thinking that it was too bad the Arabs couldn't hear him. Gordon wasn't a wuss anymore. Wasn't a pussy. And if the guys who beat him up in high school had been there, he'd have whipped their asses, too.

The tall, horse-faced colonel had climbed off the tractor and was running for the only other armed vehicle: a machine-gun-mounted jeep. The platoon was firing wild, with as many rounds kicking up dust around Gordon as zinging off his armor. In the glow of the electrical fire atop the tractor, the younger captain stood unarmed, motionless, his expression not fear but fascination.

Gordon headed for the colonel. He was nearly at the jeep when behind him he heard wails of panic. The colonel stared past the LDV, and his long, intelligent face went slack with horror.

Rover was sailing through the darkness of the tunnel.

The soldiers scattered. Some tried to climb the sheer rock face. A few broke away and ran by Gordon in the direction of Spain.

Then it was quiet, the only sounds the fire lapping at the laser's insulation and the low moans of the wounded. Gordon turned to the colonel and saw him sitting with the machine gun between his legs, his arms at his sides.

Abruptly the man seemed to remember what the machine gun was for. He jerked the barrel at Gordon and let fly with a rattling burst. A few bullets stitched the ground to Gordon's right before they started slamming into him.

Gordon picked up the nearest object, the mortar, and hurled it at the jeep.

It was a good throw. A strike dead-center into the batter's box. The colonel tried to duck, but the machine gun was in the way. The mortar slammed into the colonel, and he disappeared off the vehicle, bleep, like a Nintendo character.

Gordon grabbed a rock and lofted it into the laser. It hit the coils hard, and must have hit home, because a fine mist sprayed into the air. The captain on the LDV turned, saw the mist, and hurriedly clambered down off the trailer. By the time he reached the ground, Rover was right beside him.

"Ain't we gonna see some shit fly now!" Gordon howled. "This is the fucking Day the Earth Stood Still! This is goddamned Arabs Versus the Flying Saucers!"

But nothing happened. The Arab didn't run, and Rover didn't advance. They stood there, just staring at each other. Amazement in his face, the young captain put his hand out, as if what he wanted most in the world was to touch the light.

Rover skittered backward. The captain's arm slowly dropped.

What was in the Arab's face? Reverence? Oh, my God, infatuation? He took a step toward Rover, and suddenly the light shot off down the mountain.

Gordon turned and left, his hormone high dispelled, the cries of the wounded behind him raising the hair at the nape of his neck.

The battle hadn't gone quite the way he'd planned. Nothing in life works out the way you imagine. *This ain't Nintendo*, he decided. The thing about computer characters, when you hurt them, they didn't cry.

CHAPTER 9

NEAR CALHAN, COLORADO

Early that afternoon, men came riding up from Calhan in big official vans. There were lots of men and they climbed out of their trucks wearing white decontamination suits and toting Uzis. To Jerry the scene looked eerie and unreal, as if the camp were being attacked by Mars.

The people gathered around because the men had brought food; but the officers didn't give out the food right away. Instead, a tall, gray-bearded man in a doctor's white lab coat climbed on top of a van and read off a paper.

"Pursuant to Colorado State Injunction 53," he announced in a weak, halting voice. "Public Sanitation."

"It's a bunch of shit," a voice beside Jerry said. He looked over and saw the girl.

The doctor lowered the paper and closed his eyes, apparently reciting from memory. "The State of Colorado claims the right to control disease within its borders."

Three men from the camp had made their way out of the crowd, Jerry noticed, and they were talking to the officers in the decontamination suits. The group was a small, gossipy knot, and Jerry could see the men pointing—there, there, and there.

"Carriers of contagious disease—" the doctor said and paused. He bent his head and looked at the paper again. He looked at it a long time.

The wind pushed its invisible shoulders through the camp. It rattled the paper in the doctor's hand, kicked up stinging dust, and made the tents flap and their rope supports sing.

"Carriers of contagious disease," the doctor went on in a whispery voice, "to wit: typhus, cholera, and bubonic plague—are asked to leave the state immediately or suffer the full consequences of the law."

Jerry turned to the girl. "Plague?"

"Just their excuse," she told him. "Just Public Sanitation's excuse to do some housecleaning."

The men in the white suits shoved through the crowd and the people scattered. The doctor climbed down from the van. After an embarrassed glance at the officers, he crawled inside the vehicle and shut the door.

Jerry walked up to the van and peered through the tinted windows. Through the glass Jerry could hear the clear, bell-like tones of classical music.

"Sir?" Jerry called.

The doctor looked up.

"Sir? Is there really a plague here?"

The doctor stared at Jerry, then bent over and turned up the radio.

"That was Telemann's Concerto in E Major for Flute," the radio announcer said in a somber baritone, "by the Academy of Ancient Music, conducted by Christopher Hogwood. And now for our Arts Notes—"

From the back of the camp came the pop-pop of gunfire. People began to scream. Jerry swiveled.

"—will be conducting the Colorado Springs String Ensemble in a selection of . . ."

"Sir!" Jerry shouted, slapping the window.

The doctor flinched, but refused to turn around.

Jerry went cautiously down the small rutted alley between the tents. Hearing a screech, he pivoted and saw sanitation officers dragging a woman from a tent. She was sick from the dysentery. A yellow-brown line of diarrhea ran down one leg of her jeans.

As the officers carried her past, Jerry looked into their dark visors. One officer stopped and stared back, the tinted glass of his helmet expressionless as an insect. Jerry read the shoulder patch. COLORADO SPRINGS DEPARTMENT OF SANITATION.

He licked his lips. "If there's . . . if there's plague," he stammered, "why don't the troopers wear them suits?"

The man's reply was muffled through the helmet. "We're city. You'll have to ask state."

Then they walked on past him, their stiff white suits crackling. Jerry followed. At a little ravine outside the camp the officers stopped and made the woman kneel. Other sanitation men were there, and other prisoners, a dozen or so, all of them sick.

The fretful wind had stilled. Far to the west, the mountains stood cool and aloof. The sun on the desert floor shimmered.

They couldn't be arresting them, Jerry thought. *Lord help us. They can't be going to arrest sick people.*

A loud crack. One of the sick women, who had been kneeling, went down. BOOM. BOOM. BOOM. The reports from the .45 against the bases of the people's skulls had a chilling rhythm. A few of the sick fought back, but they didn't fight well. When an executioner couldn't get a shot at the base of the skull, he fired into upturned faces.

Why doesn't anyone stop them? Jerry thought in horror. The people from the camp were standing, their hands in pockets, watching the murder with quiet discontent, like fans of a football team at the end of a losing season.

Say something! Do something! Jerry wanted to scream, but then it was too late. A sanitation officer came forward with two cans of alcohol, kicked the bodies into the gully, threw some dry brush over them and set them on fire.

The fire burned for what seemed forever. Long after Jerry had gone back to his lean-to, the greasy smoke was rising and blowing off toward the east. When he closed his eyes, he could still hear the sputter and hisses and pops of the corpses as they burned.

He opened the food packet the officers had left: saltine crackers and a slab of cheese. Stuffing a cracker into his mouth, Jerry watched the smoke climb the sky.

I can't get a fever, he told himself, and the dry cracker caught in his throat.

THE PYRENEES, ON THE BORDER BETWEEN FRANCE AND SPAIN

Wasef's arm felt as though a torturer had packed it with splintered glass. *In a few minutes*, he promised himself, *the medics will get to me with the morphine.*

He had given the order himself: Tend to the troops first. Now he was regretting the order a little, like a cranky child who wants to go back on his word.

Rolling his head to the right, he looked up at the laser. Gamal was still fiddling with it. And to his left, the medics were just now zipping Yussif into a body bag, after the long fight to save him.

Yussif is dead and Gamal should be with the troops, Wasef thought angrily. *Not fussing over a machine. So like a Westerner*, he decided. *So like. So like.*

As though he had heard the unspoken criticism, Gamal climbed off the laser, wandered over, and squatted beside Wasef. The colonel could hear, a little ways down the mountain, the flutter of another Mil Mi-8 coming in for a landing.

How many choppers did that make now? He had lost count. Surely there were too many. Their movement would raise an Allied alarm. He tried to get up. Agony stopped him. A moment later he forgot what it was he had wanted to do, and lay back, staring into the weak morning light.

"The laser may be beyond repair," Gamal said with an exhausted sigh. "How is your arm?"

"It hurts," Wasef replied. It hurt as Gamal's treachery hurt, the injury deep, to the marrow. Wasef was angry, then pain made his mind drift, as though part of him were winging over the valley.

"I'm sorry," the boy said.

"Yes," Wasef whispered faintly. The voices of the wounded and the medics echoed. "I am so sorry we have to tell your father."

Gamal was bending over him, and Wasef felt a metallic thread of fear stitch his belly. Gamal would hold a rock like a pillow to Wasef's face. He would smother him in stone. Yes. Gamal was planning to murder him the way he had murdered Yussif.

"Tell my father what?" Gamal asked.

Was that warning or suspicion in his eyes? "You killed my father," Wasef whispered, his voice barely above the noise of the wind. No. That wasn't quite right. He hadn't said it right. "Oh, God. I will kill your father."

"I don't understand, colonel." The skin between Gamal's eyes was knitted into a frown.

"It will kill your father when I tell him." Wasef wished he could get away from the pain in his arm. If he ran fast enough down the mountain, perhaps he could leave it behind. Fast as quicksilver fish, as the shifting of an eye. Oh. Rapid as a treacherous thought.

"Tell my father what?"

Wasef tried to move. Broken bones gnashed. *What am I running from?* he asked himself in confusion. *The pain? The boy?*

No, he realized as his mind cleared briefly, a patch of blue sky between gathering clouds. *No, I am terrified of hurting General Sabry.*

"I will not tell anyone," he promised. "Let your father decide what to do. I will not bring you back to Barcelona in chains. In chains. Listen. Is that another helicopter landing? I could have ordered you killed."

The boy stared at him. "It is the pain which makes your mind wander, colonel. Shock . . ."

Yes, it was shock, seeing the robot rolling through the tunnel and knowing, oh knowing, that he had made a mistake.

"You shot down the wrong satellite," Wasef murmured.

"No! I—"

A medic made his way to Wasef's side. Gamal left. Soon the morphine was oozing drowsiness though the colonel's body. His eyelids drooped.

"You have too many helicopters here," Wasef told the

medical corpsmen as they lifted his stretcher.

A man looked down. He was an Azerbaijani, Wasef saw. Old enough to have been trained by the Red Army. Realizing he was in capable hands, Wasef finally relaxed and closed his eyes.

Far away, as far as the minarets of the peaks, as distant as the pain in his arm, he heard the corpsman saying in oddly accented Arabic, "Don't worry yourself, colonel. There was an early airstrike today on Lérida, and we caught the Allies sleeping. Apparently their satellite is down."

NEAR WARSAW

Baranyk studied the plane gleaming under the lights. Not a small Cessna, he saw, but an eight-passenger craft. Through shrewdness or graft or most probably both, Fyodorov had slithered his way into big money.

As Baranyk approached the ladder, the pilot reached down and took his briefcase. "Welcome aboard, general," he said in Russian colored by the rural accent of Siberia. "We are just now receiving a call from your headquarters. Would you care for me to patch it through?"

Baranyk glanced around. The main terminal was a five-minute walk behind him, too long a time for his people to hold. "Yes," he said.

He climbed up the ladder into the spacious passenger compartment and pushed aside the curtain to the cabin. The copilot was still going through his flight check, clipboard in hand, headset loose around his neck. He did not seem about to leave his seat to offer Baranyk privacy.

The pilot reached for the radio and handed Baranyk a headset. "Patch through now," he told the tower in such fluent, easy English that Baranyk wondered if Fyodorov had hired him off a transatlantic Aeroflot flight.

How did the Russian boys learn to fly now that their MiGs were mothballed? He glanced into the young pilot's face and saw a softness he had not seen among his own soldiers in a long, long time.

Neutral countries too easily accepted the cocks shoved in

their mouths, Baraynk decided. Russia's heart might be in the right place, but her dirty hands and dirty mouth were not.

He pressed one side of the headset against his right ear. "Baranyk here."

"General?" Shcheribitsky's voice was loud.

With a worried glance at the copilot, Baranyk lifted the hand-held mike. "Major!" he said boisterously. "I am in Senator Fyodorov's new Cessna. Don't worry yourself! The pilot and copilot are with me and they seem to know what they are doing. The plane is so pretty that I am considering a career in politics."

Ah, just as he had thought. The copilot understood Ukrainian. Baranyk saw the ghost of a smile flicker across that impassive face.

Baranyk wondered if the Arab cock spewed money, wondered if Fyodorov had got fat on it. Fat enough for him to buy this plane.

There was a long, meditative pause from the receiver, then finally the major said, "It is as you had thought." Shcheribitsky had indeed got Baranyk's hint.

"Good, good," the general said happily. "You know how to place my bet."

The Arabs were surrounding Baranyk's army, and he, a timorous mouse, was running from the burning barn.

"Understood, sir," the major replied simply.

"Baranyk out," the general said, breaking the connection. For a moment he listened to the silence on the other end of the line.

"Please take your seat, general," the pilot said. "We will be taking off shortly."

With a sigh and a nod, Baranyk made his way back to the passenger compartment and sagged into one of the overstuffed chairs.

The copilot stuck his head through the curtain. "Will you be wanting something to drink? The senator has a fine supply of American whiskey."

"No," Baranyk said, then changed his mind. "Yes. Whatever the senator drinks will be fine."

The man brought out a bottle of Jack Daniel's. He set a coaster and glass on Baranyk's armrest. "Anything else? Some salted nuts?"

Baranyk waved him off.

Before Baranyk had the cap of the bottle removed, the plane's engines had sputtered to life and the Cessna began to bump down the tarmac to the runway. Suddenly the wind caught it and jerked it into the air like a kite. He looked out the window and saw the darkened buildings of Warsaw pass below.

When the Cessna banked, he took a book from his valise, pushed back the seat, and poured himself a drink. The sharp scent of the whiskey reminded him of the owl and the American. Smiling, he turned the book over and studied the author's picture. A silly-looking old woman. Her white hair stood up in curls, and her eyes were a bit too close together, like those of a toy poodle.

He turned to Chapter One and started to read.

NEAR CALHAN, COLORADO

The silly policeman didn't want to listen to a thing Mrs. Parisi was telling him. Besides being obtuse, he really looked awful in those short pants. His knees were knobby, his calves too thin. Colorado should examine their officers closely, she thought, before they put them into short pants.

"You have to have a letter, ma'am," he was saying, handing back her driver's license. "A letter from someone in Colorado saying they're responsible for you."

"I have *fans* who are *expecting* me," she snapped. The hot breeze off the desert was making her mascara run. She was anxious to roll the window up, surround herself with air-conditioning, and get back on the road. "Very, very important people who will be quite disappointed that you did not let me through."

"I'd suggest you go home," he said.

It was so frustrating. Of course Mrs. Parisi couldn't go home, but she couldn't tell the dimwitted policeman that.

"Ask your superior," she told him haughtily. "Where is your superior, young man? I'm sure he will want to speak with me."

The absurd officer in the Bermudas sighed and ran a hand across his sweaty forehead. "He'll be here tonight around eight. You can talk to him then. In the meantime," he told her, pointing at the unsightly sprawl of tents beside the highway, "park it. And stay out of trouble."

Temporarily giving up the argument, Mrs. Parisi jammed the van into petulant reverse and sent it rocking off the side of the road into the desert.

The camp was simply awful. Really, she couldn't understand how anyone would want to live in such squalor; but she supposed that some people did, the K-Mart shoppers, the less educated. She rolled off as far from the reeking camp as she could, toward a small ravine that smelled of the sort of sweetish barbecue one might buy at a Polynesian restaurant.

As soon as she was parked, a contingent of unsanitary admirers walked over. She put on her best smile; but they weren't smiling back. To her alarm, one brute of a man wrenched the van door open and pulled her out, roughly.

"I am a writer," she told him.

He must have been illiterate, too, because he shoved her toward the fender, nearly knocking her down. In an instant, like ants to a picnic, the mob was all over the van.

"I will inform the police," she told them. "They are just down the road, you know."

They emptied the van. Someone had even made off with her tires. She stood staring at the crippled van a moment and then kicked it in the door.

"Ma'am?" A soft voice.

She spun around. A young boy was standing there, his arms full of items. Her items.

"I saved some things for you," he said.

"Well, you didn't save much."

He nodded, his greasy blond hair spilling into his eyes. It was simply awful how young people let themselves go, without a thought for tomorrow or the least idea of decorum.

"I know," he said, properly abashed. "I'm sorry about them stealing your things and all." And he put the items back into the van.

Probably she should pay him something, she decided with irritation. Some suitably small reward.

"Here," she said, rummaging in her purse and bringing out her book. The paperback, not the hardcover. When she handed it to him, she saw his eyes light up.

"Yes," she said. "I am the author."

He ran his hands over the gaudy cover Tad had ordered, so impressed, so excited, that he was breathing through his mouth. "You . . ." he said. "You seen these things?"

She lifted an eyebrow. "Of course."

His eyes were an odd shade of green; quite intense. "I seen 'em, too," he whispered.

Mrs. Parisi felt her smile sink, and she fought to keep it afloat. "Of course you have," she murmured.

"I seen one last night. And it talked to me."

She nodded. "How completely fascinating," she said.

"And—and I know it's crazy and all, but it seems like ever since the sun started going down, they's calling to me again with them clattering voices." His green eyes were wide in his sunburned face.

"How thrilling for you," she said, getting back into her van. "And I do so hope you enjoy the book."

He finally went away, even though Mrs. Parisi could tell he had wanted to linger. Lying down on the carpet in the back, she felt the exhaustion of travel hit, and she began to nod off.

Banging on her door awakened her. She opened her eyes and saw the sun had gone down.

The police supervisor, she thought with satisfaction. But her watch said that it was only seven.

"Ma'am?" a young voice called.

That horrid boy had returned.

"Yes?" she asked sleepily.

To her dismay, he opened the back and crawled into the van with her. She sat up like a shot.

"Ma'am, they're coming," he said.

The mob? But whatever for? That grimy throng had taken nearly everything.

"Them Eridanians are coming. I can hear 'em. Cain't you?"

She didn't hear Eridanians, but she could certainly smell the boy. In the confines of the van, his stench was over-powering.

"Come with me." Urgently he took her hand.

She tried to jerk away, but the boy was too strong.

"The rain," he said, making no sense at all. "It's the rain. You don't want to miss it."

He pulled her out. And there Mrs. Parisi stood, the boy's dirty hand in hers, facing the desert.

"Come on," he said, leading her.

She had no choice but to stumble behind. Certainly she couldn't scream for help and expect the ruffians in the camp to come to her aid.

"I really must get back by eight to talk to the supervisor," she told him.

"Yeah. I'll get you back. They're coming now, and we don't want to miss them."

He helped her down into a ravine and then pulled her up the other side. "The sanitation men killed sick people today and threw them into the pit," he said in a hushed tone. "And then they burned their bodies. I saw it."

The barbecue smell was stronger. Mrs. Parisi finally understood the sweetish odor of the smoke.

"How disagreeable," she replied. Her stomach felt slight-ly queasy. How inconsiderate of the sanitation people to have a cremation so close to where people might be eating. "Are we almost there?"

A sliver of moon hung above. The desert floor, though, was dark. The boy pulled her along so quickly, she had no chance to watch her step.

"Just a little further," he said. "You know? Them Eridanians come over me, and I felt their cool soak down into my skin. They was interested in me, like I was somebody important, like I was wanted and all."

Mrs. Parisi crashed through a bush. "How very charming."

"I never been wanted like that before, not by my Pa, not by anyone."

"Do you think there might be spiders around here?"

"Look!" he cried.

The boy's hand slipped from hers. Something approached over the dark desert floor. A blue light. It floated toward the boy like a child's balloon that has been lost and is now coming home.

Good Lord, Mrs. Parisi thought in astonishment. She couldn't be seeing what she was seeing. Perhaps it was swamp gas. Yes. It was swamp gas the boy was running pell-mell toward.

The gas was now so close to the boy that it was washing him in cool blue. They stood that way for a moment, the blue light and the boy. His face filled with rapture, and his eyes closed as if holding his ecstasy in, afraid some jarring motion or stray thought would let it escape.

Then the light pounced. The next instant both boy and light vanished.

Heavens, Mrs. Parisi thought. *How utterly strange*. But she supposed swamp gas could do that, envelop the body and burn it to invisible ash.

Of course, that was what happened. The stupid boy had gone and got himself evaporated or something, leaving her to make her way back in the dark.

Muttering to herself, she began to walk. She was approaching the ravine when someone rudely shone a spotlight in her eyes.

"Do you mind?" she snapped.

"Mrs. Parisi?" a voice asked. The spotlight lowered, and now she could see two Colorado State troopers in their inane Bermuda shorts.

"Mrs. Linda Parisi?"

Obviously the supervisor was ready to see her now. "Yes?"

The officer said: "There are some men here from military intelligence. And they want to talk to you bad."

CHAPTER 10

THE KREMLIN, MOSCOW

As Baranyk strode down the marble hall, he tried to straighten his uniform. At the door to the Presidential office, a small knot of people were waiting. The general picked out Fyodorov at once.

He *had* grown fat, though not as much as Baranyk had expected.

"Valentin Sergeyevich!" Fyodorov cried, throwing his arms around the general and kissing him wetly on both cheeks.

Baranyk kissed him dutifully, then held him at arm's length. "You've eaten too many sausages, my friend," he said with a chuckle, glancing down at Fyodorov's potbelly.

Fyodorov grinned and slapped the back of his hand against Baranyk's belly. "And you were always stout. The age does not show so much."

An aide in an expensive French-cut suit leaned forward and said, "The President will see you now."

Two soldiers in smart uniforms stepped forward and swung back the massive doors. Baranyk gave them a dark glance. *Too clean, too stylish*, he thought, *to be real warriors*. His own battle-hardened group looked like bandits.

Fyodorov grasped his arm and propelled him forward into the Presidential suite. Behind an immense, intricately carved desk, Pankov stood to greet them.

The Russians had relearned opulence, Baranyk saw. The office was large as a ballroom and furnished with fussy nineteenth-century antiques.

"Good to see you again, general," Pankov said, coming around his aircraft carrier of a desk and holding out a glad hand. Evidently Pankov had given up the Russian greeting for the less intimate American one.

Baranyk took the offered hand. The palm was talcumpowder dry. The President smelled of woodsy after-shave, and his luxurious white hair was a shade too brilliant, as though he used a rinse.

"I met you—oh, let's see—" Pankov's generous brow furrowed in thought. "I believe it was just after the Berlin Wall came down." He smiled. The reflected light from his perfect teeth seemed to brighten the room. "You were a captain, I believe, and I was a minor apparatchik sent to liaise our troops from Europe. The West Germans fed us that year, remember? I developed a taste for bratwurst I have never been able to conquer."

Pankov laughed and stroked his flat belly. Stroked it as though it were a favorite pet.

The President's memory amazed Baranyk. The general didn't recall meeting Pankov at all. Then he realized Pankov must have been coached, and his estimation of the man fell again.

A television star, Baranyk thought sourly. *That's all Pankov is.* The hair, the teeth, would look good on the screen. The smile, too, with its counterfeit warmth.

"Sit down." Pankov returned to the tall chair behind his desk. "The senator tells me you saved his life in Afghanistan." And the smile dimmed, disconcertingly. Baranyk guessed that Pankov's smile, like his after-shave, underpants, and virgin wool suit, was something he put on each morning.

"A dark and tragic episode in our history," the President said.

Baranyk glanced at Fyodorov and saw the senator grinning, an inane, stupid grin, like a mouse who has fallen into a vat of cheese. Fyodorov wasn't listening to

Pankov, the general realized. It was enough that he was seated in the office with him.

So Vassily Petrovich was not as important as he made out. In fact he was so small a man that even reflected glory warmed him.

"When I was an officer there," Baranyk said evenly, "I believed I was doing the right thing."

"Of course." Pankov's agreement was too facile, a whore's compliment. "We all thought we were at the time."

"I *believed!*" Baranyk said, aiming a finger at the center of Pankov's face. The President's smile died, heart-shot. "I believed in it all. In the Soviet Union and her right to defend her borders. I believed in the justice of Communism. Should I feel ashamed for my patriotism? We were once bound together by law. By more than law: by history. Is the past no more than shit to you?"

A silence filled the room like a stench. Pankov looked at Fyodorov. "Why, no," he said. "We once shared a bond, of course. There's no denying that. It is just that in Afghanistan both our Russia and your Ukraine lost many young men."

The President steepled his hands and leaned back in his chair, smiling again.

"Wars are ugly," Baranyk said.

"Yes, they are. I agree." Suddenly Pankov turned to Fyodorov. "You must make certain the general tours Moscow. He hasn't been here since—what? '91? So much has changed. He will want to visit some restaurants. That one on Tversky Prospekt . . ."

"Yes," Fyodorov said brightly. "I know the one. A wonderful chef they have, and the blini—"

Abruptly, Pankov rose. "Yes, yes. Well, general, it was good seeing you."

Again he came around the desk, his hand held out in farewell. Baranyk popped up from his chair, grasped Pankov's hand and didn't let go. "I need fuel, Mr. President."

"I do not want a war," Pankov said, blandly returning Baranyk's stare. Then he pulled his hand free. "Afghanistan ruined us." He turned and walked back behind his desk.

"Khrushchev and his search for world power raped us. Brezhnev and his paranoia impoverished us. And Gorbachev presided over the liquidation sale."

He took a seat, carefully aligning the crease in his trousers. "The military ran us bankrupt," he said. "Billions of rubles buried in missile silos, billions of rubles, general, while the people were starving. Should we not learn a lesson from this? Of course Russia and Ukraine were brothers once. But children grow up. And brothers must learn to fend for themselves. How do you think the Russian people would feel if I put them in jeopardy?"

Baranyk slapped both hands on the desk and leaned over toward Pankov. "Forget morality, then. Listen to practicality. The Arabs will murder the Allies and then they will come after you."

At last, Baranyk saw, he had annoyed the man. Pankov waved a hand sharply in the air and turned to the window, the gilded dome of St. Basil and the gray Moscow sky beyond. "We have an understanding with the Arabs."

"You have *shit!*" Baranyk shouted.

Pankov spun, glared at him. All pretense of civility was gone. "The people do not want war. I've had pollsters research it. This is a democracy. What would you have me do?"

Baranyk turned to Fyodorov and saw that the senator was regarding the banded Russian flag which hung limply behind the President's chair. "He is afraid, Vassily Petrovich," Baranyk said softly. "He is afraid of losing the next election, and because of that fear the rest of Europe will fall."

Neither Russian spoke. Fyodorov studied his manicured nails. Pankov riffled absently through a stack of papers.

Baranyk went on. "One man decides the world's fate, and he is a coward. In a matter of months the Arabs will move north like a migration of birds, too fast, too numerous, to stop."

Pankov's television-star face was set in hard, unphotogenic lines. "When they get to the Rhine valley, they will settle there. They will become fat and complacent, General Baranyk. Feed your enemies, you see, and they lose the hunger for battle. It is just that the people of Russia are saying, 'Let Ukraine feed them, let Poland and Romania feed them. Let France feed them. Not us.' "

The battle was over, Baranyk realized. He was doomed, flanked like his army at Kiev. Only this time the murderers used words, not shells, and they smelled of soap and after-shave. Holy Father. How would he explain this to his men?

Wait, he thought. *There is still one surprise.* It would be a wild bluff, but Pankov had no way of seeing Baranyk's cards.

The general leaned forward. "We have been sighting alien ships. Extraterrestrial little blue lights."

Pankov gave Fyodorov a revealing, worried glance.

"There is an American general who thinks he can talk with them, bring the aliens into the war," Baranyk said. "It may be difficult for the aliens to understand combat. It may be impossible for them to understand neutrality."

The point hit home. Baranyk saw Pankov's composure crack, saw the uncertainty beneath.

"Look up at the sky, Pankov. Keep looking at the sky and ask yourself if there is something more lethal riding there than your aging ICBMs."

IN THE LIGHT

Down the gentle slope of moist St. Augustine, at the end of the pier over the lake, Jerry Casey's Pa was squatted, tying a fishing lure. Taking a breath of the rain-freshened air, Jerry walked down to him, his feet bouncing on the weathered boards of the pier.

"Hello, Pa," he said.

His Pa glanced up and smiled. The eyes, the nose, the mouth wavered a little, as though seen through wet glass.

"Sit down," his Pa told him.

Jerry squatted, too, and stared into the lake. In the clear water the fish hung suspended, like sleek helicopters in air. A few yards away, reeds clattered in the breeze. A landing mallard splashed down near them, making the fish dart.

"Nice here," Jerry said. There were ferns growing near the dock, maidenhair ferns with chartreuse coin leaves.

"Yes," his Pa told him, grinning a strange, loose grin. "I like it a lot. You want to go out on the boat, Jerry? Would you like that, you think?"

"Sure," he said, so surprised by his Pa's question, he nearly forgot to breathe. His Pa'd never called him Jerry before. He'd always called him "boy," as though he could never remember his name.

"Get in the boat, Jerry."

The reeds were clattering so hard, it sounded like rain. Glancing behind him, Jerry saw a little rowboat bobbing in the water.

Then they were in the boat in the middle of the lake, by the reeds. "Go ahead, Jerry. Jump right in."

Cool water rippled into Jerry's shirt, ran its calm hand through his hair. He thought he remembered dust and heat and people dying, but the memory was faint. He pushed his face underwater and watched the gold and red fish glide around the mossy rocks.

"Come on!" his Pa was calling, standing up in the boat moored yards away.

Jerry was in the boat, and his Pa was grinning that strange, fluttery smile from ear to incomplete ear. It was as though all those years with Pa he'd spent living with a stranger. This was the man he knew. Pa was like someone out of a television family on afternoon reruns, as familiar as Cosby or Beaver Cleaver's dad.

"Would you like to tell me about America?" his Pa asked in a television dad's voice.

"Maybe later, Pa, if you don't mind, that is."

Pa's smile broadened, grew wobbly around the edges. "No, Jerry. I don't mind that at all. Say, would you like a sandwich?" He opened the top of a cooler.

Jerry froze in horror. Now it would all be spoiled, the pretty day, the lake, his Pa's good mood. Jerry expected his Pa to pull a beer out of the ice. Instead he handed Jerry a Coke.

"Here," his Pa said. "You like that, don't you?"

"Yeah." Jerry pulled the pop-top off and drank. The Coke fizzed and burned down his throat.

"Have a sandwich," his Pa said, handing him a foil-covered packet. "I know growing boys get hungry."

Jerry took a bite. Ham and swiss with pickles on it, his favorite. The taste awakened a beast in him; he pushed his face into the sandwich and grunted like a starving dog. When he looked up from the empty foil, crumbs dropping from his face, he saw his Pa watching him.

They were in the cabin. A fire crackled in the hearth. Outside, rain was falling, tapping against the panes.

"Here," his Pa said, pushing a plate across the scarred wood of the kitchen table.

Chicken-fried steak with gravy. Nuggets of okra, crisp just the way he liked. A mound of mashed potatoes, a big slab of pumpkin pie.

"Go ahead, Jerry," his Pa said, sounding now like the man in *Father Knows Best*. "Go ahead and eat."

Jerry ate until his sides ached. He ate until he had to loosen his belt. When he was finished, he sat back from the table and watched his Pa watch him.

"Let's go outside," his Pa suggested. "Would you like to do that, Jerry? Would you like to go outside, son?"

They were standing on the porch, and Jerry saw that the rain had lightened to a fine mist. The tag ends of the shower were dripping off the roof, pattering on the stair boards. The air was aromatic with pine.

Jerry was surprised to see someone else there with them. Down the slope near a tumble-down, corrugated metal boat-house stood a man in a flight suit. A lost look on his face, he turned and walked up to the trees.

"Would you like to meet that pilot, Jerry?" his Pa asked.

"No, Pa. Not right now." Truth was, Jerry didn't want to share his new Pa with anyone. Not anyone. He wanted to hoard his Pa's love like something expensive and special, put it in a cotton-filled box and store it away.

"All right," his Pa said. "Not today. You don't have to

meet him today. But I want you to meet him sometime. It's important, or I wouldn't ask."

"Okay, Pa." Jerry saw the pilot looking at them. Then the man turned and disappeared into the dark forest.

Resentment emptied out of Jerry like sand through a funnel. Cool, moist happiness filled the space. He found himself grinning for no real reason.

"I think I'm beginning to understand fear," his Pa said, turning. To the rhythm of the dripping water, his Pa's face was changing. Jerry fought the urge to put out a hand and still it.

"I'd like to learn about sorrow now."

Jerry stopped smiling. Around him, the lawn became hushed, only the rustling of the reeds moved the air. Love swelled in him like an ache. His new dad was so gentle, so fragile, that the lightest touch could mar him. He wasn't like any man Jerry had ever known.

"Oh, no, Pa," Jerry whispered fervently. "I seen it all, and you don't want to know nothing about it."

BARCELONA, SPAIN

Careful not to drop his briefcase or bump his cast against the doorjamb, Colonel Wasef made his way into General Sabry's office. The rotund general stood up. "Are you all right?" he asked.

Wasef looked down at his plastered right arm. All day long his mind had played a tedious back-and-forth game of tennis with a ball of credulity. One moment, he would believe himself whole and reach for something; another moment, the broken arm was such a towering reality, it took up most of his world.

"Yes, sir. I'm well enough."

Perhaps he wasn't. He'd lost the LDV, and he'd accused the general's only son of treason. Glancing up at Sabry's round, concerned face, he wondered if the man would ever forgive him.

"Please. Please." Sabry pulled a chair up next to the desk. "Sit down."

Wasef took a seat awkwardly, trying to keep his heavy elbow off the armrests.

"We believe the last KH satellite is disabled," Sabry said.

As a man who sometimes pulls his dreams with him into day, Wasef experienced a brief and confusing flashback to the battle. The robot vehicle was turning, its arm raised like the most maladroit of baseball pitchers. The sight had been so ludicrous, Wasef almost laughed. Then he saw the dark shape of the mortar rush toward him. Here in the sunlit calm of the general's office, the memory was so strong, it almost made him flinch.

"Are you in pain?" the general inquired.

Wasef opened his eyes. "No, sir."

"Just to you will I admit I have some whiskey." The general grinned. "Do not pass that information on to the Shi'a or the Saudis. Above all, do not tell those arrogant Saudis. If you would like a drink here in the privacy of my office, however, I would be glad to pour you one."

Wasef began to lift his right arm in a gesture of refusal, but the weight of the cast stopped him. "No, sir. Please do not trouble yourself."

The general's smile faded with worry. "Even without the laser, we must make the assault. Not to act now would draw out the war another six months, and we can't afford that. An Iranian pilot put a missile into a mountaintop yesterday. Through his idiocy the planned route is impossible. We must use the road south of Andorra."

Wasef, cradling his cast with his left hand, nodded. "If we move at night, we can cross the mountains undetected. There are rarely Allied flights there, and the French, I believe, are not yet alarmed."

"We?" Sabry asked.

Wasef blinked, suddenly adrift. "Yes, sir. The artillery and tank battalions I am to lead."

Sabry frowned. The scowl was so unlike him that Wasef was frightened. *Allah be merciful. Gamal has told his father.*

"I am not sure about you," the general said.

Wasef was sweating now. The room was not air-conditioned, and the afternoon sun blared through the window like atonal music.

"I fear you are too ill," Sabry said.

Taking an unsteady breath of relief, Wasef shook his head. "No, sir. I am perfectly fine. I do not hold a weapon myself. There should be no fear that I am not capable."

"You are sure?"

"Yes, sir. I will lead them."

"Good, then. Tomorrow I will begin my push up through Gerona to Perpignan. This should draw the attention of the French." He chuckled. "In the meantime you will travel from Pons to Seo de Urgel. From there take the southern route to Mont-Louis and then to Prades. Prades will enter onto their flank, and we will have them trapped between us."

Sabry brought his palms together, squeezing the air as he planned to squeeze the French. "And it will be over," he whispered.

He stared at his hands in awe, then suddenly looked at Wasef. "Colonel?"

"Sir?"

"I have not yet thanked you for taking care of my son."

When Wasef left the office, his briefcase under his left arm, he found Gamal waiting in the foyer of the building.

The captain approached and fell in step with the colonel's quick stride.

"Did you tell my father?" he asked anxiously.

Wasef darted a glance at the boy. "No. Will you?"

They reached the sidewalk and the fierce sunshine. Wasef turned left. The boy trotted to catch up. "Colonel, I swear to you. I thought I was hitting the Keyhole."

Wasef halted. Gamal looked at him questioningly. "You *did*," Wasef said, ashamed that he hadn't remembered to tell the boy himself.

Wasef had not realized how tense Gamal had been until he saw him relax. "Would you care for a cup of coffee?" he asked.

They went to a small sidewalk café with brightly colored art nouveau columns. And with red and salmon geraniums blooming in narrow planters. Everywhere he went in Spain, there were geraniums, as though the plant were the national flower.

Taking a seat in the shade, Wasef slipped his briefcase onto a black wrought-iron chair. Gamal slouched down next to him and propped his elbows on the much-mended cotton of the tablecloth.

"I was afraid that you would tell him I was a traitor and that he would believe you," the boy confessed. "He loves me. That is something my father cannot help. But he trusts you, and that is a different thing."

The waiter came and asked for their order in insolent Catalan. Wasef responded in the same language, much to the waiter's displeasure.

"They hate us," Gamal said when the waiter had gone.

"It is natural. All conquered peoples hate their conquerors."

"Is it natural for us to hate so much, too?" Gamal asked, his eyes bright, his face intense. "The Allies are infidels, and the poor displaced Israelis less than dust. The Syrians are thieves; the Palestinians stupid; the Kuwaitis lazy. Why do we hate so much, do you think?"

The waiter brought their coffee, putting the small cups down so hard, the dark liquid slopped onto the tablecloth.

"I don't know," Wasef said.

"It is because we are still tribal," Gamal said, glancing around to make sure no other Arab was in earshot. "In this modern world, we are still tribal. Islam preaches brotherhood, but there is no brotherhood in us."

Wasef brought the cup to his mouth. The coffee was so sweet, it made his teeth ache.

"My father is uncomfortable when I speak of this," Gamal told him.

Wasef could understand why. He took another cautious sip.

"You see," Gamal said, "to my father, Arabs are good, Egyptians better, and family the best of all. If you told him I was a traitor, he would believe you. He would send me away, then tell you to keep silent. If you did not keep silent, he would ruin you. Even though he loves you more, he would ruin you. My father believes in family."

Wasef struggled to keep the rage and heartache from his face. It was true, all of it. What Gamal told him came as no surprise. "Perhaps we should talk of other things," he suggested.

"Doesn't it bother you?" Gamal asked, still fretting at the question. "Haven't you ever stood back and seen what we are? Arabs live in little boxes of loyalties: family and country and religion."

"I'm reassigning you," Wasef told him.

Gamal blinked his large, spaniel eyes. "Why?"

Wasef kept his gaze on his coffee cup. "The laser is destroyed now. Best that you stay in Barcelona. I will assign you to a division here."

"I want to go with you to Prades."

With a start, Wasef looked up. So once more the general had revealed strategic secrets to his son. But, then, Gamal was family.

"There is no laser for you to use," the colonel told him.

"I want to see combat."

Was the boy mad? It was one thing to think unorthodox thoughts. Wasef himself often did. But it was dangerous to voice them. And stupid to walk purposefully into the line of fire.

"Stay in Barcelona, Captain Sabry," Wasef said. "Stay here and live so that you may become a great astrophysicist."

Gamal flushed with embarrassment. "I think I will not be an astrophysicist anymore. We fight together, don't you see? Iranians and Jordanians. Saudis and Iraqis. This is more than simply the Pan-Arabism we have been awaiting. It is a true Muslim brotherhood."

"If you will not be an astrophysicist, what other career do you choose?" Wasef asked, curious.

Gamal blushed a shade darker. His gaze dropped to the coffee cup cradled gently between his hands. "One day I want to be President of the United Arabic States."

CRAV COMMAND, TRÁS-OS-MONTES, PORTUGAL

Gordon tried his best to keep his eyes open while Pelham was speaking. Even blink too long, he knew, and he'd drop off to sleep. He felt his body begin to sway and caught himself with a startled flinch before he toppled to the concrete floor.

"We want you to come down the mountain," the colonel was saying, jabbing a pointer at a map. Dully Gordon watched the red tip of the pointer zip back and forth across the roads like a crimson bee.

"We're holding Alfarras," the colonel was saying.

Gordon frowned in concentration.

"The road should be safe till there." Pelham gave the map a critical glance, and tapped it with the pointer. "Then cross-country it north of Lérida and head up to Zaragoza to the British air station, and we'll fly the CRAV out."

There was a long pause. Then the colonel shot in a whiplash voice, "You reading me here, sergeant?"

Gordon popped his eyes wide. "Yes, sir. Alfarras to Zaragoza, sir."

"Good," Pelham said, a smile breaking across his face. "Because, with GPS down, you'll have to remember this map. And I thought you were dozing off on me."

"No, sir. Wide awake, sir."

"It was good hunting you did," Pelham said, putting the pointer away. "Very good hunting."

Gordon remembered the scream of the Arab captain, the colonel disappearing from behind the machine gun as abruptly and decisively as a tin duck in a shooting gallery. *Were they dead?* Gordon wondered. He couldn't help hoping they were; and he couldn't help praying that what he'd done to them hadn't hurt too much.

"But the secret to keeping alive in battle is discretion,

son, not valor," Pelham told him, his face suddenly somber. "Without functioning missiles, you took one helluva chance."

Bullshit, Gordon thought. The colonel could have taken him out of the goggles anytime. And discretion didn't mean diddly in the face of destroying that laser.

The colonel nodded for no apparent reason. He glanced back at the map and then studied Gordon. "We'll have the CRAV refitted and back in the field again within a week. Mr. Ishimoto has promised us that."

"Thank you, sir," Gordon said. At last the colonel had got to the heart of the matter: downtime. A week. Gordon could live CRAVless a week.

"Dismissed," Pelham said softly. "Be back here at 0700 to get the CRAV on the road."

Gordon saluted, walked out the door, and trudged up the stairs into the twilight. His stomach told him to stop by the mess hall; his body told him to crawl into his bunk.

After an instant's indecision, he obeyed the directive from his aching muscles. He limped up the stairs into the barracks. The moment his head touched his cot, he was asleep.

IN THE LIGHT

In the cone of light at the end of the pier, minnows sailed the green, translucent water. Jerry watched his Pa bring the rod up, snap it down. The line purred as it was cast. With a hollow plunk the sinker submerged into the dark lake.

Jerry took a breath. The evening air smelled of silt and stagnant water and clean rain. Beyond the clattering reeds a thin eggshell of moon rose.

"I like it here," Jerry said in a low voice, careful not to scare the fish. It was important not to scare the fish. It was important to his Pa.

At his feet his Pa hunched, a half-lit, motionless boulder. "Sit down," his Pa said. "Dangle your feet in. I know growing boys like that."

Obediently Jerry took a place by his Pa. The water was cool on his toes; against his hip his Pa's body was soft mud. Jerry looked around the lawn to the cabin, the boathouse, and wonderingly up into the cherished spongy face. His Pa's nose dimpled in for a queasy moment, then swelled out again, as though it couldn't decide whether to be a nose at all.

"Fishing," his Pa said. "You like fishing, don't you, Jerry? You see? I know all about you. I know what you like."

Of course he did, Jerry thought. He was the perfect Pa.

Jerry turned and saw a man in camouflage staring at them from the bank. After a moment, the soldier walked down the pier to them.

"Hi," Jerry said.

"I'm dreaming," the man said. He was blond, with a weak chin and dazed blue eyes. Jerry noticed that the camouflage pants were tucked into high-top Nikes. He also noticed that if he stared at the soldier hard enough, he could see the trees and the lake right through him, as if the man were a ghost image on a TV screen.

"Who're you?" Jerry asked him.

The soldier didn't reply. He was frowning out across the lake, as though listening to the gossip of the clattering reeds and wondering what to make of it.

"Who's that, Pa?" Jerry asked.

His Pa jerked the rod. There was a click-click-click from the reel as it turned. "Who?" his Pa asked.

Jerry pointed at the soldier. The man stared at them, his eyes dazed and sleepy.

Pa turned around. "I don't see anyone. You growing boys," he chuckled in an indulgent television-dad voice, "you're always teasing your fathers."

When Jerry looked again, the soldier was gone and the pilot was making his way down the shadowed grass.

"That other boy. Why don't you go talk to him?" his Pa asked. "Go see if he wants to play."

Jerry found himself standing in the dark grass by the pilot. The man grabbed Jerry's elbow and hung on. "You're real," he said in astonishment. "I met someone else tonight. A sergeant. But when I talked to him, he went away. Are you going away, too?" His voice was high and frightened.

"No. You want to come meet my Pa?"

"He's an alien," the pilot said. "They're all aliens."

Jerry looked lovingly toward the bent figure at the end of the pier. "I know," he said.

The man went on urgently. "They're playing mind games. Everything's an illusion. Have you ever touched one? Have you? God. And seen how their faces change? Just look at that thing down there. Look at it. What the hell do they want?"

Jerry shook his arm free and walked away, but the man caught him, gripped him so tightly, it hurt. Jerry's Pa would never do that. He could never hurt him with his spongy hands. Even if he made a fist and hit Jerry, as his old Pa had done, the blows would fall cool and harmless.

"I told them classified information," the pilot was saying. "They didn't threaten me, they tricked it out of me. I could be court-martialed for that."

The pilot wouldn't let go. "Look, kid. I'm finally thinking straight now. I've had time to think. We're prisoners of war, you understand? You understand what I'm saying? We have to try to escape."

Jerry stumbled away from the pilot and back to his Pa, to safety. His Pa turned and saw him, the rod dangling in his shapeless hand, his eyes now so huge and dark, there wasn't much face left.

"Didn't he want to play with you, Jerry?" his Pa asked in a resonant voice that tickled Jerry's skin. A voice like the hum of an enormous engine. "Didn't you want to play with him?"

"No, Pa," Jerry answered. "I didn't like him much."

Across the lake, a loon cackled. The reeds clattered like a train rushing over tracks. His Pa returned to fishing, his head sinking into the bulge of his shoulders.

He cast the line. There was a whir, a liquid thunk.

"You're a good boy," his Pa told him in a dead, quiet voice.

NEAR PARCZEW, POLAND

"Grigori Mikhailovich Pankov," Baranyk muttered as he lifted the night scope to his eyes, "may God squeeze your balls like ripe grapes."

"What, sir?" Major Shcheribitsky asked, leaning across the darkness of the scout's deck.

"Nothing," the general sighed. "Tell A Company not to move forward so quickly. This is not a race."

The Arab artillery stuttered, the incendiary flashes going off on the horizon like glitter winking on a fallen evening scarf. An answering boom from one of Baranyk's own tanks, the flame from the barrel revealing, for a strobing instant, its hiding place.

So far, so good. Baranyk had not had the time he would have liked to develop his strategy; there had been only a day between his return from Moscow and the tightening of the Arab net.

Shcheribitsky had waited for his return, perhaps wisely. By the time he'd spoken to Baranyk in the Cessna, the southern arm of the net had nearly closed.

Baranyk would try to break out in the north, the side where he sensed weakness. Now if only the cheese of nine tank kills would draw out the Arab mouse. From his high perch the general saw promising movement. Scouts. On foot. Coming from the northeast, across the grass, less than three kilometers away.

"Company A shall hold," General Baranyk said. "Remind them, when they move, to be careful."

Oh, so careful. Cautious and tender as booted feet striding through a roomful of kittens. That morning he had rehearsed his tank squad for the punch-through, had rehearsed them until their legs ached and they had respectfully requested to sit down.

In the flat, open churchyard of Michów they had practiced, ignoring the tombstones and the dead. *Move there.*

No, captain! Are you blind? You have stepped into Artillery Battery C. Look down at your clumsy feet. See, you have killed ten of my men!

There was not enough fuel to simulate the tank battle mounted, so they'd run through it on foot, again and again, like courtly dancers at a cotillion.

Damn you, lieutenant! Are you stupid? Left! Left! Into the trees! Don't you know not to leave yourself exposed?

Now in the calm, dark evening the Ukrainian artillery was waiting in a semicircle for the opening bars of music that would signal the start of the dance.

"Very soon, sir," Shcheribitsky whispered.

"Yes," the general answered. "Very soon."

Suddenly, in the ant crawl of the Arab scouts, Baranyk saw larger moving squares.

"They're approaching. Pull Company A back in a leap-frog," Baranyk said.

He could hear the major's soft mutter into the handset. The Ukrainian tanks began pulling back in twos: the first firing and then retreating behind the second; the second firing and then retreating behind the first, each time searching for cover.

This was the time to sweat. The German tanks would be buttoned up, but in the T-80s, tank commanders would be sticking their heads out of the safety of the turrets to find the path in the dark. If they got lost, the battle was lost. Five tanks would be moving blind. They could roll over Baranyk's waiting men.

A kilometer now between his own tanks and the enemy. Only two kilometers now of withdrawing until the Arabs were surrounded and Baranyk's artillery could catch them in a fatal crossfire.

A fierce storm raged in the field. Thunder and gunpowder lightning and steel rain. Even the soft breeze seemed to tremble. The Arabs were coming, racing pell-mell, heedless, toward the nine Allied tanks.

Holy Father. Hadn't they learned anything from the Israelis' defeat of the Syrians? Baranyk wondered. The

Arabs were using the old Red Army formation. They were too exposed, too bunched.

He watched as one of his leapfrogging tanks destroyed an Arab T-72, a good clean hit that sent a ball of flame rising into the night.

The deep-throated Arab artillery roared. In answer, his own antiaircraft batteries behind him suddenly began stitching the heavens with hot thread.

Baranyk dropped the night scope and looked up. The bellies of the clouds flickered orange, reflecting the fire on the ground. *A plane?* he thought in disbelief. The Arabs couldn't be sending planes, not on an overcast night.

But over the clamor of battle he could hear it coming in fast and high. He saw nothing break the clouds, but something must have. The entire northeastern part of the field ignited into the fulminating hues of sunset.

"God!" Shcheribitsky gasped.

Baranyk threw his hands over his eyes. Too late. The intense brilliance had already been burned into his vision and now replayed the explosion in neon pink and green.

Then a soul-battering WHUMP, as of Heaven's great door slamming shut. He opened his eyes and saw the earth ripple out in concentric waves, as though the bomb had been dropped not into solid ground but into a quiet pond. In the wake of that oxygen-thieving swell, twenty Arab tanks lay dead.

"Have the Poles helped us with an air strike?" he asked Shcheribitsky in awe.

Bringing the night scope to his eyes, Baranyk saw tiny toy tanks and tiny toy soldiers burning. Nothing moved on the field but his own, and they were backing away as if Satan had leered from his pit.

"No, sir," the major said. "The Poles have no jet fuel, and even the Germans are out of fuel air explosives."

The devil's own luck. Some Arab commander with poor judgment had sent out some Arab pilot with lousy aim.

"Shall we attack now?" the major asked smartly, taking the headset from his ear. "Company A is asking, and our infantry is itching to move."

"Never lose sight of the objective, major," Baranyk said, still stunned by his good fortune. "It is good to be flexible, but one must remember one's goals."

"Sir?"

"Our objective was to blast our way out of the closing net. We have done so." Then Baranyk laughed, a hearty, belly-shaking laugh. With that laugh his anxiety drifted up and floated away like the smoke from the burning dead.

"Let us fall back toward Warsaw," he said, slapping Shcheribitsky playfully on the arm, "before the pilot discovers what he has done. Let us remove ourselves, major, before he returns with a Seeing Eye dog."

CHAPTER 11

CRAV COMMAND, TRÁS-OS-MONTES, PORTUGAL

To Gordon's astonishment Toshio picked up a junk-food breakfast on the mess-hall line. Gordon stuck to real nutrition: oatmeal, eggs, and whole wheat toast.

Gordon hated whole wheat toast. In fact, his hatred for whole wheat was in inverse proportion to his love for sausage and bacon. But he wasn't about to sit with a Buddhist and eat breakfast meat. Probably even the eggs were iffy, although when the two sat down and dug in, Toshio didn't shoot offended glances into Gordon's plate. He simply picked up his jelly donut and started to eat.

"You ever have one of those dreams," Gordon asked, "where you can *feel* things? You know, like the wind in your face?"

Toshio glanced up from his donut. There was a flake of glazed sugar at the corner of his mouth.

"And smell things, too," Gordon went on, "like flowers?"

"You dream a great deal?" the Japanese asked.

"Yeah." Gordon chased a pale yellow clot of scrambled eggs around his plate, cornered it with his toast, and scooped it onto his fork.

"And in color?"

"Yeah, most times. So," Gordon said, pursuing his subject, "I had this weird dream last night."

"Tell me," Toshio said, taking a sip of his orange juice.

Gordon gestured with his fork. "I was out at this lake, and there was a stand of pines and a lawn. And a pier, and this kid, and this pilot was there, and . . ." Gordon's voice cut out for a moment, like a Chevy with a carburetor problem. ". . . and there was this alien. He was like, I don't know, two hundred pounds of slug. And here's the funny part. The alien was fishing. He had this nice Shakespeare rod and reel, an expensive son of a bitch, like he'd gone shopping at Abercrombie and Fitch."

"A strange dream," Toshio said. "What did the pilot look like?"

"A little taller than me. Dark hair. Anyway, the next thing that was weird was that I was looking at the reeds—you know, in the center of the lake—and they were clattering just the way Rover does sometimes. Isn't that wild?"

"Air Force?" Toshio asked, putting his donut down half-eaten.

"Huh?"

"The pilot. Was he Air Force?"

Gordon thought about it. The scene was clear, clearer than any dream had a right to be. He remembered the silty smell of the lake, the springiness of the pier's boards under his feet. "Navy. A Navy lieutenant. Anyway, I just thought it was . . . Hey, you finished already?" he asked as Toshio got to his feet.

"We will go now," Toshio said. "We must talk to Colonel Pelham."

Gordon looked down at his unfinished plate. "All right," he muttered. He picked up his tray, took it to the disposal area, and followed Toshio out the door.

Toshio left him in the colonel's empty office. Sitting there, Gordon wondered what could be so important about the dream, important enough to miss half his breakfast.

Pelham came in the room so fast, Gordon didn't have time to salute.

"Did you get the pilot's name?" the colonel snapped.

"In the dream, sir?"

"Yes!" Pelham said with irritation. "Yes, of course in the dream!"

Toshio burst in, accompanied by a nervous major. Taking a sheet of paper from the major's hand, the colonel said curtly, "Dismissed."

The major hot-footed it.

"No, sir. I didn't ask his name. It was just a dream. He was there. I was there. The alien was there, and this kid."

"Is this the man?" Pelham shoved a faxed photograph at him.

Gordon took the fax, looked at it, and had trouble breathing.

"Is that him, sergeant? Is that him?" Pelham was practically shouting.

Eyes wide, Gordon stared at the colonel and then back at the photograph. "Yes, sir."

"Goddamn," the colonel said. "The Parisi books talk about dream communication. I'll inform General Lauterbach we have a first contact."

ON THE ROAD BETWEEN LÉRIDA AND BALÀGUER

Wasef stood up on the floorboard of his jeep to study the dark shapes of the tanks behind him.

"A pretty night," Gamal said when Wasef sat down again.

"Yes."

"What is wrong?"

The young captain's question was galling. Everything was wrong—and yet nothing was. "Two nights ago there was a disastrous battle at Balàguer. We may be spending the day among corpses."

He heard Gamal shift in the darkness. Behind and in front of them, the column of vehicles crept at a frustrating twenty kilometers an hour, in order not to burn out the engines of Wasef's aging tanks.

"How many dead?" Gamal asked.

"Two thousand of theirs, three thousand of ours," the colonel answered, peering into the night. The Catalan sky

was star-shot. The countryside smelled of lavender and diesel exhaust.

Gamal fell silent, either in contemplation or drowsiness.
Their progress had a mind-numbing rhythm, the soporific
growl of the engines, the monotonous rocking of the jeep.

"Before the battle on the mountaintop," Gamal said, "I
had never seen a dead man."

"You should have seen the flight from Egypt." Wasef
remembered the long lines of the starving, the sick; faces
like skulls, bodies like skeletons. Since Egypt he had
thought a great deal about his own death. He would
die, of that he was sure. How, though? Was it better
to die piecemeal, feeling life slough off your bones, as
eighty thousand Egyptians had during the famine? Or
to meet death in utter surprise, as the villagers would
in Pons?

"I am sending a Mil Mi-24 Hind ahead to Pons," the colonel said. "Tomorrow they will conduct an aerial spraying of
Sarin. No one must see us as we pass."

In the darkness he could feel Gamal's accusing stare.
"Can't we simply detain the people?"

"We kill, Captain Sabry," Wasef said mildly. "Soldiers
kill. That is their duty."

Yussif would have understood, Wasef knew. Yussif
would have agreed with the order, would have assured
the colonel he was right. Wasef needed that blind loyal-
ty now.

PONS, SPAIN

Hefting her rifle, Dr. Rita Beaudreaux walked across the
rosemary- and lavender-dotted meadow toward Pons. To her
right an olive tree caught the wind, its two-toned leaves
shifting from light green to silver.

At the side of the first house, she paused while the rest of
the platoon went on. "God," Rita prayed under her breath.
"If it's all right with You, please don't let there be bodies."

She had thought that her training as a pathologist
would have inured her, but the sheer number of the

dead at Balàguer had given her the first-year resident shakes.

They weren't lying on neat, steel tables, those dead boys. They were scattered, pieces of them scattered on the ground, like grisly post–Mardi Gras confetti.

After medevacking the injured soldier out, Rita and Lieutenant Dix and the rest of the platoon found fourteen men the light had sucked dry.

Six of the fourteen were Americans. Four of those now wore Arab uniforms.

After that grim chore and the long march, Rita was so exhausted, she trembled. When Dix popped her head around the corner of the house, Rita raised her M-16 and almost shot her.

"They all skedaddled," Dix said, smiling at the muzzle of the gun and Rita's startled face. "Come on."

Rita shouldered her gear and limped down the cobble-stoned street.

It looked as though someone had turned Pons upside down and shaken all the people out. Rita felt the prickle of ghost stares in the abandoned windows, thought she heard the tread of the missing as they walked to the village fountain. The platoon entered the village quietly, as if afraid to disturb the dead.

Dix motioned a squad to fall out. The men scurried, their gear jingling. When they were gone, Rita studied the shuttered greengrocer's, the boarded-up tailor's. Pons contained a sad, goose-bump sort of hush.

In a few minutes the squad returned.

"Just like forward OPs told us, lieutenant," Hoover said. "All cleaned up. All quiet."

"Let's take a load off, guys," Dix sighed.

BETWEEN ALFARRAS AND BALÀGUER

Gordon was keeping to the high country, thrashing his CRAV around in the juniper, not really thinking about where he was going. He was trying to remember his dream.

The pilot had seemed happy to see him, and had said something weird: that Gordon's face didn't change.

Of course it didn't change. Gordon had been looking in the mirror for years hoping his chin would grow chiseled, like the pilot's.

It still hadn't. When he shaved, Gordon saw the same dweeb in the mirror he saw in high school.

Gordon hadn't liked the pilot much, hadn't liked the guy's looks. Athletic and cocksure, like all the high-school jocks who beat up on Gordon.

Except that the pilot's self-confidence was frayed about the edges. His gray eyes were glazed with fear.

"I gave them classified information," the pilot had told Gordon. "I'll be court-martialed."

Yeah, sure, Gordon remembered thinking. Right there in the dream he'd started analyzing himself. During the screening of Freud Meets Gordon II, he concluded that the dream was about power.

The jock couldn't control his alien; and Gordon could.

He glanced around. The blue light was tagging along, bobbing over the black-green masses of juniper.

Too late, as usual, Gordon felt ashamed. He should have talked to the guy. What was his name? Justin Searles? When Gordon hadn't replied, the pilot got a look on his face as though they were choosing up sides for baseball and Gordon wouldn't be on his team.

At the top of a rise, Gordon paused and looked southeast. Near the horizon he could see the whitewashed rubble of what had been Balàguer. There had been a whopper of a battle there, a real double-decker with cheese, at least that's what the colonel told him. Curious, he blinked to bring up his telescopic vision.

Okay. So if there *had* been a battle—he wondered, surprise curdling in his belly—then what were all those tanks and trucks and artillery tractors doing under that camouflage netting?

He stopped in a clump of juniper, keeping the Arab army in his sights and waiting for instructions. When he felt the hand clutch his arm, Gordon closed his eyes, powered down the CRAV, and pried off his goggles.

CRAV COMMAND, TRÁS-OS-MONTES, PORTUGAL

"Change of plans," Colonel Pelham said the moment Gordon was free of the headgear.

Gordon sat, goggles laced in his gloved fingers, and waited for Pelham to go on.

"It looks like the trucks are all positioned with their grilles northeast. Unless the ANA has got a lot cleverer than they were yesterday, that's the direction they're headed."

Northeast, Gordon thought. Most of the Allies were southwest. It didn't take a genius to figure out what the Arabs were doing. Four or five tank battalions and a shitload of artillery. Overkill for the small force of British and Canadians near Berga.

Goddamn, the Arabs were invading France.

"Tell you what to do, sergeant," Pelham was saying. "You hurry on up the Segre river to Pons. Reconnoiter for me up there. Find yourself a good hiding place and wait for the Arabs to move though. I want a recording of this."

"Yes, sir."

"Keep out of sight," Pelham warned him fretfully. "And get me some good film I can show the French."

"Yes, sir. You bet, sir."

It was going to be Gordon Battles the Forces of Darkness all over again.

THE SEGRE RIVER, SPAIN

The Pyrenees are made up of little folds, all U-shaped valleys from Ice Age glaciation, and narrow, fjord-type gorges. After shooing Rover away, Gordon made his way down the gentle U-shaped banks of the Segre. Miles later he was trapped in a steep-sided fjord.

The sides of the river were mossy limestone, and it wasn't until he arrived at the picturesque bridge outside Pons that he found handholds where he could scoot-and-clamber up the ravine. On the bank he looked around, saw nothing but a curious sheep watching, and headed east into Pons.

At the edge of town stood a statue of the Virgin Mary, wilted flowers at her feet. Farther on down the cobblestoned road, a fountain splashed clear water into a granite basin.

The place was deserted, the fountain the only happening thing in town.

Pons was quaint, the sort of village that small, exclusive American shopping malls like to imitate. Near the center of the village Gordon found the hiding place he was looking for.

The sagging structure had been a stable once. Between the weathered boards were splintered gaps through which he could watch the Arabs pass. If the ANA were doing any sightseeing, they'd look at the fountain, at the neat stoops of the whitewashed houses, not the crumbling barn.

Making his way to the rear, he opened the slatted door and quietly rolled inside.

The place was exactly as he thought it would be: haystrewn, the interior dim except for slanting bars of sun. In the darkness of the rafters, frightened pigeons were flying.

One thing in the barn, though, didn't fit the bucolic picture. Directly in front of Gordon squatted an American captain, a grenade launcher on her M-16.

Which was pointed right at him.

The captain was fortyish, but good-looking. Gordon noticed that, too. She was tall, on the thin side, a coffee-and-cream black woman with a tight helmet of curls. She had huge bedroom eyes, although Gordon wasn't certain how large they might look in other, less startling, circumstances.

Praying that the captain wouldn't fire off a grenade, Gordon put his arms up.

WITH LIEUTENANT DIX'S PLATOON, PONS, SPAIN

"Put it away, captain!" Dix shouted from a dark corner.

Rita was nonplussed. Put the gun down? But some toy tank had just rolled into the barn. The thing had robot arms, and it was lifting them over its head in an I-give-up gesture.

"We've seen these things before," Dix told her. "It's American."

Slowly Rita let her gun drop. The small tank's arms fell with twin clinks, and curled around braces on the cannonless turret.

"Where's the guy?" Rita asked.

"What guy?"

"The guy in the tank."

"There's no guy there, sugar," Dix laughed. "It's just a robot remote. The operator's back in Portugal somewhere. Hi, honey," she said and waved at the robot.

With a slight whine of its servomotors, the robot lifted an arm and waved back. Rita found herself smiling—smiling as if Balàguer had never happened.

Pushing herself up out of the straw, she walked over to it. The robot had taken a beating, she saw. There were scratches along the turret, and the back end was a mess. As she approached, the turret swiveled toward her and the robot held out a hand.

After a hesitation, she put her own hand into the steel claw. Lightly, considerately, the claw closed. The arm lifted a little and lowered again.

Then Rita caught a glimpse of something blue, something cold, between the slats of the barn. She turned, but the blue was gone.

Her heart climbed her throat. Unless her imagination was running away with her, the alien had come back. It had followed them from Balàguer. It would corner them. It would suck the blood out of their bodies.

"What's wrong?" Dix asked.

The doors banged open. A globe of blue light sailed into the barn.

Rita dived for cover. Startled pigeons exploded into a dry-feathered maelstrom. Around her she could hear the rattle of weapons coming to bear. Then she whirled, M-16 in hand, and saw that the robot was moving between the crouched soldiers and the light. Its metal arms gestured forcefully. *Go to the corner*, the robot seemed to be saying to it.

Like a well-trained dog, the light obeyed. Hunched against the opposite wall, heart beating triple time, Rita waited, staring suspiciously.

WITH THE CRAV AT PONS, SPAIN

Don't shoot! Gordon wanted to scream.

Every gun in the six-person squad was pointed at Rover.

Desperate, he rolled toward the captain. She shied back, but the little lieutenant didn't. Instead she watched, her blue eyes wide.

He cleared a space in the straw with one swipe of his arm.

DON'T SHOOT, he wrote in the sand.

"Okay," she said, her voice taut. "Okay. Just keep it away from us, understand?"

He smoothed out the dirt and scribbled, GOT IT.

Gordon glanced back. Rover was in the corner pretending to be Good Dog. He was practically doing an imitation of Roll Over and Play Dead.

"You all *friends* with that thing, or what?" the lieutenant asked.

Gordon turned to her. CLASSIFIED, he wrote.

The lieutenant and her squad stared at the word. They looked at it a long time.

Gordon wouldn't have minded telling them more, but knew Pelham and Toshio were watching on the monitor. Rover was more than Classified, higher than Top Secret. He was Eyes-Only. Say more, and Gordon, like Justin Searles, would be the victim of a gang bang by a court-martial board.

He smoothed the sand again. GET OUT OF PONS BEFORE SUNDOWN, he wrote.

There. That was cryptic enough. Not anything Pelham could take exception to. Looking at his own sentence,

Gordon thought it sounded a bit too much like a B-Western. He could add THIS TOWN'S NOT BIG ENOUGH FOR THE BOTH OF US, but since he was wearing the best poker face of all, the squad might not understand the humor.

"In Balàguer we seen fourteen people that light sucked the blood out of," the little lieutenant said, resting her suspicious gaze on Rover.

NOT THIS LIGHT, Gordon wrote back. IT WAS WITH ME ALL THE TIME.

Rover had an alibi for the deaths at Balàguer all right, but that didn't mean he wasn't a killer. He had nailed three people in an Arab tank and one member of the LDV platoon. God only knew how he spent his time while Gordon slept.

I'LL KEEP IT AWAY FROM YOU, he wrote with more confidence than he felt.

"Make damned sure you do." The peach-faced lieutenant with the blue eyes checked her watch. "Listen. We got a couple of hours yet until dusk. My men had the stuffing worked out of 'em. You mind if we hole up here and grab some down time?"

Gordon knew little about flesh-and-blood women. His fantasies centered either around the posters of blondes in chain-mail panties he purchased at comic-book conventions or the fainthearted heroines of old horror movies. What little sex life Gordon had had contained a confusing mixture of his awe of women's fragility and his fear of their strength.

The lieutenant with the wiry forearms didn't seem as though she was about to suffer an attack of the vapors; but she didn't resemble a Valkyrie with a ray gun, either. He liked her sunburned snub nose, her candid blue eyes. DIX, the namepatch on her fatigues read. Gordon thought that if he could get over his shyness, he'd look her up sometime.

Hi, he'd say. *Remember me?* And maybe Dix would overlook his weak chin, his complete and total dweebiness. Maybe one day she'd look at him and see not the disappointing man but the CRAV's chiseled, powerful form.

As though she'd read his mind, the lieutenant smiled up into his optics, a flirtatious twinkle in her eye. "I've always wanted to meet one of you all. And the way you shook the captain's hand, like she was Steuben crystal or something. Hey. You a boy robot or a girl robot?"

The teasing look both shocked and scared him a little. Keeping his optics lifted so that the monitor wouldn't snoop on his reply, he wrote without looking: BOY.

"Well, ain't that interesting," she said.

AT BALÀGUER, SPAIN

A Palestinian NCO bent down and whispered in Wasef's ear, "Another one."

The colonel nodded and clambered up from the shade of an olive tree, whose branches had been tattered by small-arms fire. Holding a handkerchief tight to his nose and mouth, he followed the noncom up the hill.

Three thousand Arabs lay sprawled along the grassy crest, rotting in the sun. In Balàguer itself were almost two thousand Allied corpses, British and American both.

So where were the burial details? Wasef had never known the Allies to leave their dead so long. Before reaching Balàguer, he'd sent a Hind D out in a reconnaissance flight, but so far everything was quiet, terrifyingly quiet, as if the enemy intended to let their dead rot to bone.

Single file, Wasef and the sergeant made start-stop progress though the field of corpses like children playing Simon Says.

"Here, sir," the NCO said, pointing to a body.

Wasef looked down. The soldier was the wrong color, the wrong shape. The others were blue-gray, their gas-distended bellies straining at uniform buttons, their faces swollen like those grotesque American Cabbage Patch dolls.

This soldier might have been alive but for the pale cream hue of his skin, and for the bloodless hole in his forehead.

"This is the tenth one we have found," the sergeant said in a hushed voice. "All of them Arabs. Not one American or Englishman."

Wasef nodded as though he understood, but he did not understand at all. It was obvious that the blue lights were at war with the ANA. These ten Arab bodies spoke louder than a formal declaration.

He lifted his head and looked back at Balàguer, seeing the burned American M-113, its red cross still legible on one side. The red cross had not stayed the ANA missile, just as the red crescent often did not stay the killing hand of the Allies. Nothing was safe.

Looking at the bloodless corpse, Wasef felt cold terror spill down his back.

"The men are afraid," the sergeant told him.

Wasef saw pleading in the man's face.

"They think Captain Rashid talks to the lights," the NCO went on. "They think he brings this terror down on their heads."

"Ignorance," Wasef grunted.

"Yes, sir." The noncom shrugged helplessly. His face looked pinched and wan. "But in battle, bullets sometimes stray from the mark." The man's voice lowered. He glanced around in embarrassment. "And for the colonel's safety, sir, I would suggest he keep away from the captain."

PONS, SPAIN

Rita hunkered, her back against the barn wall so she could keep an eye on the blue light and also watch Dix and the robot.

The pair were nestled as close as two peanuts in a shell, and just as happily. The robot had cleared part of the dirt floor, and the two were carrying on an animated conversation, Dix speaking low and the robot responding in writing.

Rita was just close enough to read the words.

R & R?

Dix glanced around at her squad. Most were asleep. A few were sitting up, snacking, and cleaning their weapons. They were pointedly not looking in the lieutenant's direction.

When Dix glanced Rita's way, Rita tactfully turned toward the blue light.

Odd, Rita thought, how still it was. How deceptively peaceful, as cool and blue as dusk. As she watched, she heard a tapping sound start up in the back of her brain, a sound to drowse to.

Quickly she looked away and saw Dix smiling up at the robot. "Three weeks," the lieutenant whispered.

LISBON? the robot wrote in reply.

"Probably. Why? You all interested?"

Rita watched the metal finger make a slow arc in the dirt, then another arc. The heart-shape completed, the robot drew an arrow through it.

Rita felt a titter of mirth in her throat and hurriedly lowered her gaze to the straw. It was somehow hilarious, macabre, and sweet at the same time, seeing the two talking together, the large metal object and the tiny pink-faced girl.

"Lieutenant?" one of the men said. "I hear something."

Rita saw Dix erase the heart. Then she, too, heard it. A throbbing growl in the distance.

"Helicopter," Dix whispered, grabbing her gun.

Rita eased herself into a mound of straw. Around her, the rest of the squad did the same.

The sound of the helicopter went from a throb to a flutter and finally to a definite whop whop. It was coming right down the center of the village, fast and low.

"Shhh," Dix whispered.

No one moved. The robot was still as a boulder, and even the blue light seemed to dim.

WHOP WHOP

The helicopter passed overhead, the sound of its rotors dopplering as it went.

In a splash of sun, a soldier sat up. "It's raining," he said in wonder. "It's—"

From the dark roof, a pigeon fell. Then another. The soldier's trembling hand halted halfway to his face and he stared at it moronically. "Raining," he whispered.

Dead pigeons fell like feathery bombs into the straw.

The soldier gave a strangled, prolonged gurgle. He stared at Rita, eyes cartoonishly wide, face darkening to a cyanotic blue.

Rita lunged forward to help, when a pigeon fell by her outspread hand. She blinked in surprise and noticed she was seeing double.

Her muscles were weak and trembly. *Dear Christ*, she thought. *How stupid. I'm going to faint.*

Then she realized that the soldier wasn't dying from a coronary. What was killing him had felled the pigeons. And had also touched her.

Nerve gas was fatal within seconds.

She tugged at the Velcro fastener of her mask. A few feet away, Dix's small body was twitching on the straw, and the robot was trying to hold a gas mask to her face.

Rita jerked, the Velcro ripped apart, and the mask fell to the hay. She tried to pick it up, but fumbled, not able to tell which of the two images was real.

Atropine, she thought. *I have to get the atropine.* But an instant later a shudder jackhammered its way up her spine, demolishing logical thought as it went.

The world went dark, and something heavy sat on her chest. She couldn't breathe. Blindly she reached out and encountered a shuddering hand.

The blue of Dix's eyes enveloped her. Wide, staring, dead eyes. Curious eyes.

A serene, catacomb chill settled down. Somewhere water was trickling. She was in a cold blue bed in her old house in New Orleans and in the bathroom the faucet had begun to drip.

Tap-tap. Tap-tap.

CRAV COMMAND, TRÁS-OS-MONTES, PORTUGAL

Gordon ripped the smothering goggles off his face without waiting for the CRAV to power down. He fought free of Toshio's restraining hands, tore off the gloves, and bolted from the room. At the door he collided with Pelham, nearly knocking him down.

Gordon didn't stop. Gasping, he sprinted up the stairs, taking them two at a time. In the sun-drenched yard he halted, pressing his hands against the sides of his head.

Never. Never. He'd never felt so helpless. Had never seen people die like that. This wasn't the corpses of Bagnères-de-Luchon lying in the grass as if they were movie extras.

I should have died with the squad, he thought. And then his mind screamed back, *Goddamn. You weren't even there*.

The tasteless, odorless venom of reality was soaking into him. In seconds he could drown.

"Sergeant," Pelham said softly.

A hand touched Gordon's shoulder. Gordon pushed his face into the rough wall.

"Come with me, sergeant," Pelham said. "Now."

The colonel grabbed him around the chest, and pulled him backward. Gordon stumbled, almost fell.

"Come on," Pelham said as he pulled him across the yard.

Gordon's ankle bumped something. Pelham's grip tightened.

"Get me something!" the colonel was shouting to someone. "Get me a sedative for this soldier!"

Someone tried to claw his fingers from his face, but Gordon wouldn't drop his hands. This wasn't some horror flick on HBO. This wasn't something he could skip by glancing down at his popcorn.

If he looked, he would see real people. He'd see Dix and her men glass-eyed, fish-mouthed, and staring. If he listened, he would hear the gurgling of their lungs.

Pelham pushed him into a chair.

"What's wrong with him?" a female voice asked.

The colonel's reply was an angry shout. "That's fucking classified information, major! Get him something! Now!"

Gordon heard steps hurrying away.

"I can't," Gordon said, rocking back and forth in the chair. "God. I can't." *I can't deal with this*.

Pelham was calm now. "There wasn't any way you could have helped them, son. There wasn't anything you could have done."

Gordon opened his eyes and saw he was in the clinic.

"You okay now?" Pelham asked.

"No," Gordon whispered.

A woman major in a white lab coat came back with a syringe. She pulled up Gordon's sleeve and plunged the needle into his arm.

"The syringes," Gordon said dully. "I should have remembered the syringes."

"It wouldn't have done them any good," Pelham replied.

The doctor looked at them both.

"Get out," Pelham told her.

"We better put him in bed," she said. "As much Valium as I've pumped into him, he's going to fall out of the chair in a minute."

"Out of here, major."

After a hesitation, she obeyed.

"I want you to get some rest," the colonel told Gordon. "Take a day or so. Toshio will command your unit."

The drug was saturating Gordon's body with lethargy. He blinked and remembered the lieutenant's wide blue eyes. When had he realized she was dead? He'd been trying to keep the mask on her face, the rubber skirting of it around her head like the petals of an olive-green flower. Then she wasn't seeing him. She wasn't seeing anything. And never would again.

Gordon shuddered.

"Cold?" Pelham asked.

Cold, Gordon thought. Cold to the marrow. There was a lump of ice in the pit of his stomach.

"We'll have you up and running again in a couple of days."

Gordon shook his head. Afternoon sunlight flowed over the linoleum like spilled honey. "No. Not the CRAV again," he said. His lips felt thick, his tongue awkward.

"You don't want to command a CRAV?" Pelham was surprised. "Why?"

The only part of Pelham in Gordon's vision was the colonel's sinewy, folded hands. Strong, brown hands. "Alone," Gordon said.

"What?"

"Alone." Gordon had been alone all his life. In high school. Through college. All the time he'd sat in front of the Nintendo screen.

And in the CRAV he was the loneliest of all.

He hadn't known that. Not until now. The diamond-hard armor of the robot had kept out more than rockets. It had kept him from bullets of humiliation and heartache.

Gordon suddenly saw how dangerous that armor was, and how destructive the fantasy of computer games. They had made him so self-absorbed, he had become an adult without understanding consequences.

"You'll change your mind," Pelham said.

"No," Gordon said without taking his eyes from the sunlit floor. "I won't."

IN THE LIGHT

Past the pane of window glass, so old it had gone slightly wavy, stood a low, circular stone wall, its center filled with winter-brown leaves. Beyond that was a rusted swing set, its childless swings rocking in the wind.

Rita turned. Light trickled through the grand floor-to-ceiling windows, caressed the stacks, the books. Against one wall of the library a fire crackled in an ornate stone hearth.

"Hello?" she called. Her voice was absorbed into the thick, cool air. Silence dropped like dying birds from the fourteen-foot ceiling.

"Hello?"

No one answered.

"Read me your book," a voice said.

She whirled. The person standing by one of the stacks looked like Dr. Gladdings, her old professor of anatomy. But when she looked closer, his face swam, as though she were seeing it through one of the antique windowpanes.

"I'm dead," she told him.

"You know a lot about death," he said. "That's why I've asked you here. Read me a book about it."

If she were dead, she shouldn't be afraid. She shouldn't be wanting to run. The thing that looked like Dr. Gladdings took a step toward her. She blundered back, fetching up against the chill of the window.

There was a book in her hand. She looked at the cover. *Gray's Anatomical Book of the Dead.*

With a spasm of fear she tossed the book away. It hit the marble floor, making a musical, languid clatter.

So this is what the brain experiences in the moment of extinction, she thought. She had always wondered what those final synapse firings would be like. Now she wondered how long they would last.

Dr. Gladdings was at her shoulder, so close that she could feel the cold radiating from his skin.

"You always were a curious girl," he said.

She swallowed hard. Probably she should say the Act of Contrition now, but it was too late, as late as the gas mask, as late as the atropine. Beyond the glass in the windows she could hear sleet beginning to fall, rattling on the dead leaves, tapping on the empty playground swings.

"Did it hurt?" Gladdings asked with an odd, flabby smile.

"I'm sorry?"

"Death," he said. "Did it hurt? You always wondered about that."

Death had breathed at her through the gaps in the barn roof; it had sidled through the narrow breaches in the boards and clapped invisible hands over her mouth. With a grimace she recalled her terror. It hadn't lasted long. Fatal within seconds.

"Hurt?" she said. "No. Not much."

"Good. That's good."

Then he was sitting behind the librarian's desk. The sleet crescendoed. As he looked at her, his head began melting into his shoulders. His eyes. Oh. His eyes were doing something strange.

My God, she thought. *What huge eyes he has.*

Dr. Gladdings smiled an eerie, shapeless smile. "The better to see you with, my dear."

CHAPTER 12

CRAV COMMAND, TRÁS-OS-MONTES, PORTUGAL

The next morning, Gordon was awakened by two MPs. They told him to get dressed, that Pelham wanted to see him. He put on his fatigues and followed them out of the clinic.

It was when he was walking across the foggy yard that he began to wonder how his CRAV was and who, if anyone, had taken it over.

Oddly, he didn't care. Not really. Not as he cared before the deaths in the barn. Funny. Now that his life had been revealed for the comic-book fiction it was, he realized that if he had any sense, he wouldn't go back in the unit.

But people were always doing things that weren't good for them, weren't they? They didn't watch their cholesterol. They didn't exercise enough. They smoked.

Gordon's vice was that he loved the soft edges of illusion. He'd taught himself to view life through a television screen. The program was comfortable, and he'd been watching it so long he wasn't sure he knew how to change channels. Or even if he wanted to.

The MPs left him at Colonel Pelham's door and walked away without a word. Gordon hesitated, then turned the knob and entered. Pelham was standing; a stranger was seated in his chair. The sight of the four-star general was so astounding that for an awkward moment Gordon forgot to salute.

"As you were," the general said.

Gordon glanced at Pelham. The colonel looked ill at ease. The general looked pissed off.

"Sit down, sergeant," Pelham told him gently.

Gordon sat.

The general was a small man with a balding head and cat-yellow eyes. "What happened to Captain Beaudreaux?" he asked.

"Sir?" Gordon asked in alarm, looking from the general to Pelham.

"The captain who was with you in Pons," the general snapped.

It was easier looking at Pelham, so Gordon did. "She was killed, sir. If she was at Pons, she was killed."

"Bullshit, sergeant!" the general roared.

"Just answer the question, sergeant," the colonel said in a soothing voice.

"I want to know what the aliens are doing with her," the general said. "I want to know what their intentions are."

"The aliens, sir?"

"The blue light!" The general's face was cherry red with anger. "Goddamn it, sergeant! The blue light took her away!"

SEO DE URGEL, SPAIN

Wasef stepped over the bodies of the elderly couple. On the wood stove a pot of coffee was boiling over, filling the kitchen with its burnt reek. A roll of Spanish sausage, a slab of cheese, and a loaf of crusty bread sat on a counter. The pair must have been about to have breakfast when his men shot them.

He took the pot from the stove and set it aside. On the wall, a canary sang in a wooden cage, oblivious to the deaths of its masters, unaware that it, too, would soon die. Wasef picked up a paper bag and spread some seed at the bottom of the cage. After a moment's thought, he opened the cage door.

The bird didn't fly out. It cocked its head and stared at him with its glass-bead eyes.

Wasef opened the back door to the sunlit, enclosed garden. If the bird decided to save itself, Wasef saw, it would have company. In the garden, a lark trilled from the dark-green depths of a blooming laurel. By a thicket of climbing roses, grasshoppers sang.

Leaving the door open, Wasef turned away. The small house was immaculate except for the splatters of blood and brain. He looked down at the old woman. Her black skirt was up to her knees. The soles of her feet were clean.

Before he left the kitchen, he made himself a sandwich, using his one good hand. He took a jar of home-pickled olives from near the stove, stepped over the bodies, and left the house.

A few of his men were lounging under the dense shade of a cork tree, sharing bread, oranges, and cheese. Finishing his own looted sandwich in four huge bites, Wasef trudged up the hill to the bivouac area of Infantry Battalion C. On the way he passed Gamal Rashid, who was sitting by himself, reading. Wasef stopped, seeing the cover of the book.

Gamal was reading about the blue lights.

"Captain!" he shouted.

Gamal nearly dropped the book. His eyes widened with alarm.

Putting the jar of olives down, Wasef snatched the paperback from the captain's hands. *The Eridanian Way*, the cover read.

"Not a scientific text," Gamal was prattling in embarrassment, "but then not much scientific is published about UFOs."

"Damn you," Wasef said under his breath. Steadying the book between his cast and his stomach, he tore off the cover and stuffed it into the dirt of a nearby potted fern.

A blush turned Gamal's dark neck maroon. "I was hoping to find out . . ." he began.

Wasef threw the book at him. Gamal caught it. "Don't show interest in such things. The men distrust you already, and where will you be, Mr. Future President, when your constituents turn away?"

Gamal bit his lip. "I shouldn't have told you."

Something else to feel guilty for, Wasef thought. Such a number of choices: the dead he had left in the buttercups of Bagnères-de-Luchon; the old couple here in Seo de Urgel whose blood brightened their terra-cotta floor. Now he must do penance for the death of this young man's aspirations.

"My father laughs at me, too," Gamal told him. "He says I don't have a political mind."

"You don't." Wasef sat, dug his hand into the jar, and brought out a palmful of dripping, brownish purple olives. "Here," he said, offering them to Gamal. "Eat and forget about the future."

The captain frowned at Wasef's hand. "We can't forget about the future."

"Food," Wasef said, lowering his mouth and sucking up three of the slick, small olives. He chewed the bitter meat from them and spat the pits into the cobblestone road. "Food is the future. If you want your constituents not to fight with each other, you will promise them food and hide the fact that you are an intellectual. They don't want a smart man to lead them, Gamal Rashid. Only a shrewd one."

Gamal eyed him. "*You* are a shrewd man."

"Ah, yes," he laughed. "Perhaps I will be President."

Gamal didn't smile. "Perhaps you will."

Taken aback by the captain's somber expression, Wasef blinked. "It was a joke. I have no interest in what happens after the war."

"You must," Gamal retorted. "Listen to me, colonel. In a few months we will be handed the responsibility for the world. If we must drag conquered Europe down into fundamentalist ignorance, I would rather lose than win this war."

Lose or win the war. The phrase seemed made of nonsense words. Wasef knew logically that wars had their endings, but his heart told him otherwise. There was only strategy and killing, the hollow thuds of artillery and the squeak of tanks.

" 'As you are, you are led,' " the colonel recited with an acid grin. "Perhaps we get the leadership we deserve."

"I do not listen to the mullahs. You know, colonel, the prerequisite for being a Muslim should not be stupidity."

Dig into Gamal Rashid deeply enough, and the softness was gone, Wasef saw. He had struck iron. The boy was staring at him, chin high, mouth set in a firm line. He looked Presidential.

"You are a one-man revolution, captain," he said kindly. "Wait until you have someone to fight with you."

"Don't tell me to wait," Gamal huffed. "We Arabs have been waiting eight centuries for enlightenment and freedom to return."

Wasef caught a flicker of yellow out of the corner of his eye.

"A canary," Gamal said, his own head lifting in wonder. "Look! It is a canary."

Somehow the bird had made it out of the house to perch, singing, on the branch of an olive tree. Had freedom lured it from its prison, or did the smell of death drive it out? It wouldn't live long, Wasef knew. The lessons of survival were too quick and hard for a caged bird to master.

"A miracle," Gamal said, grinning.

The captain did not know the deaths from which this miracle had sprung; nor did he stop to think that in death the miracle would end.

Despite the heat of the midmorning sun, Wasef felt a chill. Gamal was wrong about the eight centuries of waiting. Only death, not the Arabs, would be so patient.

"You are going?" Gamal asked as Wasef got awkwardly to his feet.

"We must get some rest before sundown."

The boy's eyes were still shining. "A good sign, don't you think, colonel? Don't you think the canary is a good sign?"

"Perhaps."

From the olive tree the bird trilled a series of liquid notes. Wasef looked up at the branch in dread. The canary's song fluttered in his heart as though wings of darkness beat there.

IN THE LIGHT

Justin walked up the slope of the grass and into the shadowed stand of pines. A few yards into the forest he stepped out into his sunny Florida backyard.

Lemons hung on the tree like Christmas ornaments. Clouds, soft and gray as rabbit fur, scooted across the rain-scented sky. At the corner of the house, Harding was waiting for him, standing in the chill chatter of the palms.

"Did you like your visit?" the XO asked.

Harding's face was sagging under the weight of gravity. His eyes were sliding down his cheeks. Justin looked away, not wanting to see the eyes slip off his chin and fall to the ground like fat, blue tears.

"We have to talk," Justin told him.

They were in the kitchen, his mother sitting across the table from him, her hair going from gray to brown to black.

"What did you want to talk about?" his mother asked.

"I don't want to be here," he said.

The rattle of the palms grew to thunder.

"I want to go back. I think you should send me back now. You've learned everything you can from me."

"Not everything," she replied. "Sit down, Justin. Sit down and have some milk and cookies."

"Don't do this to me!" he screamed.

Suddenly they were all there: his mother, the bus driver, and Harding. Their eyes were huge, startled, and black.

"I know where I am now, don't you see? I know what's happening. Stop pretending to be something you're not!"

Time froze. Outside in the yard the clamor of the palms diminished to a breathless hiss. For an instant Justin was afraid, more afraid than he'd ever been in his life, certainly more afraid than he'd ever been during battle. Maybe he didn't want to see. Maybe the illusion was better.

A cold, wet wind blew in through the open window, soothing the tension in the room.

"I think he's had a bad day at school," his mother said worriedly.

Harding nodded. "Maybe he wants to drive the bus again. Maybe he'd like Ann to come back. Maybe he needs some milk and cookies."

The bus driver reached out and put cool jellyfish fingers on Justin's arm. "Why do you want to go back if you're so afraid to die? What are you most afraid of, Justin?"

Justin leaped from his chair, ran out the door, and sprinted to the safety of the pines. On the other side of the grove of trees it was night again. He watched a young, swarthy-faced Arab captain amble out of the trees and cross to the corrugated metal boathouse. The officer opened the door, hesitated, then entered.

When the Arab was gone, Justin trotted down the sloping lawn. "Hey, kid," he said.

At the end of the pier, the boy looked up.

"We have to get out."

The boy reeled in his line and selected another sinker from the red tackle box.

"You hear me?"

"I hear you," the kid said. He tied his tackle and cast the rod. In the still moonlight, the reeds were clinking ice-music, broken-glass chords.

"They take you where you want to go," the kid was saying, angry, "but you don't give 'em no never mind. They listen to what your heart tells 'em, but you don't give a shit. They wouldn't have took you if you didn't want out. All they want to do, damn it, is make you happy."

Justin stared at the back of the kid's head. God. He hadn't wanted out of war that badly, had he? Had he been so afraid, even more afraid than the other pilots, that the aliens sensed the difference? The alien sat, a lump of clay, next to the boy.

"What makes you think that?" Justin asked.

The kid's eyes were moss-green in the glow of the dock light. "I got it figured, and you would, too, if you had any sense. This is the genie in the bottle. This is the three magic wishes."

Justin said, "This is just some damned dream."

"It's a dream," the alien agreed in a doting-father voice, a voice perfect for little-boy confessions or for going to sleep in laps. "We want to know your dearest wish. It's wishes that call us."

Tap-tap-tap. The sound from the reeds was tender now, the noise of gentle rain on leaves.

"I want to go back," Justin said.

Its lips bubbled up into an ironic smile. "Do you?"

Yes, he told himself, hoping that he was thinking hard enough and sincerely enough so that the alien would hear that answer and not the treacherous *no* of his fear.

CRAV COMMAND, TRÁS-OS-MONTES, PORTUGAL

Gordon watched the video, sitting bolt upright in the chair, the nails of his right hand scratching the skin of his left so hard, it raised welts. On the screen the small lieutenant was dying and pigeons were tumbling from the rafters.

"Right here," the general said, pointing. "You can see it."

At the top right of the screen, the captain was fumbling for her gas mask, shaking like a drunk with the d.t.'s. This was what Gordon hadn't seen. The captain's death, and everyone else's in the squad, had been peripheral. His attention had been on Dix.

Now he saw Rover moving in, as if for the kill. The light pounced—and winked out. Where the captain had been was empty straw.

The monitor went black. Pelham turned off the VCR and looked inquisitively at Gordon. "You don't remember," he said.

"No, sir."

"Mr. Ishimoto took over for you," Pelham said. "But the light didn't return. It still hasn't."

"You have some sort of control over it. Why?" the general asked. "What does it see in you?"

"No, sir. I don't have control over it, sir."

"Don't give me that!" The general jumped to his feet, purple-faced. "I saw you tell it to go into a corner! I watched it obey you! Goddamn it, son, don't lie to me!"

Gordon glanced to Pelham for protection. The colonel was astonished.

"General Lauterbach, he—" Pelham began.

"Shut up!" the general shouted, then suddenly bent over Gordon. He was inches away, and Gordon could read a savage longing in the man's pale eyes.

"You saw the place the aliens take them," he said.

"I just dreamed about it, sir."

"You saw it. I want to know why that pilot punched out when his RIO said he could have landed the F-14. Why did he do that? Why did they take him? How did the man look?"

"Well, sir, he—"

"Did he tell you anything?" the general shot.

"Nothing much, sir. He was kind of frightened."

The general's face was so taut, his cheeks twitched. "Frightened," he said in a hollow voice. Suddenly the hazel eyes lost their predatory look and grew sad.

The general gazed around the room aimlessly, as though searching for something he had lost: his keys, a pen, his earlier anger. "Seo de Urgel," he said. "The Arabs are at Seo de Urgel, if my calculations are correct."

"Yes, sir. I'm sure that's right," Pelham said, physically shaking off his befuddlement.

"The main ANA army is moving east. They've surprised and overrun the single French battalion at Gerona. The other Arab division will begin crossing the Pyrenees tonight. It will probably take two days." His back to Gordon, the general was now studying the map, his hands folded behind him. The man's small body was still, but Gordon could see the fretfulness in his hands. They were contending with each other, two weary armies.

"They mean to attack the French western army from two sides, then," the general said thoughtfully. "The French are sending an Israeli commando squad up on the heights to catch the Arabs on the switchback at Llivia, before they reach Mont-Louis. I want the Israelis to have a complete and disastrous success. I want them to kill them all; otherwise the division will simply back down the mountain and we'll play our waiting game again."

Pelham looked warily at Gordon. Gordon himself was startled by the disclosure of battle plans and wondered if he should leave the room.

"I want this man in control of that CRAV," the general said without turning around.

"Sir," Pelham said gently. "I've given the sergeant a couple of days off."

The general didn't take his eyes off the map. His voice was flat. "I want him in control of the CRAV, colonel. See to it."

"It's okay, sir," Gordon said to Pelham. It was more than just okay. He wanted to be in the CRAV now. He had to regain the equanimity of the goggles; he had to get that safe distance back.

"I want to see if the light returns," the general was saying. "If it does, I want the CRAV to move up toward Mont-Louis, meet with the Israelis, and then block the road while the squad blows that mountain."

"Block the road, sir?" Pelham asked, incredulous. "But the CRAV's missile tubes aren't functional."

"If the light comes back, colonel, he won't need the missile tubes," the general said quietly. "God forgive me. I'm going to find out just how much the aliens love him."

IN THE LIGHT

Maybe Purgatory was simply a place where nothing happened. Rita imagined time spinning around her, trapping her in its centrifugal force. Centuries might whirl here in this limbo, this library of pale light and subdued shadows.

She took a deep breath. The air smelled of old books and the wood smoke from the fireplace. From the tall windows came the ubiquitous clatter of rain.

"Tell me about death," Dr. Gladdings said.

Slowly Rita turned. The sparse hairs at the top of the

old man's head, greased and combed to cover as much of the bare scalp as they could, seemed to be sinking into his skull. His eyes, darker and larger than life, bulged over his cheeks as though forced out by some unimaginable pressure.

"I don't know much about it, really," she told the professor.

Her response seemed to surprise him. Insistent rain beat its tiny fists against the panes.

"Of course you know," he said. "You must. Haven't I taught you anything?"

"What do you want?" she asked. "A definition of clinical death? A physician would tell you that death occurs when the brain shuts down. A biologist would tell you that cells live on, oblivious to the death of the organs."

For a moment she pictured her corpse in the barn: her cells, like an army which had not yet got word of the defeat, trying to expel the poison that had killed her.

She tried to picture her funeral; but the mourners, except for her mother, were faceless, anonymous forms, like all the acquaintances who had peopled her past.

It was an aptly lonely Purgatory she was in, she decided, empty but for a man who was lonelier still. She recalled Dr. Gladdings's solitary, bent figure striding across campus: it was wound so tight around his ever-present armful of books that the books seemed the anchor for that rubber-band body. Take them away, and there would be no center left. His arms, his legs, would fly apart; his tense mind would unravel.

For the first half of the semester she had thought he disliked her for her color; later she saw that he disliked everyone, and that the pile of books and the lecturing pointer were fortifications for his solitude.

"There must be something else to death," Dr. Gladdings said in a bewildered voice.

"What? The soul?" she asked wryly. If this scene were not being played out in the electrical twitchings of her dying brain, then this odd, spongy Dr. Gladdings must be demon or angel. But a demon should not be so tentative; and an angel would not be so lost.

Dr. Gladdings's face, as ill-defined and pulpy as a toad-stool, was drawn into an expression of dismay. "I thought you would know."

Embarrassed, she looked away. She ran her hands over the dusty spines of the books. "I'm not a theologian. I mean, that's the ultimate question here, isn't it? Does life after death exist? You tell me."

He didn't reply. The noise of the rain against the leaves outside had a dreamy, comforting quality that reminded her of damp-wool winters and marshmallows spreading sweet white foam over hot chocolate.

Rita closed her eyes and leaned her head against the books. They were solid, cool, and smooth. "Please," she implored him. "You tell me."

CRAV COMMAND OFFICES, TRÁS-OS-MONTES, PORTUGAL

Mrs. Parisi sat as primly as she was able in the uncomfortable chair the Army had provided. They'd treated her well, she supposed, although the accommodations were Spartan. Since landing in Portugal, she had found herself paying less attention to her bed and food and more to the little nuances of people's speech, their sidelong glances. She was all business now, her nerves as alert and bristly as a cat's questioning whiskers.

When she heard approaching footsteps, she leaned back to peek around the open doorway but found she couldn't see much of anything except the hideous olive-painted hall.

The footsteps stopped suddenly. Down the corridor, two men were arguing, but not loudly enough for her to understand.

"—traumatized." The husky-voiced man's word burst into the air like a single firework and hung there, sparkling with possibilities.

Mrs. Parisi was listening so hard, she was scarcely breathing. *Traumatized?* she thought. Well, it was war. That was the entire point of armed conflict, wasn't it, to traumatize as many people as possible.

They were talking again, the one giving soft, low orders, the other murmuring a plea.

There was a story unfolding there in the corridor. In life, there were always stories. She liked stories; she had made up some herself—the supposed interviews with eyewitnesses, the tales of abductees and dreamers.

Suddenly the conversation in the hall broke up. Heavy footsteps receded, the footsteps of a big man made heavier by the weight of disappointment. A moment later lighter, quicker footsteps approached the door. She jerked her head around to the empty desk before her, not wanting to be caught eavesdropping.

"Mrs. Parisi?"

She turned and saw a short, balding man enter the room. He was dressed, as all the soldiers were, in an unappealing camouflage uniform.

With a regal gesture she extended her hand. "I don't believe I've had the pleasure."

He seemed taken aback, but quickly rallied. "T. Williams Lauterbach," he replied, giving no indication of his rank. He didn't need to. There were four stars lined up like toy soldiers along his collar.

The hand in hers was firm yet dainty, like the hand of an athletic woman. "So delighted to meet you," she said.

He walked to the desk, took a seat behind it. "I've read your books," he told her.

She had surmised as much. With an effort she managed to look pleasantly amazed. "How gratifying for me."

"Tell me about the aliens," he said.

His hazel eyes were level and shrewd. The general was not a fan, she realized. And this interview had more of a test about it than flattery.

"The Eridanians are wise—"

"How wise?" he asked.

"Very, very wise." Oh, my. She wasn't getting anywhere. His face had closed into hard, suspicious lines.

"Tell me something substantial. We need to determine that what we're seeing is intelligent and not merely an atmospheric phenomenon."

Good heavens. The general was smart, but he'd slipped and handed her a clue. Atmospheric phenomenon, was it? Like the odd blue swamp gas that had eaten that horrid boy. The swamp gas had seemed to act intelligently. At least gullible, superstitious people might construe its action that way. And what had the boy said about it? She searched her mind. Ah, yes. Keeping a sweet expression on her face, she tossed out a small, teasing bone. "Eridania is a lovely blue planet. It rains quite a bit there, you know."

"Really," he said in a noncommittal voice. The general had an excellent poker face, but she could see that he found her remark toothsome. His hands, folded on the desk, tightened.

"What do they want?" he asked.

Remembering the look on the boy's face, she replied, "Love." The general's expression told her she was on the wrong track. "Of course, love is not to them what it is to us. It is more of an interest, you see. They find some of us simply fascinating."

Her words seemed to have struck a nerve. For an instant the general's eyes clouded. He unlaced his fingers and sat back in his chair.

There was pain in him when he talked about the aliens. Yet there was a keen curiosity, too. And a neediness so strong, it nearly took her breath away.

Most people were easy to read: the woman who hoped the Eridanians would give her something to worship besides a bad marriage; the man who wanted a distraction from his own failure; the person who had lost one faith and was searching for another. This general was more complex than that. Mrs. Parisi knew that when she conquered his doubts, he would become her greatest trophy.

"They love us, Mr. Lauterbach," she said earnestly.

He squinted. "Seems odd, since we've had soldiers killed by the lights."

Mrs. Parisi hid her shock, and she knew she was more successful in her effort than the general had been at hiding his need. "Yes," she told him patiently. "But don't you see? They killed them with love."

To her surprise she saw the man wince. She'd verified something, she realized, and if he had been inclined to disbelieve her before, he was leaning the other way now.

She'd have to be careful. She'd have to pussyfoot and eggshell-walk, but she'd win. Relaxing at long last, she enjoyed the victory inherent in his stunned and credulous face.

CRAV COMMAND CENTER, TRÁS-OS-MONTES, PORTUGAL

Gordon stood when Pelham entered the room. The colonel wasn't looking his way, however, but studying the floor, as though some compelling and sorrowful news were written on the linoleum.

Pelham didn't take a seat; and Gordon was afraid to get back in his chair. They stood a couple of feet apart, Gordon watching the colonel's downturned face.

"Your orders are to take your CRAV and make your way around the ANA to the switchback just past Llivia. The Israeli team will rendezvous with you there. And then you will block the road."

"But you explained to the general, didn't you? My missile tubes—"

"Didn't you hear me, sergeant?" Suddenly Pelham lifted his head. His eyes were burning.

"But . . ."

"That's a direct order. Go to your command station now."

Jesus. The general hadn't changed the orders. Block the *road?* And hope that Rover saved him? The Arab army would run him down. And then what would happen when the shell hit, when the TV screen in his mind splintered to let howling reality inside?

"With all due respect, colonel, I can't," he told him and waited for Pelham's wrath to fall.

The MPs would come next. The court-martial. It didn't matter. Gordon could retreat into himself the way he always had into comic books and fantasies. Soft edges. Distance. That was the way things should be.

Pelham didn't shout. His eyes lost their anger as he regarded the map on the wall. "I've been asked to inform you that noncompliance with this order will be considered desertion."

"I can't help that, sir. I—"

The colonel's voice was quiet, shorn of tone. "The penalty for desertion during this war is death by firing squad. General Lauterbach asked me to remind you of this."

Gordon's thoughts fell out of his brain and rolled along the floor like scattered marbles. "Sir?"

Firing squad? Surely the colonel was joking.

God. Gordon couldn't think. He saw FIRING SQUAD as though it were written on a Day-Glo billboard.

"Just a moment," Pelham said. He opened his door wider and shouted down the hall. "Major Kelly?"

An instant later, the major appeared, his face questioning.

"I wish you to remain here as a witness in case a court-martial is to be convened." Pelham's eyes connected with Gordon's long enough for Gordon to witness the pity there. For him to see the firing squad marching smartly out onto the grass.

Pelham's stare, his irises like a TV movie.

"Sergeant Means," Pelham said. "You are to go to your command center immediately. You are to engage your CRAV and follow the route given you. Once there, you are to block the road. This is an order. Do you understand? And do you understand the penalty for disobeying the order as I have explained it to you?"

"You're killing me," Gordon whispered.

Pelham's mouth worked. He said nothing.

"I'll stand there and let the Arabs destroy my CRAV, sir," Gordon said, "but it will kill me."

And without bothering to salute, he shuffled out the door.

CHAPTER 13

THE PYRENEES, ABOVE SEO DE URGEL

Zahra was standing ankle-deep in the Nile, tasseled papyrus reeds around her, *gelabia* pulled up to her knees. Her face was unveiled and she was smirking.

"Come out," Wasef told her. "And lower your skirt."

"The American women taught me secrets," she said, her dark eyes flashing with hatred. "The biggest secret of all was that you killed me."

Behind him, men were walking the dirt road, a line of ambulatory skeletons. The lustful eyes in their skulls were fastened on Zahra.

"Lower your skirt or I will beat you," Wasef said.

She laughed. Her skirt twirled higher, to the level of her thighs. He reached out to grab her, but she danced away, splashing water that caught the sun and for a moment burned like incandescent magnesium.

"Come away," he ordered, but she wasn't listening.

He had no control over her, he never had. He glanced behind him. The line of men had stopped, and they were staring because they knew. They knew he could not make his wife obey.

"You shame me," he said. But Zahra was gone, disappeared into the silent, motionless papyrus.

Panicked, he rushed after her into the shallows, scattering

white ibis, a mud-colored crocodile, and strange, flesh-pink fish. Three steps into the Nile, the bottom dropped away. He sank, clutching at water, clutching at nothing.

With a gasp, Wasef sat bolt upright in the jeep. Out of the darkness beside him came Captain Rashid's concerned whisper, "Are you all right, colonel?"

"A dream." The transmissions of the tanks behind him were whining up the incline. Ahead of him he could see the dark shapes of the peaks, the gleam of snow on their shoulders.

"War?" Gamal asked.

"What?"

"You dream of war?"

"No," he said. "Of murder."

Zahra had wanted to stay in California; but Wasef forced her to return to Egypt. He remembered the easy American girls with their foul mouths and their nakedness. He remembered how terrified he was that Zahra would be infected by freedom.

"I dream strange dreams now," Gamal said to the inattentive colonel. "There are Americans in it."

Americans, Wasef thought. Americans and their sophisticated, decadent ways. Their lives of singles bars and lonely, barren nights.

He'd thought Zahra wanted to become sinful; but realized now that what she had liked were the bright clothes, the silks, the ruffles. Perhaps she remembered dressing up when it was allowed by Egyptian law. All she wanted was to feel pretty.

"I am at a lake," the captain was saying softly. "There is a young American boy there, and sometimes an American pilot. Down at the end of the pier, just under a fall of light, sits an ill-defined thing. I think it is an alien," he whispered.

Wasef was barely listening. He was thinking of Zahra, boyish in blue jeans and a tee shirt; Zahra, a hothouse flower in a gossamer dress of red and purple. Wasef had loathed the way the American men's heads turned in her direction, the way their eyes fondled her.

He had been afraid to lose Zahra, so he brought her home to die.

"Are you all right, sir?" Gamal asked.

Wasef gazed up into the star-shot pool of sky lapping at the black peaks of the mountains. "Why shouldn't I be?"

"You sound . . ."

"I'm fine," Wasef said sharply.

The empty road before them was illuminated by a thin strip of light from the jeep's shrouded headlamps, the glow so weak that Wasef wondered how the driver could see where he was going.

They were lost; all of them lost. Wasef and the entire Arab nation was atop the black mountain of combat, with nothing, not even the gleam of reason, to light their way. No wonder he could not picture the war over. No one but Gamal Rashid worried about aftermaths.

"It is such a strange dream," Gamal told him. "Sometimes I think I should stop and talk with the Americans, but I am afraid to. I am ashamed."

Wasef glanced down the steep ravine to his right and noticed a river parallel to the road, its water silvery in the moon. Safety, sanity, was a long way down.

"To hide from the Americans, I walk into a shed," Gamal said. "Odd. It reminds me of the shed my family had in the desert. And just before I wake, I think of my father."

"Do you," the colonel said absently, remembering his last dream-glimpse of Zahra before she disappeared into the reeds. Zahra as she had been before hunger covered her beauty like the shroud of the *gelabia*.

"My father," the boy said mournfully. "He is on his way into France and I am afraid he is too old for battle."

"Too old?" Wasef sniffed. "He's only fifteen years older than I am."

When Gamal didn't answer, Wasef turned. "And I also am too old? Is that it? Do you think that war is a young man's game?"

"It isn't a game," the boy said.

The jeep struggled higher into the dark, barren rocks. On the other side of the mountains, eight hours from now, they would reach France. There would be trees there and places for concealment. Wasef needed a place to hide. At one time he thought he killed to avenge the famine. Now he wasn't sure. Perhaps he killed to avenge Zahra.

"We are all either too old or too young for war," Wasef said bitterly. "There is no good age for killing. Promise me one thing."

"What?"

"Promise me that if you ever become President, you will get rid of the *gelabia* and the veil."

Gamal's voice was thin, whining. "You have no right to make fun of my aspirations. It is—"

"Promise me!" Wasef said so loudly that the driver glanced over his shoulder. "Promise," he whispered.

Perhaps Gamal caught the pain in his voice, as subtle as the glimmer of moonlight on the snows of the colonel's reserve. Gamal cleared his throat. "I promise," he said softly.

THE PYRENEES, AT THE SWITCHBACK ABOVE LLIVIA

The CRAV hidden in the rocks by the side of the road, Gordon watched the Israelis set their explosives into the crannies of the cliff. Six were strung across the sheer limestone face like spiders; six were at the top of the cliff, feeding out line.

They worked silently, like coordinated insects, each man on top responsible for a man below. One misstep, and they would both fall.

And Gordon would not be able to catch them.

He hadn't had the heart to talk to the Israelis much, hadn't wanted to feel a tie to them as he had with Dix and her men. What would he write in the dust of the roadside, anyway? That it was a shame the price of Israel's survival was the lives of her mercenaries?

Gordon turned to watch Rover. The blue light was at his side, where it had been all evening. As though Rover was afraid Gordon would leave again.

Gordon *was* going to leave. His orders were to park himself in the middle of the road and not move, not even if the tanks rolled over him, not even if they blasted him to pieces.

And why? Because if the Arabs didn't stop for Rover and the CRAV, they'd maintain their cautious five-tank-lengths' distance. The cliff, when it fell, would get only six or seven. There had to be twenty armored vehicle kills; otherwise the tanks would simply turn around, head down the mountain, and destroy the single battalion waiting for the survivors at the bottom.

Once Gordon had basked in his near invulnerability. The CRAV was not like the Gordon of the weak chin, the Gordon who always got chosen last for sandlot baseball.

Before the CRAV, he'd always come in last. An afterthought.

But it was illusion he'd loved. He learned that at Pons. The CRAV's soft, human heart was already broken; and a few hours from now, the hard armor would rupture, too.

Tears welled up in his eyes, ran down his cheeks, collected at the bottom of his goggles. His sight fogged and he blinked to clear it, going in and out of telescopic vision. Rover was a blue blur.

Gordon felt more than saw the light's presence: steady, curious, and somehow sympathetic. The clatter in his mind was soft and questioning.

"I'm sorry," he told it.

The CRAV was the bait, the staked goat, and when the Arabs advanced to kill the robot, Rover would be forced into a decision to defend or flee.

Rover had saved him before, and the general was gambling it would save him again—save him from an entire Arab division. The question was, how much did Rover love Gordon? And, for Christ's sake, why?

CRAV COMMAND, TRÁS-OS-MONTES, PORTUGAL

Pelham pretended not to notice that Gordon was crying. "Get some downtime," he said. "We sent a surveillance drone up, and it looks like you have three hours."

Without reply, Gordon slipped the gloves off his hands and wiped the tears from his cheeks.

"The light won't go away, will it?" Pelham asked.

"I don't think so, sir."

"Good," he said, nodding vaguely. "Good."

Gordon got up and started to leave the room, but the colonel took his arm. "I want to talk to you. I got you some dinner, and there's a cot set up in the monitoring station."

Following Pelham to his office, Gordon found a meal waiting. A whole New York strip, a mound of fries, and broccoli with cheese. It looked like the colonel had ordered from the officers' mess.

"Sit down." He waved a hand toward his desk. "Go ahead. Dig in. I've already eaten."

Gingerly Gordon sat in the colonel's leatherette swivel chair. It was a big seat for a big man and Gordon felt lost in it. He picked up the knife and fork and cut a slice of the steak. Pink blood ran from the center and gathered in a murder-scene pool around the potatoes.

"The main Arab army is moving fast, so fast they're playing hell with their logistics," Pelham told him. "They're headed across the border to Perpignan."

Gordon looked up from his squeamish scrutiny of the blood.

"The French are driving their forces east to meet them, hoping to Christ we've covered their backside. General Lauterbach is deploying our own troops in Figueras. The French will drive the Arabs right into our 3rd Armored."

Gordon put a chunk of steak into his mouth. It was body-warm. Unable to swallow, he surreptitiously spit it out into a napkin.

"I wanted you to know this," Pelham went on. "I wanted you to know how important your mission is. Unless we catch the Arabs in the Pyrenees totally by surprise, they'll regroup. We'll jam their communications so they can't call ahead to warn the main army. But we can't jam them for-ever, son. We've got to take them quick and mop up."

Gordon put his fork down wearily on the plate.

"Look at me," Pelham said.

Slowly Gordon lifted his gaze.

"It's just a robot."

"I know that, sir."

"Would you like me . . ." His voice trailed off for a moment in chagrin or compassion. "Would you like me to be there? To sit beside you or something? Just as a reminder that . . ." The colonel's voice failed him again.

That I'm not really dying.

"Yes, sir," Gordon said. "That might be nice, sir."

"I know you don't like to be touched, but . . ."

"I understand, sir," Gordon said quickly, plucking the colonel from the brink of embarrassment. "If I feel a hand on my arm, I won't take the goggles off. I won't close my eyes."

"Yes," the colonel told him. "That's very important. You'll want to, I know. But you can't close your eyes."

Not close them. Not even when he saw the approaching shell.

Pelham glanced at Gordon's full plate. "No appetite?"

"Can't eat, sir."

"Well." The colonel looked distractedly around his office as though it were unfamiliar. "Want to lie down for a while?"

"Yes, sir. I'll try that, sir."

Gordon walked to the monitoring room and lay down on the cot. When his head touched the pillow, he spasmed once, as if he were falling, and tumbled off the precipice of sleep.

IN THE LIGHT

Jerry was sitting in the grass with his Pa, watching the pilot toss stones into the lake. It was either sunset or dawn. The sky was a raspberry-sherbet pink at the horizon and a deep, starry cobalt above. Birds, black silhouettes, darted across the heavens.

Dew was falling, condensing on Jerry's arms and his face, as though the solicitous breeze were pressing a cool washcloth against his fevered skin.

"I'm not a coward," the pilot said.

Neither Jerry nor his Pa answered. There was no need. Jerry knew that if the pilot hadn't wanted to come, his Pa wouldn't have brought him. Pa wasn't a forceful man, with a booming, scary voice and stinging slaps. He wasn't made up of have-to's.

Jerry watched the stars wink on. Evening. It was evening.

"I mean, everyone's scared sometimes, aren't they?" the pilot asked. "I wasn't any more scared than anyone else."

Pa turned to Jerry. "Why don't you look in the cooler, Jerry? I bet there's some ice cream there."

Jerry looked behind him and saw a Coca-Cola cooler in the grass. He lifted the lid. Inside, nestled into chunks of ice, was a white plastic spoon and a pint of Blue Bell Strawberries and Cream.

"Growing boys like sweets," his Pa said.

Jerry licked the ice cream off the paper lid. The pilot threw a stone into the lake. The concentric circles caught the candy-pink glow of the dying sun.

"You like throwing things?" Jerry asked. He popped a frozen strawberry into his mouth and sucked on it.

"What do you mean?" The pilot's voice was sharp.

"Chunking rocks. Throwing missiles."

Justin started to lunge to his feet and come after Jerry, but Pa stopped him. "Boys," he said indulgently, grabbing the pilot's arm. "Sometimes they play too rough. Sometimes fathers have to intervene. Why don't you have some ice cream, Justin? Some ice cream will take your mind off things."

With a surly tug, the pilot freed his arm. "Nobody likes killing, kid, unless he's sick. And nobody but a coward punches out unless he has to. My RIO was wrong, you know that? Tyler wasn't flying that plane. He couldn't feel the way the pole was jerking. It wasn't that I was scared of landing. We were going down," he said. Doubt fogged his eyes. "We were going down."

Then he started throwing rocks again, his movements furious.

Jerry was finishing up the pint of Blue Bell when the man in the camouflage and the Nikes came walking down the hill. He stopped near Jerry and sat, arms around his knees. He stared out into the water.

Jerry saw the man was crying. "What's wrong?" he asked.

"Guy's a loser," the pilot muttered. "A fuck-up. A real gomer."

The man swiveled. His eyes were a pale blue and Jerry could see the edge of the lake and the trees through them. "I need your help," the man said. Then his face went blank, as though the next thought had dropped through the gauzy pan of his brain.

"Let me tell you about chunking missiles, kid," the pilot said, ignoring the soldier in the camouflage. "You know when your plane's sick. You can feel it. There's this part of you that becomes part of the plane."

Jerry turned to the soldier and saw the man wasn't looking their way. Wasn't listening. He was staring across the lake, at the clatter of the reeds, an expression of longing on his face.

Suddenly the soldier in the Nikes stood up. Across the grass an Arab was walking, a swarthy ANA officer. The two confronted each other: the Arab yearningly; the American in stunned recognition. Then the Arab went to the tumbledown boathouse. Doorknob in hand, the Arab paused. Finally he shook his head and walked inside.

"You become the plane when you fly, Justin," Pa was saying. "But you don't become the plane the way this man would become the light." There was a smile, sweet as brickle and chocolate, melting down Pa's face.

"Gordon doesn't know it yet," Pa said so lovingly that Jerry felt a jealous pang. "But he would like to fly the light."

Jerry put the empty ice-cream carton back in the cooler.

When he looked again, the transparent man in the camouflage uniform was gone.

THE PYRENEES, ABOVE THE SWITCHBACK AT LLIVIA

He heard them coming long before he saw them. The
army moved with a low, grinding noise that echoed back
and forth between the limestone canyons. Like the warning
growl in the throat of a tiger.

Gordon glanced behind him. Rover hung low near the
CRAV obediently, just as he had been told. His light was
so dim, it was barely discernible from the moon-splattered
rocks.

Quickly Gordon swiveled his head around. He wondered
when the tanks would come into view. Just out of sight of
the plastiqued switchback, he wouldn't see the Arabs until
they were on him.

And then, if luck was with the Allies, the Arabs would
stop. The whole line of vehicles would stop. He imagined
them rolling blind up the sharp S-curve, each tank commander not realizing that the vehicle ahead wasn't moving until
he almost collided with it.

And when they were bottlenecked along the S-curve like
the worst of bumper-to-bumper traffic, the Israelis would
blow the limestone wall.

Gordon wouldn't hear the rumble as the cliff came down.
He'd be dead before that.

His first death had been a lightning bolt: a hot blast of
stinging shrapnel, a clap of thunder. This time he knew it
was coming. His teeth chattered. He shook so much that
the robot arms shuddered in their mounts and clattered like
Rover.

The sound of the approaching army grew louder. It wasn't
a growl anymore; it was a roar.

Gordon was going to run. He knew it. No one should
have to have this sort of courage. He was breathing hard
now, gulping air. His face wore a mask of greasy sweat.

Someone put a hand on his arm—Pelham, probably.

Gordon nearly came out of the command chair screaming.

Just a robot, he reminded himself. Sweat rolled down from his brows and dropped, stinging, into his eyes. He fought the urge to close them. He fought the intense need to blink.

I'm just a robot.

THE PYRENEES, BELOW THE SWITCHBACK AT LLIVIA

Wasef checked his digital watch. Three in the morning, he saw with surprise.

Settling back into his seat, he watched the lead tank, a ghost in the moonlight, negotiate the long S-curve of the road. Above him a limestone cliff rose to dizzying heights, its moon-soaked face marred by small fissures and rain-gouged holes.

Beside him Gamal stirred, and Wasef wondered if the boy had been asleep. If he had been dreaming.

"What time is it?" Gamal asked, yawning.

"Zero three hundred."

The road ahead, dull pewter in the moonlight, seemed to hang to the side of the mountain as though dangling by sheer grit.

"I've made you a promise," Gamal told him. "Now you make me one."

"Yes, all right," Wasef said. The jeep was fully into the switchback, and the high cliffs blocked the moon.

"If I don't get back," Gamal said, "tell my father I love him."

"You'll be there to tell him yourself when we meet his division in France."

The idea of France was so strange. There was no place for him below, Wasef knew. Spain was distant as the years-old memory of Egypt; and France was a mist-and-shadow place. Wasef belonged here, in this no-man's-land of giddy heights and dark stone.

They moved out of the end of the S and around a blind corner, the jeep hugging the wall. Below him the mountain fell away so far, Wasef could no longer see the stream. They were now even with the immense peaks, like flies bumping the ceiling of the world.

The jeep braked hard, throwing the colonel forward against the front seat. "What?" he asked. Then he heard the shouts from the lead tank.

"I don't know, sir," the driver said, turning around.

Nudging the rear bumper of Wasef's jeep, the following tank stopped. Its commander was standing up in the turret, calling to the tank ahead.

"Maybe an obstacle," the driver of the jeep said.

Wasef climbed over the front seat, the hood, and pulled himself one-handed up on the deck of the forward tank. In the muted glow of the T-62's headlights he could see something blocking the road. Lifting his night-vision scope, he began to pick out details, unexpectedly familiar details. Treads; metal arms resting about a round turret.

For a moment he thought he was dreaming. Then he dropped the glasses. "Fire!" he screamed.

The sergeant gave him a puzzled look. Did the tank commander not see it?

"Kill it, damn you! It is the American remote!"

The commander looked down into the hole and snapped out an order. The turret made a grinding noise as the barrel of the cannon moved into firing position.

The little remote stood its ground, no missile tubes showing. Was it incapacitated? Wasef wondered. Was the operator crazy?

"Fire," the TC said.

The tank shook as the shell left the tube. The jolt knocked Wasef to his knees. For a heartbeat the mountain lit up with flame, a hot strobe that cast the naked rocks in orange and hard black shadows.

The robot was no *djinn*, Wasef saw to his relief, but a solid thing of plastic and steel. The armor-piercing shell went right through it, flaying steel skin, laying open sizzling wire nerves and computer-component organs. The force of the impact swatted it around a half-turn. An instant later it burst into flame.

"Push it off the mountain," he ordered. He was turning

away when the TC began to scream.

Nightmare was back full force. A blue light had burst out of the burning guts of the robot and was making for them at dizzying speed.

The TC pulled himself from the turret and ran, pushing Wasef aside in his haste. The tank began to move, not forward to push the demolished remote from the road, but backward.

"Stop!" Wasef shouted.

No use. The tank hit the jeep with a squeal of buckling metal, crushing it into the T-72 behind. The first tank lifted as it began to climb the wreck.

In the sickly light from the burning robot, Wasef saw Gamal trapped in the accordioned backseat. The captain's eyes were bulging with terror as he pumped rounds from his sidearm into the tank's impervious armor.

The T-62's treads clanged a quick rhythm up the metal chassis of the jeep. Dropping to his knees and sliding, Wasef grasped the scorching metal of the cannon to stay his fall.

"Stop! Stop, damn it!" Wasef beat the butt of his own Glock 9mm into the decking of the driver's cubbyhole.

The tank clambered the rest of the way. A shriek of metal drowned out Gamal's final scream.

Turret closed, the T-72 was trying to retreat. Incredulously Wasef saw it collide with the tank to its rear, then watched it, transmission still grinding in reverse, slew right, and tumble off the mountain.

"Stop!" Wasef shouted.

But his men weren't stopping. They were falling back in a panic, firing machine guns at the cavorting light. Wasef heard bullets ping off the metal deck beside him, heard the peevish whines of the ricochets. With a gasp he dove for the safety of the hatch. Too late. Bullets slammed into his stomach, his legs—one, two, three—their impacts like fists. He sprawled face-up across the night-cooled metal.

"Stop," he whispered. Above him the stars twinkled like distant artillery.

No one, not even the stars, was listening. The three remaining members of the first tank crew abandoned their vehicle and fled into the darkness, through hysterical gunfire.

A cramp stitched Wasef's belly. He drew his left leg up to ease the pain. He was suddenly very tired. Too tired to move, to think.

From the switchback came an earth-shattering series of booms, so loud that the mountain shook to its foundations. Somewhere rock was falling, clattering like metal rain.

Wasef moaned as another cramp hit and bent him in two. When it was over, he lay back panting and sweating in the cold, star-struck night. He heard his men screaming but was too exhausted to go see what was wrong.

All the victims of the famine, even Zahra, had left life furtively. Sometimes he imagined he had been there when her death came. That she had passed away in his arms and not in an offical army letter.

Zahra died in black and white, embossed with a govern-mental seal.

He rolled his head to the side. Zahra was there in the reeds, an arm's reach away. The papyrus was tapping in the wind. "So tired," he told her. He was so tired of it all: the fighting, the foxhole nights.

Zahra smiled. The Nile at her feet reflected the stars. Something was burning, something that stank of smoldering insulation.

Sharp-toothed pain bit again. He raised his shoulders weakly. Somewhere under him, he knew, Gamal lay buried in a steel grave. How odd fate was. He'd thought that Gamal, not he, would be shot by his men.

It was too quiet. There was no rumble of engines, no squeak of sprockets. On the other side of the switchback something was happening to Wasef's army. Something . . .

He sucked in a breath and held it, hoping the agony would leave. He closed his eyes. Zahra was standing ankle-deep in the blue Nile, blue as the desert sky, blue as lapis stone.

The reeds were clattering.

IN THE LIGHT

Across the silent library, someone was weeping. Rita made her way down the aisle of books, books silvery in the glimmer from the high windows. At an oak table trimmed in a barley twist design sat General Lauterbach, his head in his hands.

She walked over. At her approach, he raised his head. Not weeping, she saw. Laughing. Lauterbach was laughing.

His face, unlike Dr. Gladdings's, didn't change. Muted light glinted off his balding head, off the stars on his collar. Through his shoulder she could see the edge of the stacks, the spines of the books.

"It worked," he said.

But then his face *did* alter. It went from a smile to a grimace of concern. "Rita?" he whispered cautiously, as though afraid his voice might shatter her, and the library, into silver-plated pieces.

"Rita? Is that you?"

"Too bad they killed us both," she told him and walked away.

"Rita!" he called.

She didn't stop. Dr. Gladdings was waiting for her by the fireplace. "I have a question about pain," he said.

"Really?" She cocked her head and listened: the general's calls were silenced, absorbed by the cottony air.

"Come," Dr. Gladdings said.

She followed him to an anteroom. On the marble floor a soldier was dying.

He was an Arab, she saw. An officer. One arm in a cast. Blood had turned the uniform below his waist a clotted, dirty red.

"Do you think he will die?" Dr. Gladdings asked.

Rita studied the man's injuries. Through a hole in his left thigh pumped arterial blood. The tear in the lower quadrant of his shirt suggested a serious abdominal wound. The officer was raising his knee gingerly toward his stomach, as though in great pain.

She looked at his face. He smiled weakly at her.

"Is there a hospital near?"

"No," Dr. Gladdings said.

"Then he won't make it," she concluded.

"Which is better: pain or death?" Dr. Gladdings asked.

"There shouldn't be any pain," Rita said.

Death had always been a thing she dealt with easily. Pain, on the other hand, was not. It was the babies in the hospital mewling in their sleep, it was the adults whimpering in their delirium, who had pushed her into pathology where she saw only the consequences of suffering, not its messy, inhuman process.

Dr. Gladdings's lips stretched into a sagging-dough smile. He handed her the pointer. "Kill him," he said.

She took the stick. The wood was as cold as frozen metal.

"Kill him," Dr. Gladdings coaxed. "Look how he wants you to."

The Arab was staring up at her, his liquid eyes dark with yearning, his long face tight with pain.

"It's all an illusion," she told Dr. Gladdings. "Lauterbach, this Arab. It's all some sort of game."

"Won't you play a hand of poker with me, then?" the doctor asked, teasing. "Won't you play a little, Rita? You were always such a serious girl."

She brought the pointer down and touched the Arab to the right of his sternum. His dark eyes widened in surprise. They didn't shut again.

Rita whirled and walked into the main part of the library. Outside the windows, freezing rain was covering the leaves with ice. Lauterbach wasn't there. The Arab, when she tried the anteroom a while later, was gone as well.

NEAR FIGUERAS, CATALONIA, SPAIN

Frustrated, horrified, General Sabry stood up in his BRMD scout, holding the cupola cover before him like a shield.

It was all happening so fast that Sabry couldn't think. His troops had lost their reason in the blood-soaked marshes near Perpignan. He'd called for a strategic fallback by figures. The tanks should have leapfrogged, making the French bleed for every kilometer they gained. But somewhere in that retreat they'd lost leadership just as they had lost communications—jammed by ECM and terror. His demoralized men transformed a retreating army into a scrambling mob.

The French must have been hoarding petrol. That was it. They had hoarded their jet fuel and lied to their Allies. Hadn't Sabry read all the intelligence reports? The Americans had been on their knees begging for fuel while the French insisted they had none.

Now the French were spending every stockpiled drop to kill Sabry's two divisions. Jaguars and Mirages. A never-ending deluge of fire and steel. The Dauphin helicopters stayed airborne after the initial disastrous air combat, not bothering to keep to nap-of-the-earth flight. After the first hour of battle nothing Arab moved in the skies; and now all that was Arab on the ground was fleeing.

Behind him he heard a bone-shattering boom as a HOT missile hit. A second struck a BMP nearby, sending flames and smoke rushing skyward.

Sabry pushed his bulk down from the cupola and dropped into the cabin of the BRDM. Major el-Hakim was cowering against the wall. The cramped interior of the scout vehicle was filled with the sharp stink of nervous sweat.

"The nearest town!" Sabry shouted over the growl of the engine.

"Sir?" The major's eyes were blank with fear.

"Damn you! The nearest town! What is it?"

"Figueras, sir," the driver answered.

"How far?" the general asked, turning away from the paralyzed officer.

"Twelve kilometers due east," the driver said. "We will have to go through Figueras, sir, to cross the bridge there."

"Defensible?" Sabry asked el-Hakim, raising his voice to be heard over the engine noise.

The major didn't answer.

"Where are the maps, damn it!" Sabry screamed.

"Sir," the driver said. "Figueras, if you'll recall, is a crossroad town. There are flat marshes leading to it, and a river valley. Probably very defensible, sir."

Sabry felt hot embarrassment rise in his face as he realized that he, too, had caught the panic. Hysteria was making morons of them all.

Sabry tore the radio from el-Hakim's hand. "They overran

us, sir," the major was babbling. "Where did they get so much fuel for their planes? How could that happen? And there was no artillery, did you see that? No artillery. Colonel Wasef's division should have been on the heights."

Sabry tried to raise Colonel Abbas. All that came over the radio was the roar of ECM.

Yes, Wasef should have been on the heights with his artillery and Sagger missiles. What had detained his flanking division, his favorite officer, his only son?

The radio spat static. "Colonel Abbas?" Sabry called.

Sabry could hear terror in the colonel's high-pitched shout. "Sir!"

"We regroup in Figueras, colonel," Sabry told him. There was no composure anymore, not for Sabry, not for his men. There was only a fifty-kilometer killing ground from here to Perpignan, a slaughtering floor, a place of shame.

"Yes, sir." But there was a question in the colonel's voice.

Sabry knew what that question was: How in the world do we regroup? The army had become a mass of lemmings. They might not stop until they foundered in the Mediterranean Sea.

"Send word down the line, colonel," Sabry told him. "Tell them they stop and regroup in Figueras or our own tanks will kill them and get the slaughter over with."

"Yes, sir."

Sabry put the radio down and stepped up into the cupola rim, pushing his bulk through the hole. Raising his field glasses, he made a sweep of the pale green grass, the river, and the abandoned town beyond.

A flash. Sunlight winking off metal, perhaps. A second flash, then the ripping sound of a shell overhead.

All of Figueras had begun to twinkle, a daylight sparkler.

"Artillery!" he screamed, dropping down into the cabin again. In his corner by the radio, el-Hakim sat frozen. The driver was jigging back and forth along the grass, bruising the tires on stones, slewing the rough-riding vehicle so sharply, Sabry almost fell to his knees.

Too quickly the Allied artillery found Sabry's range. The

earth shook. Red light strobed from the open cupola. Thunderous cracks—near misses.

Sabry was flanked. Turn back, and they would fall into the deadly French rain. South lay the sea; to the north, the mountains.

A shell slammed into the BRDM's side. The vehicle reeled, tolled like a bell. Sabry was flung against the bulkhead. Blood gushed from his nose, pooling warm in his lap.

The driver was shouting something, but all Sabry could hear was an angry-hornet buzzing.

He had to think. If he didn't act quickly, everyone under his command would die. If he didn't act now, the next shell would kill him.

He glanced up and saw the driver staring. Sweat had turned the boy's white undershirt dark, and blood trickled from his ears and nose. Sabry reached for the radio and screamed into it, "Surrender!"

Outside the cupola, fireworks flickered like a Judgment Day cryptogram.

The BRDM scout was motionless now. Sabry wasn't sure whether it was the engine that had failed or the courage of the driver.

"Give me your undershirt!"

The driver couldn't hear. Either the explosions were too loud or the boy, too, had gone temporarily deaf. With quick, impatient gestures, the general made himself understood.

Snatching the offered undershirt, Sabry crawled up in the cupola. He lifted the makeshift white flag in the air. At that instant the scout vehicle lunged as though trying to mount the sky. From the depths of the cabin something snatched the general's legs and jerked him hungrily down.

Sabry forced open his eyes. Blood had glued them shut. He was lying on his back in the cabin of the BRDM, afternoon sunlight from the rent in the scout's side painting Major el-Hakim in brass. An unexploded shell lay across Sabry's leg.

He tried to move. Splintery pain halted him. Outside the

ruins of the vehicle was a long, wide silence, a hush that stretched for miles.

El-Hakim, chest pinned to the wall by the thick, unwieldy point of the shell, was staring at his commander reproachfully. Blood had crusted down his chin like a dark, untrimmed beard.

"Major," Sabry whispered.

The major's glazed eyes did not shift. The grimace of pain did not soften.

Sabry could not get his mind to work. Wasef and Gamal were waiting, waiting for his army to punch through France. Yet it seemed he also remembered that in the sweet spring grass of Catalonia his army had been ambushed.

A rattle and clang at the side of the BRDM.

"Sir!" an American voice shouted. "Hey, sir? There's an unexploded round in here. And some fucking high-ranking Arab!"

A moment later, Sabry felt the ruined scout bounce. He blinked up into the face of an American lieutenant. Under the rim of the helmet, the boy's eyes were wide with awe.

What was it Sabry wanted to say? Ah, yes. He remembered. "Surrender," he whispered.

The boy left.

Later, five more Americans pushed their way inside. They bent to examine Sabry's leg, the shell, the corpse of Major el-Hakim.

"Surrender," the general said, but they weren't listening. Westerners never listened. That's what the entire war was about.

"We can't move that shell. Amputate?" a lieutenant asked a captain.

The captain nodded. "Leg's a goner, anyway."

"Surrender," Sabry said. Couldn't they hear? He was surrendering his army, the best part of himself.

The captain bent over. "What's he saying?"

A sergeant shrugged. "Beats me."

"I don't like the looks of that scalp wound. We'll give him a local. Get a tourniquet on that leg." The captain knelt beside Sabry and looked into his eyes. "General? Can you hear me? Can you understand English?"

"Yes," Sabry told him.

The captain turned to the sergeant. "Start me an IV drip, please."

Sabry grabbed the captain's hand and held it fast. "I surrender to you."

The officer moved his brief attention from the sergeant to Sabry. "Okay. You're going to be all right. We'll have you out of here in five minutes. Harris?" he shouted. "Make sure you hold that chopper."

The sergeant ripped the sleeve of Sabry's battle shirt and expertly slid a needle into Sabry's elbow. A private tore open the buttons of the general's blouse and set the cold pads of an EKG on his chest.

"Where's the lidocaine?" Sabry heard the captain ask in a voice calm as a placid lake.

Easy for the Americans to be calm, Sabry thought. The Allied army was a killing machine. The M1-A1s never broke down like the old Soviet tanks; he had never seen the Allies flee in panic. Oh, Allah. How had he lost the Western campaign?

"General? General?" The American captain was shaking his shoulder.

Sabry opened his eyes.

"You'll feel pressure, and possibly some discomfort. Please don't move. There is an unexploded shell on you. If you're in too much pain, just tell me."

Just tell him. That was the whole point, wasn't it?

Sabry heard the twin snaps as the surgeon put on his gloves. And faintly, just before he fell unconscious again, he heard the noisy whine of a saw.

"I surrender," he mumbled.

No one was listening.

CHAPTER 14

AUTUMN, WARSAW, POLAND

In the watery light, Baranyk sat on the bench, drinking Polish vodka and watching Chopin. The composer regarded Baranyk with irritating forbearance, as though absolving him for the dusty and drunken intrusion into his rose garden. There was a white streak of pigeon shit on Chopin's cheek. Baranyk wondered where the pigeon had gone and if it had ended up as someone's poor dinner.

"Fuck you," Baranyk told Chopin, lifting the bottle in a toast. "Tchaikovsky was better. Shostakovich and Prokofiev were better. Even Moussorgsky was better, and he was a goddamned lazy Russian. A worthless son of a bitch."

Leaning back on the bench, Baranyk lifted his face to the sun. November already, and the hot breeze made him sweat.

He closed his eyes and let the warm sun beat on his lids. "Fuck the Russians, too," he whispered.

The sound of footsteps on gravel. He turned toward the museum, a huge Napoleon pastry among the flowers, and saw Andrzej Czajowski making his way over. The Pole was singing "Mother of God" as he walked.

Czajowski stopped at Baranyk's side and gazed down with the gentle understanding of Chopin, of Mary. His uniform hung on him, a suit on a straw scarecrow. There were dark bags under his eyes.

"You sing your national anthem off-key," Baranyk told him.

The Pole smiled. "This is not a crime."

"It should be."

Czajowski appeared to be waiting for an invitation to sit down. When none came, he sat down anyway.

Baranyk contemplated the statue, the pigeonless lawn. "Does it bother you," he asked, "that everything we lived for is gone?"

Czajowski lifted an eyebrow.

"Communism," Baranyk explained. "Communism has become a crazy aunt Tatiana: no one in the family dares mention her name. Once it was a good thing to be a proper Communist. Once I won medals for this very reason. Now I am supposed to be ashamed of it? How is it that we speak of our former lives in whispers?"

"Oh, that:" Czajowski shrugged. "If you must know, I believe Communism was Hell designed by incompetent bureaucrats." The Pole sat silently for a while, staring at Chopin, as though waiting for the composer to scoff at Communism, too. "Perhaps the past wouldn't bother you if you didn't drink."

"Ah, but I drink to forget," Baranyk said, tipping the bottle to his mouth.

The Pole gave him a critical glance. "By now, surely, you have forgotten your own mother."

Air-raid sirens began to shriek. Neither man moved.

"General Lauterbach thinks to send a division to help break the siege," Czajowski told him, stretching his legs on the gravel walk. "He plans to meet with Weiderhausen."

"Weiderhausen would rather eat shit than get his army dirty," Baranyk sniffed. "He will dig in at the German border. Lauterbach doesn't dare send a division. He has more Arab prisoners than Allied soldiers. If he turns his attention away, the Arabs will revolt."

Czajowski had begun humming the anthem again, much to Baranyk's annoyance.

"I tell you, Andrzej," Baranyk said. "When the Arabs learn how little matériel we have, and they crush through us on their way to Germany, the Americans will see the wisdom of negotiation. Germany will not hold. Do you hear me? Germany cannot hold."

A distant smile on his face, Czajowski continued humming. Baranyk wondered how the man could find the tune amidst the shrieks of the sirens. A moment later, with a fierce rattling sound, AAA stitched the blue sky.

"If this is a Scud and not bombers," Baranyk muttered, "I will have that antiaircraft commander's balls for dinner," he said, and then guffawed, "Meat for a change."

"It would be nice to have more of the American ERINT missiles to shoot down the Scuds."

Baranyk looked at the Pole in disbelief. "And perhaps we can have Mickey Mouse climb out of his Florida ocean like a drowned rat to deliver them. And Prince Charming Lauterbach will bring them strapped to his white charger. Or perhaps your beloved Virgin can simply make more ERINTs, since the Americans have such a problem with production. Do you miss the birds?" Baranyk asked.

Czajowski turned a questioning face toward him.

"Every pigeon a roasting hen; every sparrow a squab. Warsaw is empty of rats, have you noticed?" Baranyk said. "Are you hungry enough so that you wonder at times how surrender tastes?"

In a soft voice Czajowski asked, "Do *you* want to surrender?"

"Three months we have been trapped here," Baranyk replied. "What will happen when winter comes?"

"It was winter when the Germans left Leningrad. It was winter that defeated Napoleon in Russia. The Arabs are not accustomed to the cold. Perhaps—"

"Wake up, my friend. Mickey Mouse is dead. There are no more Communists. And there are no more winters like that," Baranyk told him. "What do we fight with when the ammunition runs out?"

"We throw stones," the Pole said. "I don't know. Do *you* want to surrender? It is not your fight. It is not your country."

The alert wasn't for a Scud. Bombs began to fall east

of them, a sound like giants on the march. Baranyk took a breath. Warsaw smelled like a defeated town. It stank of cabbage and exhaustion and roses.

"Fuck surrender," he snarled.

"The men gossip that you are becoming an alcoholic."

Baranyk sat up from his comfortable slouch and looked Czajowski in the eye. Nearby, much too close, a bomb vibrated the earth. Both generals flinched, then saw each other's embarrassment.

"Fuck you, too," Baranyk laughed.

CRAV COMMAND, TRÁS-OS-MONTES, PORTUGAL

Gordon tracked a strip of sunlight across the linoleum of the clinic floor. Inch by inch, it made its way toward him, a quiet incursion.

"Maybe you'd like to talk about what happened," the doctor was saying.

Gordon put his foot out. A wavelet of sunlight splashed over his slippered toe.

"Sergeant Means?"

Gordon looked at the window. The screen divided the yard into small squares of information, like pixels. In the window, a pointless movie was playing: three Arab prisoners in a flower bed planting chubby-faced pansies under the watchful eye of their guard.

The doctor was a voice-over. "Sometimes it helps to talk about things."

Steps. A walk-on part. A new voice said: "Well?"

"No response. He's not aphasic, I think. He responds well to orders."

Gordon had always responded well to orders. Go here. Go there. Stand and die. The movie screen with the Arab prisoners blurred.

The voice-overs were silent for a moment. At his side he could feel the intense scrutiny of the camera, its lens a dead fish eye.

"The colonel's here. He wants to see him."

"I don't see why not."

Lots of quiet footsteps. An exit; an entrance. Gordon felt a touch on his arm and reflexively turned. Pelham was looking at him. "Hello, sergeant," the colonel said.

There was a creak in the sound track as the colonel took a chair.

"I brought you something," he said.

From his pocket he took a Milky Way bar and set it on the table between them. Its wrapper the same sweet brown as the man's hand.

"Hide it," Pelham said.

Hide it. Like a CRAV among the rocks.

"Go ahead, son. Hide it."

Gordon snatched the candy from the table and shoved it hurriedly into the pocket of his pajamas. Pelham was watching him. Gordon didn't know what else he wanted him to do. Gordon would do anything. Hadn't he proved that already? Why were they testing him again?

"That's right. That's good." The voice was meant to be soothing, but there was something wrong with it. Something sad and horrified. "You just keep it out of sight, son. Maybe I could bring you one of your comic books, too. Would you like that?"

Gordon closed his eyes. He was at the lake again. Jerry was fishing, and the alien sat baiting a hook.

"You're back," the alien said.

"Yes." At Gordon's feet, water lapped against the pilings. The reeds across the lake tapped out an eerie movie score. "I like this," Gordon told him.

Soft edges, that was the thing. Hard edges hurt when you fell down. You could bust your chin open. You could crack your skull.

Nintendo had soft edges: the round, pumpkin heads of the Mario Brothers, the indistinct beep-beeps as they moved.

This calm lake, this quiet grass, he knew, was an illusion without razor-edged sorrow. "I could stay here forever," Gordon told him.

The kid, Jerry, whirled around with a glare of jealousy. The alien, face sagging, dropped his sinker into the lake and smiled.

"Good," Pelham was saying.

Gordon opened his eyes.

"It's good, cheating every once in a while, don't you think?"

Gordon had lost the thread of the plot. He stared at Pelham curiously, and then turned to look out the window. To his relief that same movie with the Arab prisoners was playing, the same stars, the same extras.

Nothing at all had changed.

CENTRAL ARMY HOSPITAL, BADAJOZ, SPAIN

Rashid Aziz Sabry grasped the cold metal bars in his hands and attempted the walk back. At the end of the walkway his physical therapist, Lieutenant Alvarez, crouched in wait like a spider.

The general's slippered, mutinous feet jerked out of his control. The lieutenant stood up, reaching, as if prepared to catch him.

I'm too old to relearn walking, Sabry thought with disgust. And far too fat for the small lieutenant to catch. He grimaced, braced himself more firmly on the bars, and began his slow, painful shuffle.

"Good. That's very good," Alvarez was saying.

Sabry glared at his recalcitrant feet, searching for any sign of rebellion.

"Excellent. I can tell you're making progress."

Wouldn't the woman shut up? It annoyed Sabry to be patronized. To be cajoled. And Alvarez was a patronizing, cajoling woman.

"Good. Good. Just a few steps more, and— Good morning, sir."

At the surprise in Alvarez's voice, Sabry glanced up and almost lost his footing. The pin in his hip pinched, reprimanding him for his inattention.

An American general was standing at the end of the walkway, a small, spare man. Sabry froze, seeing the four stars lined up on the man's collar. But then he doggedly lowered his head and resumed his agonized, halting shamble toward the reprieve of the wheelchair.

"I didn't mean to disturb you, sir."

The American had a clipped voice, but it was somehow not unkind. Sabry halted in the middle of the walkway, panting. He looked at the man again. Odd, that the American should look so tired now that the western campaign was over.

"You do not disturb me," he replied stiffly. Then, with a self-deprecating laugh, he added, "The artificial leg disturbs me. The pin in my hip disturbs me. Living my life in pajamas disturbs me. Not you."

Sabry was astonished to see embarrassment in the man's face. Suddenly the American turned to Alvarez. "Is he finished with the operations?"

Keeping his eyes on his wayward feet, Sabry continued the slow, sickroom march. The stump below his knee was a burning agony now. And there was a cramp in his hip.

"He'll have the final skin graft in two days."

Reaching the end of the walkway, Sabry fumbled desperately for Alvarez. But it was the American general who grabbed him tightly under the arms and wrestled his bulk into the chair.

Sabry sagged into the seat, massaging his thigh.

"I'm T. Williams Lauterbach," the general said.

"I know," Sabry told him without looking up. Sabry knew more than the American general's name; he knew his manner of fighting.

"Perhaps it would be good now to send the lieutenant away," Sabry suggested. "Perhaps we could talk alone."

The lieutenant left. The room was empty except for a paraplegic American moaning under the harsh ministrations of his therapist.

How strange, Sabry thought, to be sitting with his enemy, so close that he could smell his sweat. He glanced down and noticed that Lauterbach's boots were scuffed, his BDUs mud-spattered and wrinkled. Sabry wished he could have met his adversary in uniform rather than in a robe and pajamas.

"I have been told nothing," Sabry complained.

"That's in keeping with the Geneva convention, sir."

Sabry brought his palm down hard on his leg, a little punishment for its earlier defiance. "To hell with the Geneva convention, General Lauterbach. What happened to my division in the Pyrenees?"

He saw the answer in Lauterbach's cautious face. "Our countries are still at war, general."

Tears welled in Sabry's eyes. Lauterbach had seen Sabry's army slip from his control; and now witnessed his body's insubordination.

"My son was on that mountain!" Sabry snapped.

Lauterbach froze. Then nodded curtly. "Give me his name," he said. "I'll find out for you."

"Gamal Rashid. He was—is a captain." Sabry looked away, avoiding the American's weary face. There were answers there, but even more questions.

Yes, Sabry decided. Something was very, very wrong.

CENTCOM, BARCELONA, SPAIN

Mrs. Parisi heard the guards at her door snap to attention and knew that meant the general had come back. Since her move to Spain, he came to her a lot. She had been good at the Game, and he had become so needy that now the other officers resented her. She was "the general's pet palm reader," she was "that split-tail Rasputin," and when she took her daily constitutional around the base, she could feel the heat of the officers' displeasure.

"Good morning," the general said stiffly. He was always formal with her, and she hadn't bothered to correct that. She wanted him formal, she wanted a little distance. Good Lord, the man was like a fly at a picnic.

"Oh, hello," she said, as though surprised. "How nice to see you."

He didn't bother with pleasantries. He never did. Instead he took a seat on the government-issue sofa and got right to the point.

"I dreamed about the library again," he said.

"How stunning. This means, of course, dear, that the Eridanians like you. Otherwise, they would not let you visit so often."

He waved the compliment aside as usual, but Mrs. Parisi persisted. Men's egos were bottomless pits. And a general's ego must be even deeper. "It's very rare, you know. They've taken quite an interest in you."

"I'm no closer to communication," he said. "They don't come to me, damn it. They won't speak to me. This is the chance of a lifetime, one of the most important events in history. God, don't they know how I feel?"

Lauterbach was frustrated, Mrs. Parisi realized with a thrill of alarm. The Game had traps and pitfalls. There came a perilous moment in it when the subject vacillated between faith and rejection. The general was at that point now. She could read disillusionment in his hazel eyes, along with an addict's keen yearning.

"Well, dear. It's just a matter of time."

He startled her by shouting, "Goddamn it! There isn't any time!" Abruptly he stood and walked to the window. Outside, in the yard, a lethargic rain was falling, turning the prefab walls of the neighboring hospital dark.

She stared at his back, hating him with such an awesome, mind-numbing intensity that she was surprised he could not feel it.

"Warsaw is about to fall," he said. "Before the Arabs have a chance to march into Germany, the President wants to negotiate a peace. He'll give the Arabs half of Europe. I've . . ." For an instant his voice failed him, a disorienting skip in a scratched record. "I want the Eridanians to help us. If I have to stop the Arab advance myself, I'll stop it ugly . . . The aliens' civilization is centuries older than ours. We must seem like children to them. Tell them we need them. For Christ's sake, explain that we're powerless."

"Well, dear. They think war is silly."

She'd lost him. She could see his shoulders slump.

"You must concentrate on dream communication," she said, knowing she must keep him busy at a task. This

Game was the longest and most grueling she had ever played. Let her concentration falter, and she would lose him completely.

He didn't turn. She sat staring at his accusatory back. "I don't understand why you can't tell them yourself," he said.

"The one who wants the help must ask directly, and they're trying to give you that chance. Follow the printed instructions I've given you. Record your dreams every, every night. That's the important thing."

"Sometimes I wonder," he said softly into the open window. The rain-swept breeze tugged at his voice.

"Wonder what?"

"I wonder why I come back."

Mrs. Parisi knew, although she dared not tell him. She was Scheherazade, and he was addicted to her stories. He had to keep coming back to find out how it would end.

IN THE LIGHT

Justin stared at the poster of an angular black F-117 riding the clouds. Above him, attached to the square light fixture, dangled the slender dart-shape of an F-22.

His room was as he remembered it: filled with model planes and toy soldiers. A Bible sat open atop the nightstand, beside the Bugs Bunny lamp. He took a breath. The room smelled the same, too: a mixture of paint and modeling cement.

"Get your bat and glove, Justin," his mother said.

He turned to see her framed in the doorway, a melting form of blue dress and pink flesh. There was no way to tell where the material ended and skin began, or which part was alive.

"Get your bat and glove," she repeated. "Someone's come to play."

Outside the open window, cerise bougainvilleas tapped their enameled petals against each other, impatient nails on wood. He opened his closet and grabbed the bat by its taped handle, his pitcher's glove by its thumb.

"They're waiting," his mother told him.

Without looking into her face, he brushed past her and went into the yard. Mike Johnson was there.

Mike hadn't grown. His blond hair trailed over his forehead the way Justin remembered. He stood in his usual sprung-hip, twelve-year-old stance. Freckles came and went like twinkling dark stars across the pulpy expanse of his cheeks.

"Hi, guy," Mike said.

Justin looked away from Mike to the clouds looming over the neighboring roofs. "I've figured out what you are, you know," Justin whispered. "You're daydreams. You let me see everything I want to see, only nothing's quite right. My F-14 wasn't on fire like I saw out of the bus window, was it? The truth is, I punched out because I didn't have the right stuff anymore."

"Let's choose sides," Mike said. "Let's play some ball."

Justin looked into the street. Beyond the shade of the mango tree five boys were ringed like worshipers about a weak-chinned, skinny soldier. "You brought the gomer?"

"I want to choose sides now," Mike said.

As they walked over, Mike told him, "You choose first."

Justin pointed to a pale imitation of a kid. "Him."

Mike flinched, as though Justin had slapped his spongy cheek. "Well, I want Gordon."

The gomer blinked. Through his uniform, his skin, Justin could see the line of the sidewalk and the grass.

"Oh, don't bother," the sergeant said vaguely. "That's all right. I don't think I need this anymore." He turned and walked away.

When the gomer was out of earshot, Mike turned to Justin. "Why didn't you choose Gordon?" he asked angrily.

"I don't know." There was no way Justin could put his objection into words. He simply didn't like the sergeant's type. The softness in his eyes, the timidity in his hunched shoulders. "What's the big deal with him, anyway?"

"He won a battle all by himself," Mike said. "And then we let him die."

"Too bad," Justin said. He dropped the glove. Grabbing the ball away from one of the kids, he tossed it in the air and hit it with a solid crack from his Louisville Slugger. The ball, of course, flew over the rooftops.

"I don't want to play anymore," Mike said. And all the kids walked away, leaving Justin standing by himself. He stared after them, hurt and frightened by their rejection.

So the gomer had won a battle, and for that the aliens had let him die. The one thing Justin had learned from the aliens was the nature of illusion. But war had taught him that as well. There was no medal of honor worth death, no streets-of-gold reward, no God there to catch him. And in the F-14, Justin had been alone, just he and his decision.

"Yeah?" Justin whispered bitterly. "So you don't want to play anymore? Well, that's too fucking bad."

CRAV COMMAND, TRÁS-OS-MONTES, PORTUGAL

Gordon walked along the beach, the sand sucking at his shoes. Somewhere a gull was cracking a clam against a rock. If he listened closely, he could hear it, a persistent tap-tap.

The boy named Mike walked beside him, scuffing his feet into the water, sending sand-colored crabs racing. Seeing the pallid crabs run was eerie, unsettling, as though Gordon had caught the movement of ghosts at the edge of his vision.

"Gordon?" a voice called.

He opened his eyes. Toshio Ishimoto was sitting next to his bed in the clinic, a frown on his round face.

"Did I wake you?" Toshio asked.

Gordon looked down the bed at his blanketed feet. Past the line of cots, two nurses walked, pallid as crabs, silent as specters.

Toshio's voice was hushed. "I never explained what I saw when the CRAV was swallowed by the light."

Gordon closed his eyes. He was on the beach again, and Mike was staring up at him, his huge eyes dark with affection.

A touch on his arm. Gordon looked around. In the clinic, the movie with Toshio was still playing. "The aliens weren't attacking," Toshio said. "I understand that now. What they offered me was Nirvana, and I was afraid."

Confused by the movie in the clinic, Gordon closed his eyes again. On the shell-laden beach, Mike was talking about the ocean.

"Each molecule is unique," Mike said. "And yet it is part of a whole. When the raindrop hits the waves, it believes it is lost, but only for a frightening moment. Equanimity. Distance. This is what makes you brave. But are you brave enough, Gordon?" He laid a damp, flaccid hand on his arm. "Do you have enough courage to ask for what you want?"

Toshio was saying urgently, "Listen, Gordon. Listen to me."

With an effort, Gordon pulled himself from the beach to the rain-scented clinic, where Toshio was waiting.

"I think you have found such a place," Toshio said. "A sort of Nirvana. But you give yourself too easily, as you gave yourself to the CRAV. Gordon, please. Before you lose yourself completely, come back."

"Come back," Mike whispered.

Gordon closed his eyes and watched the long breakers hiss and foam against the shore. He cocked his head. In the roar of the whitecaps he thought he could hear Toshio's summons.

"What is it?" Mike asked.

Gordon didn't answer; and after a while the sea forgot his name.

CHAPTER 15

IN THE LIGHT

The library held a bell-jar silence. A rainy-day glow silver-plated dust on the sill. Taking a breath that tasted of mold and old books, Rita turned away from the window. The swollen knob of tweed and flesh that looked like Dr. Gladdings was watching.

There was a keen hunger about him.

The real Dr. Gladdings had been a dry soul who sucked up parched answers, a parasite attached to the paper and ink of his books. The replica of Dr. Gladdings sucked her living thoughts.

The touch of the pointer had killed the Arab. The officer's face had changed in an instant from moist brown to desiccated beige. Which had answered some questions. Angels, even those consigned to Purgatory, didn't kill people. And only one thing killed like that.

There were no dry paper-and-ink answers here, just clammy-mouthed ones. If she squashed this Dr. Gladdings, he would leave a stain on the wall, like a leech, a tick, a vampire.

"But he wanted you to drink of him," the false Dr. Gladdings said. "You felt it and responded. You're a good girl, Rita. A kind girl. You always were."

"Shit. I didn't even know he was real. Nothing seemed

234

to matter then. I'm not sure it does now."

Dr. Gladdings's forehead puddled into a frown. "I'm sorry to find you're so cynical, my dear, since you tasted him, too."

She looked away, remembering the oddly pleasant sensation as the pointer fell. The silent stacks of books were leaning slightly toward her, as though their interest had been piqued.

"The Arab had a fine, rich flavor, don't you think, Rita? A taste of date palms and rivers through deserts."

A glissando of fear ran down her back. "Are you going to kill me, too?" she asked.

"If we did, you would taste spicy," Dr. Gladdings said, smacking his rubbery lips. "All shrimp creole and hot jazz."

She kept her gaze on the falling sleet outside the window, in order not to see the blow when it came. She expected to feel the sharp stab of a proboscis, a viscera-deep tug, a sudden, deadly suction. But nothing touched her, only the chill breeze seeping around the edges of the glass.

"Will you?" she asked.

His answer came from a safe distance. "Because you wanted so badly to live, we took you. Why should we kill you now?"

"So why didn't you take the others? Why didn't you suck them dry?" *Or had they?* An image of Dix the color of spoiled cheese.

"They were too close to dying to savor; and death should taste, my dear. In your spice I think there would be a certain carbolic flavor," he said. "A tang of cayenne and formaldehyde."

She hugged her arms and shivered. The sleet made a soothing clatter against the glass.

"Don't be afraid," he told her with mild annoyance. "I soak up fear and blood and longing. The blood tastes sweet, the fear rank."

The sleet was mesmerizing. She closed her eyes and suddenly she found her mind drifting back to her mother's house, to her own tall, wide bed.

"Ah, yes," he said in a hushed voice. "The flavor of

memory is best of all. It is a varied jambalaya. Think about your past, Rita. Your old house. Would you like to go there?"

If the aliens had drawn so apt a caricature of Dr. Gladdings, capturing his weaknesses with a few deft strokes, she wondered what horrors they would show her in her mother. "Don't do that," she snapped. "Don't try to sell me your damned make-believe. You and I both know New Orleans isn't there anymore."

"Shhh," he soothed. "Shhhh. Think about the kittens suckling in your childhood closet. You remember the calico you named Miss Patch? That's good. I taste milk and warm, purring fur at the back of your mind."

Rita walked away through the stacks of books. By the oak table, General Lauterbach was waiting again, an unchanging caricature of a man. She wondered what truth the aliens wanted to tell her about him.

"I envy you," the general said. "What makes you so goddamned special?" Suddenly he blinked. His hazel eyes lost their whetted edge and seemed simply unsure. "I shouldn't have put it that way."

"Leave me alone," she said. "I don't want you here."

Rita wondered how the general would taste. Of cordite, most probably. And the flat flavor of hot steel.

"I'm sorry," he whispered.

Embarrassed, she let her eyes drift to the tapping sleet at the window. The ghostly, translucent Lauterbach was as disturbing as the flaccid Dr. Gladdings. She had remembered the general as neat and self-possessed. Now he was messy, gale-tattered.

"I remember the first time I met you," he said in a dreamy voice, a voice so private, she felt she was sipping at his thoughts. "Standing there," he murmured. "A strong woman amid the smell of burnt bodies. Strange how admiration can come in the oddest places. Do they love you? The aliens? What can I do to make them love me, too? Please," he said in a gasp, as though he had just then awakened. "Help me."

She turned. "What do you want me to do?"

His face creased into a puzzled frown. "I can't seem to remember. I dreamed earlier about falling and then about fire. The people in Warsaw. The President . . ." The knitted weave of his thoughts faltered, dropping a stitch. "Listen to me, Rita," he said urgently. "I need the aliens. Don't you see? Tell them I'm sorry about what happened in the Pyrenees, what I forced them to do. I just want to talk. To explain things. I have something here . . . something . . ."

Hands trembling, he took a piece of paper from his breast pocket. Unfolding the page, he smoothed it out on the polished wood.

"I need . . . I need . . ." His voice died in miserable confusion.

And he evaporated. She looked at the table and the blank white paper lying there.

WARSAW, POLAND

The sun was rising, turning the leaden sky a pinkish gray. Smoke from burning buildings made a sooty streak across the clouds.

Baranyk got to his feet. From where he stood he could see the ruins of Stalin's Palace of Culture. Once, not so long ago, the old Georgian's muscular, revolutionary-style erection had dominated the city. Stalin had always been an invincible prick.

"After Stalin, we are all impotent," he muttered into his vodka bottle.

"Sir?" Zgursky asked.

"You are a good boy," Baranyk said, clapping his arm around the aide's shoulders. Under the general's weight, Zgursky sagged. "A good boy."

"Yes, sir," Zgursky answered. "Thank you, sir. Wouldn't the general care for some breakfast now?"

Baranyk hugged the sergeant tighter, crushing the boy's head against his chest. "No," he replied. "The general wouldn't care for breakfast." Impulsively, he kissed the top of the aide's cropped head.

When Baranyk released him, Zgursky staggered away,

a stunned and disapproving expression on his peach-fuzz face.

Baranyk's booming laugh echoed amid the ruins. "I love you, Zgursky. I love you so much, I want you to accompany me to the artillery emplacements now."

Zgursky sighed, wiped the top of his head, and nodded. "Yes, sir."

Baranyk put down the empty vodka bottle and walked, the aide tagging after. The side street Baranyk chose was miraculously intact, its tree-lined length serene. A block later, they began picking their way through rubble. Along with the tang of smoke, the general caught a whiff of putrefaction rising from the shattered buildings. Not a dead cat. Not a dog. They had long ago been eaten. Only one thing left in Warsaw could smell like that.

The morning's vodka rushed up his gullet. He leaned over in time to keep the flood from splattering his uniform. The pale vomit was streaked with red.

"Are you all right, sir?" Zgursky asked hesitantly.

"Of course." He waved the solicitous sergeant off and walked on, Zgursky a little camouflage shadow at his shoulder.

"Perhaps you should go back to barracks and lie down, sir. You might need rest."

Did the boy know how poorly he slept? Baranyk wondered. The aide's cot was in the next room, close, so Baranyk's low call would rouse him. Perhaps he had heard the creaks of the bed as Baranyk tossed and turned. The general darted a glance in the sergeant's direction, but Zgursky had his head down, watching where he put his feet.

"Am I a bad commander?" Baranyk asked quietly.

Zgursky's head came up fast.

"Tell me the truth, sergeant, good Ukrainian boy that you are. Do the men say I am a good commander or merely a drunken one?"

Much to Baranyk's astonishment, a gamin smile spread across Zgursky's face. "The men think you are a better commander drunk than any ten sober Arab generals."

Baranyk stopped. Zgursky backed away quickly, as though fearful he might be kissed again.

"Kiev—"

"Forget Kiev, sir," the sergeant said in a voice so sharp it flirted with insubordination. "Can't you forget Kiev? You shout orders in your sleep, and I know you are fighting the battle all over again."

After a moment, Baranyk asked, "I talk in my sleep? What do I say?"

"You try to call the tanks up, sir. You try to order the infantry back. Sometimes you call Major Shcheribitsky's name so loud, he wakes up and comes down the hall to see what is wrong."

Baranyk took a deep breath that tasted of vomit and soot. "I see."

"Sir? You are the best commander I have ever served under," Zgursky told him. "You don't lose your temper. You always listen to us. That is the important thing. Forgive me for speaking frankly with you, sir."

"Yes, of course," Baranyk murmured as he began picking his way through the rubble.

He rarely lost his temper, except in defense of his men. That much was true. Unlike a Patriot missile, he never exploded at his mark; rather, like the ERINT, he used the power of his own bull-necked kinetic energy to crash his way through. He had risen through the ranks with an unerring radar for seizing opportunity, and with an unstoppable stamina.

Now all of that was gone. The Arabs had surrounded Warsaw, outnumbering his army five to one. The ANA wouldn't launch a frontal attack, wouldn't meet them like men, head-on. Why should they? he asked himself bitterly. The bombing, as it had during the Great Patriotic War, would again wear Warsaw out. When the Arabs crossed the Vistula, they would be met with apathy, not bullets.

The street emerged on a fussy little square with a fountain. On the western side, the side that had been hit, ruined buildings stood like movie-set façades, their blank windows open to nothing. Five women and a mob of filthy children were rag-picking in the charred ruins. Zgursky at his shoulder, Baranyk walked over to the fountain and washed out his sour mouth with the algae-covered water. Then he scrubbed his face.

"Now," he said, straightening his uniform. "Do I look presentable ?"

"Very presentable, sir."

"My eyes not too bloodshot?" he asked. "I do not smell too much of vodka? I do not stumble or slur my words?"

"No, sir. Not at all, sir."

"You would tell me, Zgursky? We will go see Colonel Jastrun now. It would not be good for the Poles to see me drunk. I do not wish my men to be ashamed of me."

Zgursky's young face tightened. "Sir," he said, "your men will never be ashamed of you."

CENTRAL ARMY HOSPITAL, BADAJOZ, SPAIN

Just before dawn, the American general came back. Amazed to see him so early, Sabry turned his wheelchair from the window, tearing his gaze from the unlighted staff offices and the huge, floodlit prisoner compound beyond.

"Sorry to disturb you, sir," Lauterbach said. "But the nurses said you were awake."

In the dim light from the bedside lamp Sabry noticed that the American's face was drawn.

"No bother," Sabry told him. He gestured at a vacant chair. "Please. Sit down."

Lauterbach glanced at the chair, hesitated, remained standing at parade rest.

"General Sabry," he began in a soft but formal tone, "I regret to inform you—"

Fear pulsed through Sabry like the cold touch of anesthesia. "Sit!" he said so loudly that a flicker of astonishment crossed the American's face. "Please," he added. "Please sit. It is always hard to give such news. I've done it many times. Indulge me, please. I want to talk."

Lauterbach perched on the edge of the chair, hands on his knees, as though poised for escape. The wind shifted, carrying predawn cool and the scent of pine through the open window.

"Do you know the problem with Westerners?" Sabry asked, staring at the fierce halogen brilliance of the prisoner compound, the tall spires of the guard towers. "They don't listen well. Had we won the war, we would have taught you to listen."

"A rather bloody lesson, don't you think?"

The hospital quiet was thick, like the silence at the bottom of the ocean. Far down the hall Sabry could hear faint clinks of metal on metal as the medication nurse began rounds.

"I loved my son. He is dead, isn't he?"

"Yes."

Sabry glanced around the small, antiseptic room. "It is too quiet in this hospital, you know. Your doctors and nurses never argue and rarely laugh. Five Arabs in a room, and there is bedlam. Allied soldiers, even as they are dying, I have noticed, scream hoarsely, as though ashamed."

Perhaps he was making the man uncomfortable. Perhaps he had said something he shouldn't. Lauterbach's face was impassive.

"My son, Gamal, understood Westerners," Sabry told him. "He received his doctorate at Cal Tech. I sent him to the Pyrenees. Perhaps he screamed there as you might: an inhibited, apologetic scream."

"Don't do this to yourself, sir. Our job demands we put people at risk. There's no evil in that. No reason to feel guilty. If you're a good commander, you try to minimize the risk. That's all you can do."

An inexplicable, overwhelming sorrow filled Lauterbach's face.

"Gamal changed, you know. When he was a boy, I would take him out to the desert. We had a place there, little more than a shack. Those were simple times."

Lauterbach made a noncommittal grunt. The man was no longer listening; he was thinking about something else, his expression as contrite as it was pensive.

"When my son was older, and came back from the States

for his visits, I could see him growing less and less simple. Sadder as well. How did he die?"

The question roused Lauterbach from his thoughts. He shot a cautious look at Sabry. "Quickly," he said.

Sabry knew the American was lying. A terrible death, then. He shifted his gaze to the window and saw the lights of the compound dance through his tears.

"You know, I am very much a Muslim—"

"Tell me what disposition you would wish for his remains. He's been buried, but I'll make sure that—"

"Listen to me!" Sabry shouted. His tone was so preemptive, so harsh, that a guard opened the door and looked in. Lauterbach waved him away.

When the soldier closed the door, Sabry leveled angry eyes at the American. "Do not interrupt me with your damned, cool reason! You do not know what I was going to say."

"Yes, sir," the American said. "You're quite right. I'm sorry." And leaned back in his seat.

"The mullahs promise Heaven to those who die in battle, but the battle must be holy, and I'm not sure this war was. In any case, I can talk to Gamal no longer. What good is heaven, I ask you?"

Amazingly, Lauterbach smiled, irony in his eyes. "I'm sure I don't know, general. I lost a wife through divorce and a daughter to cancer. I believe at the time I asked myself the same thing."

"Did Colonel Wasef survive?"

The American seemed puzzled. "Excuse me?"

"Colonel Qasim Abdel Wasef. He was in the Pyrenees, too."

"Oh, yes. The commanding officer. No, sir. He did not survive the engagement."

"And how did he die?"

Lauterbach's face shut down and for a long moment he was silent. Could it have been such a terrible death, Sabry wondered, that even the American was awed by it?

Finally Lauterbach took a long breath. "Friendly fire," he said.

WARSAW, POLAND

Baranyk put his cup down with a wince, trying to ignore the fire the coffee had reignited in his gullet. By the bunker wall Zgursky stood chewing hungrily on a sweet roll, a look of intense enjoyment on his face.

"Well, colonel," Baranyk said, turning to Jastrun. "No bombings today if the weather remains socked in. Those Arab pilots cannot find their cocks with two hands."

At the fancy German phased-array radar screens, one of the specialists tittered. Jastrun's lips curled into an arch though indulgent smile.

"Warsaw is a big target," the colonel said. In the forced tolerance of the Pole's gaze Baranyk saw questions. Jastrun was wondering what the Ukrainian was doing here.

"Perhaps Scuds." Baranyk looked at the green radar screens.

"Yes. Perhaps Scuds." The colonel shifted on his feet uneasily. Baranyk wasn't sure what made the man nervous: the possibility of missiles or the Ukrainian's presence. "Would the general care to see something else?" Jastrun asked at last.

A polite way of indicating that the tour was at an end. Baranyk ignored him. "Tell me, colonel. If you could ask the spirit of Kazimierz the Great for one gift, what would it be?"

The colonel's smile vanished: Baranyk had made a poor joke.

"Targets?" Baranyk suggested.

The Pole's eyes narrowed. He was thinking furiously now; he was considering his situation.

"Forgive me for being ignorant of this miracle of German engineering," Baranyk said with a slow, cunning smile. "But is it not true that if the Arabs shell, this radar can track the incoming shell and find the Arab emplacement even before they hit here?"

The Pole held his back stiff, as if awaiting a blow. "Yes," he said, drawing out the word into three cautious syllables.

"So the Arabs bomb instead."

A pause. Jastrun's eyes were asking questions so fast, so furiously, that Baranyk imagined he was looking through them into the working guts of a computer. "Yes."

"I am thinking that if I mounted a small attack, a small one, you understand, we might provoke them into shelling."

Jastrun leaned forward in interest. "Have you discussed this with General Czajowski?"

"It is just a thought as yet," Baranyk told him, making a lazy, dismissive gesture with his hand. "I thought I would speak to you first, to see how you liked the idea."

Jastrun pursed his lips judiciously. "Perhaps you should speak to him and then to me."

"Ah, yes. Chain of command," he said with a sly, ironic grin. "I remember how important that was in the Red Army. Good day," he told the insulted Pole cheerily before the man would come up with a rejoinder.

Zgursky followed him out the bunker door. "Allies," Baranyk laughed, slapping the aide's belly with the back of his hand. "God preserve us from allies." He pointed toward the hushed and opalescent east. "Not even the Arabs hate me so much."

Still chuckling, Baranyk made his way past the sandbags at the side of the bunker and walked across the packed-dirt yard to the sheltered tanks. Gutzman was at one of the Hammers, performing some arcane maintenance ritual. At their approach he glanced up, an oil rag in his hand.

"Has the general come back for another lesson on the Hammer?" the lieutenant asked.

Baranyk regarded Gutzman, who seemed pleased, and then Zgursky, who decidedly did not. "I think I should be the driver today. Let us have the sergeant be the gunner. And you, who have more experience, will be our tank commander. Choose our vehicle. I am under your orders, lieutenant."

Gutzman climbed onto the tank's deck. Baranyk climbed to the driver's hatch and eased himself into the plush reclining seat, pulling the hatch closed behind him. Just before he put on his goggles, Baranyk turned and saw Zgursky staring at him in dawning horror.

"We are armed and fully functional?" the general asked, slipping the headgear on.

In his ear he heard Gutzman's calm voice: "Armed and ready, sir."

Baranyk started the engine and put his hands around the steering T. His palms, he noticed distantly, had started to sweat.

At one side of his vision were the gaily colored gauges: red for the reactor heat; blue for the kpm; yellow, a cautionary, cowardly color, for his directionals.

He turned the tank south, a cautionary, cowardly route. In his ear he heard a relieved sigh. Zgursky.

The Hammer moved like a huge, fat luxury car: a Russian Zil or an American Cadillac. At twelve kilometers per hour, he drove past the countersunk munitions bunkers.

"Where to, sir?" he heard Gutzman ask.

"I thought we might try something different today."

A gasp in his ear. Zgursky knew. He'd known from the moment Baranyk had mentioned the plan to Jastrun.

Ten meters, twenty, Baranyk counted, hoping he had found his mark. "Brace yourselves!" he called and floored the accelerator, slewing the big tank left. He muscled it over the barricades.

"Sir!" Gutzman's voice was so loud, it hurt Baranyk's ears. "Sir! What did we hit?"

"Keep your eyes on your instruments, Gutzman," Baranyk said quietly. "We will be feinting toward the enemy to draw artillery fire."

A groan from the headset. Gutzman's this time.

Out in the open, mine-dotted field, Baranyk reviewed his mental map of their path. He wound the speed to 80 kph and angled toward the road. In his ear, a crackle of static, then the enraged voice of Jastrun, "Who the hell is in Hammer 8?"

"Tell him," Baranyk said.

Gutzman's voice was high-pitched with panic. "General Baranyk, Lieutenant Gutzman, Sergeant Zgursky."

The tank mounted the road, and Baranyk accelerated, watching the kilometers flick by on the display. He set the stud on the steering T to telescopic vision and saw guideposts: the stand of pines, the shattered, burned farmhouse.

Three kilometers, three and a half, he counted.

After a long silence, Jastrun asked, "Who is this on the radio?"

"Lieutenant Gutzman."

"You are tank commander?" Jastrun barked.

"Yes, sir."

"Then turn that tank around immediately!"

"But sir," Gutzman said miserably. "General Baranyk is driving."

"Fuck General Baranyk!" Jastrun screamed, his fury apparently overcoming his religious awe of rank. "Doesn't he know there are mines out there? And four hundred thousand Arabs? I will call General Czajowski! Tell him that! I will call General Czajowski! My hand is on the phone now, General Baranyk! Do you hear me? I am making the call right now!"

They went over a crater in the road, the suspension easing them through it as gently as a farm girl carrying eggs.

"Lieutenant?" Baranyk said. "Sergeant?"

"Sir?" they answered in nervous tandem.

"It is not too late. If you want to go back, tell me now."

"Sir," Zgursky said, his voice shaking. "I trust you, sir."

A pause. Then Gutzman's hesitant, "No, sir."

"Then, Gutzman! Tell that bugger of farm animals, that lazy Pole, to pay more attention to his radar screens than to his telephone. At ten kilometers in, we'll open fire. I suspect the Arabs are no more than sixteen kilometers from the perimeter. He should begin preparing to orchestrate response."

"Firing in . . ." Gutzman began and stopped, evidently consulting his own readouts. "Oh, my God!" he screamed. "Firing in two minutes! Colonel Jastrun! Prepare to conduct response!"

They barreled up a hillock, the Hammer going airborne for a moment before coming down with a buttocks-bruising slam that even the suspension couldn't cushion. Before them extended a grassy plain dotted here and there with islands of birch and pine.

Holy Father, Baranyk thought in horror. He was lost. He checked his display again nervously, imagining mines ahead, imagining all sorts of things. Perhaps the Arabs didn't have the old artillery standbys: 2S5s and 2S3s. If they had the longer range BM-27s, the emplacements would be too far away to hurt. If 2S1s, Baranyk would be right on top of them.

"Gunner. Prepare to fire," the general said.

"But—where, sir?" Zgursky blurted.

Baranyk steered the tank off the asphalt and ran parallel to the yet unseen Arab artillery. Was this the way or not? "Fire now! Six kilometers due east!"

Baranyk heard the turret turn on its well-oiled gears. It took a moment for the tank's computers to calculate wind direction and speed, then the 120mm cannon boomed, rocking the tank. The sound nearly brought Baranyk out of his seat. A *mine*, he thought, then realized what the noise had been.

"Fire!" Baranyk shouted. "Keep firing, Zgursky!"

The recoil momentarily tore the steering from the general's hands. The eastern horizon began to twinkle.

"Response! Six-point-five kilometers!" Gutzman shouted.

A shell hit so close that Baranyk gasped. Instantly he was sober. *Mother of God*, he thought. *My drunken stupidity will kill us all*. He pulled the steering T into a desperate right turn and angled for the town, heedless of the mines. Directly in front of them a train station burst open, spilling guts of smoke.

He raced around a prerevolutionary building to hide, to let Zgursky fire again. There was no need. In the air above the artillery bombardment there was a flash. From the exploding Allied shell, submunitions arced out, making a weeping-willow pattern of fire. A heartbeat later, the bomblets went off, their downward blasts as sudden and hard as pile drivers.

All along the sparkling perimeter, Allied shells exploded, a border of incandescent flowers. From the ground, flames blossomed, meeting the glow from the sky. Baranyk's pulse began to slow. The tightness in his chest eased. He smiled. *Not bad for an old Communist who finds his courage in a bottle of vodka.*

The barrage from the east dwindled to sporadic mortar fire. Still grinning, Baranyk turned the tank west and, carefully following his own tread marks, hurried back to Warsaw.

By the time he rolled over the barricades and brought the tank to a halt, both barrages had ended. Jastrun, hands on hips, was standing outside the bunker, his officers and men around him. Pulling the goggles off, Baranyk fought his way out of the driver's compartment and up the deck. The eastern horizon was dark with smoke.

He whooped. "See there!" he cried, pointing. "And they call the American general crazy!"

Gutzman and Zgursky joined him. Zgursky's eyes were swollen as though he had been crying, and a wet spot covered the front of Gutzman's pants.

Baranyk felt his smile falter.

"General Baranyk?" Jastrun said.

Baranyk looked down at him.

"Commander Czajowski is on the phone. And he wants to talk with you now."

IN THE LIGHT

Jerry was not happy to see the soldier come back. It was plain as day that his Pa loved that soldier; and Jerry could imagine a time when his Pa's love would drift from him like a distracted gaze.

They sat on the grass watching the stars come out in the bruised sky. Next to Jerry's hip, his Pa shifted weight and laid a moist, calming hand on his arm.

"Debts, Jerry," his Pa said in an Andy Griffith voice.

"Yes, sir."

The hand squeezed his, the soft fingers molding themselves around his flesh. "No one should ever forget debts."

The soldier was sitting next to the kid named Mike, and he was staring off into the clattering reeds. He never said much, the soldier. Never said hello, never said goodbye.

Jerry didn't like the pilot. Didn't like the way he thought about war. But it struck Jerry that the pilot must be right. The soldier was a gomer. A second-rate target in a kill box.

"Look," Mike said.

One of the blue lights was coming over the lake, a rising cerulean moon.

Mike pointed his boneless finger. "See there, Gordon?"

"Yes," the soldier said.

"I live in the light," Mike told him. In the dim glow of the pier Jerry could see Mike's eyes bulge with fierce hunger. "We all do. We make it come. We make it go." He waved his hand. The blue globe of light bobbed back and forth, as if it were a kite and Mike were holding the string.

"It is our eyes," Mike said.

But that was a lie, Jerry thought. Mike's eyes were oozing down his cheeks.

"From where the light is, I can see the other side of the lake. Do you understand?" Mike asked the soldier.

The gomer screwed his face up into a confused frown.

"We drive it."

The soldier's bewilderment smoothed out, was replaced by surprise.

"Would you like to drive one?" Mike was asking, leaning into the soldier so that their bodies pressed together. Mike's soft bones gave way. His chest swallowed the soldier's right side. "Would you?"

"I would, Pa!" Jerry said quickly before the soldier could answer. "I'd like to see the other side of the lake in that thing."

"Shhh," Pa said.

"But I'd like to go, Pa. Please, can't I go?"

"It's not for you, Jerry," his Pa said. "It's for Gordon. We make this offer for Gordon."

But it would be a fine ride, Jerry knew. Better than bumper cars. If his Pa gave him everything he ever wanted, he should let him drive one of those lights.

"I want to drive one, Pa," he said.

Pa wrapped him in his arm, and for the first time Jerry realized how heavy that arm could be. With an angry tug, Jerry freed himself from his Pa and glanced around.

Mike was regarding the blue light thoughtfully. The soldier was gone.

WARSAW, POLAND

Taking a deep breath, Baranyk walked into the office. Czajowski was sitting behind his desk, a drowsy-eyed spider. "Shut the door, will you?" he said.

Baranyk pulled the door to. Czajowski stood. "Valentin, Valentin," he said, shaking his head. "There was a mine field out there. And four hundred thousand Arabs."

"Yes, Andrzej. And none of them killed me."

"Not for lack of your trying."

"Someone should try something, I think."

The Pole looked either sick or exhausted. He limped over to a plush armchair and fell into it. He massaged his leg. "My arthritis bothers me again."

"I am sorry to hear it."

"*You* bother me," Czajowski said, concentrating on his knee.

Baranyk looked at the ornate cross hung above the Pole's desk, and the statue of the Virgin in blue and white beside it. The Mother of God had her face lowered, her hands outspread, as if welcoming to her bosom a child or a pet dog.

"We must save our ammunition," Czajowski said.

"Yes. We can make rings out of it. Bracelets, the like."

At Baranyk's acid tone, the Pole glanced up. "I could strip you of your command. Do you know that?"

"If we obey you, Andrzej, we will let all of Warsaw become rubble. Have you forgotten what happened during the Patriotic War?"

Czajowski's face flushed. He jumped to his feet, nearly toppled again, grasped his thigh. "Goddamn," he growled. "Shit. May my leg be fucked. Yes, Valentin, goddamn you. I realize the Red Army sat back and let the Germans level Warsaw." Breathing heavily—more from pain, Baranyk suspected, than from fury—the Pole dropped into the chair again. "General Lauterbach is sending a division. When he arrives with the Germans, we will need every shell we have."

Baranyk studied the commander. The Pole's cheeks were pale, his jaw taut with pain. A man so weary of battle, it seemed he was ready to fall into the Virgin's porcelain, unfeeling arms. It was a dangerous faith that Czajowski had. A deadly one. "God, Andrzej," Baranyk whispered. "Don't you see? Lauterbach is lying to us."

"He will come," Czajowski said. "The Germans will come. Warsaw is too important to fall."

"The Germans hope the Arabs will be satisfied with Poland, and they are probably right. They will write a peace on our corpses."

When Czajowski did not respond, Baranyk went to the opposite chair and sat. The office was smaller than Pankov's, but in its way just as opulent.

"Look at me," Baranyk said. "Won't you look?"

The Pole kept his eyes on his offending knee. "I am angry. If I look at you, I will be angrier still."

"Then don't look. Listen. Lauterbach has no fuel. How can he move a division so far? And if he got here, what good would a division be? Four hundred thousand Arabs surround us and Arab planes own the skies."

Czajowski's hair was flaxen and silver. At the very top of his cranium, pink scalp shone through the sparse strands.

"I know Lauterbach," Baranyk said. "I understand his mind. He is devious, and no fool. It is easier to lie. A lie gains him time. He lets us think help is coming and— oh, Andrzej. Don't you see?" The small office was filled with the hush of resignation, the sour stench of defeat. "Lauterbach dangles the carrot."

Baranyk glanced up at the bronze figure of Christ on the Cross. The statue's muscles and tendons were delineated, its face sagging, like Czajowski's, with pain. Christ, Baranyk thought bitterly. Christ had dangled the carrot, too.

The Pole massaged his knee. His voice was the soft, acquiescent voice of a saint facing martyrdom. "Lauterbach will come," he said.

CHAPTER 16

CRAV COMMAND, TRÁS-OS-MONTES, PORTUGAL

"I came to say goodbye," Toshio said.

Hunched in a chair in his pajamas, Gordon let his gaze rest on Toshio's face. This was obviously near the end of the movie, the sad part. But Gordon couldn't remember the rest of the film and didn't know why he should be unhappy.

"You're being transferred home," Toshio told him. "Colonel Pelham brought the papers over this morning."

Someone died. That was what happened in the sad parts of movies. Who, though? Then Gordon realized that the dead man was himself.

Toshio looked away, because people never look at the dead for very long. "He'll be in to see you in a few moments."

A hush settled over the room, airy and light as the glow from the windows. Gordon closed his eyes. Mike was standing on the beach, ankle-deep in the waves.

"Are you ready?" Mike asked. He put out his hand, and Gordon grasped it. The small mouths of Mike's nails sucked at his palm.

"No family," Toshio said.

Gordon opened his eyes. The man was regarding him, his black eyes turned warm obsidian.

"You have a mother somewhere, but you were never close to your family. No girlfriend. I read your psychiatric file. There is no one who cares for you. I think the colonel makes a mistake by sending you home."

Home. Gordon suddenly knew that Mike was coming to take him home. He sat up straighter, listened hard, stared out the window.

"Gordon?" Toshio asked curiously.

Everyone in this film was dead. That's why it was sad. The world was full of mummies and vampires and zombies. The dead peered out of movie screens. Somewhere Bela Lugosi laughed, a lazy heroin chuckle. And the tall ghost of Christopher Lee strode.

"Gordon? What is it?"

Mike was coming.

Beside him Toshio was as hazy as a TV with bad reception.

Gordon leaped to his feet.

"What's wrong?" Toshio asked, rising with him.

In the back of Gordon's mind, he heard the clattering of sleet, whispered vows, the combined troth of the community. He felt a tug of longing as though his heart were being sucked from his chest. Mike was close, riding on eddies of air, on volumes of wind, drifting over the alien green fields.

Gordon ran to greet him, knocking over a table, shoving past a nurse. At the entrance to the clinic Pelham glanced up, startled.

Stumbling down the steps and across the gravel in the yard, Gordon soared like an untethered balloon, no family, no ties to hold him. An armed MP and his group of prisoners stopped to watch him pass.

"Damn it, Gordon!" he heard Pelham shout.

Gordon halted in the yard, taking in a ragged breath. Mike was there. The blue light was sailing into the compound. Arab prisoners scattered; the MP screamed for them to stop.

Strong, desperate arms grabbed his pajamas, clawed at his neck. "No!" the colonel shouted. "No, son! That thing will kill you!"

Then Pelham's arms were wrenched away. Bewildered, Gordon turned and saw Toshio and the colonel wrestling in the gravel.

"Let him!" Toshio said. "Let him go! Gordon needs someone now. Let him go."

Gordon whirled. Mike was right beside him, cool and wintry blue. Closing his eyes, he plunged into the azure Atlantic, the salt smell of the waves, the keen, clattering shrieks of the gulls.

WARSAW, POLAND

Baranyk awoke to the sound of sirens. It was black in the room, and the general, still half asleep, imagined that the rises and falls of sound were slow ocean waves bearing him into the dark.

He turned over in bed, the cheap army-issue frame creaking. He scrubbed his face and finally sat up, letting the warmth of the covers fall away. A shadow stood at the door.

"Sir," Zgursky said. "Would you care to go to the basement?"

The AAA had not started up. A Scud, then, not bombers. He blinked at Zgursky, a man-shaped blot in the night.

"No," Baranyk said. Had he been dreaming again? he wondered. The bedclothes were in a sweated knot. From the open window flowed a cool breeze and the drumming sound of November rain.

Groping toward the top of the nightstand, he found his vodka bottle, screwed open the cap, took a swallow. The liquor laid a hot trail down his throat.

"Your gas mask, sir?"

"No. You go ahead," he told his aide. "Get your mask. Go to the basement. I'll be there in a minute."

The shadow in the doorway didn't move. Zgursky probably knew he was lying. "One minute," the aide said.

"I understand." Zgursky was counting. They had three minutes from the first moan of the sirens to the strike; two minutes had already gone by. The aide lingered, a clock-watching death angel.

Other than the sirens and the slow rain, Warsaw was silent. No dogs barked. No cars passed in the rubble-choked streets.

Then the shadow moved. Zgursky raised his head, listening.

A belly-wrenching explosion—much too close. The floor shook. Dull red light sparked at the window. The blast rolled on, an incredible, ceaseless timpani. Baranyk's small Tensor lamp jittered across the nightstand and fell over with a crash.

He stood in the dim orange light and fumbled for his pants. "Close the drapes," the general gasped. "Turn on the lights." Under his bare feet the floor still shuddered.

"Sir?" Zgursky called.

Holding his trousers in one hand, Baranyk hurried to the window. From the east rose a column of fire. Another quake struck, rattling the curtain pulls, making the springs in the iron bed sing.

As Baranyk hurriedly began to dress, he heard a dry click.

"Electricity's out, sir," Zgursky informed him.

Baranyk buttoned his uniform blouse as well as he could with shivering, blind fingers. The door to the hall swung open with a squeal.

"General?" Major Shcheribitsky whispered.

"You will come with me, major. I wish to inspect the eastern emplacements. And order the Humvee to be brought up, please, sergeant."

Baranyk put on his calf-length woolen coat, searched in the dark for the nightstand, found the bottle and took a deep, calming drink.

Outside of the officers' barracks, Zgursky was waiting. Baranyk, ducking his way through the rain, climbed into the shelter of the Humvee. The warning sirens had fallen silent, but from a nearby street came the tenor wails of fire trucks.

Two blocks from the fire, Zgursky stopped. In the steady downpour, Jastrun stood with some Polish officers watching the inferno. Across the street three fire trucks were parked in a line, the firemen gathered around, confounded and useless.

"Have you called up the tanks?" Baranyk shouted at Jastrun.

The Pole, too, Baranyk noticed, had been dragged out of bed. His wet uniform was awry. "What?" the colonel snapped, in his foul mood overlooking formalities.

"Call tanks to this location, man! Get spotters on the roofs! If the Arabs take the advantage, they will attack at this location!"

A series of angry bass booms thundered as the flames reached more stockpiled shells. Jastrun and his men flinched. The firemen ran for cover. An instant later hot debris rained down, hissing through the mist, pinging on helmets and the Humvee.

"Colonel Jastrun!" Baranyk shouted.

Ducking, the Pole made his way to the side of the Humvee. Even in the lurid glow from the fire, the man's face was pale. "Yes?"

"Which munitions, colonel?"

Jastrun blinked. "The smart shells, I believe. I—"

"Does Czajowski know?"

"Of course. I informed him immediately. I believe he has telephoned the Americans and plans—"

"Shit!" Baranyk screamed. "Mother of God! He would tell the Americans?"

The Pole was utterly confused. "Why not?"

"Your brains drip out your asshole, Jastrun! Because, *tovarich*," Baranyk said, falling back into old habits, older suspicions, "now Lauterbach will begin drafting Poland's surrender."

He rapped on the door frame of the Humvee. "Get us to the commander's office now, sergeant. Get us there quickly, before Czajowski makes his mistake."

It took almost fifteen minutes to reach the command center. Before the Humvee came to a stop, Baranyk had jumped out and was sprinting up the steps. The power was back on; the hall he raced down was brightly lit. He reached Czajowski's office at a dead run and flung open the door.

The Pole was just putting down the secure phone's receiver. There was a bemused, frightened expression on his face.

"Did you tell him?" Baranyk shouted. "Did you tell Lauterbach of our situation?"

Czajowski stared at the phone. "Do you know what he said?" he asked softly.

Baranyk was still breathing hard from his run. It seemed that his tight throat meant to strangle him.

"He said he would get back to me," Czajowski said with an anxious twitch of a smile. "I told him we had lost half our munitions, and he said he would get back to me. Blessed Mother," the Pole breathed. His grotesque smile vanished. "Doesn't he realize there will be no one to pick up the phone?"

CENTCOM WEST, BADAJOZ, SPAIN

Banging and shouts at the anteroom door. Jolted from sleep, Mrs. Parisi sat up and looked bleary-eyed at the clock. Good Lord. Twelve midnight, and they were waking her up. The Army simply had no sense of decorum.

It was cold in her room, and that made her even more out of sorts. She turned on the bedside lamp, but before she could put on her robe, she heard footsteps, and there was Lauterbach in the doorway. He looked a fright. His hair was mussed, his face wide-eyed and pale.

"The main munitions dump in Warsaw has just been destroyed," he said. "Out of bed. We need to contact the aliens."

Suddenly Mrs. Parisi was aware that all she had on was her filmy nightgown, the one with the tiny pink and blue flowers all over it.

"Let me get dressed," she said, pulling the blanket over her shoulders.

Much to her astonishment, the general lunged across to the bed and grabbed her upper arm so tightly, she knew it would leave bruises. He shook her, and she was shamefully conscious of the water-balloon sway of her braless breasts.

"Listen to me, lady!"

Furious spittle flew, misted her cheeks.

"I'm sick of all this New Age crap you've been feeding me!" He shoved his face into hers. "It's all over with, all right? This is do-or-die time. You said in your books you can contact the aliens. Well, goddamn! Get to it!"

"Not everyone comes at your silly beck and call," she said, overriding her fear of him and returning his glare. "The Eridanians are not your ridiculous toy soldiers."

For a moment it looked as if he might actually strike her. He was breathing so hard that his chest heaved.

"You're lying, aren't you?" he said with a sound between a moan and a gasp. "God. You've been lying to me."

Her heart was hammering terribly now, so loud, she was certain he could hear it. His grip on her arm made her fingers tingle.

"You simply haven't been able to sleep deeply enough to reach them," she told him. "Don't blame me for that."

His eyes took on a faraway look she didn't like.

"I know you!" Her voice rose now, strident with desperation. "You catch a couple of hours here and there. I can see the effects of sleep deprivation in your face. Really. You look just awful. How do you expect . . ."

He dropped her arm; stepped away. "I take sleeping pills. That's not it." He looked around, at the dresser, the bed, like a child who has strayed from his mother in the busy confusion of a shopping mall. "You've been lying."

She stood up, ignoring the sheerness of her nightgown. "You stupid, egotistical little man!" she said. "You can't talk to the Eridanians if you've been taking sleeping pills."

His eyes sparked in renewed anger. Faith took a long time to die, she knew. It sickened and decayed into a prolonged half-life. She realized, at that moment, Lauterbach still yearned to believe.

"Did you take pills tonight?" she asked.

"No, I just—"

"Go straight to bed," she said curtly. "You're living on drugs, that's what you're doing." She had never played the Game so boldly and so well. Her skill gave her a giddy sense of pride. "No wonder the Eridanians can't understand."

His shoulders sagged. "For Christ's sake, lady. I can't sleep."

"Well, you'd just better, hadn't you? You'd just better try."

He straightened. His gaze became Machiavellian. She hadn't seen that shrewdness in his face in a long time. "You're lying," he told her.

"How will you ever know?" she smirked.

For a moment he stood, regarding her skeptically. Then he whirled and stalked out.

"Sir?" a waiting aide asked. "Will you call General Brown now, sir? To arrange the ordnance for the B-2s?"

The door slammed on Lauterbach's reply.

IN THE LIGHT

Rita turned the corner of the stacks and saw Lauterbach. His eyes were red-rimmed, his face a sickly gray.

"I have a message," he told her, his expression intent.

"Fuck you," she answered. "What do you expect me to do, salute? You want 'Yes, sir, what is the message, sir?' Well, up your four-star ass, sir. I didn't ask to be sent here."

"There isn't much time," he said. "You need to ask them to help."

"Who, the aliens?" she laughed. "Help with what?"

He scrubbed his hand over his face, pinched the bridge of his nose. "Help. Yes. Help."

"Ask them yourself." She turned to go.

"Goddamn it!" His rage stopped her in her tracks. His body, she saw, was stress-fracture brittle.

"*You* have to tell them, Rita. They *like* you. I can't find my way around the library. The stairs go nowhere, and the elevators bring me back to where I began. No matter which direction I take, I always end up at this table. They won't come to me. They won't listen to me. You've got to do it."

"I don't understand."

He looked around wildly, began yanking books off shelves. They landed on the marble floor with wet smacks.

"What are you doing?" she asked.

"Getting their attention!" He took *The Collected Works of Alfred Lord Tennyson* and hurled it at the window. It hit the glass with a wind-chime sound.

"Stop!" she screamed.

He didn't. The books, covers open like wings, swatted the windows, one after the other, birds flying to their death.

Lauterbach would tear the library down around her shoulders. What what would happen then? What horrors would stand revealed when all the illusion was gone?

A weighty volume of Shakespeare smacked against the pane with an ice-pellet rattle. "I have to get their attention!" the general shouted. "Quick!" He lunged at her. "Give me a pen!"

She backed away. He turned and waded though the fallen books, to the table.

"A pen!" he called into the pewter air. "For Christ's sake. I told you I was sorry. What else can I do? Give me a goddamned pen!"

"There's a pen in your pocket," she told him.

Surprised, he glanced down, patting his uniform. He grasped the pen, then began looking around frantically.

"What the hell are you doing? And what are you looking for now?"

"Paper! I need paper!"

She gestured with exasperation at the floor. They were both ankle-deep in books. "Jesus. Can't you see? There's paper all over the place."

He looked up at her with pathetic gratitude. Bending, he picked up the Shakespeare and scribbled something on the flyleaf. "Here," he said, handing her the book.

She took it.

"Please. Please. Give it to them. Tell them— Tell them how much they mean to me. Tell them how I've pinned my hopes—"

His voice faltered. His expression was imploring. After some hesitation she waded though the fallen books and out of the labyrinth of stacks. Dr. Gladdings was waiting for her at the librarian's desk.

"I have a message," she said.

He looked up, his tarry eyes melting down his cheeks.

Opening to the flyleaf, Rita handed him the book and glanced at the meaningless scribbles Lauterbach had written there.

Dr. Gladdings smiled up at her. "Oh, the message." He shut the book with a slap and looked out the windows at the barren trees. "We have the message. We've known it for quite a while."

WARSAW, POLAND

The cold nudged Baranyk awake. He opened his eyes to ashen light. Wrapping the blanket around him, he went to the window. Ornate ferns of frost etched the glass. Below him, Warsaw lay covered in hoary ice.

Teeth chattering, back hunched, he got into his uniform. Hiking his coat over his shoulders, he walked into Zgursky's room. The aide was still asleep, shivering under his blanket.. Gathering his own blanket from his bed, Baranyk threw it over the sleeping boy.

In the common room, Shcheribitsky was seated at the table, hunched in his coat, his gloved hands encircling a glass of tea.

"What weather, general," the major said in wonder. His face was pallid but for two spots of winter rouge, one on either cheek. He sniffed and wiped a glove across the end of his nose. "Some breakfast?"

Baranyk gestured at him to keep his seat and began rummaging through the barren cabinets. "Any news?"

"Jastrun moved tanks to the perimeter. It appears we have lost four of our nine munitions dumps."

Baranyk picked up a jar of pickled herring, hesitated, put it back. There was fig jam, he saw, but no bread. "Polish idiocy, to put the dumps so close together."

"Yes, sir."

Baranyk grabbed the fig jam and a spoon. He poured himself a glass of tea from the pot the major had made. His breakfast balanced in his hands, he sat down.

"It is quiet, sir," Shcheribitsky observed in an uneasy voice.

Baranyk spooned a little jam into his mouth. "Too quiet," he agreed. "I find it incredible that the Arabs have not yet—"

A noise. Baranyk turned. Zgursky was in the doorway, his eyes wide.

"Look outside, sir!" he shouted. "General! Look out the window!"

Shcheribitsky leaped to his feet. His chair toppled, hitting the wooden floor with a 20mm bang.

Baranyk was on his feet, too, but was afraid to look, afraid that, without his knowledge, Warsaw had fallen, that he would see Arab soldiers among the buildings, BTR-80s full of troops, and columns of T-72s.

"It's snowing!" Zgursky cried.

Incredulously, Baranyk walked to Shcheribitsky's side and stared out the fogged pane. November. A Greenhouse November, yet snow was coming down in the streets like gentle falls of angels.

CHAPTER 17

CENTRAL ARMY HOSPITAL, BADAJOZ, SPAIN

Sabry opened his eyes to discover that he had survived the operation. It appeared, too, that he was out of recovery and back in his own room. But then again he might be dreaming, because Lauterbach was there. The American general was standing with the surgeon.

Sabry caught the tag end of the general's sentence. ". . . just for a few minutes."

And the doctor's reply. "Don't stay too long. We had a bit of a surgical complication, and I imagine he'll be tired."

Surgical complication. Sabry's dulled mind played with the phrase. He rolled the words this way and that, until the words became too heavy and his mind grew too exhausted to hold them.

Something shoved him awake. He saw Lauterbach bending over him. The American looked sick. Sabry wondered if he had had a surgical complication, too.

"What is the readiness of your nuclear response, sir?"

The question amused Sabry. He wanted to grin at the American, but his lips wouldn't work. The room, Lauterbach's face, faded to gray.

The American shook him. His tone was impatient. "General Sabry! What is the readiness of the Arab nuclear response?"

It must be a dream, Sabry decided. Left to themselves, his eyelids shut. A slap on his cheek woke him. He was still dreaming about Lauterbach.

"I will pull you off this fucking bed, sir, unless you answer my question. There isn't any time."

A nonsensical dream. Sabry turned his head to look out the window. Through the slats in the blind he saw that it was raining.

Lauterbach slapped him again, harder. The blow should have hurt, but it didn't. Nothing hurt, not the stump of his knee, not his hip.

"Answer me!"

"I will answer you with bullets," Sabry replied, his anesthetized tongue lolling in his mouth. He laughed, too, but the laugh sounded strange.

Three quick blows like impatient applause: clap-clap-clap. Sabry's head jerked hard with each impact. Not a dream, he thought, a nightmare. But a nightmare that left him more irked than afraid.

"ICBMs!" Lauterbach cried.

Sabry tried to will the wild-eyed, furious American away. "No ICBMs," he muttered.

"What about the twenty-five Russian nuclear scientists? They didn't help you build a delivery system?"

Sabry laughed again. "Russians." The Russians were dead, he remembered, shot by a mob during the famine. Shot because they were foreigners. *Gamal was right*, he decided. *My son was right. We are xenophobic idiots.* Sabry closed his eyes. Strong arms clutched the front of his hospital smock.

"Listen to me!" Lauterbach hissed.

The American's hot breath smelled of mint and coffee.

"Goddamn you! Don't go to sleep again! Don't you go to sleep again on me! Open your eyes!"

An angry little wasp, that's what the American was. An annoying little nightmare.

"I don't have anything left to lose, General Sabry. And I want a goddamned answer. What about your nuclear delivery system?"

"Nothing works," Sabry mumbled. His army had broken down like the Russian tanks. Had the scientists survived the mob, what they made would have been shit, too.

Lauterbach shook him again. "So if we used nuclears, the ANA could not respond in kind."

Wait a moment, Sabry thought with a flicker of alarm. Something was wrong with this dream. But he could not quite put his finger on the problem.

"You could not respond, sir? Is that what you're saying?"

"Respond?" Sabry asked, blinking. It was very important that he wake up now, he knew. He reached over to pinch his own arm, dragging the IV with him. The pinch didn't hurt, either.

"Answer the question," Lauterbach barked. "Why didn't you nuke us?"

"I wanted to," Sabry groaned. Oh, how he had wanted to. He leveled a glare of hatred at Lauterbach. "I wanted more than life to kill you."

A moment later the American left, and Sabry dropped off to sleep. He didn't dream again.

IN THE LIGHT

The reel purred as his Pa brought in the line.

"No fish today," Jerry said.

"No fish," Pa agreed. He set the rod. In the pool of light on the pier his mottled fingers caressed the lures, the sinkers, before closing the tackle box.

"You'll be leaving now," he told Jerry. Then Pa was up and walking away.

Jerry stared after him in disbelief. When his body could work, he scrambled to his feet and ran after, his heart in his throat. At the other end of the pier, Jerry caught him. His fingers sank into his Pa's arm.

Pa turned around. His face looked stranger than ever. The eyes had sagged, and his mouth, too. His nose was a long horned beak.

"What are you talking about? I'll never leave you," Jerry said.

"You know, Jerry?" his Pa said in Ward Cleaver's voice. "You know what you do with wild things when you capture them?"

Jerry knew. He had seen all the programs. "You let them loose so they can be free."

Pa's rubbery arm slid out of Jerry's grasp. He turned and headed back to the house.

"But damn it, I ain't no bird or lion or nothing," Jerry said, rushing to catch up.

On the lawn, Pa stooped and laid the rod down, put the tackle box beside it. "You'll grow up soon," he said without looking up. This time he sounded like Bill Cosby. "Boys get interested in girls, you know. And their fathers aren't so important anymore."

"Not me, Pa." God. Wouldn't his Pa look at him? If he looked, he would see the need in his face. Need was a kind of glue. It had held Jerry to his old Pa, even when he'd got drunk and beaten him. Now it held him to his new Pa like a fly in honey.

"I'll be good," he promised, his voice a whine. "I'll never do it again. Whatever it was I done, Pa, I'll never do it again."

It didn't seem that his Pa was listening. Jerry had the frightful thought that maybe his Pa didn't love him anymore. Maybe he loved the soldier.

Pa stood regarding the red tackle box. "You'll want to go home one day, and we won't be able to bring you back."

"No, I won't. I won't. Really. Pa, look at me. Why don't you look?"

Pa looked up then. His face was even stranger. The black eyes had a multifaceted sheen. "We've learned everything we could from you." He didn't sound like a television dad now. He didn't even sound like a human.

"No, Pa. No. Please. I can show you lots of things. Fireworks . . ." His mind jittered a dozen different ways, all his thoughts tangled in the panicky idea of abandonment. "You never seen fireworks."

A dull pop at his back made Jerry turn around. A red chrysanthemum burst streamers into the night sky. A whistler went up next, riding a wavy ribbon of brilliance. It exploded into blue and then orange and then green, the sparks racing toward Jerry so fast that he stepped back in surprise.

Pop. In the sky, purple flowers bloomed, their fallen seeds glittery crimson.

"You'll see. I promise," Jerry said. "I can show you lots of things."

Pop. Another chrysanthemum swelled until it filled half the sky. Suddenly Pa's cold arms were around him. Pa pressed his spongy body against Jerry's back.

"Tell me," Pa whispered into his ear.

Something sharp and hard dug into the meat above Jerry's collarbone. He held his breath and forced himself to stand very still. "Shoeing horses," he said, tripping over the words in his rush. "Fixing cars."

The sharp thing pressed harder, stinging a little. His Pa's cold, sodden face was right next to his, cradled in the crook of his neck.

Then Pa released him. Jerry turned around, rubbing his shoulder. There was a tiny hole there, like an exploratory bite.

"We use you, Jerry." His Pa's voice was a pulsing bass, like the hot throb of some huge engine.

"That's all right," Jerry told him.

"And we're not what we seem to be."

"That's okay, too."

"As long as you understand what's happening."

Jerry knew what was happening. It had to do with love and stuff. It had to do with gluey need.

His Pa bent to pick up the fishing gear. "What do you want for dinner?" he asked.

Jerry studied the cherished and ever-changing curves of his Pa's back. "I love you," he whispered fervently.

Pa looked up, surprised. "I love you, too," he said in Bill Cosby's voice.

WARSAW, POLAND

Baranyk got out of the Humvee and waded through the snow, Shcheribitsky and Zgursky at his heels. The wind was bitter, and the temperature, unless Baranyk was imagining it, was still falling.

At the eastern perimeter the main street was cluttered with tanks. Skirting the traffic jam, Baranyk made his way down an alley.

"Like January, sir, isn't it? The way January used to be," Shcheribitsky said, his breath coming in puffs of fog.

Baranyk caught a glimpse of something green deep in the rubble. He stopped, bent, and peered into a small cavern. A girl was lying there, curled in sleep like a cat. One of Warsaw's army of orphans.

"Sir?" the major asked at his back.

"Just a moment, Shcheribitsky."

The general reached in a hand to touch her face. She *was* cold, he saw. As stiff and hard as the bricks around her, and her face as gray as the masonry dust.

Quickly he got up and dusted off his gloves.

"Sir?" the major asked.

"Nothing," Baranyk answered and continued on.

As they reached the ruined perimeter, Baranyk saw that most of the earthworks were gone. Where the munition stockpiles had been was a smoldering crater. Four blocks away from the wreckage sat the radar station, its door wrenched off its hinges. A line of soldiers like worker ants were carting equipment from the building to a sooted apartment house nearby.

Baranyk followed a burdened lieutenant up the stairs. In the living room of a vacant apartment, a fire was blazing in the hearth. Jastrun, surrounded by computer components, was muttering orders to his men.

In the neighboring bedroom stood Czajowski, a phone to his ear. "I am on hold," the commander said with a droll smile.

It was too hot in the apartment. Baranyk slipped his coat from his shoulders and draped it over a swivel chair.

Jastrun turned his irritable attention to a sergeant. "Where are the cables? You were going to get me the cables."

Without a word the sergeant turned, his every movement weary, and trudged out of the room, leaving snowy footprints in his wake.

"No," Czajowski said into the receiver, his English words clipped with irritation. "I will not leave a message."

Baranyk glanced at the commander, but Czajowski was no longer looking his way. He was standing ramrod straight, staring at the snowdrift on the bedroom windowsill.

"Has there been any movement of ANA troops?" Baranyk asked Jastrun.

The colonel glanced up from his appraisal of a keyboard. "What? Uh, no. No movement as yet, general. Captain?" The captain was on his hands and knees searching for a plug. "You will do a diagnostic on this, please."

Baranyk caught Shcheribitsky's eye. "Perhaps the snow confounds the Arabs."

The major shook his head doubtfully. "They are Afghanis and Cossacks and Iranians, sir. They understand cold."

Baranyk studied the room. On one side stood the gleaming computers, the radar screens. The overstuffed and ugly furniture, tattered anachronisms, lay piled against the opposite wall.

"Whose apartment?" he asked Jastrun.

"Who knows?" the colonel said, not looking up from his work. "They are dead, they are gone away? Who knows?"

Most of the pictures had been taken down; Baranyk noted their pale, square ghosts on the wallpaper. Yet the Poles had let a cross remain, along with a saccharine painting of the Virgin.

Czajowski gave a sudden loud and joyous cry. "General Lauterbach!"

Baranyk turned to the bedroom.

"You were to get back to me . . . What? No, not yet. Are you . . . Yes, I know it is difficult. You must understand our difficulty as well."

Baranyk looked at the mute, gray plastic speaker on the table.

"What is that?" Czajowski asked. "No, sir. I do not think we can hold against an enemy attack for more than a couple of hours, perhaps less. Yes? You . . . Well, I see. I understand, but . . ."

Striding into the bedroom, Baranyk hit the button on the speaker. Lauterbach's calm, amplified voice suddenly filled the small apartment. The men at the computers looked up.

" . . . wish you all the luck in the world," the American was saying.

Baranyk's pulse jumped. A vein beat madly in his temple. "Shit!" he shouted into the speaker. "You feed us shit!"

There was a pause, then the American asked, "Valentin Sergeyevich? Is that you?"

"Yes, T. Williams. That is me." He looked at Czajowski's pained face and then back at the speaker. "Have you told him?" he asked.

Another pause from the gray square of plastic. "Told him what?"

"That America plans to drop its pants for the Arabs."

"Valentin," Czajowski said, his tone cajoling and embarrassed.

"Tell him, T. Williams!" Baranyk shot. "Tell him the truth! You are right now drawing up plans for a negotiated peace."

Lauterbach's answer was curt and quick. "We are not."

"You are not sending a division," Baranyk persisted.

A short hesitation. In that brief silence Baranyk could hear his world crumble. "No," Lauterbach admitted.

"You never were."

"No."

"You will let the Arabs have Poland, to keep Germany safe. Tell him, T. Williams. Admit it."

Over the speaker came the sound of Lauterbach clearing his throat. The apartment was hushed now, except for the crackle of the fire. Soldiers were seated on the living-room floor, their terrified eyes on the speaker.

"I cannot allow that to happen," Lauterbach said.

"What?" Baranyk pulled his gaze away from a young Polish boy's blanched face, the memory of the little dead girl following like an afterthought.

"I said I cannot allow the Arabs to have Poland. It will upset the balance of world power. You have to look to the future, Valentin Sergeyevich," he was saying.

Baranyk was trying to understand. The future? But there was no future. Didn't the American realize that? There was no tomorrow for Warsaw. There were only eventualities.

"I'm looking ten, twenty years ahead, as America should have done after the Second World War . . ."

"What shit," Baranyk whispered. His eyes went to the window and the softly falling snow. Suddenly an idea came to him. It was a nasty idea, and it moved in him as a worm through a corpse. "How do you plan to stop them?"

"You must understand the necessity," the American said.

Baranyk exchanged a horrified look with Czajowski.

The American was saying, "I don't make this decision lightly. I've tried everything. God. I've tried. Believe me . . ."

"Don't ask me to believe you!" Baranyk shouted. "How can I believe you? You will not let the Arabs have Poland, so no one may have Poland. You will make it unlivable for a thousand years!"

"It will be a surgical strike. Low yield."

Now that Lauterbach was finally speaking, he wouldn't shut up. Baranyk wanted to clap a hand over the speaker as if it were the American's mouth.

"There's a chance for you," Lauterbach was saying. "There will be some warning. I can't tell you more than that. Get into the basement. Take food and water. Maybe you can ride it out. I wish . . ." His voice foundered, struggled to go on. "I wish you all the luck . . ."

Lauterbach must have hung up, because Baranyk realized that he was listening to the hum of an empty line.

He looked around. None of the soldiers had moved, and for a moment he had the frightening thought that they were dead, all of them dead, their insides crisped to cinders.

IN THE LIGHT

"You must leave now," Dr. Gladdings said.

Rita was standing in the entranceway before the heavy double doors, Dr. Gladdings beside her.

"They're coming. You have to leave," he told her.

Her hand dropped to one of the scrolled knobs. Cold. Cold. Like the touch of frozen flesh. Ice sweated from the pores of the metal skin.

"No," she whispered, snatching her hand away.

But suddenly she was outside, at the curb, in the dull, gray day. Above her head the ice-bound branches chimed softly. On the ground a few dead leaves caught the wind and sailed scrape-stop-scrape along the asphalt.

"Dr. Gladdings?" she called, turning to the closed, unlit building.

Around her sleet began to hiss on the gelid ground.

"Dr. Gladdings?"

Something huge was coming down the wintry, tree-lined street, its headlights bright halogen stars in the gray afternoon. It crawled along, scattering drifts of brown leaves. Over the dark square of the driver's window was a sign that read CHARTER.

The bus stopped at the curb, brakes groaning. The ribbed metal of its sides wore a matte finish of dust.

A hydraulic sigh. The door opened. On a high bench seat sat the driver, a lump of ill-shaped clay.

"Get in," he said.

She blundered back, back down the sidewalk, toward the safety of the library. Her shoulders and the rear of her head bumped against the inside of the windshield.

The bus stank of stale air and mildew. The windows were dry, but rain chattered and gossiped on the roof. In the middle of the banked rows of seats a man was screaming.

"We going to fuck now?" a boy asked.

She whirled. In the front row a Navy flier sat, smiling bitterly. "Hey, driver," he said. "You want to order us to the backseat so the captain and I can fuck?"

The bus lurched as it drove off. Rita grabbed the frigid steel bar of the driver's seat and hung on. The screaming man was an ANA private, a Turk, too old for his rank, too old, it seemed, even for the service. He was ranting as he shrieked, a hopeless, futile babble. Beyond him in the shadows was another ANA soldier. A young Libyan corporal.

"Look, honey," the pilot said. "I don't have anything against dark meat, but could you make your breasts a little bigger?"

Warily, she sat across the aisle from the American pilot as the bus drove into the night. *Don't make a sound*, she thought. *Don't move. Don't draw any attention.* She sat like a child in church, hands folded in her lap, deciding that, if she stayed very still, danger might pass her by.

The sound of rain on the roof grew heavier. The driver turned on the wipers.

"Hey," the pilot said, leaning toward the driver. "Where's my F-14? Or did I learn that lesson already?"

Rita looked out of the corner of her eye and saw they were in a desert. On either side of the road, black sand dunes hunched like waiting assassins in the dark.

"Gosh, folks," the young, dark-headed pilot said. "You already taught me I'm a coward. I just can't wait to see what you're going to teach me now."

Behind her the screaming man's voice rose to a keen, thin garrote of a wail, then lowered to a blunt-instrument moan; an unending assault of sound.

The bus pulled up next to a tapestried tent agleam in torchlight. The door wheezed open. A Saudi officer, a hatchet-faced, cruel-looking man, boarded; he gave one curious glance to the pilot and another to Rita before he strode down the aisle. Very slowly, very cautiously Rita turned and peered over the seats. The Saudi skirted the screamer and sat down beside the corporal.

Now the wailing man was beating his head against the window. Along with the ever-present rain, there was the hollow-melon drumming of a skull on glass.

"Please. Where are you taking us?" she asked the driver politely, in the voice one uses to address the powerful: a priest, a president, a murderer.

He didn't answer. They were moving out of the desert and into the chill, waiting stars.

"It's all an illusion," the pilot laughed.

The stars gathered, as though for warmth, in the center of the windshield. A moment later they sprang away. Rita saw the bus was landing, coming down in a moonlit forest.

With an imperious snap the door opened. A cold wind whipped in the doorway, carrying with it confetti flakes of snow. There was no sound now, except for the old man's howls.

"Last stop. Get out," the driver ordered.

The pilot stood.

Fearing to be left behind, Rita got to her feet as well. "I think we're home," she whispered to the pilot.

The boy's lips twisted into a patronizing smile. "Just play along," he said. "It's easier that way." He walked down the steps. Then the two Arabs left, abandoning the hysterical old man.

The driver turned in his seat, his eyes flicking by Rita and resting on the screamer. Below those pitiless, bulging eyes, his nose was a daggered beak.

The driver started to rise, but Rita said, "Please. I'll get him, I'll get him."

The driver settled into his seat like so much khaki ice cream. In the dead, oblivious silence, she inched her way down the aisle.

"Shhhh," Rita said. She grabbed the old Turk's wrist. His flesh was firm, his skin feverish. His eyes were wide and blank.

"It's going to be all right now. They brought us home," she told him gently, even though she knew he didn't understand a word.

CENTRAL ARMY HOSPITAL, BADAJOZ, SPAIN

Sabry rolled his head listlessly to the side when he heard the door open. The doctor coming in with a shot of Demerol, he hoped. His hip was starting to ache, and there was a tingling foretaste of agony in his thigh.

It wasn't the doctor, it was Lauterbach.

The American was followed by a blond man in a business suit. Sabry caught himself staring. How long had it been since he'd seen a three-piece suit? Five years? Six?

"General Sabry," Lauterbach said. "This is Mr. Thornson from the International Red Cross. He's here to observe the treatment of prisoners, and I've told him you wish to make a statement."

The man's eyebrows were cottony, his eyes a faded blue. He took a small tape recorder from his pocket and set it on the nightstand.

"I have been told you were beaten," Thornson said. "In violation of the Geneva Convention. Is that correct?"

Sabry looked at Lauterbach. The general was standing, hands clasped behind his back, facing the night-darkened window.

Thornson, too, looked at Lauterbach. "You told me you struck him."

"Repeatedly," said the American.

The tape recorder was running, Sabry noticed in disbelief.

"Why?" The man from the Red Cross sounded mildly irritated.

"I was angry," the American replied. "He would not respond to my questions."

"The man was coming out of anesthesia."

"That's correct, sir. I slapped him to wake him up."

"I see," Thornson said. "Would you care to make a complaint, General Sabry?"

There was remorse in Lauterbach's face, but a remorse too keen to have been caused by the manner of interrogation. No, the guilt was for what Lauterbach had learned.

I told him too much, Sabry realized, his own guilt making him flush. He glanced at the man from the Red Cross to see if he had caught any hint of the shared sin. But Thornson was staring in pity at the IV in Sabry's arm.

"Perhaps it would be best if you left the room, General Lauterbach."

Lauterbach started. "What?" he asked faintly, and Sabry saw then that under Lauterbach's crust of guilt lay a soft, unbearable pain.

What drives a man to despair? Sabry wondered. Shame, of course, but that was an Arabic answer. Maudlin Americans grieved most over unrequited love.

Thornson said, "He's obviously afraid of you. I doubt he wants to lodge the complaint with you in the room."

"I understand." The American nodded, spun on his heel, and walked out.

When the door closed, Sabry asked, "Did he tell you that he hit me?"

"Yes, sir."

"Did he tell you what questions he asked?"

"No, sir. He told me he considered your conversation classified."

Sabry motioned Thornson closer. His eyes narrowed with cunning; his smile grew edged. Lauterbach wanted to commit a sort of suicide and was asking Sabry to be the gun. But sometimes a gun's aim was off. Sometimes the bullet didn't kill; it maimed.

"He never touched me. We talked of the weather, of my leg. Just between us?" Sabry whispered. "I think the man is insane."

CHAPTER 18

EASTERN RADAR ARRAY, WARSAW, POLAND

The room was dark. Outside, the clouds had cleared. Zgursky stood in the window of the command room, caught in a shaft of moonlight.

Baranyk recalled that the flash of the Hiroshima camera had cast sooted shadows on walls, a portrait of the dying. He looked around the room and wondered what snapshots the flashbulbs of Warsaw would take.

At the radar screens, technicians hunched, a line of trolls in the green radiance of their VDTs. Near Zgursky sat Major Shcheribitsky, some trick of the warring lights—green and moon-pale—making his pock-marked face seem young.

Behind the closed bedroom door voices rose and fell, the sound of Czajowski's and Jastrun's argument. Baranyk wondered if the incandescent glare would catch their Punch-and-Judy silhouettes, too.

Baranyk asked Zgursky quietly, "Do you remember when I gave you your stripes?"

In the moonlight, Zgursky turned, the enchanted heir of a doomed kingdom.

"Do you remember, sergeant? I had the major call for you. Remember that, Gennady Ivanovich?"

Shcheribitsky slowly raised his head.

"To tease you, the major acted very distressed, and from

the look on your face, I'm sure you had decided I was about to blame you for everything, for the fall of Kiev, for the crucifixion of Christ, perhaps. You were shaking in your boots, and I had no idea why." Baranyk gave a soft laugh. Shcheribitsky chuckled with him.

Zgursky managed a smile.

"We have had some good times," Baranyk told them. "Haven't we? Despite the war, some good times."

"Yes, sir," Zgursky whispered.

Baranyk knew what portrait the blistering camera would make of them: three resigned figures, an image of good friends.

"Should we go into the basement, sir?" Zgursky asked.

Shcheribitsky shook his head, a beam of moonlight toying with his chestnut hair. "Quicker this way," he said.

Very quick: a flashbulb. Baranyk pictured the winter melting into a second, momentary spring. In her cubbyhole of ice the dead little orphan would thaw and then burn.

"Remember when Corporal Lozhovska's team was to move the T-80," Baranyk asked. "But it was raining so they closed the hatches? And the Tatar driver ran over the car of the Minister of the Interior because he couldn't see? It was hell trying to convince the Poles the Muslim was a loyal Ukrainian and the destruction of the minister's new Volvo an accident."

A grin tugged one side of Zgursky's mouth.

"Remember the good times," Baranyk said.

The argument beyond the door crescendoed. Shcheribitsky raised his head like a fox sniffing the air. Jastrun burst into the room, still raging.

"We must surrender!" he cried.

Czajowski was at his heels. "I will get on the phone again to Lauterbach. I will talk to him. He will listen to reason."

The colonel whirled on his commander, his face so twisted that in the green light of the radar screens he resembled a terrorized demon. "He does not answer the *phone!*" Jastrun screamed. "Damn you! He does not come to the *phone!* We will surrender now. Don't you see? Lieutenant—" He snapped his fingers. "Lieutenant—"

An officer stood up, awaiting orders. It was obvious that Jastrun had forgotten the man's name.

"Lieutenant. Get to the radio station immediately. Send out a message to the Arabs that we offer terms. And tell the citizens of Warsaw to go to their basements . . ."

"Ignore that order," Czajowski told the man as the lieutenant took a hesitant step to the door.

"You will kill them!" Jastrun screamed. "If you do not tell them what is coming, you will murder everyone!"

The men at the radar screens watched fearfully, uncertain which officer would win, and whose orders they would obey.

"I will try Lauterbach again," Czajowski said.

"You have sucked the American's cock!" Jastrun shouted. "And now they kick you for a whore!"

Shcheribitsky roared, "Shut up!"

Baranyk was taken aback by his aide's vehemence. To Shcheribitsky, apparently, sins were not all equal. For the Americans to bomb Warsaw was a transgression to be sure, but for the colonel to admonish his own commander—that was an offense in the sight of God.

"Be reasonable, colonel," Baranyk said. "There is nothing to be gained by surrender. The Americans will bomb anyway."

"Don't you see?" Jastrun threw his arms wide, as though to carry them all into the mutiny with him. "If the Arabs know what is coming, they may shoot the planes down."

Baranyk's stomach curdled. Holy Father. To help the Arabs hunt the Americans down. The idea had a certain ugly seduction.

It struck him suddenly that what he most wanted in the world was a drink. He wondered if there was time for Zgursky to find him a bottle, and if he dared give the boy such an order.

"A good soldier knows when to fight. He also knows when fighting is useless," Baranyk said.

"*You* dare tell *me* what a good soldier knows?" Jastrun blurted, turning on Baranyk. "You and your Ukrainian fatalism? Will you let Warsaw fall as you did Kiev, with your head stuck in a bottle of vodka?"

A blur at the corner of Baranyk's vision. Shcheribitsky had launched himself from his chair. Head lowered, the smaller major hit the tall, thin Pole in the stomach, driving him backward. The breath exploded from the colonel's lungs in a loud *oof*.

Arms locked, the two men staggered into a table and then into a pile of helmets. They went down. Helmets clicked and rolled like skulls.

Furious grunts from the struggling men. Fists smacked flesh. The wooden floor creaked. Jastrun, the victor, sprang up and ran for the door.

"Colonel? I will shoot you," Czajowski said mildly.

Jastrun whirled, his hand on the doorknob. The Polish commander had drawn his sidearm, a blue steel Makarov, and was aiming it at Jastrun's chest. On the floor, Shcheribitsky was getting up, cradling his bleeding face.

"I beg you to sit down," Czajowski told the colonel. "There is a bullet in the chamber, and my arthritis makes my fingers stiff. I haven't the control of the trigger that I would like."

Jastrun froze. Prudently keeping his head down, Shcheribitsky was crawling away.

"Colonel?" Czajowski asked.

"Please," Jastrun whispered. Tears glistened on his cheeks. "Please. We will never forgive ourselves if we do not warn them."

Was this the way the flashbulb would catch them? Baranyk wondered. Was this to be their last testament? Would tourists, years from now, marvel at the silhouettes of dying men with hands at each other's throats?

"Target acquired," a technician said.

Czajowski's gun hand fell limply to his side.

"Target acquired and tracking now, sir."

Baranyk went over to the technician. "One?" he barked.

"One, sir," the man replied, his voice a little hopeful. "No IFF. Too slow to be a missile. A plane, then. At fifty-five thousand feet. Too high for a bomber, don't you think, sir? It might be an Arab recon."

Baranyk said, "A gravity bomb. On an old B-52."

Some sixteen kilometers distant, Arab AAA began to rattle.

"Let us fire our last missiles!" Jastrun begged. "Please let us fire our last few missiles to bring it down."

"No," Czajowski said.

The white mark on the screen inched closer and closer, approaching along the polar route.

Suddenly Czajowski spun and went to the bedroom. "I will call Lauterbach again," he said. "I will call the Americans, and they will listen to reason."

The Pole slammed the door. The crash made Baranyk flinch even though he was expecting it, even though he knew it was not the last sound he would hear.

"I remember when I was a boy," Zgursky said, "and we had a cow who didn't like to be milked. She would piss on you, isn't that funny? When you got close to her flanks, she would piss." His laughter fluttered high, higher, dizzily out of reach. "I remember—"

"Twelve kilometers out," the technician said.

Baranyk held his breath. The Arab AAA rattled angrily beyond the window.

"I traveled once to St. Petersburg," Zgursky was saying in a rush. "My father became angry because we were lost. Such a big city. My mother laughed at him. I remember . . ."

Quicker than a heartbeat, Baranyk thought. One blinding flash, and they would all be soot on a bare, standing wall.

"My sister was allergic to oranges," Zgursky prattled. "And what did her new boyfriend give her? But she ate them anyway. Welts all over, and still she ate them."

Not burned to death. Vaporized. Baranyk rolled the idea around his mind like a bitter cherry.

The tech's voice rose. "Moving away now! Sir! It is moving away!"

A flat bang. Gasps peppered the living room. Baranyk turned to the mute bedroom door. In three strides he was there, his hand on the cool knob, his heart in his throat.

Blue smoke layered the brightly lit bedroom's air. Czajowski stood, pistol in hand.

The phone lay in pieces, its plastic cover burst. "He wouldn't speak to me," Czajowski said with an apologetic shrug. "Lauterbach wouldn't come to the phone."

KAMPINESKA FOREST, NEAR WARSAW

The world was shades of film-negative gray. Across the snow, moonlight cast latticework shadows. The old man's shrieks echoed among the pines.

"Why doesn't somebody shut him up," the pilot muttered.

The two Arabs, arms folded, danced a jig of cold.

"Hey!" the pilot shouted. "I'd like to go to Florida now! You hear me, you assholes?"

A sharp rattle. Rita turned. Two soldiers in calf-length coats emerged from the gathered trees, AK-47s in their hands.

"Oh, hey," the pilot said. "This is good. This is creative."

The soldiers' frightened gazes brushed Rita and fixed on the shrieking man. The screamer fell to his knees. Guttural orders from the soldiers. A Slavic language. Russian? Czech?

"No," the pilot said. "No, really. This is great."

The Saudi officer was inching away. Any minute he would run and the soldiers would kill them all. The soldiers' voices grew shriller, more alarmed. The Saudi froze; but the old Turk got to his feet. Arms outspread, he made his cringing way toward the soldiers like a dog coming to heel.

A shout. A warning? Then an end-of-the-world crack as an AK spat flame. The top of the screamer's head exploded. He dropped. The pilot stumbled back whimpering, his cheeks chicken-poxed with the screamer's brain.

A firefly mass of bobbing lights hurried through the forest. A voice snapped in Slavic-accented English, "American? You are American?"

Aimed flashlights struck bullet-blasts of color: the aqua of the pilot's shoulder patch; the strawberry spill of blood on his cheeks.

An officer pushed his way into the barrage of light, his boots squeaking in the snow. Two angry lines bracketed his mouth. The muscles in his jaw worked.

The pilot lurched in wind-up-toy circles. He stumbled over the body of the screamer and fell into a drift.

The officer stepped over the corpse and pulled his sidearm from its holster. Grabbing a fistful of the pilot's hair, he shoved the 9mm to the boy's throat. "American pilot!" The officer's words emerged in cartoon-balloons of fog. "What are you doing with Arabs? Will you kill us and then betray us to the enemy, too? What are your orders?"

"I don't remember," the pilot babbled. "I can't . . . Maybe it was a CAP mission for the bombers. Maybe . . ."

"Where are your bombs? Your plane?"

"I punched out! Oh, Jesus! I punched out! I didn't mean it. And I told them stuff. I told them everything! I'm sorry if I—"

"General Lauterbach will want to see us!" Rita said.

The officer turned.

"You're allies, aren't you?" she asked.

"Once I thought we were." His eyes were arctic blue.

She stepped toward him and stumbled. Her numb feet seemed to have merged with her boots, so she couldn't tell where leather ended and skin began. "Help us," she told him. "We're going to freeze to death."

"We will all be dead in a few minutes." Skirting the dead body, the officer walked into the circle of blinding light. "Stand him up, captain! Stand the pilot up."

The Navy boy, frenzy consumed, had fallen facedown.

"If we shoot him on the ground, we will make a mess of it."

"Wait!" Rita gasped.

A barked order. The dry rattle of cocking guns. The Saudi officer, ablaze in the light as though already transcended to Heaven, covered his face and moaned.

"Wait a minute!" Rita shouted. "For Christ's sake wait

just a minute! What's the matter with you people?"

It was a trick, that was it. Any moment, Dr. Gladdings would walk out of the hazy, monochrome moonlight to ask what she thought of death.

It sucks, that's what she'd tell him. Death was a crock.

Her nose was running, the mucus freezing on her lips. Wanting to plead, she opened her mouth. The icy breeze stole her breath.

Beyond the screen of trees came a loud *chug-chug*. Fire stitched a red seam across the night.

The forest was thinner than Rita had imagined. Beyond the fringe of pine, buildings were etched in the glow of the barrage.

The flashlight beams lowered, casting polka dots on the snow. The soldiers stood swathed in moonlight, their rifles pointed down, their heads lifted to the flashing sky.

"What is it?" she asked. "What's happening?"

Bitterly, the officer laughed. "The fall of Warsaw," he said.

EASTERN RADAR ARRAY, WARSAW, POLAND

"Sir?" a tech said. "We are experiencing ECM."

Baranyk wiped his face. His palms came away greasy with sweat. Czajowski stopped his incessant silent praying to lean over the tech's shoulder. On the screen, too many bogeys, appearing and disappearing. A green fishbowl of fireflies that came and went.

"It has been a pleasure to serve with you both," Baranyk told his aides.

The major nodded. His face was puffy and bruised, his russet eyes resigned.

The room was deathly silent, all the people in it still, as though awaiting the glare of the flashbulb.

The Arab AAA started up again, furiously this time. Its glare lit the room. In his corner Jastrun sat huddled, a toddler playing hide-and-seek, his face in his hands.

"Sir?" Zgursky asked, grabbing Baranyk's arm. "Do you think it will be fast, sir?"

The general put his hand on the aide's. "Very fast. No. Don't look out the window now. Look at the wall there. See the places where the pictures were? Those pale squares?"

"Yes, sir?"

"I want you to look at them very hard, Yuri Vassiliyevich. Stand right by me and look. I want you to tell me what sort of pictures you think they were. Shcheribitsky?" he asked. Lowering his voice to the point of halting affection he said, "Genya? Will you not tell me what pictures you see?"

"Flowers, sir," the major said in a squeezed voice. "I think there was probably one of flowers in a meadow."

"Yura?" Baranyk asked gently, "What are the paintings?"

The aide's voice came out in staccato gasps. "I don't know, sir."

"Look!" Baranyk's voice was made so harsh, so loud, by his own terror that Czajowski glanced up. "Look at the wall, Yura, and imagine the paintings. One of a troika in the snow, don't you see it? Don't you see how the woman is laughing, how the man shouts to his horses? Look! There is a picture of a family, can't you see? The frame done up in gold leaf? There is the father, and there the pretty mother in braids, and there . . ."

His desperate words died heart-shot. Outside the window came a low bass boom.

The aide began to pull away, but Baranyk held his fingers tight. "Quick! Look there, Yura. Look at the wall. See the flowers? The laughing people? There is a dog there beside them, can you see that? A spotted dog, a small one. See how the child reaches down . . ."

A boom so loud, it shook the building's foundations. The cross swayed on its perch and fell.

"We should not be hearing this!" Baranyk shouted. "Why are we hearing the bombs?" He dropped Zgursky's hand and turned, Shcheribitsky snatching at him. Baranyk turned, thinking that the flash would strike him blind.

The horizon was aflame. Bombs were falling, bleeding fire into the night.

"Oh, look," Baranyk whispered.

No flash. No blinding light.

In hushed wonder he breathed, "Look. Lauterbach lied again."

TRÁS-OS-MONTES, PORTUGAL

Momma's going to be mad at me. It hurts. When Momma finds out, she's going to be mad.

Pain brushed them. Death perfumed the wind.

Don't touch anything, Momma told me, but when I picked up the funny green ball, it bit me. It bit me because I was bad.

The need became louder as they drifted through the early morning fog and the trees. In the glade the grass was empty except for a little girl, and she was dying.

It hurts, the little girl thought.

Bleeding stumps where her hands should have been. A carmine ruin of a chest below round, childish cheeks. The little girl sensed their approach and turned her face, their blue reflected in her eyes.

They hoped she would think of something else now, something other than her terror at seeing them. Dying had a rich flavor when mixed with memory; and a bitter one when mixed with fear.

Tender as air, light as a last breath, they settled. One acrid taste of fear, and then—

Watching the goats leap over each other in the meadow. Bouncing like balls. Like furry balls. How funny. If goats could laugh, they would—

Her thoughts were on the goats when they took her. A ripple moved through the gathering, a shock wave of satiation. A moment later, they rose from the husk and hovered, the sweet aftertaste lingering. Some small, nearly forgotten chore nagged at their minds.

Moving down now, down through the mist-choked mountains, not savory death drawing them, but something almost as powerful. Something alien.

Faster. Need building to an ache. Flying through fields and pines and cow-dotted meadows.

Exotic things. Familiar things. Buildings that were barracks. Men who were prisoners and men who were not.

They—he—suddenly remembered who he had been.

Cramping desire rocked him. He saw faces like moons in the windows of the mess hall. He heard screams from the Arab prisoners and shouts from the MPs.

Two men on the porch: a tall man the color of chocolate; a short man with onyx eyes. There was something he should remember, he knew, but recollection came slow.

It was Toshio who came forward across the yard, even though Pelham put out a hand to stop him.

"Gordon?" he whispered, putting his hand into Gordon's blue, glowing flesh.

Gordon shied from the touch of Toshio's longing.

I'll tell you what you'd taste of, Gordon thought. *Sushi and incense and calm rivers. Pelham would taste bittersweet.*

The colonel was coming down the steps now, striding out to the gravel where Toshio stood. Gordon felt an undefined, paralyzing need, one as strong as the thirst he was learning.

"It is Gordon," the Japanese told Pelham. "He has come to say goodbye."

That was it, Gordon thought. Yes. That was what had brought him. He had come to say goodbye.

Satisfied now, he melted into the ranks of the community. Small chore done, they moved away, gaining speed over the gravel, hurrying through the wire barricades and up into the waiting sky.

WARSAW, POLAND

No one spoke. In the silence of the room, Baranyk's thoughts lost direction, bent back on themselves and strayed.

Toward dawn the bombs stopped. Gray smoke feathered the peach horizon.

Baranyk glanced at Zgursky, who was running his palm monotonously up and down his thigh, up and down, reading the warm, living Braille of his own body.

"Who are they?" Zgursky asked.

No one answered.

"Are we all right now?" Zgursky asked.

A fluttering rumble snapped Baranyk's attention back to the window. When he caught a glimpse of the helicopter speeding toward them, he stiffened. Grabbing his coat, he ran down the stairs, Czajowski behind.

In the cold, late-morning air he halted. Not a Chinook, he saw with troubled confusion. A Hind.

The huge chopper settled on its landing gear like a brown dragonfly. Through the rotor-driven blizzard Baranyk caught a glimpse of a figure walking, head ducked, coat flapping. Baranyk squinted, furiously wiped the blown snow from his lashes, and looked again. A Russian general emerged from the maelstrom, brushing fussily at his coat.

"Oleg Tolmachov at your service," he said in passable Polish as he approached. His heavy, peasant's face was high-colored from excitement and cold. He pulled off his gloves, shoved them in his pocket, and held a hand out to Czajowski.

The Pole's inattentive eyes drifted toward the helicopter, toward the curling smoke of the Arab emplacements. After an awkward moment, the Russian dropped his hand.

"We caught the Arabs squatting over the shit-hole, bare-assed and mouths open," Tolmachov said. "The early snow scared them, it seems. The prisoners tell us there were mass desertions ever since the cold snap. Like fleas off a dog, you'll be plucking Arabs from the woods for years."

"Did you see no other planes?" Czajowski asked.

"Other planes?" The Russian general cocked his head to the side and blew on his cupped and reddening hands. "We sent a high-altitude recon through before the airstrike. That one?"

"Other bombers," the Pole whispered.

Tolmachov glanced at Baranyk and gave the Pole a curious look. "A pilot reported sighting a B-2 above him, between him and the moon. But if it was there, it left during the bombing runs."

"I see," Czajowski said, nodding vaguely. "Thank you."

The Russian stamped his feet to get the circulation going. "A long night," he said in a subdued voice. "I wouldn't mind a glass of something. Tea. Vodka would be better yet. I'll take you to our headquarters. I have a surprise waiting for you there. We can celebrate."

"Yes," Czajowski said absently. "Perhaps we can celebrate." Not looking at either man, the Pole plodded to the chopper.

Tolmachov took Baranyk's arm. "Everything is all right now. You understand?" he said, switching to Russian.

Russian made the words nearly credible. The sound of the language was as cozy as Baranyk's old feather bed, his goose-down comforter. He watched Czajowski, hunch-backed with exhaustion, climb into the Hind. Baranyk took a deep breath that tasted of ashes.

Suddenly he felt hungry and remembered that he had missed breakfast. Missed dinner the night before. So many months of stingy meals. His uniform hung on him, not like the well-tailored uniform of the Russian. He felt ashamed and touched at the same time, as if his wealthy, estranged mother had picked him up from the orphanage to enjoy a pleasant day in the country.

Remember the good times, he thought.

"Does the Pole think we invade?" Tolmachov asked. "We have no intention of that." He shook Baranyk's arm. "What is the matter with you people? Listen to me. The war is over."

No, Baranyk thought. *It cannot be as easy as this.*

"You are Lieutenant General Baranyk, are you not?"

Baranyk caught himself tugging painfully at his ear, as if milking belief from his skeptical body. He stopped himself and nodded.

"President Pankov sends you a message."

The Russian's epaulets were a crisp blue. His brass buttons gleamed. There was not a speck of dust on his coat; not a rent; not a worn patch. Not a drop of blood anywhere.

"He wanted me to tell you that he has looked up into the sky as you told him to do. He says he has seen the early snow and asks if the American general will put in a good word for him now. Do you know what he means?"

Baranyk's lips twisted. "I will take that vodka now," he said.

They waded through the snow and got into the Hind. The chopper lifted with a scream of turbines and banked east. Staring out the window, Baranyk saw smoldering emplacements pimpled by black craters. Nearby, Arabs stood knee-deep in snow, dirty sheep abandoned in a meadow. Their camouflage uniforms were gray with frost, and they huddled together for warmth. Thousands and thousands of them, waiting motionlessly, their rifleless arms wrapped around them, their blank faces upraised.

By an outlying country house, the Hind landed. Baranyk followed Tolmachov out into the stinging, snow-blown wash.

"Their supply lines, their logistics were shit!" the Russian shouted gleefully. "Their trucks broke down miles back in the snowfall. Stupid Arabs. They hadn't planned for the sudden winter. They were using the wrong antifreeze, the wrong grade of oil."

In the yard, Russian soldiers were stacking corpses. The Arab bodies had stiffened into improbable, puzzling positions: a brittle hand upraised there, a knee bent as though in sleep, an open mouth gorged with snow. A few wore frozen blood on their cardboard clothes like spills of cherry jam. Most bore no mark at all, no sign of what had killed them, other than the frost veining their blue-marble flesh.

"Where are their coats?" Baranyk asked.

Tolmachov cupped a hand to his ear. "What? Yes. A grand victory."

"No. I asked about the Arabs' coats. Their gloves."

In front of the piled corpses young Russian boys were laughing. Callous as children, they brandished unfired rifles and posed for heroic pictures to send home.

"Oh," Tolmachov said gruffly. "That. The coats went the way of their food: caught in transit, as I told you. If we wait a few days longer, the Arab question will be solved, don't you think?"

Should he tell him? Baranyk wondered. Is it possible he didn't know? Such a grand victory it was: Tolmachov bombing the dead.

After a final look at the corpses, Baranyk trudged into the warmth of the house. In a quiet back room a fire crackled in the grate. On the table stood a tray piled with poppyseed cakes; a platter burdened with sliced sausage.

"Vodka, then?" Tolmachov asked as he shrugged out of his coat.

Baranyk watched the amazed Czajowski pause at the table, saw his gloved hand go out and snatch at the tray of meats. Mechanically, without a hint of delight, the Pole shoved slice after slice into his mouth.

A frown crossed Tolmachov's face. "Vodka!" he shouted.

An aide came in toting a heavy silver tray. Baranyk downed his offered shot glass and waited until the Russian placed the bottle on the table. With trembling hands Baranyk picked up the bottle and drank from the neck.

"I had intended a toast," the Russian said in quiet disapproval.

"A toast!" Baranyk cried. Feeling dizzy, he held the bottle up and saw he had drunk nearly a quarter. "A toast, Andrzej," he said brightly, nudging the Pole so hard in the ribs that Czajowski stopped chewing.

The Pole picked up his glass and drank. Then reached for the sausage again.

Tolmachov turned away. "Well," he muttered, as if Baranyk and Czajowski had ruined the party. He shouted to the closed door, "Bring in the generals' surprise!"

Sharp clicks of polished boots on a polished floor. The door swung open, and two smartly dressed officers marched in, herding a bearded, sniveling ragamuffin.

The man's cheeks were flushed with fever, his feet swaddled in stained cloth. A Russian Army blanket hung around his shoulders. Baranyk saw the uniform under the folds of olive wool and caught his breath.

Switching to English, Tolmachov asked the threadbare man, "Do you not have something to tell them?"

The man shivered, leveled hostile eyes at Tolmachov, swiped angrily at his nose.

The Russian turned to Baranyk. "He speaks. I know he speaks. Tell them, General Shuqairi. Tell them how you regret this."

Baranyk felt an electric jolt of familiarity. *I know him*, he thought. *An Afghani?* he wondered. His mind rolled back to all the Arabs he had ever met; all the Arabs he had fought.

No, he realized at last. The man was familiar only because the eyes were commonplace. They were the same haunted eyes he saw in Zgursky's face, in Czajowski's, and in his own shaving mirror.

"Tell them," Tolmachov insisted. "Tell them as you told me, when you were begging us not to shoot you, when you were crawling on your hands and knees weeping. Tell them!" he barked.

Baranyk glanced at Czajowski. The Pole was still chewing, staring into space, as though he were waiting for angels to herald the victory.

Suddenly the Arab's dark gaze found Baranyk and began to take him in: from his scuffed boots to his soiled coat, and up the tarnished buttons to those overly familiar eyes.

Haven't we met before? asked that hollow, exhausted gaze. *Don't I know you?*

In the hearth, the quiet fire snapped, scenting the room with pine smoke. The snow on the Arab's matted hair was melting, and water ran down his fevered brow, his temples, like rain.

"I am sorry," the Arab muttered in English.

After a moment, Baranyk replied, "I am, too."

CHAPTER 19

LEBANON, TEN YEARS LATER

Wheezing, Rashid Aziz Sabry climbed the white limestone steps to his garden, a stiff breeze from the Mediterranean nudging his back. From the patio of the house, Irací called, and he paused to look up, shading his eyes.

His young Brazilian wife was standing in the shade of the blue Fiberglas overhang, dappled in undersea color. She was patting her head, a reminder to put on his hat.

He ignored her, ignored the pain in his stump. He climbed higher. The moss roses were blooming, he saw.

"Your hat!" she shouted.

He waved her warning away. A cool sun now, that was what the scientists said. A serendipitous lessening of solar flares. Sabry couldn't tell the difference. A bead of sweat slipped from his balding head and dropped, stinging, into his eyes.

"Well, at least get dressed for the visitors!"

Irací was wearing an abbreviated red dress. Her shoulders were exposed, as were her long, taut legs. He winced, imagining what the old mullahs would say.

But marry at all, as the new saying went, and wed a foreigner. Too many Arab women had died.

"Yes, yes," he said dismissively.

Irací persisted. "They will be here any minute. I'll ask them to dinner—watch your diet, remember—and I won't let you sit down at the table with your filthy gardening clothes."

"Please, don't ask them to dinner," he groaned. But she was already turning away.

Foolishness in his old age, to obey the summons of his loins and in so doing make himself captive. He contemplated the sway of his wife's hips and decided, with a sigh, that the imprisonment was worthwhile.

The sound of a car drew his attention to the bottom of the cliff. On the ocean road a Saab pulled up and parked. A spark of brown and crimson against the white steps: Irací was going down to greet them.

Sabry stood, his jaw set. A tall coffee-and-cream woman emerged from the driver's seat. She went to the passenger side and helped out a small, feeble man.

The American was wearing a striped shirt and jeans. Perhaps it was the lack of uniform, Sabry thought, that made him look powerless. Turning his back on the visitors, Sabry began to weed. The beetles were after the strawflowers again, he noticed. And aphids dotted the purple lupines.

"Thank you for seeing me."

The voice was close behind him. Lauterbach had climbed the steps so stealthily that Sabry had not heard his approach. Whatever else had changed, the American was still furtive.

Sabry turned and saw that the man's skin was stretched tissue-thin over the bones of his skull.

Do I look that old? Sabry wondered. He thought not. The same fat face stared back at him in the morning mirror.

Lauterbach is ill, Sabry realized.

No. He is dying.

"The women went up to the house," Lauterbach said, at a loss. He paused, awaiting an invitation. On the gnarled hands, on the insides of the man's bony elbows, Sabry could see the angry pinpricks of a doctor's needles.

The bald dome of the American's head had already turned pink from the heat, and he was sweating. He looked utterly miserable. Grudgingly, Sabry waved to the covered patio. "Come. Sit," he said.

Lauterbach followed, his pace slower than Sabry's own limp. They sat in wicker chairs under the blue-tinted shade. Sabry watched afternoon clouds build over the ocean.

"Beautiful spot you've picked," Lauterbach said. "It's more stark, of course, but it reminds me of our farm in the Texas hill country. Why Lebanon, general?"

"Too many memories in Egypt. People should change their lives as they change clothes, I think," he replied.

Had Lauterbach changed his clothes? Sabry wondered. Or had memory stitched itself to him? He wondered if the needle marks on Lauterbach's arms were the ice-pick scars of history.

"Your wife is gracious," Lauterbach told him. "And very attractive."

Sabry shrugged. "She is young. I am surprised to see you, too, have married again."

Irací had been ten when the war ended, and knew it only from retrospectives on TV. Sabry wondered if Lauterbach had met his wife during wartime. And if so, what sad, nostalgic prison marriage had become for them both.

Lauterbach said softly, "Four Americans were captured by the aliens. Two stayed with them. One committed suicide soon after his return. My wife was the only survivor."

Sabry shifted in his chair, uncomfortable with the mention of aliens. For a short time even he had believed, but then the Parisi books were revealed as fakes, and the blue lights found to be a Greenhouse phenomenon.

"They covered it up," the American said ruefully. "Amazing what care they took. Did you know the reporters even accused me of sleeping with the Parisi woman? Jesus Christ." His laughter died in a strangled cough. "But I know for certain that someone else's body is buried in Sergeant Gordon Means's grave." Lauterbach's ruined face was alight with the same conspiracy-theory glow Sabry remembered from the TV interviews. "And how else do you explain Lieutenant Justin Searles's last words before he jumped: 'The light was better than this'?"

Wishing the American would change the subject, Sabry looked off into the sun-shot clouds, the distant gray veils of falling rain.

"No matter how dangerous it was, I wanted the aliens to find me interesting, too," Lauterbach said. "I wanted them to talk to me. Wanted the war to end. I wanted so many things that my need probably overwhelmed them. Maybe cooling the sun and ending the Greenhouse heat was what they thought I had asked for."

With a pang of compassion Sabry realized how much Lauterbach had paid. First Parisi and the blue lights, then the news of the aborted bombing of Warsaw had leaked. No one had stood by him, not the President, no one. Even Sabry, in his Red Cross deposition, had added to the chorus that the man was insane.

"You should have been made a five-star general," Sabry told him. "You deserved better." *Right or wrong*, he thought. *The man deserved more than ridicule.* Lifting his head to the freshening breeze, he drank in the smell of coming rain. In the west the clouds were swelling, their pregnant bellies gray.

"Thank you," Lauterbach whispered.

Allah manipulated fate in strange ways. Lauterbach had won the war; Sabry the peace. While Lauterbach was still struggling for exoneration, Sabry had negotiated a quiet armistice here in Lebanon with Irací, with his flowers.

"You will stay for dinner, of course," he said. Rummaging through the dark closet of the past, he found the old clothes of his humiliation. They didn't fit anymore, and it was time to throw them away.

In a hoarse and halting voice, Lauterbach said, "I would like that very much."

The afternoon darkened, clouds drifting over the new, cooler sun. The first fat drops of rain pattered on the Fiberglas.

"You know? Before people die, they try to put things in perspective." The American's tone was so intimate that Sabry felt he was privy to the man's most pitiful, most terrible secrets. "I mean—I wish—I've questioned my life a lot. But whether I was right, whether or not it was even worthwhile, I'd have to repeat it all. Every order, every mistaken belief, every damnable lie. I would betray the aliens' trust again. I would teach them more about war than they wanted to know. And no matter how much I longed to keep them here, I would again frighten them away."

"We did our best," Sabry told him. "It is all we could do. There is no guilt in that, remember? Remember preaching so to me?"

But Lauterbach wasn't listening. "Wishes, you see. My wife says the lesson the aliens taught her is that wishes suck you dry. But, my God, isn't there more? All that wisdom. A universe-full of knowledge. Why did Justin Searles die screaming that the light was better? What could Sergeant Means have discovered that made him want to stay? I can't begin to imagine what miracles . . ."

When the sentence broke, Sabry turned. Lauterbach was weeping, his face lifted to the blue roof and the incessant clatter of the rain.